ISIS TRILOGY

BOOK TWO

THE
EMERALD
TABLET

ONE LIFE IS NOT ENOUGH

S. L. GORE

2018.03.05 Edition

ISBN 978-1-940304-01-4

Published by Tajine Publishing, Las Vegas NV
This book is available in eVersion

Author website: www.SLGore.com

AUTHOR'S NOTE
This book is a work of fiction. Names, characters, places and incidents are the product of the author's imagination or are used fictitiously, and any resemblance to actual persons, living or dead, or events is entirely coincidental.

"A romantic time travel fable with a gorgeous strong sexy heroine who conquers all with grace and intelligence. I love the way Gore writes two stories at the same time. She's brilliant at taking the reader back to the Oracle of Delphi—or to a bar in Copenhagen!"
Anna – Copenhagen DK

"Erotic, romantic, edgy historical adventure for the intelligent reader."
Barb – Las Vegas NV

"Gore's a painter. She paints a story with words."
Hillie - Amsterdam NL

"What a gallop. It's wonderful. Getting more and more complex and fascinating as these lives spill into the future and back."
Ann – Los Osos CA

"I loved the richness of the story and the atmospheres Gore creates while weaving history, action and suspense."
Leslie – Ann Arbor MI

"The scene between Athena and The General in chains is a triumphant tour-de-force. Terrific suspense."
Len – Arroyo Grande CA

"Ancient history combined with magical transitions from one lifetime to another. I could see the Lighthouse of Alexandria against the pale dawn."
Suzanne – Boston MA

"What a great education wrapped up in romantic intrigue. Isis has evolved to Athena ~ smart, classy and in control."
Phyllis – New York NY

"The Emerald Tablet is the perfect sequel to The Red Mirror. The story continues with the same powerful characters coming back in surprising ways. Lots of unexpected twists and turns."
Eric – Montreal QUE

"Gore has created her own genre – sensuous, historical, philosophical and New Age."
Elaine – Easton PA

"Gore's second book, The Emerald Tablet, is just as amazing as The Red Mirror! Athena is another sexy smart lady. Can't wait to meet Elektra."
Paul – Chicago IL

"The Red Mirror was wonderful, but I loved The Emerald Tablet more. Please hurry and write the next!"
Caroline – San Luis Obispo CA

"The Emerald Tablet is every bit as good as The Red Mirror – maybe better. Still passionate, erotic, informative, and thrilling! I love the way Gore blends spiritual possibilities, shifting realities and time travel. Thank you again!"
Carol – Shell Beach CA

My gratitude to the Greeks for their brilliance.
Thank you to Jesper
for traveling the journey each bumpy step of the way.

Thank you to the Muses.
May they continue to whisper and sing.

TABLE OF CONTENTS

MAP OF EASTERN MEDITERRANEAN
200 BC

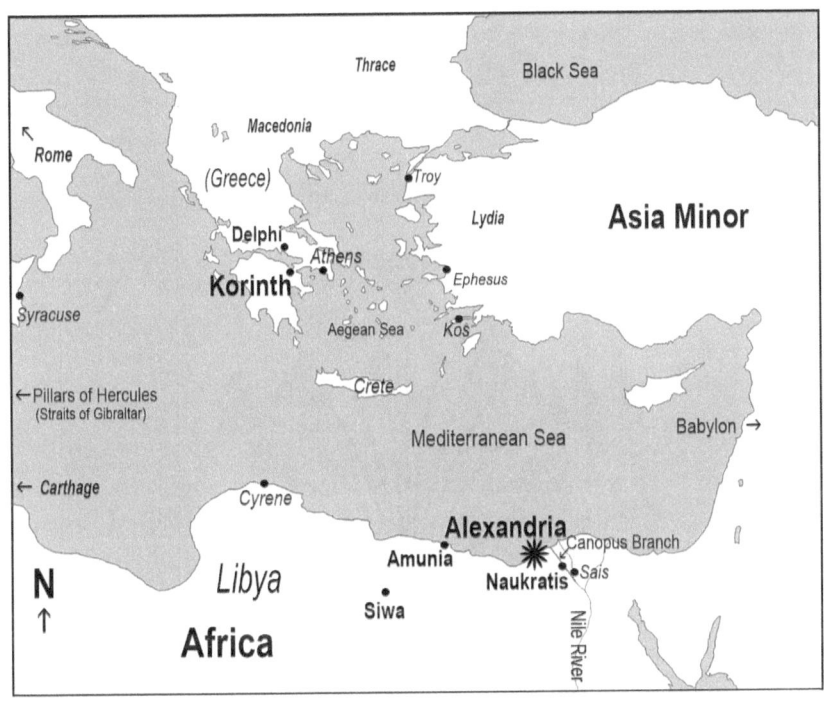

"As it is above, so it is below.
All things came from the One.
Everything is one."
– The Emerald Tablet

PROLOGUE
ISIS AND THE RED MIRROR

"Reality is fragile as glass." – Gore

A red mirror in a Las Vegas antique mall. I never suspected the dusty sheet of glass set in a funky, red-lacquered, vaguely Chinese frame with tarnished struts and stars would change everything.

Before the Red Mirror, I'd always believed that we live only once. I hadn't considered that circles of souls linked over time are destined to meet again and again. Like a cast of the same actors playing different roles in changing dramas, we encounter each other until we learn what we need to learn.

The first time I saw the exotic green-eyed woman in the Mirror, I didn't realize she was me. I know now to look deep into the eyes—the mirror of the soul—but I didn't have the Sight then. That night she beckoned, and I followed. When I came back, I was never the same. Not me now. Not me in the past.

You might ask how I'm able to cross from this reality into another. Someone else might explain the transition in terms of a complex multiverse ruled by quantum mechanics. Tony could do that. He's the rocket scientist.

For me, the Red Mirror is simply magic.

PART ONE
THE HATHOR RING

CHAPTER 1   YELLOW SILK DREAM

"I know men in exile feed on dreams." – Aeschylus

I call it my yellow silk dream. It always starts out with buttery satin sliding on my bare skin. The room is bathed in white moonlight shining in from a terrace open to a canopy of stars.

Sometimes gentle waves slurp pebbles from a near shore. Mostly the world is silent.

Then the men come. Four of them. Their bodies are formed in every perfect detail, but I can't see their faces. Coalescing from the shadows, they draw nearer and nearer to cover my warm body with kisses before disappearing through green doors inscribed with words I don't understand. I know I am meant to follow and everything depends on choosing the right door, but it's never made clear to me precisely why.

What should be an erotic whimsy turns each time into a kind of mild, nagging nightmare. Instead of savoring the touch of the men's lips on my secret places, I wake agitated and dissatisfied.

The yellow silk dream doesn't come each time I sleep, but often enough that I lie in bed before dozing off and plan which door to pick. But in spite of my determined preparation, a decision always eludes me.

Even Aisha is fed up. She's taken to deserting my restless bed to curl up a safe distance from whatever madness stalks my sleep. Seeing that I am myself again, she brushes her white whiskers across my cheek and purrs a welcome-back melody in my ear.

"I'm here, Aisha," I soothe her. "But not for long."

Barb eyed with suspicion the Cadillac margaritas with Grand Marnier floating on top. She rarely allows herself more than a single glass of wine at lunch.

"Are we celebrating?" she asked, "Or drowning our sorrows?"

I was saved from an answer by Felipe arriving with his cart of black pumice bowls filled with diced onions, tomatoes, chili peppers and chopped cilantro. He scraped the insides of a ripe avocado and added garnish until I said, "Stop." Next he squeezed in fresh lime juice and finished with a generous sprinkle of rock salt. The pumice bowl of fresh guacamole went on the table between the two margaritas and next to a basket of warm house-made wheat tortillas.

He stepped away. I took a long sip of the sweet limey margarita and plunged in.

"I need your help, Barb. Please don't say no right away."

"Well, that doesn't sound promising. Help with what?"

"I'm going back."

"Back?" Her look was one of total disbelief. "You surely can't mean back *there*? You said you were through with that mirror stuff." She paused; her top teeth, tiny and laser-treated white, bit into her lower lip. "Have you forgotten how *terrifying* it was?"

What I hadn't forgotten was how it felt to be *her* instead of me. Isis. Isenkhebe Nefrusobek. High-Priestess. I drained the last drop of watery lime and tequila, licking the salt from my lips. I would have ordered another but knew Barb would command, "Too fattening!"

"I know you think I'm a little crazy—"

"A little? I think you've gone raving mad. And you dare ask me to help you!"

"There's...uh...something else." It took a moment to muster my courage. "I need you to cover for me with Hector."

"Hector?" Her eyes blazed. Incredulous had turned to indignant. "No! Absolutely not. I won't lie to him. He doesn't deserve it."

"You probably won't have to tell him anything. I'm going to tell him... something. I don't know what yet. You're just a kind of...insurance."

"Why not tell him the truth? It's not as if he doesn't know about these trips. He went through the mirror for you. He saved your ass. Or have you forgotten that, too?"

"He won't understand, Barb. He'll take my going as...well...that he's not enough."

"One might see his point of view," she said acidly.

Someone somewhere scored a goal, and a crowd roared on a flat screen. A dish fell to the tile floor behind me, but neither Barb nor I looked.

"Only one day, Barb. What's twenty-four hours?"

"Long enough to get in trouble. You said time is different there."

"Yes, but nothing that happens on the other side can actually hurt me," I argued. "I mean, my body's still *here*, isn't it?"

She exhaled hard out through her nose, making a little snorting sound—her way of dismissing a rationaliztion—or showing disgust. Then her eyes narrowed. "There's something you're not telling me. Has this got anything to do with Rasheed?"

"No," I lied. Almost everything had to do with Rasheed, but I wasn't going to admit it. "He dumped me. Remember?"

"I seem to recall that's what he does." Finally, she took a sip of her margarita, only a small one. Her eyes never left mine. "I bet you think you're going to find him again. And that he'll be different. That it'll be different between you. *River God*," she sneered. "*Puh-leeze.*"

I didn't bother to tell her it was a lot more complicated than Rasheed. God knows, I'd tried often enough to explain. She just didn't get it. How could she? She'd never been a High Priestess—that she knew anyway.

"And if you lose Hector?"

"I won't," I said stubbornly. "Not if you help."

Her platinum helmet hair, cut short and neat with bangs straight across her eyebrows, shimmered in the sunlight. How odd that the burgundy of her sweater matched the red of the leather bench. I had the strangest vision of a talking head suspended in space, detached from her body. But it was me who was detached. Detached from this world.

"You're not even sleeping with him," she accused. "You won't give him a chance. I can't believe he puts up with it."

"You know how it is with him, Barb. All or nothing. We've talked about this. I'm not ready to commit."

"Commit?" She made that little snorting sound of hers again. "Remember finding Mr. Right? Seems that's all I ever heard."

"Things have changed. It's not that simple anymore."

She glared at me from across the table. "I don't think anything has changed. What I think is that you're not capable of happiness. That you can't be satisfied."

I didn't have an answer. I don't know how satisfied feels.

"Well, you know what I want?" she snapped. "I want to go back in time before you bought that damned mirror. Bad enough that you're obsessed with *Mr. Mystery Man—always breaking your heart—Rasheed,* but you're pining away for some lifetime that's been over for centuries. You even call yourself 'Isis' now. It's sick."

"Will you help me, Barb?"

She looked at her watch and grabbed the check. "I've got a client waiting for me. You get the tip."

"*Please*, Barb. I'm going with or without you." I tried not to sound desperate but determined. "I need you. You make me feel…safer."

"Safer? I thought everything was going to be fine. Listen to yourself!"

Not saying anything for fear it'd be wrong, I held her gaze, hiding my panic. How would I get back without her? I could get stuck there.

She slid out of the booth then and stood to her feet. We stared at each other for a moment, me hardly breathing; her china doll blue eyes were ice and fire at the same time.

Whatever she saw in my eyes caused her to relent. "Okay. One day. And I mean it. 24 hours. And don't screw things up with Hector," she threatened. "You'll regret it. Trust me on that."

So like a woman scheming ways to meet her lover, I planned my deceit.

Hector had been waiting for my Skype. Lounging on a black leather sofa in his apartment in Buenos Aires—BA as he called it—he balanced his laptop on blue jeans-covered thighs, screen tilted up. A bold-colored abstract painting hung above his head; his mahogany tan glowed against a lemon yellow polo shirt.

"*Lastima*, Isis, but I can't get back this weekend," he was saying. "There are some problems with my uncle's estate. I have to meet with the attorneys on Monday."

"Actually, Hector, that works out great," I said so smoothly. "I should fly up to Bend and see Sylvia. She's back in the hospital." I paused for a second and then added, "I'll probably be off the grid for a while."

Each single part was the truth but, when combined, made up a lie. I scared myself a little that I was so devious.

We chatted for a while about inconsequential stuff. Hector had eaten a huge steak at *La Cabaña* and been to a new tango bar in *Las Milongas*.

"I want us to take tango lessons as soon as I get back to Vegas." Hector was his usual enthusiastic self.

He didn't suspect a thing.

Just as the sun was setting, Barb arrived and poured two glasses of an oaky chardonnay she'd discovered. We sat opposite the Red Mirror and stared at our reflection, sipping our chilled wine, not saying anything.

A single polished silver strut gleamed against the red lacquer; the other thirteen, spaced evenly around the rectangular frame, were dull. One tarnished silver starburst anchored each corner. In the way the blue, white and green paint covered the metal strips, I knew the sprinkling of delicate Chinese chrysanthemums had been added sometime later.

"I'm going to stay to see you go," Barb announced bravely, but her too-tight mouth and pale face told me how nervous she was.

"I always rubbed the same strut and always went back to Isis. What do you think will happen if I choose another one?"

"Why not try a couple, and we'll see what comes up?" A note of excitement had come into her voice; a bit of color was in her cheeks.

I chose a random strut and rubbed it with the cotton rag dabbed in olive oil. Seconds passed before a fragile-looking girl with slanted eyes and a golden orchid behind her ear appeared.

Did she paint the chrysanthemums on the Mirror's frame?

She wasn't actually crying, but her eyes told of an unspeakable sadness. If this broken girl was indeed me, I had no desire to revisit.

"Can you see her, Barb?"

"See *who*?" she asked in utter frustration. "Is there someone in the mirror? I see only us."

I closed my eyes and breathed slowly and rhythmically, relaxing my mind, focusing on the reddish glow inside my head, right behind my lids. The buzzing in my cells started in the fingers and then spread up my arms, until, finally, I tingled all over. With a will of its own, my hand moved to the strut below the one that led to Isis.

The robust new woman in the mirror was far from tragic; golden curls framed a perfectly proportioned face with a high forehead, curvy lips and straight nose. The clear look in her intelligent green eyes said, I know exactly what I'm doing.

"That's the one, Barb. She's where I'm going. Wake me up in 24 hours."

CHAPTER 2   INVITATION

"I'd like nothing better than to achieve some bold adventure, worthy of our trip." – Aristophanes

T he transition was immediate. Or if not, I wasn't aware of any time lag. First came smell—a scent of rosemary mingled with salty sea. Next came sound. I kept my eyes closed for a moment to listen to the haunting notes of a distant flute amid the cries of seagulls.

The air held a slight hint of chill, yet the warm rays of a strong sun caressed my shoulders and bare arms and penetrated deep to the bone.

A lark trilled, and I opened my eyes to a vast expanse of blue sea joining blue sky at the curve of the earth. White puffy clouds hung near the horizon. My seat was a marble bench standing on a carpet of red poppies at the edge of a steep cliff. Offshore floated a scattered handful of islands.

Volumes of royal blue wool, soft as cashmere, draped the curves of my generous breasts and thighs. A wide, silvery border gathered in sumptuous folds at my feet. My sturdy sandals, trimmed in silver, laced up the leg.

While Isis had been reed-slender with narrow hips, this body was lush. My muscles were toned, though, and my flesh firm. Like Isis, I must walk a lot. I didn't often bask in the warmth of the sun; the skin on my arms was milk-white with a spattering of tiny freckles.

I reached to feel my hair twisted into a thick knot at the nape of my neck. All mine—no wigs in this lifetime. Wispy strands of shimmering gold blew across my face.

My head was remarkably clear given that I felt my own feelings and thought my own thoughts at the same time I felt and thought hers. This woman was calm, centered and focused. Confident. I let myself slip further into her.

Below, at the base of the cliff, dozens of wooden ships with rows of oars and bright-colored sails filled two harbors, one on either side of a narrow isthmus. Men tiny as ants, straining on long ropes, hauled a massive *bireme* from the protected port on the gulf side along a stone causeway to the windy harbor on the open sea.

Red tile roofs of a small white city crawled part way up my hill. All around rose low mountains punctuated with dark green glades of tall, pointy cypress trees. Everywhere in the chaulk white stone grew bunches of yellow broom.

I might have sat there for hours gazing at the sea, listening to the windsong in the trees, but footsteps crunched on the gravel behind me. I turned to a woman so bent with age, I immediately christened her 'Ancient One.'

"Your Grace, the delegation from Alexandria has arrived," she announced in lyrical Greek.

I understood every word.

Your Grace. I liked the sound of that.

Once past rows of ornate Corinthian columns and inside the great marble Temple, the air was hushed. Not even the sound of the wind entered here.

We crossed a small flowery courtyard with a gurgling fountain and entered a wide corridor with an ochre ceiling. Geometric-patterned bands of bright blue and gold leaf trimmed the tops of tomato red walls and around open doorways.

At the end of the hallway, a pair of mammoth oak doors on heavy bronze hinges swung open. I stepped into a great hall with sunlight streaming through a circular opening in a high domed roof. More blue and gold geometric designs framed an azure sky.

All around the room, among the brightly painted statues and vivid-colored columns, a chorus of pastel-robed priestesses strummed lyres and sang softly.

Directly under the overhead oculus sparkled a pool with a glass mosaic of the cupid-god Eros riding a dolphin through white-crested waves.

On my right, facing the length of the hall from a dais, a two-story lavish-painted marble statue of Aphrodite, Goddess of Love and Beauty, towered above us.

Voluptuous and utterly feminine, the defender of Korinth poised frozen in perfect balance—weight a bit forward on her right leg, torso twisted slightly to the left, arms lifted with hands holding a massive gold shield.

Shiny hair, crafted in gold, gathered into a wavy bun at the nape of her neck. Lustrous gold nipples tipped flesh-colored breasts. The carved marble gown, painted royal blue, draped around her hips and thighs, tumbling in luxuriant, chiseled folds to her ankles.

"Athena of Korinth, Supreme Priestess of Aphrodite," announced an extraordinarily tall woman with a ringing voice. Painfully thin, her long ivory *peplos* hung on bony limbs unrelieved by a single curve.

A dozen or so clusters of men, clean-shaven and richly robed, quieted and bowed their heads in my direction. My first impression of the Alexandrians was an arrogant lot holding themselves proudly under a crushing weight of gold. A handful glittered in studded military vests and shiny-winged helmets, but as was custom in the Temple, they were unarmed.

The music stopped. All attention focused on me as I glided across the marble tiles to the dais. I felt perfectly at ease; Athena was accustomed to this. Three steps led up, and I settled in a tawny, vine-carved cypress chair at the feet of the Goddess. Our gowns were the same rich blue.

I saw him almost as soon as I was seated. Tall, broad-shouldered, oozing virility, he held himself in the confident posture of a charismatic man born to privilege. He stood not far from the dais next to an older Alexandrian distinguished by a heavy gold chain of office round his neck.

My first thought was that Hector had come through the Red Mirror again. I caught myself staring quite openly at him, trying to decide if he recognized me. Arching his right eyebrow, he returned my stare with a bold, inviting look.

I turned quickly away, signalling the bony priestess to begin, but not before seeing Hector and the older man exchange satisfied glances.

Tapping a golden staff briskly on the marble tiles, the Amazon priestess boomed, "Kadmos of Alexandria. Esteemed Envoy from Ptolemy *Philopater*, divine Pharaoh of Egypt."

Kadmos turned out to be the older man with Hector. He stepped up in front of me and with the appropriate show of respect, bowed his head, chin touching his chest. His salt and pepper hair had been carefully barbered into tight curls around a fleshy face. A gold sunburst secured a purple cape at the left shoulder; wide bands of scarlet embroidery trimmed the neck and hem of his ankle-length white *chiton*. The thick, heavy gold chain of a court officer glittered on his chest.

In his hands he carried a yellow silk pillow. On the pillow perched a miniature gold chest. I bestowed the smile of a Supreme Priestess— gracious and detached.

"Be welcome, Kadmos of Alexandria to Korinth and the Temple of Aphrodite," I pronounced in the golden tones of Greek. "We pray Poseidon granted you fair passage."

"The Gods have been most generous in Their favor," he crooned with another bow of his head.

He straightened and met my eyes directly. "We are most grateful for the audience today, Your Grace, and beg you to accept this humble gift from our Pharaoh, the beloved Ptolemy *Philopater*, Osiris-on-earth, Horus the God."

The bony Amazon took the ankh-encrusted case from Kadmos and passed it to a young girl who mounted the steps. The tiny latch came easily undone, and I opened the lid. Inside, nesting in red silk, gleamed an antique gold ring with twin horns holding a grape-sized, deep blue lapis lazuli stone.

Icy calm, I slipped the ring on my right middle finger. It fit perfectly. There could be no doubt. This was a Hathor Ring—only two in all Egypt! One had belonged to me as Isis, the other to my mother, Sit-hathor.

I believe I kept my face a mask and again turned my gaze on Kadmos. He gave no indication that he knew the significance of the ring but droned on without pause, his lips reciting an endless stream of titles and adulations until, at last, he came to the purpose of his visit.

"The Oracle of Amun has revealed that His Most Gracious Ptolemy is willed by the Gods to build a glorious new Temple in the Great City of Alexandria—more glorious than ever beheld. A Temple in honor of Her Sacred Goddess Aphrodite, patroness of the illustrious Korinth."

He paused. I waited to hear what this project had to do with us. Surely they hadn't travelled all this way for me to recommend an architect? More likely they sought permission to copy our temple design as Athens had done for the Parthenon. It turned out their purpose was every bit as startling as the gift of the Hathor ring.

"It is Your Grace, Athena of Korinth," Kadmos announced with great theatrics, "whom the Gods desire to guide the Temple's construction in Alexandria."

He had the look on his face of a man bestowing a laurel crown to a prize athlete.

I believe I hid my surprise well enough, although it was clear from the sudden hush in the hall that others didn't. A *woman*—a *Korinthian woman*—in charge of building a temple in Egypt?

I was still processing his astonishing pronouncement, even wondering if I'd understood him correctly, when he motioned to a red-headed youth of about fifteen who hurried over with a papyrus scroll bound in silver tassels.

"The terms of the Royal Commission," Kadmos went on in the informative tone of a man attending to administrative details, "are contained in this personal letter from the Great Ptolemy Himself. We are confident that Athena of Korinth shall find the offer most advantageous."

The boy held out the papyrus to the Amazon who took the scroll, as she had the ring, and moved to give it to the young girl.

I held up my hand, and she stepped back, still holding the scroll.

"We are greatly honored by the Pharaoh's trust and confidence," I heard myself say, "but it would be premature to consider terms."

Kadmos blinked and shifted his weight slightly. In the silence, I heard water splashing in a fountain. Hector, or rather this incarnation of him, stood even more erect than before. Like everyone, he fully concentrated on me.

I don't believe there was anything about me that signalled my irritation at these arrogant Alexandrians who'd arrived in their gilded, ponderous *trireme* without prior inquiries and proper behind-the-scenes negotiations. If they had conferred with the League of City-States, I hadn't been apprised. Why should I leave my duties behind and risk a voyage to Egypt? Ptolemy was reputed to be a madman.

When I broke the stillness, I used what I sensed was my standard response when not wishing to commit.

"The wishes of the Goddess—not our own—must be considered. As in all matters of great import, we must first seek to know Her will."

I let another moment pass to give my words the appropriate gravitas.

"We hold the Oracle of Amun in the highest regard. All that remains is to seek asssurance the Gods speak with the same voice. We shall consult our own Oracle so that we may know the divine course of our destiny."

"Certainly, Your Grace," Kadmos acquiesced without a pause. No Greek, not even a presumptuous Alexandrian, could object to consulting the Oracle of Delphi. "It shall be as the Gods ordain."

"My duty and pleasure are to bring glory to the Goddess always," I responded in the most solemn of voices.

After delivering a string of blessings for the House of Ptolemy, I stood to signal the conclusion of the audience. I had no doubts as to the outcome of the prophesy. I would simply interpret the nonsensical verses of prophecy as they suited me.

The mood in the great hall morphed quickly from somber to playful. Young girls appeared with golden cups and silver pitchers of wine. The chorus of pastel-robed musicians strummed again on their lyres and sang.

Gliding with the grace of practiced dancers, the most accomplished of my priestesses flowed in clouds of musk among the men. Silver bells tinkled at their ankles; bells rang in their soft laughter. Trained singers all, their voices had a musical cadence alluring to the ear.

A few teasing words reached me—they were setting up appointments for this evening. Now that the business portion of their visit had concluded for the day, the Alexandrians were intent upon enjoying the pleasures of Korinth.

Hector lost no time approaching me. I could guess by his swagger and bold eyes that he didn't know me but intended to. He most certainly hadn't come through the Mirror.

His hair was the same rich chestnut, but instead of brushing the thick waves back from his brow, he wore barbered curls that fell on his forehead and around the ears. His white teeth blazed. Polished bronze greaves covered long shins up past the knee. A scarlet cloak hung off his bare shoulder. All toned muscle, he had the rich mahogany glow that comes from training daily in the nude.

Surely Apollo the Sun God gave him his shine.

"Please accept my respects, Athena of Korinth. I am Hektor of Naukratis. I had come today anticipating great beauty, yet I find myself more awed by your wit and grace. In beauty and youth, such intelligence is rare."

Charming words came easily to him. He delivered them in a most natural way, confident and without pretense.

He dared to touch my bare skin above the elbow, on the back of my arm. It had been a very long time since Athena had felt that thrill. I eased away from his hand, not a real rejection, but clearly signalling that he moved too fast.

Far from being discouraged, he seemed amused by my attempts at aloofness. I suspected that as much as Athena was accustomed to masking her thoughts, I didn't hide them very well. He saw through the mask; he read the signs. Barely hiding his triumph, he arched his right eyebrow and with another of those bold looks, had the audacity to invite a Supreme Priestess to a *symposion*.

"I am the houseguest of Xenon," he went on grandly, not missing a beat. "He begs you accept his invitation to an evening of music and poetry. The wine and the company shall be the best the city offers. And as the world knows, the best of all pleasures is found in Korinth."

He handed me a small scroll waxed with Xenon's seal.

When I answered very coolly that I would perhaps drop by for a cup of wine, Hektor smiled without a trace of surprise. I'm certain that few women resist his charms.

Just before he went through the door with his crimson cape swirling behind him, he turned back to catch my eyes admiring his broad shoulders and muscular thighs.

He nodded and smiled knowingly, again arching that eyebrow.

The spot on my arm where he'd touched me burned. So much for Athena the Ice Queen.

CHAPTER 3   SYMPOSION

"The vine bears three kinds of grapes; the first of pleasure, the second of intoxication, the third of disgust." – Diogenes

A lavender sky deepened a shade toward violet, and the first star came out. I took my place in the center of the atrium beside a massive bronze brazier on tripod legs. Red embers glowed. When the wind gusted, sparks flew like fireflies.

Every woman in the circle wore a dark green wool cape and a wreath of flowers in her hair. No one spoke; I heard no quiet whispers.

The Ancient One appeared with a silver chalice embossed with leaping satyrs. When I tipped the powder into the brazier, white dust hit the red hot coals and exploded in dancing glitter.

We sang. All of us, in perfect harmony.

O Aphrodite, O Goddess sublime, O perfect beauty among all beauty.
Leave the golden palace of your father Zeus.
Sail the heavens in your chariot yoked to feathered wings of doves.
Enflame the cold, empty heart,
Bring lust to lonely loins hungering to flower.
Light the dark that wild desire be persuaded to passion.

I sprinkled more powder, more dazzling sparks rose in the air, and the ceremony finished with the priestesses lighting clay lanterns. In a long chain of twinkling lights, hundreds of sacred prostitutes began winding down the steep slope of the *Akrokorinth* to persuade the city to passion.

It was not a difficult task. Both harbors were crowded with ships, all the inns full. The Alexandrians had booked my top priestesses. With the blessing of the Goddess, it should be a most profitable night for the Temple.

Polished oak beams crisscrossed the turquoise ceiling of a dressing chamber with tangerine walls. A gilt band of golden dolphins swam around the crown molding. In one corner stood a triptych screen splashed with curvy dancers with thick manes of yellow hair cascading down their bare backs.

The masseuse pumiced my body hair and then massaged my stinging flesh with hyacinth-scented oils until my skin glowed as if bathed in moonlight.

The barber first arranged my hair in coils and elaborate twists with ivory pins. His assistant heated fat iron spikes to coax soft, seductive curls around my face.

A cosmetics priestess shadowed my eyelids with a mixture of charcoal and olive oil and brushed a brown paste across the tips of my lashes. Mulberry juice reddened my lips to invite a kiss. In truth, everything about me was inviting. The sunny sheen of my long chiton of crocus-colored silk molded to my curves like a wet gown clings when rising from the sea.

A necklace of delicate gold chains joined at my throat at a *Herakles* knot, symbol of the force of love and the power of love over force. The matching thigh band on my right upper loin glinted through the sheer silk. The metal was cold on my inner thigh before it warmed.

Unlike the twittering young neophytes who attended me when I was Isis in Egypt, the dressing was quick, efficient and solemn with no giggling speculation about who would be at the party and what they would wear.

The priestesses were a somber group who looked me directly in the eye when they spoke. No one prostrated themselves as they would for an Egyptian High-Priestess. The only acknowledgment of my higher station had been an initial bowing of the head and a momentary lowering of the eyes.

The Ancient One glowered from a nearby tripod stool.

"Does Your Grace think it wise to attend a symposion? And what do we know of this Alexandrian?"

"Wisdom has very little to do with it. I go but from curiosity. I have heard much of Xenon's parties. They are said to be tasteful and restrained. As for the Alexandrian, he is merely a means to my amusement."

To myself I was thinking, *This is Hector. I can handle him.*

"I remind Your Grace that you are the Goddess on Earth. A Goddess is unattainable. Therein lies her power."

"Do not worry yourself unnecessarily. I shall be in control."

I slipped the Hathor ring on my middle finger and at once felt its power. As Supreme Priestess of Aphrodite, I made my own rules.

The lamp boy arrived. He carried a long pole with a bronze oil lantern. About twelve years old, he wore a slave's rough wool chiton and coarse leather sandals laced up his shins. His hair was cut short but not professionally barbered; uneven pieces hung around his ears and on his neck. His thin shoulders were bare. I wrapped myself against the spring night's chill in the dark green cloak of a priestess.

A million bright stars filled the moonless sky. The wind had died after sunset, and the night was quiet. Gentle waves tugged on a rocky beach at the base of the Akrokorinth. A few wood doves cooed. Just once, I heard the hoot of a faraway owl.

We covered the two hundred-foot descent and arrived quickly at the city. The streets were dark with closed shutters. Only lamp boys leading couples and singles travelled the narrow, winding alleys. We met one group of rowdy young men coming from the Street of Taverns. They shouted for me to join them, then laughed and moved aside to let us pass.

Our steps fell quietly on the cobblestones. Feral cats fought over garbage until we came near and they disappeared into the shadows.

Two-story, whitewashed houses with red tile roofs clung to each other in a meandering maze. Only the color of the doors was different. Red, green or blue. I would never have found my way without the boy. The promise of another copper *obol* ensured he would wait to lead me back home.

Turning down an alley barely wide enough for two, we stopped at a green door with a red frame. Hidden behind the tall white walls was a gracious fountain courtyard with grapevines clambering up an arbor. Three long-legged hunting dogs lazed under a rough wooden table. Accustomed to visitors, they didn't bark.

This was not Xenon's home but his pleasure house. From the sound of the laughter and wild shouts, I judged the symposion in full swing.

A dozen or more couches were arranged flush against the cobalt blue walls of a large rectangular room. I recognized a handful of flute girls from the Temple. Barely past puberty, they circulated among the guests, shy nymphs trilling high notes on their pipes. They would linger a moment to let eager fingers explore young thighs and slim waists before gliding coyly away. Long garlands of ivy trailed in their scented hair.

Xenon, the wealthiest man in wealthy Korinth, greeted me.

"Welcome, Athena of Korinth. You honor my humble villa with your presence."

Hektor was by my side at once. He exchanged a look with Xenon, arching his eyebrow slightly as he slipped the cape from my shoulders and handed it to a boy slave. I saw Xenon's wry smile as the look of a gambler who had lost a friendly bet.

This was not the first invitation I had received from Xenon, but it was the first I'd accepted.

Hektor's unashamed eyes travelled from my ripe breasts, down past my curvy hips and along my lush thighs to my pumiced and hennaed toenails before returning on my face.

"There are not words written to describe your beauty," he announced with a flash of white teeth, "so I shall seal my lips and let my eyes tell you what my heart feels."

Not a full minute passed before the *hetaera* Omphale left her group of admirers to touch Xenon's arm. Her sheer silk gown, the color of her olive complexion, was a second skin. The red tips of her breasts matched her cheekbones, lips and mound. She wore a strand of gold beads and white pearls the size of chickpeas.

A spoil of war from some long-forgotten Lydian campaign, Omphale had risen quickly from slave to courtesan. Renown in Korinth as a shrewd businesswoman, she held the rare, respected position of what is commonly called a 'woman of property.' Rumor was she owned many houses in Korinth and Athens—and countless chests of jewels. All gifts from admirers.

When Xenon introduced me to her, she spoke in a soft, husky voice, the slightly accented Greek flowing like honey from her lips. She turned her dazzling smile on me, but her exotic yellow-green eyes, turned up at the corners like a cat, warned me to stay away from her man.

I kept thinking that I knew her from the other side of the Mirror but couldn't place who she was. It was obvious that she, like Hektor, didn't recognize me. Her wary eyes saw only a rival.

From what I'd heard, Omphale had no cause to be concerned. She'd bewitched Xenon the first moment he met her; the sum he supposedly paid for her contract could wage a small war. She went everywhere with him, even to battle. It was well-known in the city that he kept her better than his wife.

Hektor and I settled on a sofa of carved cypress covered by red cushions woven with yellow flying cranes. Crowded and noisy, the room was already too hot. I kept my feet on the footstool, my spine straight, and rested my elbow lightly on the high armrest.

A slave boy brought a gold chalice embossed with Dionysus capturing bare-breasted Ariadne in his muscled arms. Swan heads formed the two handles. Twin nude boys, carrying a silver *krater* inlaid with golden sunbursts, ladled wine into my cup. The wine was sweet, dark and hardly watered. Xenon intended for a wild night.

Hektor leaned back against the blue wall, drinking from his silver ram's head goblet and smiling at me over the top. His long legs, free of bronze greaves, stretched out along the divan. True to his word, he let his eyes speak; they said he was ready.

The room fell almost silent when a boy with chestnut skin and matching curls, nude body draped in garlands of poppies, plucked the strings of a *kithara* and sang verses from Sappho. His voice was that of an angel, high and sweet.

Here recline the Nymphs
at the hour of twilight,
Back in shadows dim of the cave,
their golden Sea-green eyes half-lidded,
up to their supple
Waists in the water.

Hektor's hand moved to my waist. I stiffened, and he moved his hand away. When I met his eyes, they still smiled.

"*Kallistei!*" Hektor toasted me. "To the most beautiful."

Each guest raised his *kylix* to me and then rushed to name another beauty. The toasts triggered a competition with the first man beginning an ode to his lover then passing the phrase to a second—then a third and so on—to complete the verse. The finish of each recitation ended with a toast. Xenon's guests were fast becoming roaring drunk.

I sipped slowly at my own cup.

Immersing himself in the party, Hektor cheered out loud when merited and booed without pity when drunken words fell over each other and lost their sense. He joined in the heckling when young men competed in tossing their wine across the room to splash into a *krater*.

Although he often touched my arm and, more than once, the thigh band visible under my gown, he was patient, drawing me slowly from my shell with his confident and unhurried presence. Like a comet falling inexorably into the sun, I began to fall under his Apollo spell.

Small boys carried trays with stuffed dates, candied rose leaves, sesame cakes and raisins. The fish stew was flavored with fennel; a whole roast lamb appeared in an aromatic cloud of rosemary and garlic. It was most unusual to serve food at a symposion, but Xenon, too, made his own rules.

I had no appetite and scarcely took a bite. Both the unwatered wine and Hektor made me a little giddy.

Young men moved in close to older ones and let hands explore under chitons. A pair of nude youths wrestled in the center of the room, sweat glistening on their golden skin. The handful of *hetaerae* settled with their patrons to discreet acts of intimacy.

All the time, the musicians played double pipes and strummed the strings of lyres.

His palm warm and dry, Hektor stroked first my shoulder, then slowly down my arm and back up again. His touch was that of a master sculptor molding my flesh. I closed my eyes and let his warmth defrost me, one degree at a time.

His fingers on my cheek turned my face into his. Flecks of red gold floated in the warm brown of his eyes; shiny locks the color of polished cedar curled on his forehead.

"Athena of Korinth," he whispered, "why do you lock your fire inside marble? You have the face of a goddess but the too-serious expression of a woman past her prime. Have your duties aged you? Do you ever laugh?"

His words stung because they went straight to the truth. The Temple employed more than a thousand women to be fed, clothed and cared for, even unto death. While the Goddess promised love and pleasure to others, my days were filled with petty squabbles, leaking roof tiles and unsettled debts.

"We do not always have choice in our lives," I answered too defensively. "I was a child when my father delivered me to the Temple. But I have worked all my life, and the Goddess has blessed me. When the Gods appoint, we must obey."

"You are far too intelligent to believe in that superstition, Athena of Korinth. Gods do not reward or punish—or ordain our lives. Epicurus says that we are but atoms moving in space. We can only hope for pleasure and avoid pain. Why not accept pleasure for its own sake? Who can say that he shall still live tomorrow?"

Sliding his arm around me, his hot palm moved onto the sheer bodice of my gown and took my breast in his hand. In one smooth, effortless motion, he reached down and eased my legs from the footstool to the divan, pulling me back into him, turning us on our sides, a little upright against the armrest. His manhood was a stone post at my back.

I held my breath while he cupped my other breast and his lips found that spot on my neck that opens all doors. I didn't try to suppress my moans of pleasure. I purred like a cat.

Hektor simply took me in his expert hands, doing exactly what I wanted but hadn't dared ask. My nipples grew hard in an instant under his fingers and rose in tight peaks through the yellow silk.

He shocked me with a splash of wine on the mound of my breast. Before I could think to stop him, he sucked away the wine, leaving a dark circle. I ran my fingers through his curls, forgetting everything— where I was, who I was.

His long fingers eased up the back of my gown, sliding under the gossamer silk. He lingered for a moment to stroke the golden thigh band before caressing my hip, my inner loin, and then slipping into the wet. He went straight to a spot in my canal that I never knew existed.

Heat spread instantly through my pelvis and buttocks and down my loins. The atoms of my body, moving in space, melted into a pool of warm oil.

I'd heard of such a spot but thought it was a myth. I gasped out loud when his finger rotated; he covered my mouth with his other hand to still my cries. His lips and warm breath were on my neck soothing me with whispers in a low and husky voice.

"Sh-h-h. Relax, Athena of Korinth. You are so beautiful. Let me pleasure you."

I would have promised anything if his touch on that spot would never end. Surrendering all, I tumbled without sense of head or foot; rolling waves washed over me. The release was so needed, tears wet my lashes. Hektor kissed them away.

My mind stilled; I had no thoughts or cares. I lay utterly at ease with my body molded into his.

He had softened somewhat but was still hard. I reached back for him, but he stopped my hand.

"I shall take care of that later."

His tone sounded too matter-of-fact for a man lost in passion. He straightened the long skirt of my gown, pulled us upright and handed me the golden chalice. I felt dizzy and disoriented. I'd had too much wine and not enough to eat.

"You shall love Alexandria, and Alexandria shall love you," he was saying as if all had been decided.

I suddenly hated his smile. Rather than charming, I saw him as smug. Was this the strategy? Send Hektor to seduce me, and I would follow him back to Egypt? Did they honestly think me so weak that I could be tamed by an orgasm?

I willed my eyes to ice when I passed the golden goblet back to him. The lapis lazuli of the Hathor ring on my hand was almost black in the low light. Hektor's hands with knowing fingers were now occupied with his wine cup and mine.

"You have serviced me well, Hektor of Naukratis," I thanked him politely, frost hanging on every syllable. "You have most ungraciously reminded me that I must attend to my needs more frequently."

Turning my back on him, I called for my cape to cover my wine-stained breasts and bid good night to a sober Xenon. Then with my back straight as a sword and head held high, I followed the lamp boy up the steep slope to my sacred hill with the Temple that reveres women.

CHAPTER 4   ORACLE OF DELPHI

"Great deeds are usually wrought at great risks." – Herodotus

Bright blue shutters stood open to brisk air filled with the sweet scent of herbs. A pair of larks sang out to each other.

The warm morning sun streamed onto stacks of scrolls scattered about my cypress writing table. Following a sunbeam, a butterfly landed next to my hand, his pale wings not much lighter than my milky skin. The sky was deep blue with cotton clouds moving quickly from the sea over the land.

I had pushed last night's humiliation from my mind and concentrated on sorting petitions according to time-sensitive, less urgent, and capricious, when the Ancient One scratched at the oak door to my office.

"Hektor of Naukratis requests an audience with Your Grace. He waits at your pleasure in the reception hall."

The nerve of the man.

"Tell him that I prepare for my journey to the Oracle of Delphi. My purification rites allow me no visitors."

When the Ancient One returned, she carried a small ebony box. Inside, on a bed of saffron silk, coiled a double-serpent bracelet of gold. A large oval garnet gleamed from a *Herakles* knot formed by the curling tails of entwined twin cobras. Both snakes had glinting emerald eyes.

A tiny scroll of papyrus tied with a yellow silk band rested on top. The script was in a fine, artistic hand, the words almost those of the final stanza of a Sappho verse from last night.

She of yellow hair was the Nymph Athena,
And the lilac-tressed were Iphis and Io;
How they laughed, relating at length their ease in
Evading the Satyr.

Hektor had substituted yellow hair for orange and named the nymph Athena. And yes, I did consider him a satyr.

Fear the Greeks even when bearing gifts. First the ring from Ptolemy and now a bracelet from Hektor. My first impulse was to toss the box aside, but instead, I lifted the bracelet and let the serpents twist around my forearm. All the magic of Egypt had been crafted into the exquisite gold work. I twisted my arm back and forth, watching the sunlight play off the delicate detail.

I argued with myself that I should send the bracelet back immediately, but already knew I would keep it. I sighed. Perhaps my price was less than I thought.

Setting the empty box at the corner of my desk, I went back to work. There were at least a dozen scrolls requiring my attention before we sailed for Delphi. But my eyes kept going to my writing arm with magical cobras coiled around the hypnotic garnet stone.

It was an easy sail across the Korinthian Gulf to the port serving the Temple of Apollo on the slopes of Mt. Parnassus. From there I rode a mule until we began the final ascent on foot. I climbed endless stone steps passing through rows of terraces lined with squat treasury buildings.

The Sun God Apollo had first come to Delphi as a dolphin, a *delphis,* to vanquish the ancient spirits. He chose his Oracle from among the oldest and purest of the peasant women, christening her Pythia. Each new generation of the Oracles of Delphi bore the same name.

The Oracle was the official stamp of approval for all important decisions and weighty affairs of state. Even the young Alexander the Great came to her. When she refused to speak, the teenager had grabbed the old woman by the hair until she screamed out, "Let go of me; you are unbeatable!" And so he almost was.

One could always arrange the desired prediction with a generous offering to any of the terrace treasuries. The phrases uttered in trance were so obscure that they could mean anything. In hindsight, almost any verse could be construed to fit the events that followed.

I didn't bother to prearrange a prophecy. Although Ptolemy's Royal

Commission was indeed tempting, an unheard-of opportunity for any woman, Hektor had turned me off the idea. I didn't like being manipulated. I'd have to swallow my pride to go to Alexandria now. Consulting the Oracle was a formality. I'd already decided how I would interpret her words—whatever they were.

The sanctuary of Apollo at Delphi perched on a rocky spur overlooking a green valley with groves of cypress, oak and olive. Austere Doric marble columns rose in tall, circular shafts fluted with parallel grooves. Each pillar was topped by a plain capital with square abacus supporting the long beam of the roofline.

Three carved cautions greeted the truth-seeker at the entry to the sacred courtyard. KNOW THYSELF, NOTHING IN EXCESS and A PLEDGE, AND RUIN IS NEAR. I took the last as a warning of the demise of so many Greeks in defense of that cruel master, honor.

A crowd gathered under the shade of a covered *stoa* constructed with ribbed Ionic columns. These capitals were carved in the coils of a scroll, each pillar a single megalith rather than the usual stacking of thick marble discs. The back wall of the arcade was inscribed with the names of thousands of freed Athenian slaves and the justification for their manumission.

Inside the courtyard, it was eerily still. The muted voices of the crowd murmured among the marble columns and echoed quietly against the stony hillside. White doves fed on bread offerings.

The Oracle was late. She might yet be deciding which petitions to grant. I was certain I would be among the chosen. One high priestess wouldn't refuse another.

The sun was sliding into the west and the shadows long when the Oracle at last appeared from the *naos* of the Inner Temple. Silence fell across the courtyard; even the birds hushed and flew to the trees. Anticipation sharpened the air as before a storm.

Two strong priestesses in unbleached wool held the Oracle upright between them and settled her on a tripod stool above a small opening in the earth. The two kept beside her, one on each side, supporting her arms.

Her ancient shoulders sagged under the weight of her robe. Drool oozed from the corners of her slack mouth. Her head rolled from side to side. Her lids fluttered wildly over gleaming white eyes with no trace of irises.

She was in a trance, of that I was certain, but whether it was self-induced or brought on by a psychotropic drug, I couldn't say.

Starting slowly and then pivoting faster and faster at the hips, her torso gyrated wildly in circles. Without the two women holding her, she would have flown from the chair. We all watched, mesmerized. There wasn't a sound save the windsong in the cypress. I thought I could hear the crowd breathe as one.

Suddenly, she lifted her head and sang out a long single note, not forming any word but exhaling *O-o-o-o-o-o* until the last of her breath. Her white eyes appeared to look in my direction. Those standing near me stepped away.

When she spoke, her voice rocked me. It was fierce, not at all what I expected. Not a man's voice exactly, but too deep for a woman. Her words boomed against the stone buildings and then, echoing from all directions, bounced back.

"Athena of Korinth! Approach that thou mayest know thy Path."

My head throbbed. I felt light-headed. There was a rushing sound in my ears.

Pythia closed her eyes, and when she opened them again, her irises were the palest of gray rings around small black dots. She stared at me, but her expression was blank; I wasn't certain she actually saw me.

"Thou camest in this Form to learn thy Destiny," she intoned in that vibrating voice of no gender. "Know that all is written on the Green Stone buried in the Sands."

As she spoke, droplets of saliva spewed from her lips. The wind shifted and brought a chill that blew through my wool cape.

"Await not!" she roared.

My heart skipped a beat with her urgency.

"There are two Roads," she warned. "Choose carefully. One leads to Honor. One to Slavery."

She closed her lids for a brief moment and opened them wide. Her sudden, direct stare went right to my soul. The Oracle clearly saw me now—the real me.

And I saw her. Kiya, nursemaid and protector of Isis.

"Athena of many faces and many times," she called to me.

I heard myself gasp. What next would she say?

"Make thine own Nature, not the advice of others, thy guide in this

Life and all others."

This life and all others. Would anyone question what she meant? Already a wide circle had formed around me, a circle of fear. Oh, how I dreaded what Kiya might reveal. Surely she wouldn't expose me.

But I needn't have worried. As if drained of all her energy, she hung her head. Limp strands of gray hair covered her face.

I thought she'd fallen asleep when she looked up and hissed, "A crocodile spells the End and the Beginning."

As if on cue, the sun moved behind the peak of Mt. Parnassus, plunging the courtyard into deep shadow.

"The Voice is stilled. It is finished," Pythia whispered. She was just an old woman again; her blank stare was back.

Kiya no longer looked into my soul.

The two priestesses helped her down from her tripod and led her back into the *naos*. Mine was the only message today.

The crowd broke into small grumbling groups. Many had journeyed from Athens and beyond; they would pass yet another night at a nearby inn.

Contrary to my expectation, much of what the Oracle said was far from a riddle. She warned clearly not to wait. She declared without any doubt that my destiny was on a green stone—what could she mean but the Emerald Tablet? I interpreted the sands as Egypt. But two paths? One to honor and one to slavery? And the crocodile?

Distracted, I brushed against Ptolemy's envoy Kadmos, who bowed his head and murmured an apology. Ever the diplomat, he didn't mention the Oracle's message, but he looked exceedingly pleased with himself.

Hektor stood behind him; his curls burning deep red in the late rays of the sun. I glared into his eyes for a moment before I turned away. His confident smile was gone.

I'd reached the terrace below the sanctuary when Hektor caught up.

"Athena!" he called out at the same time he took my arm.

I pulled away with no attempt to be gracious and faced him. It crossed my mind to keep going, but I was certain he would follow. It was best to confront him and be done with it. I signaled to my companion priestesses to wait down the path.

"I know what you think of me," he said. "I tell you that you are wrong."

He spoke earnestly and sincerely, so that for a fleeting moment, my resolve softened; I was almost swayed to trust him. His eyes looked honest enough, without a hint of his usual arrogance.

"No, Hektor of Naukratis, it is you who is wrong," I said with perhaps more coldness than I felt. "I think of you not at all."

He was still bold enough to put his hand on my shoulder as I turned to leave. When I lifted my hand to move his aside, the garnet in the double cobra bracelet on my forearm caught the sun.

We both looked at it. Hektor had the good sense not to smile, but the confidence was back in his eyes. I wore his gift—a victory for him. I felt myself blush. Another victory for him.

When I went down the path, he didn't try to stop me, but I sensed his eyes following my descent and could only guess for how long. I didn't once turn to look, not even when I made the bottom of the hill and found my mule driver waiting impatiently to get home to his supper, now sure to be cold.

CHAPTER 5   ANCIENT ONE

"Happiness is a choice that requires effort at times." – Aeschylus

Once resolved to go to Alexandria and having procured the blessing of the League's *strategos*, who could never deny the prophesy of the Oracle, I experienced a sense of exhilaration, even liberation. I was to see Egypt again. I was to see the Nile again. I found myself laughing at silly jokes. It had been days since my last headache.

My change in mood didn't go unnoticed. I caught the Ancient One casting me sly looks when I hummed and smiled.

"Your Grace seems in better spirits since the symposion."

"The symposion? I've quite forgotten that," I replied with a dismissive wave of my hand. "I look forward to this new challenge, that is all. I am aware of no other woman blessed with such an opportunity."

Not being an architect, I wasn't sure how I would oversee a construction project. But the Oracle of Delphi left no doubt about my destiny—it lay buried in the sands of Egypt.

I would not sail with the delegation but travel later on a trading ship owned by Xenon; his yearly tribute to pirates guaranteed safety. With the winter storm season past, our route went straight south across the Mediterranean to Cyrene in Libya with a stop on the island of Crete. After Cyrene, we would sail east, hugging the North African coast.

There was much to arrange before my departure. Ptolemy's Royal Commission didn't require I give up my authority in Korinth, and I had no intention of doing so. I had worked all my life to attain the position of Supreme Priestess.

I poured over the details required to manage the Akrokorinth from Alexandria. My staff was well-trained; I'd seen to that.

Delegate. Delegate. Delegate.

After careful deliberation, I named competent Irene of Samos, too loyal and weak to usurp me, as manager in my absence.

The Ancient One scratched at my office door.

"Your Grace, Hektor of Naukratis requests an audience. He is prepared to wait."

"Tell him that I am occupied with my duties."

"Do your duties ever allow you to enjoy the theatre?"

We both swirled at the sound of Hektor's male voice here in the most private of sanctuaries, my office. The Ancient One clutched her chest. I jumped from my chair to grab her arm as her bony knees hit the tile floor.

"How dare you enter my chambers?" I demanded. "Men are forbidden on the Temple grounds."

Mine was a small house at the back of a white-walled garden, the last building after a cluster of brick dormitories and storage rooms. My office with its window on the sea was up a steep flight of open stairs. Hektor had penetrated deep into sacred grounds.

His broad shoulders filled the doorway; he had to duck his head under the oak lintel. His chiton, ending at mid-thigh, fell on tanned, muscled loins. Leather sandals laced up to his knees. The scarlet cape on one shoulder was fastened with a golden lion that matched two armbands around his powerful wrists.

I resented that he was such a magnificent specimen of masculinity—and even more, that I noticed.

"You must leave at once," I insisted. "Your presence here offends the Goddess."

But instead of leaving, Hektor helped the Ancient One from the floor and settled her on a three-legged stool. Without any hesitation, he found the water urn and bent to a squat to put a clay cup to her lips, holding it for her while she sipped. She squeezed her eyes shut as if frightened to see what evil filled the room.

Her breathing slowed. He asked if she were hurt. She shook her head and opened her eyes. She actually looked at Hektor with gratitude, seeming to forget it was his audacity that had caused her to fall.

I glared at him, but he looked at the Ancient One, not at me.

"Do not blame her," he commanded me. "I followed her here."

"I blame no one but you."

Satisfied the Ancient One was revived and unharmed, he rolled back on his haunches and faced me.

"I sail the day after tomorrow, Athena. You shall not see me for weeks." He spoke as if we were long-time lovers. "Come to the theatre with me. There is a performance this evening of Menander's *Double Deceiver*."

I had to give him credit for persistence—and that tantalizing self-assurance. He appeared oblivious to my power as Supreme Priestess; men usually cowered in my presence.

"You need a break from your work, woman. I fear your frown will etch itself forever into your brow."

The Ancient One turned wide eyes on me. It was clear she waited for my response. That surprised me—we both knew there could be only one answer.

"I have no time to waste," I snapped impatiently.

"At last, she acknowledges the truth! Indeed, my sweet Athena of Korinth, you have *no* time to waste. Each moment that passes is gone forever. The difference in men's lives is simply how moments are passed. Do you choose to pass them in pleasure or pain?"

"And if I choose not to go to the theatre, does that mean I prefer pain? Perhaps time spent with you is more pain than pleasure?"

Hektor smiled. We both knew any pain he caused was born of the pleasure he'd given me. There was no point in pretending the symposion never happened.

He had a disarming and infectious enthusiasm about him that bordered on boyish. For a moment, I envied his freedom to choose pleasure. My desk overflowed. Piles of scrolls and wax tablets nearly buried the floor mosaic of a nymph struggling in the arms of a satyr.

Yes, I was tempted, I really was.

"In any event," I said with more conviction than I felt, "we live not as we wish but as we can."

"Sad words from a beautiful woman who could have anything she wished. I ask you only to the theatre. Leave all this behind for a few hours. It shall be here when you return."

"You do not strike me as a man who lacks for company. There must be many women who would be pleased by your attention." I really didn't want so much frustration in my voice, but there it was. "Why do you pursue me with so much persistence?"

"Why pursue you? Because, beautiful Athena, you beg to be pursued. Your signals are subtle but unmistakable. And I love a challenge. Is it not harder to conquer a woman than to subdue a wild beast?"

A challenge. And a conquest. I was accustomed to that kind of thinking. What I resented was that he saw me as needy. Begging to be pursued.

The Ancient One sat quite still and made no move to leave; she hadn't said a word. Did she hope to protect me—or that Hektor and I would forget her and play out our drama as if alone?

Her presence didn't at all deter Hektor.

"Life is too important to be taken seriously," he said, taking my shoulders in his big, strong, warm hands. "We have only this moment—only here and now."

Hektor never once kissed me at the symposion but had conquered me with his lips on my neck and breasts. How easy it had been for him. I saw my own head mounted on a wall among his trophies of lion and wild boar.

I tried to move away, but he held me firmly without being forceful.

"Pleasuring you gave me pleasure in a new way. I want more. *You* want more. Listen, Athena—your need speaks to you now."

His hands stroked slowly down my back, his long fingers molding my waist and spreading across my hips. He cupped my buttocks in his palms and pulled me into him. I felt my arms slide around his neck.

Lowering his head slowly, holding my eyes, I knew he was going to kiss me, even with the Ancient One looking on. What I didn't know was whether, with the Ancient One looking on, I would open my lips and welcome him.

CHAPTER 6   ISABEL

"Once made equal to a man, woman becomes his superior." – *Socrates*

Instead of a warm kiss, icy water splashed my lips. I opened my eyes to Barb's face, not Hektor's, inches from mine. Her eyes were wide with relief.

"Sorry about the water, but you wouldn't wake up. I didn't know what else to do."

I blinked. My head was spinning. Why had she brought me back so soon?

"It's been 24 hours."

Only one day had passed here? What would a week be like? I looked around my place with the eyes of someone coming home from a vacation. Only no dust had accumulated. The roses in the vase on the dining room table were still fresh.

"Please talk to me!" she demanded. "Are you okay?"

"I need a couple of minutes to adjust. You pulled me out of the middle of something."

"What something? Was it good or bad?"

"I think good, but I may never know."

"Hector's tried to Skype you twice. His message says it's urgent."

It was uncanny to talk with Hector in Buenos Aires while all the time I saw him as Hektor of Naukratis with curls on his forehead and one bare shoulder.

"I can't get away, Isis. I need more time with the attorney. But my mother arrives in Vegas tonight. I want you to meet her."

"I'd love to, Hector," I lied.

I'd heard too much about Hector's mother. He sang her praises quite loudly; they were obviously close. Too close in my opinion. He was her only son; he'd never married. According to Hector, Isabel de Segovia was an astute businesswoman, a renown art collector and a gourmet cook—a real mother-in-law from hell.

"She'll be staying at the Bellagio and wants you to join her there for a drink. Get to know you *un poco*."

I bet she can't wait to find everything wrong with me.

"How long is she in town?" I asked as casually as I could. *Please don't say she's coming just to meet me.*

"Only a day or two. There's an art auction at the Venetian. I asked her to take you. She said she's looking forward to it."

I'm sure it's the last thing she wants to do.

"I've told her all about your place and what a great eye you have." He positively beamed with pride.

Knowing Hector, he hadn't held back any of that enthusiasm with his mother. *Doña de Segovia* was primed to hate me.

I settled on a Dior suit from my favorite vintage shop and a Gucci bag from the swap meet. From deep in my closet, I dug out a pair of low-heeled black patent pumps with discreet gold buckles. The navy blue blazer with box-pleated skirt and a white silk blouse, open at the neck with a strand of pearls, made for a Caroline Kennedy look that would have pleased most mothers.

The Petrossian Bar at the edge of the Bellagio lobby was packed, but I spotted her right away at a prime table set in a curved balustrade alcove. Waiters circled around her like drones to the queen.

To set the stage perfectly, a pianist with shoulder-length hair played a complex, full keyboard rendition of "This Guy's in Love with You" on the Steinway piano.

Isabel was ready for me. A bottle of *Moet & Chandon* chilled in a sterling ice bucket; two flutes waited on the small glossy table.

I recognized her suit as Fendi; it was definitely not secondhand. She wore her rich black hair, streaked with glorious silver, pulled back severely into a bun, like a prima ballerina. Her beauty was still quite stunning. I hoped that I look half as good at her age. Of course, she had the benefit of money and South American cosmetology.

It wasn't until I sat opposite her that I saw who she was. Sit-hathor's eyes bored straight into mine. She had been my mother twenty-five centuries ago in Egypt; now she was Hector's. Was that a good thing or bad?

If I looked surprised, she didn't.

"*Encantada*, Isis. It is a pleasure to see you at last."

The formality of her tone said that it wasn't a pleasure at all.

For an instant, the Petrossian Bar morphed into Hathor's Temple, and she wore a silver-tasseled wig, her flashing dark eyes lined with *kohl*. She didn't wait for my response but plunged ahead, taking charge, directing our drama.

"You may call me Isabel. That is my name in this lifetime. We won't bother with formalities. No *Señora de Segovia*. Hector would not like that."

She was not warm. I didn't sense any of the love she had for me in the past, but then she had been as cold in her temple in Thebes the day I challenged her will.

"Isabel and Isis." She said Isis in the Spanish way so that it began with the same 'ee' sound as Isabel. "Do you not find that an interesting coincidence?"

Again, she didn't wait for a response.

"Do you believe in coincidences, Isis? I do not."

"What have you told Hector?" I asked.

"I haven't spoken with Hector of our past lives together. It isn't for me to make him aware. He must be ready himself to hear. If he is not ready to believe, it doesn't matter what I say."

My first thought was that she was wicked to keep something so remarkable from him, but on consideration of my own lies and secrets, I concluded I was a bit wicked, too. Like mother, like daughter.

"So you see, Isis, I am in an awkward position. I know you far better than my son does. I have never seen him like this. He is altogether enamored of you. But then, you know that."

Her musical Spanish accent and deep voice gave her a continental mystique.

"Did you use the Power to entrap him, Isis?"

Her abrupt question threw me a bit off balance. I didn't like 'entrap' but decided to let it go. I would have told her that it was Hector who pursued me and, that not only did I do nothing to entrap him, I found his attention rather overwhelming. But that isn't something one says to a mother who dotes on her son—and certainly not to Isabel.

"No, I didn't use the Power, Isabel. I didn't need to."

She settled back in her chair and studied me with black shiny eyes framed by long, spiky lashes. Emerald studs set in antique gold pierced her ear lobes.

When she took a taste of champagne, an old-fashioned Asscher-cut diamond flashed. The stone was easily five karats, but the ring didn't look the least ostentatious on her regal finger. My guess was a family heirloom, passed down from mother to daughter—or daughter-in-law. The Hathor rings had once been ours in Egypt. Was she displeased that yet another ring might come to me?

A white-jacketed waiter brought Beluga caviar on shaved ice to be served on tiny squares of toast with miniature silver spoons.

"I do care for you, Isis. The feelings tug at my heart. But my first priority in this lifetime is my son. I cannot tell you to love him, if you do not. But I must warn you to be careful."

She waited for me to say that I loved Hector and, when I didn't, she sighed and took another sip from her glass. The red of her long nails matched her lips. Her makeup was exquisitely applied, just enough to highlight angled cheekbones and arched eyebrows and give blush to her ivory skin.

"So that is how it is. Well, Isis, what do you propose we do now?"

I returned her Sit-hathor look with an Athena one.

"I propose you let Hector and me work it out."

That brought a raised eyebrow and her smile that never showed teeth. There was a tiny flicker of respect in her eyes before they hardened again.

"It seems I am expected to help you in a new career. Let us focus on that—to please Hector. The rest will unfold as our destiny dictates."

She had one more piece of business.

"Hector tells me that you have the Emerald Tablet. That he was with you in the antique shop when you uncovered it by chance. Is the Tablet safe?"

"I believe so."

So Hector had told her about the Tablet. That made four of us who knew—Isabel, me, Hector and, of course, Barb, who knew no more than Hector, which was very little. And that was how I wanted to keep it.

My story was merely that the Tablet was extremely old and quite valuable. I was discovering that the best way to hide the truth is to keep as close to it as possible.

No, I wasn't interested in selling. Not now, anyway.

Hermes Trismegistus had been clear when he gave the Tablet into my protection to carry out of Egypt. *You are the Chosen One, my daughter. No one must know its power. The world is not ready.*

The world wasn't ready twenty-five hundred years ago and didn't seem any more ready today.

Isabel raised her glass. She looked so like Sit-hathor in the Temple, compelling me to look into her dark eyes, reminding me that she had not only been my mother, but also my superior, the Highest-of-High of the cult.

"To Hector."

But when we had both sipped our champagne, she added, "Tread carefully, Isis. My son is not the man you think he is."

CHAPTER 7   BIDDING WAR

"The secret of happiness is freedom. The secret of freedom is courage." – Thucydides

Traditional oil paintings still covered the foyer walls of the former Guggenheim Gallery at the Venetian where the auction was being held. Inside the venue, gilt chairs with plush red velvet backs and seats stood in ten rows, about twenty chairs in each, with an aisle down the center.

The registrar recognized Isabel and stood to greet her. Without looking her name up in the computer, he handed over a white paddle about the size of a square Chinese fan with the number 103 in bold black font. His assistant gave each of us a glossy, bright-colored catalogue printed on the most expensive of papers.

Each painting on sale this afternoon was featured in full color with a physical description of dimensions and other technical data along with its *provenance*, the history of ownership tracing the painting back to its creator and first owner. The last piece of information was the expected price range of the sale. If there was to be a minimum bid, that was also listed.

We took our seats near the rear of the room, on the outside, closest to the door, in velvet cushioned chairs marked 'Reserved.' Isabel, no doubt, chose these seats for fast exit.

The crowd was of mixed ages, largely well-dressed and formal; a few looked artsy with longish, slightly unkempt hair. The handful of businessmen types I guessed to be private collectors.

Isabel saw someone she knew. Her eyes went slightly wide, and her right eyebrow arched almost imperceptibly.

"What is it?" I whispered and turned to look.

Standing in the aisle, about ten seats from us, was the General. I hadn't seen him since that night at Caesars Palace when his words severed Rasheed from me with the precision of a surgeon. Before that, I hadn't seen him since I slit his Persian throat in a desert tent.

His expensive Saville Row suit flattered his bull frame; the cashmere caressed his thick shoulders and chest without pulling. He wore a conservative tie with discreet ivory polka dots on blood-red silk.

First he bowed his perfectly coiffed head to Isabel and then to me. The amused smile on his face was an odd mix of Cheshire Cat and Mona Lisa. He turned and took his seat on the other side of the aisle, also near the rear.

"Do you know him?" I asked Isabel.

"I was going to ask you the same thing."

She looked at me in a way that said she expected me to divulge first.

"I met him through an old boyfriend. I think they do business together." There was no reason for Isabel to know anything about Rasheed.

"Hm-m-m." She obviously sensed there was more to the story but didn't press.

"Well," I asked. "How do *you* know him?"

"He is often at auctions," she said vaguely. "I see him everywhere."

I glanced over at the General. He appeared absorbed in his catalogue. In truth, I'd expected to find him trying to menace me from afar.

"He has excellent taste." Isabel had decided to tell me more. "And he is not shy about using his fortune to acquire exquisite pieces. He never buys anything himself but always uses proxies. *Corsican*," she finished in a hushed tone.

I decided that Isabel found the General intriguing.

"The source of his income is reputed to be—shall we say?—on the shady side."

Shady. As far as I knew, Rasheed still did business with the General. It explained the bodyguards. It explained Rasheed's secrecy.

"He believes he has anonymity," she confided. "But the only unknowns are what he will buy and how much he will pay. He always buys. He is an addict."

As it turned out, Isabel was after a small impressionist painting, a rather minor piece in the collection. Still, the price range was impressive to someone like me who picks up my art at antique malls and flea markets.

Stretching the full length of a long table on our left was a row of laptops manned by chic thirty-somethings dressed all in black and armed with smartphones. The podium and easel were at the front of the room at what Isabel called 'the block.'

Stragglers wandered in from the gallery and took the remaining seats. There were about thirty people standing behind us at the back of the room.

Once the British auctioneer got started, the bidding was fast-paced. He opened with a minimum, upping the bids by increments proportional to the price range: thousands, tens of thousands, hundreds of thousands. Potential buyers raised their paddles marked with their respective numbers.

When the competition narrowed and intensified, a bid took only the slightest of nods. I imagined a game of tennis with the players using their heads to keep the ball moving.

The auctioneer never let the final two bidders off easily; he was slow to bring his hammer down, directly asking if the other wished to go higher before declaring, "Sold!"

Isabel commented on each piece as it was introduced. Who would be interested. How much they would pay. She bid casually on several items, lost some to the live bidders, some to the phones. Finally, at a price in the mid-range of the scale, she succeeded in winning the Mary Cassatt oil she had come for. Never hesitating, Isabel relentlessly drove the other bidders until they dropped out. She acknowledged the applause like a duchess.

We rode together in a taxi from the Venetian back to the Bellagio; my car was at the valet there. Isabel seemed pleased with her acquisition. She knew someone in Buenos Aires who would be delighted to purchase it from her.

"Do you mind if I ask how much commission you'll make?"

"As much as I can."

We didn't talk about Hector.

She said goodbye in the lobby next to the Petrossian Bar where we had sipped champagne. Correct and courteous, she treated me like an assistant, not a possible daughter-in-law she disapproved of. I saw why she was successful; she didn't mix feelings with business.

I was watching Isabel weave her elegant way through the tourists and gamblers, when a man stepped up beside me.

"May I offer you a drink?"

The General laughed just a little when he saw the expression on my face. Surprise and fear, I imagine, is what he read. That's what I felt.

"Somewhere safe?" he suggested. He glanced in the direction of the Petrossian Bar. "Here?"

I stood there like a dummy, trying to decide if I should run.

"Are you afraid I'll throw a cloak over your head and carry you off?" he chuckled.

"The thought did cross my mind."

Then his smile came—the same as in the tent in the Persian camp, the smile that crinkled his eyes.

"Come, Ishtar. No tricks. I promise."

He called me Ishtar, the name he gave me when I was his sex slave. My first impulse had been to get away from him as quickly as possible, but instead, I sat for the second time today at a table in the Petrossian Bar.

The waiter smiled big and said, "Welcome back." Isabel must have left a nice tip.

I ordered a Plymouth martini, and the General told the waiter to make it two.

He was more handsome than I remembered. His rough and pitted skin was appealingly savage; no matter how well-groomed, he couldn't hide his animal power. He had the chest of a bull, even in his tailored suit. He wore his hair a little long in the European way. The deep red tie at his throat brought vivid visions of gushing dark blood.

His tone with me was conversational, even friendly. He appeared perfectly at ease. I saw him reclining in his desert tent in silk robes, beard carefully curled and tied with colored ribbons.

He swallowed a gulp of his icy martini and took both giant olives in his mouth, chewing with a smile and studying me, nodding his head slightly.

"It would seem we move in the same circles. First Rasheed, and now Señora de Segovia. Las Vegas is a small world."

"Señora Segovia is mentoring me," I replied, although not sure why I felt compelled to explain. I wasn't his captive anymore.

"And Rasheed?" That's when his eyes got serious and locked onto mine. "Rasheed is none of your business."

He raised his eyebrows and smiled a little. I couldn't tell if he knew Rasheed had dumped me that night at Caesars. I wouldn't give him the satisfaction of learning that his not-so-subtle insinuations had succeeded in driving Rasheed away.

"He doesn't know anything about us, General. I'd suggest you keep it that way—if you want to do business with him, that is."

My warning seemed to amuse him. I studied his face, trying to gauge what he knew, wishing that he might tell me something about Rasheed. Had he seen him? Had he mentioned me? *Would he ever come back?*

But before I could try to draw him out, he put his thick fingers under my chin and turned my face slightly sideways and up. His eyes travelled from my hair, around each feature, and ended by looking in my eyes.

I held my breath for one long moment while the scene in his tent played like a hologram between us—my ride on a comet. I felt it. He felt me feel it.

This was too close to what I'd feared would happen. I willed my voice to be firm, uncompromising and devoid of fear. I wanted to be absolutely clear.

"I'm not going with you—and you're not coming with me. This is not going anywhere."

Why was I sitting here? Why hadn't I run when I saw him?

He chuckled a little at my declaration, as if it were the last thing on his mind. Then he leaned forward the tiniest bit.

"I have a proposal for you, Ishtar. I know you like a challenge."

He had to know that he used the same words a couple of thousand years ago when he laid out my narrow path to survival.

"I am a collector of fine things. I find it more successful if I do not show interest in any item by openly bidding on it. I employ agents who do the buying for me. They earn a respectable commission on each purchase, and of course, I pay all expenses."

I stared at him. I'm sure my face was sheer astonishment.

"Are you offering me a job?"

"I am offering to pay you for your services. That should make a pleasant change for us."

I laughed. How could I not? He joined me, and I felt close to him for a breath. We had shared the most intimate of experiences—passion ending in death.

"Why would you want to hire me? Or do I want to know?"

"All you need to know is that I want to acquire a number of artifacts that will be more sought after if word gets out that I am interested. There are those who would outbid me simply for the pleasure of seeing me lose."

"And that's all there is to it? You want to buy something and don't want the price driven up? That's the reason for the cloak and dagger?"

'Cloak and dagger' slipped out quite innocently. I blinked after saying it. Until now, we'd never mentioned my slitting his throat and escaping in his cloak.

I hadn't meant to be funny, but for the second time tonight, he laughed out loud.

The General was a lot more relaxed in this lifetime. I laughed with him, and he signalled for another round of martinis.

The Petrossian Bar filled up. There was only one seat left at the bar. The hum at the adjacent gaming tables grew louder as evening players began to show.

"I do have choices this time, General. I don't have to accept your offer."

"No, you don't, but you will."

"How can you be so sure?"

"Because you accepted having a drink with me."

His eyes smiled at me across the table.

"That tells me that you are searching for something. Why else would you play games with a man you so feared that you killed him? You *are* playing games with me, aren't you, Ishtar?"

"I'm more interested, General, in learning why you are playing with me." I wasn't going to let him control the conversation. He'd taught me that. I'd learned from the best.

He surprised me with a flicker of tenderness in his eyes, saying, "I had forgotten why I find you so compelling. As afraid as you are, you show no fear. There are few who stand up to me—and no other woman."

His voice lingered over 'no other woman' in a wistful way. Then he smiled and raised his glass.

"I, too, enjoy a challenge, Ishtar. That's yet another thing we have in common." His eyes twinkled; he loved baiting me with unsubtle reminders of our shared taste for dark passion.

We sipped on our martinis. He relaxed back in his chair. He knew my decision, and I knew it, too.

I was sick of my job. I was tired of scraping by every month.

"If I decide to work for you, then work will be it," I cautioned. "Nothing more. Don't expect anything else."

"I expect you to be you. What else could I expect?"

I wasn't so happy with his response; it left open a lot of doors. He was skilled at easing the way, though.

"We won't tell Rasheed about our arrangement, *ma bella*. That *is* what you want, isn't it? For Rasheed not to know about us."

The General reached out again and slowly traced his middle finger down my cheek. His eyes were hypnotic. I didn't pull away.

"This will be our secret." His voice was low, soft for him, mesmerizing. "You can trust me."

He let the spell linger a moment before placing a business card on the table with his cell number and email address. I couldn't take my eyes off the crocodile logo printed in the upper right hand corner. The end and the beginning. But of what?

"Send me your email, and I will forward you the specifics."

When we stood to go, I repeated, "Strictly business. Expect nothing."

And then as if another person were speaking, I heard myself say, "Unless you can convince me otherwise."

I couldn't get to my car fast enough. I half expected him to follow me—or send his little army of bodyguards—but he didn't.

Barb was right. I was crazy. I don't know why I said something like that, except I seemed to have developed a taste for playing with fire.

CHAPTER 8   FRONT MAN

"First secure an independent income, then practice virtue. " – Greek Proverb

I didn't waste much time sending the email, and the General didn't waste any time replying. An upcoming antiquities auction at Bonham's in New York included a rose granite and bronze ibis, listed simply as Pharaonic Egyptian.

Why would he choose me, with no experience, to be his agent? His expertise in game playing being far greater than mine, I was at a loss to see his strategy. It no longer seemed like an accident that we ran into each other at the auction. He lay in wait for me at the Petrossian Bar.

The General probably knew where I lived. A man like that could find out anything—know everything. And then there was that crocodile on his business card.

I decided then and there, I would have nothing more to do with him.

But I weakened when I read his offer again. As promised, he would pay well for my services. His proposal included first class airfare and a hefty retainer up front. I could make more money acquiring his 'fine things' than I'd ever imagined possible.

Athena managed a huge temple with a thousand initiates. I had been her. *I* had managed a huge temple. I was certainly capable of buying a few items at an auction or two. Isabel kept her feelings separate from business. So could I. I would keep my relationship with the General on a 'strictly business' basis.

I chose to believe that the crocodile signalled the beginning of a new life. And the end of my old.

When I clicked on the link to the auction and saw that the ibis looked exactly like the Abydos statue Isis had intended to give to her father, I took it as a sign that destiny was pointing the way.

I prayed it wasn't the road to slavery.

Barb was incredulous. She couldn't believe I would consider any contact with the General.

"You don't know anything about him. Everything you told me points to some kind of criminal activity. You don't mess around with these kinds of people. They play for keeps."

"What he's asking me to do is...legitimate. Collectors use front men all the time to protect their identities."

"But where does the money come from?" Barb insisted. "You could be laundering dirty money from drugs—or human trafficking."

I didn't have a ready answer to that. *One road leads to honor.* But even I couldn't rationalize the General as honorable.

"What if I agree to one auction and find out what I can about him before continuing?"

"What if he won't let you out once you're in?"

That sounded an awful lot like slavery. But like two sides of a coin, I also saw the General's offer as a chance to be free, my own boss.

"I'm a slave now, Barb. I barely make enough money to survive. I'm saving nothing for the future. What's my plan B? Marry money? Isn't that a kind of slavery?"

"You're being ridiculous," she snorted. "We both know marriage to Hector would hardly be slavery."

"We don't know that, Barb. I already feel like a slave to Skype."

Barb and I had been round and round about Hector; there was no point in talking more about him. We sat quietly for a few minutes. Norah Jones crooned in the background while we sipped Merlot; Aisha curled in my lap. Barb curled up on the red sofa with her long legs tucked under her. Her pale hair was luminous in the low light. I watched her expression change from exasperation to acceptance.

"I can see you've made up your mind. I'm done trying to convince you to sanity. When the shit hits the fan, I'll be here to say *I told you so.*"

"Then you'll help me go back again?"

"What! God, you really know how to push the limit."

"I'll need 48 hours this time."

"Two days! I haven't even agreed to one."

But she didn't put up any more resistance. We could go through the same arguments—she with the cons, and me with the pros—but we both knew what the final outcome would be.

Changes *were* happening in my life. But I didn't have the kind of power I'd imagined. Possessing the Tablet wasn't enough. Something was missing. And there was only one way to find out.

The General was most accommodating with my suggestion for a trial period. I'd go to New York for the auction of the ibis, and we would take it from there.

"You are a free woman, Ishtar. The commission from this purchase will buy you even more freedom."

Did he mention freedom because he knew about the road to slavery? I stopped myself. I was getting paranoid. The General couldn't possibly know about the Oracle of Delphi. Coincidences *do* exist; I couldn't discount them.

Hector was still in Buenos Aires. I flat-out lied to him with an excuse for my absence. If he knew I was hiding something from him, I didn't sense it.

But Aisha sensed the coming change. She insisted on lying on my laptop keyboard or trying to hold my left hand with her paws while I typed.

I felt good. I felt strong. I was ready for Athena.

CHAPTER 9 BORN OF THE SEA

"Faithful earth, unfaithful sea." – Ancient Greek Saying

My airless, windowless cabin reeked of mold and salty damp. Straining wood groaned and creaked in the violent swells pitching us from side to side. Muffled voices shouted above a howling wind.

I made my way up the ladder to the deck where tall waves broke over the gunwale and sprayed sea water like driving rain. Sailors had secured ropes around their waists to lash themselves to masts and railings. The long rows of oars were shipped, and the shackled men clung to the wood beams to keep their seats.

The captain came to me at once and shouted in my face to stay below. We clutched the ladder handrail with both hands as the deck listed deep to port.

Water flooded over the side and swamped the shackled oarsmen. They cried out to be released, but no one moved to help them.

It was spring; the season of storms should be over. Greeks never sail on the open sea in the winter, and no matter the time of year, prefer to hug the coast. The islands of the Aegean ensure they are almost always close to land, but after Crete, the journey south to Libya meant open water. It also saved weeks at sea.

"Poseidon is angry! The Luck Gods have forsaken us," the captain shouted. "Pray to Aphrodite to save us!"

His eyes were desperate; he grabbed my upper arm, begging for intervention. "You are Her priestess. Convince Her to calm Her lover, God of the Seas."

Before I could answer, another massive wave hit the ship and tossed us deeper to port. Only the captain's grip kept me on my feet. The list was so steep that the red sails dipped into the foaming white crests before the mast righted itself again.

I saw everything through a curtain of rain. Water rushed across the deck, around my legs, and nearly swept me below. Sailors shouted vainly into the wind, and the cries of the chained oarsmen grew to a wail.

"Release them," I screamed to the captain.

"They are slaves," he shouted back, his face inches from mine. "Save the ship!"

I would gladly have called on Aphrodite, except at that moment, rope bindings broke, and a mountain of *amphorae* collapsed. Hundreds of clay jars, heavy with wine and olive oil, shot across the deck with the force of missiles, knocking sailors overboard and crushing others.

A clay jar hit the captain's right leg, knocking him off balance and causing him to release his hold on me. I grabbed his thick forearm as he fell and tried to drag him forward; he screamed when his shin bone burst through the skin. His shoulders were so close to the hatch that I believed I had saved him. He grabbed the balustrade with his free hand while I gripped his other wrist with both hands, using all my strength to try to haul him below deck.

The winds twisted and ripped the drenched sails; torque on the mast splintered the wood. The snap of the mast cracked the air like a giant thunderbolt. The massive wooden beam with yardarms and gaffs fell with a thundering crash, pinning screaming sailors to the deck.

The wind roared, and the sea raged, but still I could hear injured men pleading to the Gods for mercy.

The captain didn't make it. First his hand slipped, and then mine. As hard as I tried, I couldn't hold on. I watched helplessly as he slid along the wet angled planks, over the side and into the sea.

"O Aphrodite!" I cried out to the Goddess. "Born of the Sea, Daughter of Zeus, give ear. Save us from the wrath of Poseidon. He loved You once. Offer Him whatsoever He desires, and I shall make sacrifice."

Within minutes, the wind, having raged in full fury, was spent. The great trading ship, with its rows of broken oars, was still afloat and rocked in harmony with the waves. I didn't realize the sea could calm so quickly. The storm, which had come out of nowhere, disappeared just as suddenly.

Bodies of the injured and dead littered the deck. Dark blood mixed with oil and sea water. Galley slaves slumped over oars, buried by chunks of broken clay *amphorae* and drenched by saltwater and wine. Desperate pleas for help came from all sides.

Miraculously, I was unharmed. My worst injury was a sprain in my wrist from my efforts to drag the captain's heavy body to safety. I believed in that moment that Aphrodite, indeed, watched over me.

The weight of my wool cloak and *peplos*, soaked with rain and sea, dragged at my shoulders. I struggled to make the last steps up to the deck, dropping the green cape at my feet near the hatch. The air, still brisk from the storm, chilled my bare arms.

The sun came out from behind fast-moving clouds, glared off the glistening deck, and sparkled on a plum sea. The sky and sea had been so dark, I thought it was night and was surprised to see the sun still above the horizon.

In the west, near the bright sun, not far in the distance, loomed two square black sails. I watched for a few moments, using my hand to shield my eyes from the sun's glare. The ship headed for us.

O Aphrodite! I shall never doubt you again. Not only had she appeased Poseidon, she had sent help.

I did my best for those who were still alive. It seemed I was the only one left standing until a cabin boy—not more than eleven or twelve years old—surfaced with clay jars of drinking water. We circled the deck together, lifting debris off broken limbs when possible, and holding cups of water to the lips of the conscious.

The three priestesses who travelled with me were not on deck or below in our cabin. Accepting that they had faced the same fate as the captain, I gave a prayer to Aphrodite to deliver their spirits from Poseidon.

Still, a few of the wounded galley slaves might yet be saved. I sent the cabin boy in search of the special tools needed to remove the shackles from their ankles.

A slave's wretched life was spent chained to the bench, rowing in daylight and slumping over the oars by night. Many of those miserable lives were now ended. Great waves had washed over them followed by an avalanche of cargo and equipment that rained down on their trapped bodies.

We worked without pause as the sun dipped into the sea. There was not a cloud in a sky first gold, then mauve. We floated without a ripple in magenta satin water.

The ship with black sails was almost upon us when the cabin boy saw the red flag emblazoned with a black falcon.

"Get below deck," he pleaded, tugging desperately on my wet gown. "Hide!"

The pounding of feet on the deck above my head was the first sign we'd been boarded. Then I heard men's voices speaking loudly and coarsely in a guttural language not at all unfamiliar, but I couldn't make sense of any words.

I clutched the cabin boy to me when the screaming started. A wail might be followed by a splash as bodies were thrown overboard. I couldn't tell if the shrieks were death cries or the protests of the injured being tossed into the sea. The intent of the invaders was clear—leave no one alive.

Pulling the boy tighter into my body, I covered his mouth with my hand, but he wouldn't stop sobbing. I would have sobbed too, if he hadn't needed me to be strong.

The screams finally ended. Night must have fallen; the hold of the ship, always dark, was pitch-black. Then, men with lamps moved among the sacks and chests of cargo, heaving heavy loads up on deck. So far no one had come near the narrow shelf where we lay, covered with filthy rags on a bed of straw crawling with vermin. I didn't know which was fiercer, my fear of discovery by these monsters or my dread of the bite of a plague-carrying flea.

After a long period of silence, I dared look out from under the rags into the blackness of the hold. The men were still onboard; I heard their muted voices and heavy feet on the deck above our heads. A faint whiff of smoke reached us, and the boy and I both stiffened. Fire! They were burning the ship.

The flames started near the center of the hold, above the keel, but spread rapidly as spilled oil ignited. I wasn't certain we could make the ladder before the fire reached it, but if we didn't move quickly, we were sure to burn.

We held onto each other's hands as to a lifeline. My *peplos* dragged through oily water so deep it reached mid-calf; I prayed a random spark wouldn't ignite the sodden wool. We reached the bottom step seconds ahead of the flames. The heat seared my ankles as I climbed, pushing the boy ahead of me, hurrying to escape the tongues of fire licking at our feet.

Near the top, in sight of the stars, the boy was snatched from me. There were more shouts in their language. The cold metal of a sword flashed in the torchlight, and the boy's terrified scream ripped my ears.

"Stop!" I shouted. "Do not harm him!"

The group of men, dark shadows in the dark night, turned toward my voice—a woman's voice. A woman speaking Greek. The surprise on their faces was visible even in the flickering light.

"He is but a child," I reasoned.

The longest of moments passed. No one moved. The heat of the fire below deck seared my feet and legs. I stepped onto the deck into a circle of gaping men.

My soaked gown clung to every curve of my body. The yards of fabric were almost too heavy for me to stand, but I kept my shoulders back and my spine straight.

Rain, wind and sea had washed my barbered curls into a wild mane of unruly blonde waves. Thick tendrils, red gold in the fire, blew across my face and lifted around my head.

"Medusa!" whispered one of the shadows.

The stare of Medusa is said to turn a man to stone if he meets her eye. The men in the circle immediately looked away.

But the giant among them showed no fear of Greek legends. Gripping the cabin boy by his thin arm, he moved closer with a torch. His skin was so black, I could see only the white of his tunic in the dark and then the whites of his eyes. He towered over me, massive as a basalt statue.

"What is the boy to you?" he growled in crude Greek.

Goliath! The Universe had sent Goliath! Once, the Nubian would have done anything for Isis. How could I make him see she was me?

O Aphrodite, sweet Goddess, whisper in his ear.

The crackle of burning wood turned into a roar; we couldn't stay much longer. The ship was so drenched in oil, it might burst into flames at any moment. Death by fire or drowning? I rejected both choices.

The Gods help them that help themselves; I couldn't rely only on the Goddess. I grabbed Goliath's massive wrist.

"Take us with you," I pleaded.

In the torchlight, the lapis lazuli stone of the Hathor ring was blue-black against my white skin. Goliath stared at my hand, pale as snow against his ebony flesh, his eyes fixing on the ring. First he looked puzzled, and then surprised. The whites of his eyes showed all around the black centers. I was certain that he recognized the ring.

When he looked into my eyes, the mirror of the soul, I willed my soul to reveal itself. I'm not sure he fully understood the connection, but I knew in that moment that he wouldn't leave me behind.

He grunted guttural words to the men, and one of them seized me by the arm, dragging me forward. I stumbled on a pile of cloth that was my green wool cloak, the cloak of a priestess of Aphrodite.

"My cloak! Let me take my cloak."

Goliath passed the torch and the cabin boy to a man with a terrible scar on his cheek that ran from eye to jaw. With my cape over his shoulder and his giant hand tight around my upper arm, Goliath led his men to the starboard side, where we slid down ropes to waiting boats.

I clung to his neck for the three-story drop to an inky well, closing my eyes and visualizing the day in another lifetime when Goliath found me in the desert and held me safe in his arms.

The sea was perfectly calm. Only a few hours ago, high waves drowned men on the slippery deck and washed others overboard.

The boats filled quickly, and we rowed toward the mammoth shadow of a ship standing by. We barely floated above the water line; the sea spilled into the boat. Two men bailed constantly. The boy clutched my hand as if he would never let go.

The flames on the trading ship swelled higher and higher; giant fingers of fire clawed the night sky. A wall of heat blasted us. The sea turned red all around; dozens of bodies floated face down in the blood-red waters. As I heard no screams from the ship, I consoled myself that the galley slaves had died before the flames reached them.

Thank you, Aphrodite, for that small mercy.

Balanced atop wooden chests, rough sacks of loot and stacks of *amphorae*, I wept quietly for my priestess companions. So many lives and so much lost. My rare and priceless scrolls. The precious gifts for Ptolemy gone.

But the boy and I lived and were unharmed—at least for now.

CHAPTER 10   BLACK FALCON

"Remember that with her clothes, a woman puts off her modesty." – Socrates

Jupiter, bright white and unblinking, peeked in the tiny window up near the low ceiling. The planet of good fortune was framed for an hour or so before disappearing. I refused to take any meaning from its brief visit. We are all atoms moving through space.

Goliath had locked the cedar door from the outside. I bolted it from the inside and wrapped myself in the wet woolen cloak. It was better than the filthy blanket they gave me; at least the dirt of my cloak was a filth that I knew.

I demanded to have the boy with me, but he never showed. I wouldn't let my mind imagine what they might do to him. He was so young. How had he come to a life of such hardship, working every waking hour on a ship of rough men?

"Open the door!"

The words were shouted in heavily accented, angry Greek. Metal clanged on the other side. Whoever was there got a shock when the door didn't swing open. The iron bolt on this side rattled and shook as someone pushed and banged.

"Not until you bring me my slave!" I shouted.

These men had ruthlessly killed every survivor left breathing on the ship. I reasoned they would do with me as they wished, no matter how compliant I was. I saw no advantage in cooperating.

The voices on the other side argued; I went to the door and listened through the thick plank. The rhythm and sounds of their language were vaguely familiar, like words I might once have known, but now forgotten. Footsteps retreated, followed by silence. Had they gone to fetch an axe?

Minutes passed, and no one came back. My ears strained to hear voices—sounds—anything to tell me what was happening. The waves of the sea lapped lazily against the cedar hull. An edge of the moon showed in the window, dividing the cabin into white light and black shadow. When the moon filled the window frame, the boy begged through the door for me to give in.

"Mistress, please open the door." His voice was high-pitched with fear. "They will hurt me if you don't."

The ship beneath my feet swayed as gently back and forth as a cradle rocked by a mother's hand. I pulled at the rusty bolt and opened the door.

The boy was there, in front of me, but I barely saw him. Holding him by the shoulders, the boy's head to his chest, was Rasheed.

He wore a blue and white striped headdress and gold armbands at his wrists; a belted white tunic covered his chest and down to his knees. Deep lines etched his hard face bronzed almost black by the sun. I saw no trace of tenderness in his sculptured mouth or his burning eyes, but I did see plenty of rage.

No one spoke. Goliath stood stone-faced to Rasheed's right, towering over us all. When I looked into the giant's eyes, he looked away, but not before I saw pity. Fear welled up from my belly and into my throat; I tasted bile. The Nubian's look had been one of regret that he couldn't control what was going to happen.

Without a word, Rasheed drew a curved dagger, put it to the boy's throat. A tiny drop of bright red blood appeared at the point. The boy's eyes filled with terror were a startling clear hazel; tears rolled down his cheeks. He was so thin and so pale. He didn't cry out though, and I thought him terribly brave.

Rasheed glared at me; I saw nothing but hatred in his face. Why? If he truly desired to kill the boy, would he not be dead now? What did he want? To terrify me? To make me beg for the boy's life?

I closed my eyes and envisioned the Hathor ring while I took one long, slow breath and summoned the Power.

I felt a flush of heat; my eyelids fluttered. I grew light-headed and a little woozy from the energy pulsing through my body.

When I opened my eyes again, Rasheed still glowered at me, but the dagger had dropped an inch and no longer drew blood. I took courage from that tiny concession.

"Please do not harm him," I pleaded in the softest of honeyed whispers.

I touched the hand holding the dagger. My fingertips were as light as butterfly wings. His flesh burned so hot, I might have touched fire. I said nothing more, but my eyes told him that he could have anything he wanted from me, if he but let the boy live.

Time slowed. It was so quiet I heard every breath—my own, the boy's, Rasheed's, Goliath's. Even the sea breathed. The roll of the ship steepened. So many dangers in one day. Had we come this far to die now?

Rasheed shoved the boy into my arms. I held the shaking child tight against my breast and looked back with gratitude into Rasheed's stony face. His cheekbones were razor-sharp in the dim light. I could read nothing in his eyes. There was an emptiness there that frightened me more than the rage.

Goliath looked shocked, then relieved. Was the plan to kill us both, but first the boy, to torture me?

"May we have food and water?"

If we were to live, we deserved that.

Rasheed blinked. He hadn't expected me to be so bold. I pressed my advantage.

"And may I have dry clothes and water to bathe?"

He didn't answer but turned and marched down the passageway, his steps pounding the planks. I watched him until he reached the ladder and climbed up to the deck. He never looked back.

Goliath removed the bolt from the inside with an iron chisel, stepped out and pushed the door shut, locking it from outside. His smoky eyes caught mine for a heartbeat before the door closed; a small smile curled his lips. I had an ally.

O blessed Aphrodite! Thank You for Your protection.

The boy calmed in my arms while I rocked him back and forth, singing a little lullaby Athena knew from her wet nurse. I asked him if I might call him Jason, like the captain of the ship *Argo* who brought home the Golden Fleece after many trials at sea. He smiled.

"The angry man with the dagger is Black Falcon," he said. "He is an evil pirate. All the ships sailing this coast fear him."

He must mean the African coast.

"Are we close to Cyrene, Jason?"

"I do not know, Mistress. But the Black Falcon and his men speak Egyptian."

Jason and I slept wrapped in my damp cloak until dawn when the sound of seagulls awakened me. Did gulls mean we were near land? Jason stayed curled in a tight ball, eyes closed, snoring lightly when I rose to use the slop bucket. The rattling of metal startled me, and I hurried to arrange my *peplos* as the heavy cedar door swung open.

Goliath carried a familiar chest and set it gently on the cabin floor. On the lid was carved my name, Athena of Korinth—Αθηνα Κορινθος. Inside were my gowns and robes.

A man followed with a second chest, this one with my papyri. I didn't ask about my chest of jewels, knowing it would never be returned by pirates. I still had the Hathor ring on my finger and Hektor's gold snakes on my forearm—at least for now.

A young boy brought a jar of beer, a loaf of hard brown bread and two plates of hot gruel.

"Thank you," I said to Goliath with as much gratitude as I could put in my voice and my eyes.

I knew the chests and food could only have come with permission of the Black Falcon, but the Nubian delivered them with pleasure.

Before I could ask, he cautioned me that the bath water would be salt and not heated. I gave him a relieved, grateful smile, and he smiled back, his teeth white as ivory in his black face. I wanted to shower him with kisses.

My bath was the sea. Goliath and Jason lowered me over the side in a rough fishnet sling, holding me at the surface of the glassy waters. Brisk but not cold, the salty sea washed the smoke and sweat away.

The sky-blue linen chiton ballooned around me in gossamer swirls. I envisioned a giant but gentle jellyfish protecting me from the dangers of the deep.

Jason scrubbed my filthy *peplos* and cloak, his small hands tugging at the heavy wool and pounding it with stones and a brush of stiff boar bristles. Hung over a boom to dry, the yellow gown and green cape flapped like colored flags when the wind came up.

The sunshine was strong and almost hot, more intense than the spring sun we left behind in Greece. Seagulls circled the ship scavenging for garbage. I reasoned we were quite close to the African coast but couldn't begin to guess which part.

Goliath could loosen the ropes at any moment and let me sink into the sea. No matter how strong a swimmer, I would never survive if they left me. This was indeed trust. Little Jason waved from the deck far over my head, and I waved back.

A dolphin broke the waters not six feet away. If I grabbed his dorsal, might he deliver me to Cyrene as Apollo had come to Delphi? I put my head back in the cool sea. My hair streamed around me in long seaweed-like tendrils; I imagined myself a mermaid. At one with the moment, a hot sun warming my face, I savored the pull and tug of the current. *Each moment that passes is gone forever.* Is that not what Hektor had said?

Who can say that he will still live tomorrow?

Jason handed me the clean cloak to wrap around myself. But in the brief moment I stood on the deck, wet chiton molding to my body, my nipples erect, silver seaweed hair cascading down my shoulders, I saw Black Falcon watching me. Hunger and yearning softened the harsh line of his cheek and jaw. But he turned his back with triangular torso of broad shoulders and narrow waist when our eyes met.

Little Jason stood first in awe, then clapped his eyes with glee.

"Mistress, you are Aphrodite rising from the sea!"

I laughed as I wrapped the heavy cloak around my wet body and pulled him into my breast, kissing his forehead. How could I possibly feel so happy, captive on a pirate ship, with no idea of the future?

It was as Hektor said. *We have this moment only. There is only here and now.*

We were allowed to roam freely on deck. I stayed in the shade of an awning that Jason built for me out of two of my gowns. He was uncommonly quick with language, the way children often are. He told me the names in Egyptian of 'water,' 'sea' and 'ship.' He would run to ask a crewman new words and then carry them back to me, and I would practice, knowing my accent filtered through his.

The food was atrocious—fish and gruel—but it was the same fare as the crew ate, so we were not maltreated. I saved the fresh water for Jason and drank the strong beer that the men called 'Libyan wine.'

The evening came, and the night passed, and still Black Falcon did not send for me.

My morning sea bath became a ritual on the second day. This time I slipped out of the net and swam around the ship. We anchored off a rocky coast that didn't look much different than Korinth, only there were no islands in sight. Goliath hauled up the net and lowered Jason; we splashed in the water—Jason dragging me beneath the surface by my feet. My behavior was not at all that of a priestess. I felt good. I felt free.

In the early evening, when the sky was the deepest of blues and Venus still glittered above the western edge of an inky sea, Goliath came with the message. Black Falcon wanted me in his cabin.

Jason helped me dress my hair. With no curling irons to calm the waves, it billowed around my face and shoulders like angel hair. He held the bronze hand mirror while I wrapped a headband of gold silk across my forehead and tied it at the nape of my neck, grabbing the thick mane of waves into a covered knot.

My gown was of the finest silk, dyed a turquoise the color of the sea in a white sandy cove. My only jewelry was the Hathor ring and Hektor's snake bracelet. I gambled that Black Falcon would leave me these when he had the rest of my gold and jewels.

When I told Jason not to be afraid for me, he said ever so earnestly, "No one could harm someone as beautiful as you."

Black Falcon's cabin was at the stern, up four or five steps from the quarterdeck. At the top of the steps, a polished cedar door glowed in the lamplight. Yellow light streamed through the cracks around the closed shutters of small windows.

Members of the crew rested against the railings, talking quietly with occasional bursts of laughter. They stopped when I passed. I felt their eyes follow me all the way to the door.

Goliath knocked lightly, and we entered another world. Rich carpets spread over the floor; tapestries of verdant marsh scenes woven with dozens of species of bright-colored birds covered the cedar walls. A tall standing brass lamp with cutouts stood in the corner; the walls and furniture dazzled with tiny stars. I had expected austerity from a pirate, but these were the quarters of a Pasha.

Black Falcon sat behind a cedar plank table polished to a high sheen. An ornate silver ewer and two chalices were on the table in front of him. Six-pointed stars like those of the Hebrews bordered the rims.

He didn't rise when I entered; he barely looked at me before signaling Goliath to leave. The door closed quietly behind me, and we were alone. I waited for him to speak, which seemed to take a lifetime. His eyes were cold and cloudy; the lines in his face were deep and harsh, yet still I found him handsome without equal.

"Sit."

I took the other chair at the table, across from him. The arms and high back were carved ebony, the seat cushioned in rust-colored wool. If I had reached forward I might have touched him, but Black Falcon wanted to keep his distance. In spite of his attempt to be cold, his heat seared me.

Leaning back in the chair, I placed my hands on the lion heads at the end of each arm and looked directly—boldly—into his eyes.

Without asking if I wanted to drink, he poured dark red wine into the two chalices and slid one over toward me. The hands were the same. I could feel them on me, the touch of Rasheed—the touch of River God. Black Falcon must have it, too.

He took a sip of wine and wetted his lips. I thought of his mouth on my body, and my nipples hardened. Leaning forward to pick up the goblet, I shifted my weight in the chair, bringing my pelvis forward, twisting my spine to raise my breasts. The chiton bodice molded to me like a second skin, showing deep cleavage. In the yellow light, my skin was the palest of ivory.

Jason had told me the turquoise of my gown matched my eyes. I turned them on Black Falcon as I lifted the chalice to my lips.

My heart pounded, but I carefully controlled my breath, waiting for him to speak. Being this close to him, feeling his heat, made my pulse run wild.

"How much do you think you are worth?" His Greek was reasonable, his tone businesslike, without emotion, frigid with no warmth at all.

Not exactly what I had expected to hear, I blinked and sat back in the ebony chair.

"Worth?" I asked dumbly.

He looked impatient. When he spoke again, his tone was curt.

"How much ransom will your people pay?"

In truth, I had no idea—and no idea of his expectations. Talk of ransom was hardly what I hoped for. Had he sent for me only to negotiate terms?

"I am certain they shall pay whatever you require. Name a number, and I shall tell you if it is reasonable."

He didn't hesitate.

"Two hundred talents of silver."

The number stunned me. I wasn't a royal princess.

"Too much. Ptolemy might give you fifty and no more."

Black Falcon produced a small roll of papyrus and a writing stylus with ink bowl.

"Write the letter. Ask for one hundred fifty."

"One hundred."

He shrugged, nodded and took another drink from the chalice. He avoided looking directly at me.

One hundred talents of silver was a fortune. I could run the Temple in Korinth for five years on that sum. Why did he need so much? Was I a windfall to retire from piracy? He couldn't have planned on my capture. Goliath might have left me behind to burn, never knowing the ship they pillaged carried a Greek priestess under the protection of Ptolemy, Pharaoh of Egypt.

Jason couldn't have told them much; he was a child. Then I remembered the chest of scrolls delivered to my cabin. Black Falcon must have read the Pharaoh's writ guaranteeing my safety and defining the terms of the Royal Commission.

"Why do you ask so much? You risk they do not pay."

He looked at me then, surprise on his hard face.

"They will pay, because they know I will kill you in a most unpleasant way if they do not."

Black Falcon saw an outcome, however improbable, that would require him to be merciless. He couldn't afford an attachment. That's why he avoided looking at me. He didn't trust himself, so he hid behind his armor, one which I chose to believe I could penetrate.

He said nothing as I scribbled the ransom letter and signed it, pushing it back across the cedar plank with my right hand, the one with the Hathor ring on the middle finger. He seemed to notice it for the first time. His eyes widened; he stared at the ring for a long moment before looking up at me.

"Why do you wear the sacred Hathor ring?"

"It was a gift from Ptolemy."

There was no point in subterfuge. If he had read through my papers,

Black Falcon knew everything about me.

"Then it goes with the ransom letter."

"No," I said too quickly and pulled my hand back. I relied on the ring for my strength.

"Better the ring alone than the finger with it," he said in a flat, cold voice.

If there was a shred of mercy in him, he buried it so deep, I couldn't see it.

The night was still. I heard no more laughing on deck and supposed that the crew slept. Waves crashed on a rocky beach not far away. I wondered if I could swim to shore but feared what they might do to Jason if I escaped.

I took the ring off and placed it on the papyrus letter. His expression didn't change. He didn't even look down at the ring. I almost hated him then, but still I refused to believe in his inhumanity.

"You are so hard." I spoke softly, in the intimate tones of a lover. "What has happened to you? What pain have you suffered to build this shell? Can I not reach you at all?"

I didn't think he could grow more grim, but his face darkened a shade, and his eyes went flint-hard. He looked away to stare stonily at the star-cut lamp.

His bed, broad for a single man, was covered with an elaborate woven cloth. His chambers were too tidy and well-appointed for a man. I looked around, half expecting a woman to appear from the shadows.

"Return to your cabin. I am done with you."

Cold. He didn't even look at me when he said it.

Just before I opened the door, I turned back, slightly self-conscious in the shimmering, clinging turquoise silk meant to seduce him. I was desperate to make one last effort—loosening my hair—anything to make him want me, anything to feel his touch on my skin, his lips on my body, his heat next to me. I knew I could convince him, if he touched me and I touched him.

I closed my eyes, visualizing the Hathor ring resting on the ransom letter, summoning the Power.

"I have secrets," my aura teased, "wonderful secrets that only I can share."

I willed him to look at me, but he only stared at the lamp. A muscle twitched in his jaw, and I took a step toward him. Even from across the room, I saw the tic in his eye that signaled he was fighting for control.

My body radiated animal sex mingled with the potent allure of intense sensuality—and deep mystery. Sensuous waves rolled through the cabin. The warm, buzzing field around me expanded, pushing back the icy cloud protecting him. I took another step.

"Do not try your sorcery on me, whore priestess." He spoke without turning his head, refusing to look at me.

I had nothing left. He was always the one man who could resist.

"Why do you despise me so?"

He turned slowly; the deep lines in his cheeks were crevices chiseled in stone. Cold hatred burned in his eyes.

"You are Greek," he spat and looked away again.

I went through the door to find Goliath waiting outside. Black Falcon had never intended for me to stay.

CHAPTER 11   NIGHT VISIT

"The greatest pleasure of life is love." – Euripides

Metal rattling very slightly on the door waked me. I wasn't certain if I heard or dreamed the sound, but the creak of the wood from a step affirmed someone entered the cabin. It was so dark, there were no shadows. I could hear shallow breathing, quiet and controlled. Should I lie still and pretend to sleep or sit up and confront the intruder?

The hand came out of the darkness, but instead of grabbing me, it reached for Jason. I clutched him to me, and he awoke instantly, a young animal alert for danger.

"No," we shouted in unison, but the hand dragged him from my arms and stood him to his feet.

"Get out," Black Falcon commanded.

Jason refused to move.

Black Falcon lifted him, pushed him across the threshold, firmly closed the door and moved a chest to block the entrance. I only saw vague forms; his eyes were more adjusted to the dark than mine.

When Jason's sobs came through the thick wood, I rose from the mat and put my lips to the narrow crack to soothe him.

"Do not fear for me, Jason. Go sleep with the Nubian."

But to Black Falcon I hissed, "Why do you come to me like this? Why do you frighten the boy?"

"He is a slave."

"He is *my* slave."

His fingers were in my hair, loosening the braid, releasing the thick waves to fall around my shoulders and down my back. He lifted a handful and buried his face in my scent.

I traced the deep lines in his cheeks with my fingertips and then outlined his lips, recalling with sweet memory every kiss of River God, of Rasheed.

Black Falcon's breath was hot and moist on my fingertips. I explored his tongue, tugging and pinching gently. He bit down with equal gentleness and sucked.

The knot of his loincloth melted at my touch, and the linen fell away.

Swaying on tiptoes, pressing my breasts into his chest, feeling him hard against my belly, I kissed his lower lip, drawing the flesh between my teeth, matching his soft bite on my fingers. I licked his throat where his Adam's apple bulged slightly.

His body was so tight I thought he might shatter into a thousand shards of glass.

Taking my time, my hands glided along his shoulders and down his biceps, caressing his forearms to his wrists. When I raised his thumbs to my erect nipples, he quivered and jerked. Hot semen sprayed the front of my gown.

Only steps from the wall, I nudged him with my palm on his chest to lean against the damp, rough bulkhead.

"Sh-h-h, let me love you," I crooned in the soft, irresistible cadence of a lullaby.

All the while I breathed promises in his ear, my fingers loosened the tie at my right shoulder and then the left. The milky gown slid past my breasts and hips to pile silently on the floor around my ankles. The flowing waves of my hair lay heavy on my naked back.

Mesmerized and breathless, he allowed his thirsty eyes to drink in my breasts glowing white in the starlight.

With the most loving of touches, with my lips hot on his bronzed chest, I took his hands in mine and placed his fingers in my hair.

There was no place that I didn't taste; I savored his salty sweetness with my tongue. I suckled first one nipple, then the other, my fingers toying at the thick nest of hair at the bottom of his belly. Entangled in my waves, his fists pulled and twisted. The low rumbles of his moans filled the silence.

The muscles down his spine were as tight as knotted rope under my fingertips. I willed my hot palms to ease him, stroking down his back, past his narrow waist to his hips and hard thighs. I willed my lips to excite him. My wet tongue went into his navel, and his manhood swelled into my face.

I circled the engorged knob with my tongue, licking and nibbling. He writhed against the wooden bulkhead, his feet spread wide, hips thrusting toward me. But before I could take him into my mouth, he pulled my face up, his fingers still in my hair, and kissed me.

Only his kiss could carry me to that warm liquid world of rose-colored water and sky. I floated to the narrow mat on the floor, weighing nothing, nothing at all.

There was no rage in him now, only need. He vibrated against me; every cell in his body cried out for me, but still he resisted, refusing to flow into me as I flowed into him.

Arranging me as an artist does a model, he spread my hair out around my head. He caressed first the length of one thigh and then the other, stroking between my loins, spreading my legs. His fingers dipped in my wet and then spread me on his lips before kissing me long and deep, his tongue probing mine.

My hands were everywhere; I couldn't stop touching him, couldn't stop exploring all those familiar places.

Not in a hurry—I have never known him to hurry—he rediscovered every inch of me. He kissed my toes, my ankles, the back of my knees, but waited to enter the gate to pleasure. He kissed my fingers, my palms, my wrists, inside my elbows, the base of my neck, but waited to touch my breasts. I thought of a thousand places I wanted him to taste but surrendered to his pace. He would find them all.

I cared about nothing else in that moment. I wanted to be nowhere else. If I could have changed anything, it would have been to give him two mouths, that he might kiss my lips and my body at the same time.

The swells of the sea rocked the ship in the languid, seductive rhythm of the Mediterranean. The night was mild and silent. I could hear my hungry breath mingling with his; the purr in my throat reverberated in my ears.

When his lips returned to that magic place in the hollow of my neck, the spot that opens all doors, I took his face in my hands and breathed, "Trust me."

I retraced with my own lips on his perfect body every kiss he had given me. I felt him hold himself back, struggling for control while my caresses opened the tiniest chink in his armor.

"I shall not hurt you," I pleaded, I offering him my soul to meld into mine.

I took him in my hand and pumped slowly, very slowly, the length of my body rubbing against him with the same rhythm.

We have this moment only; there is only here and now. Hektor's words were in my head—but not Hektor. For the briefest of instants, I saw his Apollo smile flash and felt his warmth, and then he was gone. Here and now belonged to Black Falcon.

He gripped my wrist, stilling my hand. "I want it to last."

Waves whispered against the cedar planks separating us from the sea. Starlight gave just enough light for me to see the intensity in his face. His eyes smoldered; his arms were dark and lustrous. Long coils of my hair shimmered on my white arm and shoulder. Far away, in another world on the other side of the door, Jason snored lightly.

I wet my finger and traced around his ear. With his hands under my buttocks, Black Falcon lifted me into him and drove in one thrust to fill me. He stopped. Neither of us moved.

I felt him shudder ever so slightly—not in climax—but in relief to be home. No matter how many centuries and lifetimes passed, it was always the same between us.

I waited, breathless, until I felt him surrender. Every muscle in his body relaxed; he flowed into me, at last, as I flowed into him.

Back and forth, in and out, rocking with the hypnotic pulse of the sea, he moved my hips with his. I clung to the nape of his neck, my fingers stretched out on his shaved head. Our mouths were one, breathing each other's breath, mingling our cries.

I reached for his full sacks with my fingertips, and he exploded with a great shaking and trembling. Dropping his head, he sucked in air with huge gulps. The heat of his shoulders seared my palms; his sweat glistened.

"Touch me, please touch me," I whispered.

His broad, moist tongue on my nipple left hot saliva that tingled as it cooled. He circled and licked and teased before he sucked. I imagined my hot milk spilling into his mouth.

There was nothingness all around me; I lost myself in the vast void as the wave rose and rose, until it crested.

"O-o-o-o-o," I sang, clinging to him, my lips at his throat relishing his salt.

The ship rocked; the wood creaked and strained. A seagull called out. We lay perfectly still on the narrow mat, breathing together, two bodies so entwined we might have been one.

When the stars faded and we saw the first lavender light of dawn framed in the cabin window, Black Falcon rose and put on his loincloth, tunic and kilt. As I watched him from the mat, the scene at the Wynn played in my mind. That day Rasheed had walked away with no word for the future.

Well, he couldn't leave me now. We were on a ship. He had nowhere to go.

Kneeling beside me, he lifted one of my long locks and put it to his lips, kissing me through my hair. There was so much tenderness in his eyes. He stroked my face in exactly the same way as he'd caressed me the morning he disappeared two thousand years from now. I stiffened in dread of his next words.

"The Nubian will move your things to my cabin."

O Aphrodite! I shall make sacrifice at your altar the rest of my days!

Still, I wasn't too spellbound to ask, "What about the boy?"

For the first time, I saw Black Falcon smile. Not a real smile, but the turned-up-corners half-smile of Rasheed.

"He shall not sleep with us."

And then he moved the chest, opened the door and stepped over Jason curled up outside.

As Heraclitus says, the sun is new each day.

CHAPTER 12 AISHA

"No one steps twice into the same river, for it is not the same river and not the same man." – Heraclitus

I dozed until Jason shook me awake. But when I opened my eyes, there was no roll to the ship and no salt in the air. Barb was shaking my shoulders and telling me to come back.

"No, Barb! No!" I shouted in panic. "Don't bring me back. Not now!"

I jerked her hands from my shoulders and shoved her hard, squeezing my eyes shut, willing her to disappear, willing myself not to be here, to be back on the ship.

Surely two days hadn't passed. But I could have been gone an hour—I could have been gone a week.

Barb recoiled, shock on her face. "I *had* to wake you." She had a wary look in her eyes I hadn't seen before. "When I came to feed Aisha, she ran out the door. It's been overnight. I can't find her anywhere."

I heard her words but couldn't believe them. Barb brought me back for a *cat*?

As soon as I thought the thought, I was ashamed. What was wrong with me? Barb never wanted any part of this, and I nearly assaulted her.

Of course, she had to wake me. What if I came back and blamed her for leaving me in the past while Aisha was lost?

"I'm so sorry, Barb." I was just holding it together. A flick of a finger and I would have dissolved into tears. "Please forgive me. It-it was just such a...jolt." I took a breath. "I can't believe I pushed you."

"I didn't know what else to do," she said in an uncommonly quiet voice.

We looked for Aisha together, calling her name in the parking garage, walking the gardens, going through the long, open-air hallways of the seven buildings, each four stories high. I fought my growing desperation. I loved Aisha, but every minute here might be an hour on Black Falcon's ship.

Then, in a miracle moment, Barb's cell rang. It was security. They'd found Aisha. In an act of kindness, a woman in the penthouse of my building had taken her in last night when she meowed at her door.

Barb looked at me; there was a hint of guilt in her expression.

"I didn't go door-to-door."

"Of course you didn't. I wouldn't expect that. That's my job." In my mind, I seethed. *She didn't need to bring me back, after all.*

To avoid a repeat with Aisha, I asked Sonny next door if he could keep her for a few days. His Burmese, Oscar, was lonely all day, and the two cats got along.

Aisha glared at me with narrow green eyes and twitched her thick black tail. She knew.

I skyped Hector, and he popped up on my laptop screen. He wore his usual polo shirt, this one royal blue. The wild-colored abstract painting, work of a local artist, hung behind him.

He was going to be in Buenos Aires at least another week. Couldn't I arrange to come? There were so many things in BA he wanted to show me. Surely I could get time off work.

That's when I told him about the auction in New York and that I had a business opportunity I wanted to pursue. He was excited for me and didn't press for too many details, so I didn't have to lie that much.

"My mother is going to be at that auction. She'll be at the Plaza. Why don't you stay there?"

"That would've been fun, Hector," I lied again. "But I've got reservations at the Intercontinental. Pre-paid."

The last thing I wanted was to stay in the same hotel as Isabel.

"The Plaza's right down the street. You can have dinner. I'll tell her to contact you."

Once again I made it through a conversation without any suspicion on his part. At least, none that I could tell. I was a two-faced, lying bitch, and I accepted it.

The voicemail from the General said it was business. He answered on the first ring.

"Ishtar. We should meet to iron out some details."

"No," I said firmly. "I don't think that would be a good idea."

He laughed.

"Are you still afraid of me? If I wanted to steal you away, Ishtar, I could at any time. I'd like to think kidnapping isn't required for me to have a woman."

When I didn't respond, he said, "I rather fancy that I could please a woman—that she would freely choose to be with me. What do you think, Ishtar? Can I please a woman?"

If he wanted me to take the bait, I disappointed him.

"I can't meet you right now. I have other commitments."

"Ah-h-h. A busy woman, but not too busy to go to New York, I presume?"

"No, I'll be in New York. I'll get the ibis for you."

The General chuckled again.

"I look forward to working with you, Ishtar. Have a good trip."

Good trip. Did he mean New York? Of course, he meant New York. I was paranoid. The General couldn't possibly know about the Red Mirror.

Barb was so livid when I told her I was going back that very day, I was afraid she'd refuse to help me.

"This. Is. It. Do you hear me? I mean it. I'll do it this one last time. But no more. You're scaring me. My best friend is an addict, and I don't know where to send her for help."

"I don't have to be in New York until Tuesday," I insisted. "The hotel and plane are booked; I've registered for the auction."

"It's got nothing to do with all that practical stuff, and you know it."

Her aura was all prickly. I saw her as a tall, spindly cactus covered with spines.

"I need to do this, Barb," I begged, knowing exactly how pathetic I sounded. "I have to be with him."

She glared at me; her lips curled in disgust.

"*Rasheed.* It's always *Rasheed,*" she complained. "He'll ruin your life. He may already have."

I didn't answer her. What could I say? She was so close to the truth.

CHAPTER 13   THE SHELL

"Happiness is brief. It will not stay. Gods batter at its sails." – Euripides

I went back to a perfect Mediterranean day of blue sky, blue water and warm sun. Seagulls circled overhead. Dolphins splashed in a flat sea. The late spring sunshine splintered the shimmering waters into millions of dazzling diamonds. On the nearby shore, rich green cypress dotted the rocky hills, reminding me of Korinth. No wonder the Greeks had settled Cyrene. Save the intensity of the sun and the long sea voyage, they might have been home.

When I entered the cabin, Goliath and Black Falcon stood close to each other, talking quietly; they both turned toward me at the same time. I didn't like the expression on their faces—too solemn, too grave.

"What has happened?" I asked innocently.

And then I saw my chests standing by the door. I looked from the trunks to Black Falcon. He stared back, unblinking; his face was as hard as I'd ever seen it. Goliath stared at the floor.

"You will go with the Nubian," Black Falcon said in the voice of an automaton. "Your ransom has been paid."

I couldn't quite process his words. Did he say he was sending me away?

"Go?" I must have seemed like an imbecile who couldn't understand the most simple language.

"The ransom has been paid," he snapped. "You are free."

"Free? I am *free*? No! Do *not* say I am free. You send me away. If I were free, I would not leave."

He just stood there, so rigid he might have morphed into a statue. "You care more for silver than for me?" I asked in disbelief.

There was not a trace of tenderness about him; he had hardened himself for this. But I knew his inner struggle. I saw the telltale twitch in his eye.

How many times in how many lives would Rasheed tear me apart? What was it Barb had warned? *He will ruin your life, if he already hasn't.*

"Answer me!" I shouted.

His jaw set; a muscle knotted and unknotted. The luscious lips that knew my whole body formed an unforgiving line. His face was a mask of harsh angles. Oh, he was capable of more cruelty than I'd ever imagined.

Avoiding to look at me, Goliath moved past and out the door. Black Falcon and I were alone, facing each other. I couldn't stop trembling.

"Do you desire silver so much that you would sacrifice what we have?" I used all my will to keep from begging. "Do I mean nothing to you?"

"The silver is not for me, woman! It is for the cause." He spat the words at me.

"Cause? *What* cause?" The shock numbed my brain; I felt retarded. Simple phrases were too complicated; their meaning went right over my head.

"You Greeks made a whore of Egypt. You came as saviors from the Persians and made us no better than slaves. We who built pyramids while you were barbarians in the forest!"

"But I cannot change that I was born Greek, any more than you can be other than Egyptian. What has any of that to do with us—with what *we* have together?"

When he had no response, I turned angry.

"What woman has given you more pleasure?" I demanded. "Say you do not desire me."

He stared at me from a stony face and refused to answer.

"I live to please you, and you trade me for silver. Tell me. *Who* is the slave?"

"The ransom will buy weapons and feed an army," he said as if that explanation explained everything.

Army? No one had spoken of an army. I had a thousand questions but there was only one that mattered. How could he do this?

I didn't have to wait for the answer.

"I have known from the beginning that this day would come," he told me. "Nothing can change our fate. The Gods have set us on our paths. It is impossible to escape what is destined."

What was this destiny of which everyone spoke? If this pain was destiny, I wanted nothing to do with it.

If only I could have hated him, but as cruel as he was, it didn't lessen my need. I moved a step closer, thinking that if I might only kiss his lips or touch his cheek, he would relent.

But if Black Falcon needed me as I needed him, he buried his feelings too deep for either of us to reach. I wondered if he even had a heart; I imagined some beastly artificial organ mechanically pumping icy blood through his veins.

"Nubian, come!" he barked in Egyptian.

When Goliath came back in the door, he glanced at my face and then quickly away. Black Falcon switched to Greek, but I barely realized he talked to me; I heard his words through a fog.

"I assume you wish to prepare for the rendezvous. Ptolemy has sent an envoy for the exchange."

Then he said to Goliath in Egyptian, "Make ready to leave. Give her half an hour, then collect the chests and take her off the ship."

My Egyptian had improved enough that I understood each painful word. The way he said *her* was a knife through my heart.

"The boy?" I managed to ask through a throat so tight that air barely passed.

"The boy is your slave. He goes with you."

Black Falcon brushed past me; it was as if I were no longer there. I was reminded of a Tarot card from the '60s that read, "There is no you."

Now, Barb, now. Bring me back now! I didn't want to be here another minute, but of course, Barb couldn't hear me.

Ptolemy's envoy would expect to see a Supreme Priestess worthy of the exorbitant ransom. I dressed in my best *peplos* of lavender wool soft as cashmere. My only jewelry was the snake bracelet from Hektor; the two serpents with emerald eyes and garnet center coiled around my forearm. I dressed my hair the best that I could without a barber. The same silk scarf of gold threads I had worn the first evening in Black Falcon's cabin tamed my wild tresses, bleached the lightest of blonde by bathing in the sea.

Too much in the sun, my skin was no longer white. I chose not to use lead powder on my face or eye shadow on my lids for fear of streaking; I struggled to control my tears.

He wasn't on deck when we left the ship. At least, I didn't see him. He wouldn't give me a last chance to change his heart.

Most of the crew stopped their work; many gathered around, not speaking, faces somber, but not looking directly at me. Having witnessed our joy, they didn't wish to see my sorrow. They might have been attending a funeral. In a sense, they were.

As I climbed into the fishnet sling to be lowered over the side, Black Falcon's second-most-trusted man pressed a delicate pink seashell into my palm.

I managed a small smile of gratitude and kissed him lightly on his cheek, my lips brushing the thick scar than ran from his eye to his jaw.

"Thank you," I whispered gratefully in Egyptian.

Scarface whispered back, just loud enough for me to hear.

"He loves you, but he loves Egypt more."

CHAPTER 14   SILVER SHOALS

"Nothing has more strength than dire necessity." – Euripides

The rendezvous with Ptolemy's men was to take place in a small cove of snowy sand with rocky hills all around. The water was the exact same shade of turquoise as the gown I wore to Black Falcon's cabin the evening he rejected me but couldn't resist coming in the night. The memory was so painful, I couldn't bear to look at the sea.

Jason held my hand in the little skiff with red sails; another boat with several oarsmen followed. Goliath sat directly behind us. I felt his eyes on me, but when I turned, he looked away. I was so numb that I didn't cry—or didn't cry hard. I couldn't stop the tears from welling in my eyes. Poor Jason stroked my cheek from time to time and squeezed my hand.

"I shall kill him one day," he announced.

"Sh-h-h," I told him. "It does not matter. It is but another moment in our lives. The uphill is followed by the downhill."

Of course, he didn't believe me. I said the words as much to encourage myself as him.

The skiff came as close to shore as possible; the bottom of the boat scraped the sand. Our second boat hooked up with two other boats anchored nearby, unmanned, laden with small chests and heavy in the water. When the lids were lifted, the flash of metal exploded in the bright sunlight. It was then I realized the sheer volume of silver being exchanged for my release.

Two of our men carried my clothing and papyri chests to the beach and quickly returned.

Goliath stayed on the skiff. He gave me his hand to rise, lifted me over the side, and stood me gently in the water. He said nothing, not even goodbye, but his face told me, *I am sorry*. Deep sorrow was in his eyes.

I mouthed, *Thank you*. I didn't trust myself to speak.

I was fighting hard not to break down in front of Black Falcon's men, in front of Jason, in front of Ptolemy's delegation.

Drawing in a deep breath, gathering sandals and the hem of my *peplos* in one hand, Jason holding onto my skirt, I faced the shore and the waiting men.

I was Athena of Korinth, Supreme Priestess of Aphrodite and agent of the Pharaoh of Egypt, Ptolemy IV, Ptolemy *Philopater*. There would be no more tears.

The stark sun on sand and water blinded me to the tall figure who scooped me up from the water to carry me to the beach.

"You!" I exclaimed.

"Me," Hektor answered with a dazzling smile. His cedar-colored waves and curls glowed red in the sun.

I was surprised by how glad I was to see him; I locked my arms around his neck. He held me longer than necessary before setting me gently to my feet on the white beach.

"I am pleased to see you in good health, Athena of Korinth. I would not have believed it possible, but you are even more beautiful."

If he noticed my red eyes, he was gentleman enough not to show it.

Two brightly painted boats bearing Ptolemy's cartouche on yellow sails were beached a few yards away. I didn't understand why Ptolemy's men didn't seize the small skiff and take me without paying ransom—they must be bound by the rules of a game long lost in time.

Hektor appointed himself my guardian and was always by my side. He didn't make conversation or ask me anything about my captivity on the ship, but from time to time looked at my sad face and then away at the sea.

A welcoming party awaited my arrival on the Pharaoh's customized *bireme* anchored on the other side of the headland. Two levels of oarsmen, one over the other, stood ready to strike out immediately for Alexandria. Yellow and red flags waved in the breeze. Gold sparkled everywhere;

even the tops of the masts were gilded.

Designed for comfort, the deck was exceptionally broad with an Egyptian-style bowsprit and stern that turned up in giant wooden columns carved into gilt-covered reeds. This floating temple of pleasure was my first real taste of the vast wealth and extravagance of the Ptolemies.

Long mahogany tables laden with roasted meats and fowl, fresh fruits, cheeses, olives and wine stood under yellow and blue striped canopies hung with silver fringe.

The feast was accompanied by endless speeches and toasts. I played my role well, thanking Ptolemy's men for my rescue and praising the Pharaoh for his generosity and protection.

My head pounded. I waited until I could bear no more. Protesting fatigue from the strain, I excused myself to go to my cabin.

Hektor insisted on accompanying me to the door. When I looked up to thank him, he took my chin in his fingers in a most familiar way and studied my face intently. I found myself counting the red specks in his eyes to keep him from reading my shame.

"The Black Falcon has a reputation for cruelty. Surely one would expect joy in your eyes today at your release and not hidden tears? What has he done to cause such sadness?"

"You presume too much, Hektor of Naukratis. I almost perished at sea. I have seen suffering and death. My ordeal have exhausted me."

Hektor held my face for a moment longer, as if he might see through to the truth if only he looked hard enough. Nodding his head slightly, he dropped his hand to touch the blood-red garnet of my bracelet with his middle finger.

"It pleases me that my humble gift survived your trials."

How strange that the bracelet I had almost tossed aside in my office would be the only jewelry left to me.

"I do not believe in talismans," Hektor confided, "but would like to think my little piece of Egypt gave you strength and brought you luck."

"Thank you, Hektor of Naukratis. Our Temple is most grateful for all that you have done."

"So formal now between us." He frowned slightly. "You have changed, Athena of Korinth."

Then he smiled his broad smile of blazing white teeth. "A new challenge. I embrace it with pleasure."

The sunny morning in my little house on the Akrokorinth seemed so long ago. I must have welcomed Hektor's kiss that day for him to remark on my formality, but as hard as I tried, I couldn't remember more.

Ptolemy had sent a dozen slaves to pamper me with warm baths, massages of gardenia-scented oils and every delicacy to eat. The Greeks of Egypt enjoy a far more exotic cuisine than those in the Peloponnese who consider roast lamb, stewed eggplant, fresh figs and olives to be a feast.

I retreated from the world to nurse my wounds. Jason was always at my side and slept on the floor at the foot of my bed like a pet. Hektor spent as much time with me as I would allow, playing the Egyptian game of *senet* and telling me about Alexandria. As if he sensed I was too fragile, he made no advances and kept a formal distance.

He didn't ask me more about Black Falcon, but I often caught him watching me with a knowing look in his eyes. He didn't press for details; perhaps he didn't want to know the truth. He was attentive and even kind, keeping his ego in check, although his self-confidence always shone through; it was what gave him his Apollo light.

But I still couldn't trust him. I would not trust easily again.

PART TWO
ALEXANDRIA

CHAPTER 15 LIGHTHOUSE

"We hang the petty thieves and appoint the great ones to public office." – Aesop

Pharos Lighthouse, glowing like a bright star on the far horizon, was the first sign of the great city of Alexandria. It grew brighter with each hour we sailed through the night. I couldn't sleep and stayed on deck, reclining on a sofa with Jason curled up on a rich Persian carpet at my feet. The Milky Way blazed across the starry bowl of the night sky.

I marked the hours by Jupiter's wandering along its path through the constellations and tried not think of the nights on Black Falcon's ship. The moon rose and was still up when the sky lightened to pale coral in advance of the sun. A new day. I could choose, as Hektor said, to live in pleasure or pain. I wanted no more pain.

The ship skirted the treacherous sandbars off the city's coast and rounded the island of Pharos. Hektor joined me on deck, and together we watched the Pharos Lighthouse, named after the island on which it was built, grow closer and taller—taller than most towers in Las Vegas.

Ptolemy's palatial *bireme* was but a speck beside the Pharos. Built in three levels of granite blocks faced with gleaming white marble, the Lighthouse's square citadel base supported an octagonal midsection with a soaring circular tower. A cupola housed the giant bronze mirrors and polyzonal lenses that reflect the sun by day and a colossal bonfire by night.

Mammoth marble statues of Greek gods and goddesses ringed the top level; statues of philosophers, griffins and sphinxes marched around the second. A lavish hanging garden of lush flowers draped the base.

With the typical pride of an Alexandrian, Hektor was eager to tell me everything.

"Sostratus of Cnidus, the architect of the Pharos, was a mathematician at the *Akademy*. I studied there, of course. All men in Egypt do."

He didn't bother to explain that 'all men' meant those of social status and wealth. Mainly Greeks. Most likely no Egyptians.

"Ptolemy the Second dedicated the Lighthouse to his father Ptolemy *Soter*. Three hundred slaves worked seventeen years at a cost of more than 800 talents."

I quickly calculated that, with inflation, my ransom might have paid for half the citadel base.

"And there, Athena of the mighty Akrokorinth, is *our* Temple to Aphrodite. The one Ptolemy deems too small and insignificant." Hektor leaned slightly across me over the starboard gunwale to point out the Egyptian style pylon quite close to the Lighthouse. "They say it was once a shrine to Isis, the Egyptian Goddess."

"It is lovely," I admitted, "but our Goddess deserves more, certainly her own temple and not in the shadow of a colossus like the Pharos."

"Normally I would find any temple adequate to worship our silly gods. But in this case," he whispered in my ear, "I am delighted that Ptolemy's superstition has brought you here."

I stared straight ahead, thinking that I hid the thrill of his hot breath on my neck. His small smile of satisfaction told me otherwise.

To a slow, steady beat of the drum, the galley slaves pushed and pulled the long oars through the narrow passage between Pharos Island on the west and the tip of the slim, palace-covered Royal Promontory to the east. The narrow neck opened into a vast and congested harbor dotted by a score of small islands with exquisite, red-roofed villas.

Hektor really was a master in the art of women. He had a casual and confident way of directing my attention with light touches on my arm and shoulder that kept the energy between us vibrant. Yet he never went so far as to offend or make me uncomfortable. I had the sense he foresaw an inevitable outcome for which he had only to be patient.

"There you have the Royal Residences," he pointed out. "And over there—can you see the great mass of buildings just beyond the Royal

Yacht Harbor?—is the Library. And *that* beauty is our Theatre."

From the architecture, we might have been in Greece, but the flat terrain was nothing like Korinth save for the vast blue of the Mediterranean. A solitary hill to the south was crowned with a splendid monument painted in dazzling jewel greens and blues.

"Our fabled *Serapeum*, Athena. The so-called *Grand Temple* to the half Greek–half Egyptian God Sarapis. Entirely invented by the first Ptolemy in a vain effort to unite Alexandria. I'm sorry to say most of the fools in the city worship him, even the Greeks who should know better."

To the west, a line of warehouses and docks ended at a mile-long causeway connecting the mainland to the island of Pharos.

"The *Heptastadion*. Built by Alexander the Great's army. When Alexander arrived, there was nothing here but the fishing village Rhakotis. Mud hovels, really, at the mouth of a dried up finger of the Nile. Alexander founded this city and built the land bridge to create two harbors—the Great Harbor on this side and *Eunostos* on the other."

He added unnecessarily, "We built everything you see."

By we, he meant, of course, the Greeks.

"One day soon, I shall take you to Lake Mareotis at the southern end of the city, and from there, a pleasure barge down the great canal to the Canopus branch of the Nile. You will love it there. The river is wide and lush. Only fifteen miles, but another world."

"I am here for my work, Hektor of Naukratis. I need not remind you that I am far behind schedule."

"We are not going to have *that* conversation again, are we?" He started to say, "*We have only this moment—*"

I completed the words for him, "*only here and now.*" Then I threw in, "*Pleasure or pain?*"

He threw back his head and laughed.

Oh, Hektor. How I envied his Apollo optimism. I don't believe he'd ever known disappointment.

And then, at long last, my long journey that had started with the Oracle of Delphi came to an end at the Royal Yacht Harbor with its flotilla of opulent vessels decked with polished woods and gleaming metals. A giant red and yellow cobra billowed on a grass green sail.

Although I had never been to Alexandria—it hadn't existed 300 years before—I felt the exhilaration of coming home. Egypt.

An official greeting party waited under an enormous awning at the end of the wharf. Marble buildings and green gardens aflame with flowering trees covered the Royal Promontory. As Hektor had pointed out, the palace grounds flowed into those of the Library with its *Akademy* called the *Musaeum,* home of the Muses.

It took forever to disembark. Oars shipped and lines were cast amid the thunderous creaking of wood and a great deal shouting back and forth between the land crew and our own. Finally, the lumbering *bireme* moored parallel to the stone quay, hemp ropes secured to granite posts mounted with winged sun disks. The sounding of trumpets carried across the water.

A wide gangplank of polished cedar spanned the short gap from the ship to the top step of the quay. Gentle waves splashed up and bounced back again. Nut-brown Egyptians in snowy white kilts and headdresses rolled thick wine-red carpets onto the walkway, then more carpets along the quay.

The slaves had spent hours on my toilet. I bit down on cloth while they pumiced, then plucked away pubic hair. A cooling salve with honey offered some relief. Masters of their craft, barbers used several sizes of hot irons to create the curls framing my face and the deep waves spilling down my back. Ropes of pearls and emerald green ribbons twisted into a traditional Greek wreath around my head.

The Pharaoh had sent chests of gowns sewn of the finest linen, cotton and silk; I chose a purple silk chiton that turned my hair to spun gold and my eyes to jade. Hektor's cobras still coiled around my forearm.

There was nothing I could do about the tan. A Greek beauty treasures skin as pale as the whitest ivory, but when slaves rubbed me with oil until I gleamed, I didn't think anyone would find me unattractive.

Four Nubians arrived to escort me under a yellow and white striped awning with gilt wooden cobras at each corner. Hektor called me "Goddess" and followed behind with Jason at his heels.

If only Barb could see the splendor, she might understand.

I had my first moment of dread when I saw him. Dressed more Egyptian than Greek, with a golden collar, bare chest and stiff white kilt to his knees, he waited at the head of the welcoming party. A gold band across his forehead pressed on his black barbered curls. It was Setne the Scribe. There was no mistaking he was the same soul who had sought my death 300 years before. In spite of the fresh breeze off the sea and the shade of the awning, my skin caught fire.

"Athena of Korinth, Supreme Priestess of the Temple of Aphrodite, allow me to present myself. I am your humble servant Sosibius, Lord Chancellor to the great Ptolemy *Philopater*, Osiris-on-earth, Pharaoh of Two Egypts."

He bowed from the waist, a sign of deep respect. If he recognized me, he didn't show it.

"On behalf of the Pharaoh, we welcome you to Alexandria. May the Gods be praised and may all Egypt and Greece rejoice at your safe delivery into our hands."

I returned his greeting with a bow of my head.

If we keep meeting the same souls until we learn our lessons, I feared what this man, once Setne the Scribe to Psamtik III, now the Lord Chancellor to Ptolemy IV, had yet to teach me.

And I was glad Barb wasn't here.

CHAPTER 16   PTOLEMY PHILOPATER

"Often an entire city has suffered because of an evil man." – Hesiod

I was to be a guest at the Royal Palace in an elegant two-story villa near the Library and right on the beach. My chambers, bath and reception hall opened onto curved marble balconies overlooking the Royal Harbor. The Lighthouse rose in grand splendor above cobalt water. Even by day, the beacon blazed.

The waves rolled onto shore in that special slow, sensuous rhythm unique to the Mediterranean. Seagulls circled the Great Harbor; flocks of songbirds nested in the garden's myrtle and fig trees.

Ptolemy *Philopater*, Ptolemy father-lover, was indisposed; my audience with him had been postponed until the next day, which didn't disappoint me in the least. The more time I had to put Black Falcon behind me, the more strength I could garner.

I spent an hour in the rose marble bath with pillared portico open to the sea breeze. Swirling arabesques of pink granite tiles covered the floor. Murals of the Isthmus and Gulf of Korinth as seen from the Akrokorinth covered the walls. I suspected Hektor was responsible; he had seen the exact vista from my office.

As if merely thinking of him caused him to manifest, a male slave announced that Hektor of Naukratis had arrived.

Jason smiled. He liked Hektor. Hektor had made certain of that, spoiling him with sweets and not boxing his ears when he spilled a goblet of dark Delta wine on Hektor's snow-white chiton.

The slaves dried me with sheets of linen and wrapped me in a citron silk robe tied with a red-tasseled sash. I slipped into gold sandals and went to meet Hektor in my reception room, Jason trailing behind. A few coiled curls wet from the bath hung on my neck and back.

"Thank you for seeing me without previous arrangement," Hektor said with the self-assurance of a man who always feels welcome.

He was so warm and confident, I couldn't help returning his smile. His eyes travelled from my face, down over my breasts, past my waist and hips, along my thighs to my ankles, to my pumiced and hennaed toenails, and back up again to my eyes.

"Meow."

A little mound moved under his cape; Hektor reached in and pulled out a black kitten with white paws. I cuddled the fluffy ball in the base of my throat.

"May I offer you some wine, Hektor of Naukratis?" I asked, knowing his answer.

I settled onto a low sofa upholstered in tangerine wool and waved for a slave to serve us. A small pile of pillows in a rainbow of colors supported my back.

Hektor took the matching sofa across from mine, relaxing his long legs the length of the divan and resting his body half-turned toward me, one arm slung over the carved ebony armrest. Ankles crossed, sandals laced to the knee, his big feet stuck out like boats. He looked prepared to stay.

"How did you know I like black cats?"

"I would say a little voice told me, but I do not believe in such things. Though I must admit, I sometimes know a truth without knowing why."

Jason sat on the floor beside me, and we both played with the kitten, laughing and giggling at its antics.

"You have a most familiar relationship with your slave," Hektor remarked. "Did you have him in Greece? I do not recall seeing him in Korinth."

"No," I said vaguely. "I acquired him on the sea voyage."

I wasn't sure about the legal status of a boy I claimed to be my slave. Did I have to buy him from someone or could I pick him up, like a spoil of war?

"I think I am jealous," replied Hektor with a smile and raised eyebrow.

Glossy, thick chestnut curls coiled on his forehead and around his ears.

It struck me that he had an arrogant nose, perfectly straight, high-bridged and a little large for his face—but not enough to detract from his appeal.

I must have been staring at him, because he gave me one of his bold looks inviting me to take the next step. Avoiding his eyes, I busied myself with a sip from my chalice.

The evening passed pleasantly enough. We played *senet* and gambled copper *obols*, drinking excellent watered Cypriot wine. A slave served small silver bowls of *ambrosia*—almonds, walnuts and honey mixed with yoghurt—said to be the food of the Gods on Mt. Olympus. The Lighthouse flame burned bright above the harbor.

A nightingale sang outside the balcony; the night air was mild with no hint of chill. The long tendrils of my hair, trailing on my bare shoulders, dried into silken threads of gold. In truth, I liked being blonde. I felt lighter, like a sunbeam, as if my vibrations moved at a higher rate. But still, I couldn't dispel the heaviness in my heart.

The kitten slept against the curve of my belly; Jason dozed on the green woolen carpet on the floor between Hektor and me. I toyed with the idea of encouraging Hektor but decided against it. If I had allowed myself, I might have let him wash away the pain of Rasheed. But I chose not to. I still was not ready to trust.

So instead of suggesting another game and cup of wine, I announced in a cool, formal voice, "I fear I must part with your company, Hektor of Naukratis. I find myself quite in need of rest."

He leaned back on the high arm of the divan just long enough that I thought he might not leave. He studied me; I did my best to meet his gaze with a detached look.

"We have only now, Athena," he said in a low voice. "There is nothing else. You know what pleasure I can give you. Why do you squander this moment?"

He didn't wait for an answer but rose gracefully to his feet. The lamplight cast shadows on his long form, highlighting his lean muscles and strong limbs. His cape glowed deep red. He stepped over Jason on the floor.

I watched him, mesmerized, unsure if I would have the strength to resist if he insisted.

Bending down on his haunches, he put his hand under my hair, on the side of my neck, and drew my face to him, kissing me lightly, barely brushing my lips, not waiting for me to respond or reject.

Taking my chin in his long fingers, the fingers that knew the Spot, he held my eyes for a long moment before he said in an earnest tone quite unlike him, "*I* would not trade you for all the silver in Egypt."

He knew! I don't know why I was surprised. Women, after all, are Hektor's area of expertise. I felt myself redden in shame.

"How long are you going to hold yourself pure for him? He does not merit you."

Then he kissed me lightly as before, straightened his knees in the smooth movement of a practiced athlete and exited, his crimson cloak flowing behind him.

I rose before dawn to watch the sky and sea change from dark purple to lilac and finally to the palest of shimmering blues. The Pharos loomed massive and tall at the entrance to the harbor. In the last minutes before the sun rose, a golden fog enveloped the palace grounds; white marble softened to butter.

The palace complex was built mainly in Greek fashion with painted triangular cornices, terracotta roofs, and hundreds of the most ornate marble columns. More ornate even than in Korinth.

Luxuriant flowering trees and exotically-sculpted bushes bordered wide walkways passing under massive arbors heavy with vines. Purple irises bloomed among sparkling fountains and vast glimmering pools. The palm trees and the scattering of obelisks, sphinxes and mammoth statues of pharaohs never let me forget I was in Egypt.

A ceramic mug of hot posset steamed on a brass tray table with ebony tripod legs. The new kitten, yet to be named, played with the fringe of my shawl and nibbled with sharp baby teeth at my toes.

How playful and carefree she was—like me during the days on Black Falcon's ship. Black Falcon. Where was he now? I was certain he ached for me as I did for him and willed with all my might that regret stalked his every waking moment. But try as I did, I couldn't hate him.

Today I faced Ptolemy. My mind raced with his possible questions, devising believable responses that wouldn't reveal any details of the ship, its the crew or, most of all, Black Falcon. Never would I say anything to betray him.

At the earliest sign of dawn, the harbor came alive. Even before the last star had dimmed and night become day, dock workers swarmed like ants along the curved line of wharfs. Smoke from cooking fires blended with the early morning mist.

On the other side of the *Heptastadion* glistened the waters of the second harbor. Rhakotis was there. The Egyptian Quarter.

I used work to dull the pain, sitting at my marble desk and sorting through piles of correspondence that had arrived while I was on Black Falcon's ship. My staff at the Temple in Korinth was to send me monthly reports with a full accounting of all income and expenditures. Using a stylus and red ink, I flagged certain line items with requests for more information.

The personnel reports were routine. Agape was ill and couldn't perform her duties. Chloë was with child and in love with the father. Doris, whose uncle had brought her to the Temple only weeks before, had run away. There were a few discipline issues to decide. Antigone was frightfully in debt. And as usual, everyone complained about the food.

The most serious concern was an outbreak of fever that had arrived with a Phoenician ship from the East. My assistant, Irene of Samos, wisely declared the harbor off-limits to sacred prostitutes until the City gave the port a clean bill of health.

The embargo would substantially impact the Temple's revenue. I authorized the use of a contingency fund set up with the first installment of Ptolemy's Royal Commission. I then further instructed Irene to approach the organizers of the upcoming Isthmus Games for placement of our priestesses and acolytes at the many *symposia* celebrating the athletic competitions. The fields around Korinth would be packed with the tents of spectators and contestants. There should be no lack of clients.

It was clear I needed a local secretary immediately, as well as a small staff that could cipher and write. I added 'staff' to the list of requests to submit to the Pharaoh.

Satisfied with the morning's work, I felt positive about this new adventure in Alexandria—positive except for the painful memories of Black Falcon, the questions Ptolemy might pose about my captivity and my instinctive dread of the Lord Chancellor, once the evil Scribe who plotted my death by Persians.

Dressing my hair went quickly; I had slept with my neck on a wooden block. The slaves twisted my thick waves into a knot at the back of my head, leaving a few ringlets around my face and several long coils to trail on my shoulders.

I chose from my own chest a traditional *peplos* of the finest and softest cream wool. A full-length, polished brass mirror reflected yards and yards of fabric, twisted and tied with white cords and golden pins. It draped on my body, falling in folds, showing my curves to advantage in spite of the volumes of cloth. My only ornament was my Gods-given mane of spun gold.

I quelled the butterflies in my stomach with the knowledge that I would appear to Ptolemy as a Supreme Priestess, image of the pure Goddess in white, a deity not to be questioned.

A frightfully thin Egyptian wearing an elaborate beaded collar and a yellow and white striped triangular headdress greeted me in perfect Greek. His eyes were outlined in *kohl;* his earlobes stretched under the weight of golden ankhs. I followed him down the marbled arcade to the high gilt doors that opened into the Pharaoh's Presence Chamber.

Neither precisely Greek nor Egyptian, the throne room was decorated more in the gaudy Syracuse-style. I didn't realize so many colors and patterns of marble existed; Ptolemy's architects must have scoured the world to place them all in this flamboyant, overindulged space.

Gilded swags connected pillars topped with sphinx heads and palm fronds. Wild-colored hunt scenes plastered the walls behind life-sized bronzes of nude athletes. Garish, clothed statues of the Ptolemy family stood about like extras in a tawdry play.

At last, I approached Ptolemy *Philopater* himself, my footfall on the marble soft and noiseless, the heavy hem of my *peplos* trailing behind me.

He was a small man in a robe of lush purple with a crown of gold oak leaves perched on thin, dishwater curls. The throne's massive gold sunburst back and lion armrests dwarfed him.

I wasn't even that surprised to see Psamtik the Crown Prince. Right out of a bad dream, he was Ptolemy. The evil pair, Psamtik and Setne, now Ptolemy and Sosibius, were together again.

Two leopards, secured by heavy silver chains, lounged at Ptolemy's feet. They stared at me with yellow eyes.

"Greetings, Athena of Korinth. Be welcome in Our Presence," he said in the accent of a Greek who had always been in Egypt.

His tone was congenial enough. Thank the Gods, like Sosibius, he didn't appear to recognize me.

"Your Majesty's grace is beyond measure." Whatever anxiety I felt wasn't in my confident voice. "The Temple of Aphrodite of Korinth is forever indebted to Your Majesty's generous patronage resulting in my release and safe progress to glorious Alexandria, world city of splendor and great learning."

"Yes," Ptolemy chuckled, "your capture was a most unexpected— and unpleasant, We are certain—twist of fate." He smiled indulgently before continuing.

"We feared the Gods might have been angered by Our ambition, but the priests assured Us that the Oracles yet foretell a favorable outcome. All voyages and new ventures are fraught with peril. Difficult ordeals do not spell failure, but success comes to those who are strong and who persevere—and whom the Gods favor, of course."

Ptolemy then spoke expansively to the room, extending an arm weighed down with massive gold bangles.

"We look forward to the great Temple that We shall erect to the glory of the Goddess, to the glory of Our city, to the glory of the Greeks, and to the glory of Our House of Ptolemy."

The room echoed in one voice, "To the glory of the House of Ptolemy."

Pleased with himself, Ptolemy relaxed further into his massive throne and grinned benignly at me, even showing a glimpse of his yellowed teeth with one missing incisor. He showed no interest in my time on the ship. He asked nothing about Black Falcon. I dared to speak out.

"If Your Majesty pleases, and if I may be so bold to suggest, I have a small list of requests to assist me in my duties."

"You shall have whatever you require, Athena of Korinth. The Lord Chancellor shall see to the details. We have instructed him to remove all obstacles in your path."

"Your Majesty is most benevolent. May the Goddess bless Your Eminence all the days of a long and bountiful life."

Ptolemy's satisfied smile broadened, exposing more teeth stained from narcotic herbs; a second tooth was missing on the bottom.

At a nod from Ptolemy, Chancellor Sosibius announced in a grand, booming voice intended to reach all present, "May we present Antinous of Kos, Royal Mathematician, Astronomer and Engineer."

A blond muscular Greek in a short white chiton reaching mid-thigh stepped forward.

Antinous had the same perfectly proportioned wrestler's body, the same sun-streaked curls, cleft chin and startling blue eyes as when we married three centuries before and escaped on a Phoenician ship. Like the others from my circle of reincarnating souls that I'd met in this life, he gave no sign that he recognized me.

"His Majesty," Sosibius explained, "has graciously assigned the *Musaeum's* most esteemed architect to assist in this momentous endeavor."

I inclined my head slightly to Antinous, who bowed his head deep, then I turned back to Ptolemy.

"May I beg Your Majesty's indulgence to accept a meager gift? Our poor offering is not worthy of Your Grace, but the gifts so carefully selected in Korinth and blessed by the Goddess were lost at sea."

I signaled to the Egyptian who had acted as my usher, and he waved for the guards to open the gilt doors.

Jason in a new chiton, curls freshly barbered, carried a vermilion silk pillow. On top was a much-yellowed papyrus scroll hung with gold tassels.

"This scroll, Your Majesty, is the original, annotated edition of *Elektra* written in the hand of Euripides himself. Although scarcely deserving of Royal Attention, it is our most precious possession. Your Grace's own playwriting certainly has no need of inspiration, yet I dare to believe that the Muses whisper still louder when drawn to the genius of the great tragedians."

But Ptolemy barely glanced at the priceless scroll. His eyes were locked on Jason, and I knew I had made my first mistake.

CHAPTER 17   FIRST STRIKE

"The Gods are not averse to deceit in a holy cause." – Aeschylus

Antinous had joined me to dine when Hektor showed again without warning. There were a few awkward moments while the house slaves moved in a third divan.

The two knew each other from the Musaeum and had attended lectures together when students at the Akademy.

"I have not seen you of late at our drinking parties," remarked Hektor.

"I have little time for other than my lectures and research."

"Of course. Perhaps we might wrestle one afternoon. You do have time for exercise, I assume, if not for other pleasures?"

If Antinous knew that Hektor baited him, he didn't react. He appeared slightly distracted—not in a rude manner, but as if part of his mind were somewhere else, far beyond our conversation.

My cook prepared a Greek meal of grape leaves stuffed with raisins, mint and cracked wheat, followed by a roasted newborn lamb smothered in olive oil and rosemary and served with a rich fig sauce. Two slaves stood by, ready to refill our silver cups. I had instructed the heavy Delta wine to be watered 2:1; the evening must be lucid with no one stepping out of line.

"I came to study when a teenager," Antinous replied in answer to my question, "and never returned to Kos. The Library has everything I require—the best minds in mathematics and philosophy are here."

"Korinth does not lack its own charms," Hektor interjected, giving me the intimate smile of those who share secrets. "I found the city well deserves its reputation for the highest standards of culture—and pleasure."

"Of course, Greece is still home to many great thinkers," Antinous hurried to say. "But Alexandria is where I must be. Ptolemy has been most generous to provide whatever tools I need for my work and study."

"There is nothing more noble than study—unless it is sport." Hektor beamed at Antinous and then turned to me. "But we must not forget theatre, which might be the noblest pursuit of all. I believe Athena of Korinth would agree."

Giving me another of his conspiratorial smiles, he said with easy confidence, "You must allow me to introduce you to Alexandrian theatre. A Menander comedy perhaps? I much prefer comedy over tragedy." He paused and then added with a grin, "Pleasure over pain."

Antinous ate sparingly. He talked about the temple project, the advantages and disadvantages of the two proposed sites and the availability of marble.

"At a minimum, we need to import two hundred stone workers from Athens and Ephesus. Ptolemy has assured me that expense is not a consideration."

Hektor ate with gusto but listened carefully. He watched in a casual way, looking back and forth between us. He was clearly more interested in gauging my reaction to Antinous' commentary than following our discussion. When I glanced at him during a particularly long, enthusiastic exposition by Antinous, he rolled his eyes ever so slightly.

Jason played on the floor with Hektor's kitten he had named *Kallisto*, meaning 'most beautiful.' They both slept before the barley cake and black dates stuffed with almonds arrived.

The hour was not late when Antinous excused himself.

"Thank you for a most wonderful evening, Athena of Korinth. My assistant will call for you in the morning. I look forward to showing you my preliminary plans."

To Hektor he said, "Good night, Hektor of Naukratis. I trust we have not bored you with dreary construction details."

"Not in the least, Antinous of Kos, it would be impossible for me to be bored in the presence of one so beautiful and wise as Athena of Korinth."

Hektor appeared altogether too comfortable on his divan, so I smiled at both of them and said, "Yes, it has been a long day, gentlemen.

Tomorrow promises to be eventful."

Hektor accepted his dismissal with his usual good humor. "Thank you again for your hospitality," he said with a hint of tease. "I look forward to showing you our theatre and accompanying you to another symposion."

If he meant to demonstrate to Antinous his claim on me, I'm not certain he achieved the desired effect. I saw no reaction to the implied intimacy of 'another.'

Instead, Antinous said in a matter-of-fact tone, "Yes, Athena of Korinth, our theatre employs the most modern of stage mechanics. We shall make it part of our tour."

They both stood to their feet, Antinous with a bowed head, while Hektor bent over my hand. His rich mane of cedar waves glowed in the lamplight. I caught the faintest whiff of an exotic, woody scent.

"It seems that I have competition," he said in a voice too low for Antinous to hear. "I welcome it. It makes the sport all the more thrilling."

Then the two men, one golden and beautiful as a Polykleitos statue, the other virile and confident as Apollo, left together.

The next morning the nightmare began. Before I had time to ready myself for the Library, a slave announced Ptolemy's Lord Chancellor Sosibius. Dread gnawed at my stomach as I left my preparations to join him in the reception chamber. He stood impatiently by the open terrace.

"Excuse my early intrusion," he apologized insincerely. "I am here on behalf of the Pharaoh."

"Do you wish refreshment?" I asked politely, indicating he might sit in one of two gilt chairs nearby.

He declined the slave's offer of a chalice with a dismissive wave of his hand and remained standing.

"I have engaged a secretary whom I believe meets your requirements." His black eyes were hard and shiny.

I refused to give him the pleasure of seeing my surprise. My request had been for funds only; naturally, my plan had been to engage a secretary loyal to me.

He obviously meant to surround me with spies and had no shame in letting me know. If I didn't make a stand, he would usurp my authority. He was not an ally. Anything but that. He scarcely maintained civility when speaking to me.

"You are most kind and efficient, Sir. Only last evening, Antinous of Kos suggested I might find the members of my staff from among the many talented persons at the Akademy whose familiarity with mathematics and engineering would be invaluable to our project. You have spared me the arduous task of interviewing all possible candidates."

The corner of his vile mouth twitched, and his face darkened a shade. He stood perfectly still. The room was quiet save for the chorus of birds feeding in the tamarind trees by the balcony. Sounds from the waterfront drifted up from the shore.

"I am most certain, Sir, that the Pharaoh understands an excellent support staff makes all the difference to the speed and success of our endeavor. I am grateful for your assistance in selecting my personal secretary, but perhaps Ptolemy might provide me with a budget for the rest of my staff? I have always found it useful to have realistic parameters before making decisions."

He had no comment to my request. I sensed he was content for the moment with his secretary spy. He glanced around the chamber. His predator eyes missed no detail.

"His Majesty was most impressed with your gift of the Euripides papyrus," he remarked slyly. "An excellent choice."

Then Sosibius shifted to a confiding tone, as if to let me know a little secret that would further my favor with Ptolemy.

"His Majesty was perhaps more impressed with your slave boy." He looked at me with his nasty beady eyes and waited.

I'm sure he expected me to say right away that I would gladly offer my slave to the Pharaoh, if it should please Ptolemy.

"His Majesty's keen perception is most impressive." My smile must have blinded him. "No doubt the Pharaoh saw the hand of the Goddess on the child. It is an astonishing vision for those who are gifted with the Sight to see."

His lids drooped. His nose was crooked and sharp. He almost had no lips. I thought his face was that of a vulture.

"Aphrodite gave the boy into my protection," I continued without mercy. "He is a special gift from the sea. His well-being is a sign of the continued blessing of the Goddess. We regard the child as a most favorable omen of our good fortune that Aphrodite is pleased with the Pharaoh's Temple plans."

This was not the response he had anticipated, but who could argue with the will of the Gods? His black aura trailed behind him when he at last bid farewell. I didn't delude myself. I might have won the first round, but the match wasn't over.

CHAPTER 18   THE LIBRARY

"A library is a repository of medicine for the mind and a hospital for the soul."
– Ancient Greek Saying

The world-renowned Library of Alexandria turned out to be not one structure, but a gardened university campus close by the Royal compound. Untainted by Ptolemy's gaudy taste, the elegantly appointed buildings adhered to the strict harmonious aesthetics dictated by the mathematical canons of Greek architecture.

Antinous' assistant led us directly to where he waited in the shade of a portico surrounding a grand Quadrangle planted with tall cypress and flowering rose bushes. He greeted us warmly and was particularly kind to an awed Jason.

Aside from the occasional bearded Cynic with long gown and straggly gray hair to the shoulders, the men in the Quad were clean-shaven, wore short chitons and sported neatly barbered curls. The three females I saw dressed modestly in subdued colors with hair arranged in neat buns. A Korinthian would never allow his daughter to attend an Akademy; she would be tutored at home where proper Greek women passed their lives.

Antinous spoke briefly with a girl about sixteen, introducing her as Phoebe, daughter of Eioneus, a physician at the Medical Akademy.

"She has great promise," he confided afterwards. "Her hope is to treat disease in children, if her future husband permits."

Clearly, Greek dress was *de rigueur*, with the only exception being a sizeable minority of bushy-bearded Canaanite Jews in heavy, striped woolen robes and shawl head cloths over long, rather messy hair. If there were any Egyptians studying at the Akademy, they had adopted Greek dress.

"It appears you have an interest in the theatre, Athena of Korinth. I suggest we start there."

I thought Antinous might mention Hektor's invitation last night or at least his unexpected arrival, but he remained engrossed in his monologue about the Library—walking rapidly, gesturing with both hands as he guided us across the campus.

"The Library collects not only books, but also plants and exotic animals from as far east as the Indus Valley and west as the Pillars of Hercules. You must spend a full day in the botanical gardens to appreciate the extent of our collection."

Antinous knew everyone, and everyone knew him. When we approached, conversation stopped, students stood and heads bowed.

The Library theatre was a gleaming white jewel in the Alexandrian morning sun. Sited on the harbor shore, the columned open portals of the four-story marble *skene* were designed to catch fresh breezes off the water.

Unlike Greece or Cyrene with steep hillsides to carve out seating, the land here was flat. A massive earth-and-stone curved berm, faced with countless tons of marble, had been erected to support a giant *theatron* of tiered bleachers.

"A seating capacity of ten thousand," Antinous said with pride. "Quite a feat of engineering, given the confined space."

Blinding white light reflected off the shimmering facade. The sun, casting short shadows, was only midway to zenith and the day was already hot. I'd been foolish not to bring the umbrella my slaves had tried to press on me.

We entered into blessed filtered shade through an arched gateway adjacent to the requisite statue of Dionysus, the God Protector of Theatre. In the circular *orcheisthai* at the foot of the stage, a company of dancers and chorus singers rehearsed a scene from the Sophocles tragedy, "Oedipus the King."

Double flutes wailed. Tambourines clashed.

The Director stopped the rehearsal immediately upon sighting

Antinous and introduced himself with a dramatic bow from the waist.

"Please give me the honor, Sir, of showing your guest our stage machinery. I believe the Lady will find it surpasses anything in Greece—even Korinth."

The usual giant cranes, pulleys and levers needed for special effects and change of scenery were housed in the four-story *skene* directly behind the *proskenion* where the actors perform. Dressing rooms overflowed with elaborate costumes. The sacred mask room contained an impressive number of costly bright-painted masks, each displayed on its own pedestal.

At the Director's insistence, an earthquake machine shook the stage so hard, I might have been back at sea in the storm. I grabbed Jason at the same time Antinous grabbed me.

We laughed in a most natural way, without any trace of self-consciousness. Antinous might not have any memory of that life when we were married, but he couldn't avoid sensing the familiarity and ease between us. He held me a moment longer than necessary, and I didn't hurry to move away.

"If the Lady would care to descend below the *skene*," the Director suggested, "I would be most pleased to demonstrate the world's largest thunder drum."

Two slaves oiled the axis of a bronze cylinder twice the volume of ours in Korinth.

"I would advise the Lady to cover her ears."

At his command, four muscled, sweaty slaves put their shoulders to the machine. The cylinder turned, and the heavy stones inside tumbled against the metal. Boom! Boom! Boom!

Jason's eyes danced. In all the weeks I'd known him, I'd never seen him this happy.

"And now, with the Lady's indulgence, I have saved the best for last." The Director led the way up the steps again and snapped his fingers for a singer to mount the stage.

The man's deep voice filled the air. Certainly anyone sitting in the farthest top row would have heard his words clearly.

"The very latest in sound technology, Lady, and far superior to the caves and artificial tunnels used in Syracuse or Greece. Do you see the bronze tubes?" He pointed to an intricate weaving of pipes snaking their way from the stage to the open-air theatre. "We can thank the

Akademy and our esteemed Antinous of Kos."

"Not me, Sir," Antinous objected, "but our engineers."

Antinous didn't need much encouragement to wax on about the cutting-edge engineering projects at the Library. He was particularly animated about siege machines and Archimedes screw pumps.

I feigned interest in his cylindrical cavities and spindles while Jason hung on every word, posing questions I would never have thought of.

The lecture rooms of the Akademy turned out to be largely centered along the shady porticos around the Quad where we earlier met Antinous.

Teenagers only a few years older than Jason were in heated debate over the merits of dispassionate Stoicism versus elitist Sophism. Lectors discussed the mathematics of Euclid, Pythagoras and Thales or the geography and astronomy of Eudoxus and Eratosthenes.

A group of boys much younger than Jason sat under a sycamore tree taking turns reciting the *Iliad,* Homer's epic poem of the battle of Troy. After the memorization of Homer would come the writings of Socrates, followed by his student, Plato, and then Plato's student, Aristotle.

But it was at the athletic field where laughing boys raced that I saw the deep yearning in Jason's eyes. He watched their easy comradeship with the hungry look of a child who had never tasted friendship.

"Classes are nearly finished for the day," Antinous said. "In another hour or so, the *paleistra* will be filled with competitions."

"I see no Jews," I commented. "Will they come later?"

"The Jewish students are exempt from athletics. Nudity is offensive to their god."

Shortly before midday we went to the private office of Antinous with its massive oak shelves, stuffed to the brim with scrolls. More papyri, mostly unrolled, covered a large marble slab desk. Papyri were everywhere—stacked on the floor, piled on tables.

An open door gave onto a garden where birds chirped and a fountain splashed. Bright sunshine poured through a half dozen small windows trimmed with blue borders.

When an assistant arrived with a small scroll, Antinous sat Jason on a tripod stool at a small cypress table and put the scroll in front of him.

"Now you will learn to read, if you wish."

Jason looked up at me, his innocent hazel eyes enormous in a hopeful face. I nodded yes. His smile was like the sun breaking through clouds.

The look I exchanged with Antinous over Jason's head told me that he was pleased with my consent, but if he desired me, he hid it well.

The preliminary sketches of his proposed design showed a classical Greek structure, exquisitely proportional. I was polite but not impressed. The architecture was very much like Aphrodite's Temple in Korinth and the Goddess Athena's Parthenon on the Athenian Acropolis. Perfect in every way but not original.

My sense was that the Pharaoh expected something new, something that would awe—a statement uniquely Alexandrian. Perhaps the fusion of two worlds as his great grandfather had achieved with the God Sarapis.

"We must decide on the site, Antinous, before proceeding with a plan. We cannot design in a vacuum, without context, but only for a specific location. The temple must be a monument to nature as well as the Goddess."

"The Pharaoh has proposed two locations," he explained, showing me on a map. "One is here beside Alexander's Tomb and the other next to the *Serapeum* on the rise behind the city."

"I must be truthful, Antinous. Neither will do. The Temple cannot be in the midst of the city—nor should Aphrodite compete with Sarapis. Alexandria has no Akrokorinth or mountains as in Greece, but you do have the sea. Surely a suitable site can be found somewhere along the coast."

Antinous listened without being threatened. His male ego didn't rush to defend. He allowed me to make all my points without interruption.

"I shall speak to Ptolemy personally," he assured me.

I don't mind admitting that I was flattered by the admiration in his eyes.

We lunched by the sea under the rich shade of a sycamore. A slave served us melon, cold roast duck, flatbread and watered wine. Jason pored over the scroll, squealing with delight when Antinous confirmed he had learned yet another letter.

"The boy is bright. I believe exceptionally so. Would you give leave for him to attend a few hours of instruction each day?"

Antinous didn't call Jason 'slave,' but 'boy.' I agreed and thanked him for his generosity.

We rested a long time in the languid shade, quietly discussing the virtues of austere Doric columns over exuberant Korinthian capitals with their richly carved acanthus leaves. Gentle waves rolled in and out, pulling at rocks on the pebbled beach at the foot of the garden.

Our fingers touched when I passed him a silver dish of plump, juicy pomegranate seeds. He held my eyes again before turning away to answer a question from Jason. This time I had seen his pupils dilate and was certain he felt the current pass between us.

"Would you do me the honor of dining again with me this evening?" I asked boldly.

"I regret I have a previous engagement."

He said nothing more; it was his lack of explanation that I didn't like. Antinous rejoiced in explaining why and how; he lived in a universe of ideas and was always eager to communicate. What were his plans for this evening that he chose not to divulge?

I could hardly ask him what other engagement could be more important than dining with me, although I thought it.

CHAPTER 19   HEKTOR

"In nine cases of out of ten, a woman had better show more affection than she feels." – Aristotle

It was to Hektor's credit that he sent word in advance that he would pass by my quarters in the early evening to hear if there was anything I required. He wasn't so forward as to invite himself to dine, but the rules of hospitality guaranteed him at least a cup of wine.

Tonight, perhaps, was the time to start to heal my wounds.

I sent Jason to bed with his new papyrus scroll and Kallisto the kitten.

When Hektor arrived, crimson cloak over his shoulder, he looked around for the boy, and not seeing him, said, "I have brought your slave sweets."

He barely concealed his satisfaction that I had chosen for us to be alone.

We had settled on the tangerine sofas and taken a cup of Cypriot wine when he set a packet of emerald green silk on the brass tray table between us.

"For me?" I asked innocently.

"For you," he answered, raising that eyebrow.

Inside the lush folds of the silk was a heavy gold necklace. Seven exquisite gold owl charms hung from a thick chain. The owl is the symbol of Athena, my namesake, the Goddess of Wisdom. I recognized Macedonian gold work. The piece was worth a fortune. A ransom maybe.

"Do you hope to buy my attention?"

"There is not enough gold in the world to buy you or your attention. I would not be so foolish as to think a trifle like a necklace would gain me favor. You require something much more than that."

He waited a few moments. The sun had set; the sky deepened to lavender, the color of my gown. Salt air mixed with the scent of jasmine. The only sounds were the waves breaking on the gravel beach and a nightingale. Another answered. A slight wind rustled the leaves of the myrtle trees, and in my mind's eye, I saw white petals float gently to green grass like first snow.

Hektor moved gracefully around the low table to stand next to my sofa, towering over me, his shoulders so broad they filled the room. The Spot throbbed.

Taking my silence as consent, he scooped me into his arms, carried me across the pink granite tiles to my white marble bedchamber and lay me carefully on the linen spread. He removed his cloak, never taking his eyes off me. He untied the thongs of his sandals laced to his knees without once looking. But before he lifted his tunic, he noticed Jason asleep at the foot of my bed with the kitten and the open scroll.

Setting them both on Jason's stomach, he picked Jason up like a weightless doll and carried all into the next room.

I didn't move waiting for him to return. I closed my eyes, and seeing Black Falcon's lips, looked up. A delicate winged Eros, chubby and pink, smiled down from the painted ceiling above my bed. As I watched, he flitted among white doves, lyres and bunches of purple grapes. I closed my eyes again and was back at the symposion in Korinth.

My mouth was incredibly dry, but not my secret valley. The Spot burned.

Hektor towered over me once more, pulling the chiton over his head and untying his loincloth until he stood naked, the long muscles of his glorious body highlighted by the glow of a bronze oil lamp with star and moon cutouts. Tiny stars and crescent moons reflected off the marble walls and Hektor's bronzed skin. His manhood swelled and rose in the air, head glistening.

"You are so beautiful," he whispered and then lowered himself next to me.

His strong hand with long fingers stroked along my shoulder and across my throat. He caressed the tops of my breasts overflowing the bodice of my gown, not touching my erect nipples rising in the lustrous silk. Would he spill wine on me again? My heart raced, and the peaks rose higher at the memory.

I watched him as he watched my breasts rising and falling. The amber glow of the oil lamps streaked his mane of rich waves and curls with fiery red. When he saw me looking at him, he smiled slightly and put his mouth to my breast and began to suckle through the silk, leaving dark circles. The heat of his hands warmed me.

Tears welled in my eyes; my moans were soft vibrations in my throat, a quiet humming in my ears. The Spot burned hotter.

He loosened the ties of my gown and removed the gold pins; the cloth tumbled from my bare shoulders. His hands again stroked only my bare skin. Then with the moves of an expert, he eased the top of my gown to my waist.

"You are so desirable," he sang in the lowest and huskiest of tones.

I reached out to touch his engorged manhood, to feel his smooth tip, but he stopped me—like the evening of the symposion. But I had no doubts about his desire tonight.

"Let me pleasure you, Athena of Korinth."

I relaxed into delicious luxury. He required nothing from me but to enjoy his touch. When he slid my gown up my thighs, past the curve of my hips to join the cloth gathered at my waist, I parted my legs, inviting him, holding my breath in anticipation of what I knew would come next.

He focused wholly on my body; his eyes followed his hands as they caressed me.

"I could never tire of touching you."

Hektor stroked my stomach and down the slope of my thigh. He stroked my breasts and the line of my hips. His hands were strong, his touch firm and commanding. Always the master sculptor, he molded my flesh.

"You are more perfect than Aphrodite herself."

I drew a sharp intake of air when his finger went straight to the Spot. Draping my legs over his loins, I filled my hands with his thick cedar curls.

"O-o-o-o-o-o," I sang, the note rising and rising, louder and louder as his finger rotated on the magic spot that only he knew. Electric shocks spread through my buttocks, down my thighs and up into my belly.

With the sound of the nearby sea in my ears, I let the wave slowly build, wanting it not to crest but for the sensation to go on forever. When I thought the pleasure could not be greater, his finger slid along my wet valley to rotate on my lotus. The dam burst, and I swept over the falls.

I might have been Kallisto the kitten the way his hands stroked me all over.

He kissed the tears from my cheek and whispered into my ear, "Beautiful Athena. There is more."

Pulling me back into him, both of us on our side, he slipped his hardness deep into my wet. With one arm under me, his big hand with long fingers stroked my nipples; his other hand cupped my mound. The base of his palm pressed against the base of my womb.

I cried out when his manhood slid out—and again when it slid in.

His face buried in my hair, I felt his hot breath on my neck.

"I want to touch you and be in you forever," he crooned. "I could never have enough of you."

His long fingers massaged my lotus while his rod moved slowly in, and drew slowly out, as the waves of the sea suck pebbles from the shore. I pushed my hips back into his belly, gyrating slowly in the sinuous rhythm of a Persian dancer.

"Do not think of anything, Athena. Just feel."

A thrill shot through me when his tongue went in my ear. I pressed my thighs together, reaching back to grip the back of his thigh and glide with him. He filled me. We moved with a slow steady rhythm. I rode the buildup, feeling and not thinking, holding my breath until my canal pulsed, contracted and pulsed again.

Taking my face in his hands, he kissed me with a tenderness I would never have believed of him. His lips covered mine; his tongue probed deep. When he tried to pull away, I gripped the back of his neck and lifted my head to follow him, my lips clinging to his.

He laughed and kissed me lightly on the tip of my nose. And like a splash of cold water, his laughter sobered me. I had dared trust him; I had dared to trust again.

"Why do you laugh?" I whispered.

"Because you are such a delight," he said with a smile. But not his usual broad flash of white teeth. A sweet half-smile. A new warmth in his eyes replaced amusement and all arrogance; if he saw me as a trophy, I was one he sincerely cherished. He kissed me most lovingly first on my lips, then on each eye.

"Now you," I breathed in his ear.

"Do not think of me," he laughed again. "I can go all night."

I believed him. He almost did. I heard the first cock crow when he left my bed. We had not slept.

CHAPTER 20   AGORA

"What is there more kindly than the feeling between host and guest?" – Aeschylus

Making short work of the scrolls on my desk, I took an early breakfast of fresh goat cheese and warm bread infused with rosemary. The fire in the Pharos dimmed as dawn came. Ribbons of pink whipped cream streaked the sky. I just knew it was going to be a wonderful day.

The slaves dressed Jason for the Musaeum in a white linen tunic with an embroidered blue geometric band on the hem and around the square neck. They barbered his curls as if he were landed gentry and not a slave. I walked with him across the gardens and through the small red gate in the white wall separating the Library from the palace grounds. My head slave, a Syrian called Ajax with scars from the pox, carried a yellow silk parasol with green fringe.

But when we knocked at the door to Antinous' office, there was no answer. I tried again and then pushed open the polished cedar door.

Antinous was in deep conversation with a golden teen who was impossibly more beautiful than Antinous himself. No barber could ever create those luxurious strawberry blond waves; they were a gift from the Gods.

Antinous looked up when I entered. He turned immediately back to the youth, put his arm around the boy-god's shoulder and smiled at him warmly. The familiar way in which they touched left no doubt as to their intimacy.

I felt foolish and embarrassed—and regretted that I hadn't waited for Antinous to answer the door. Everyone knew about these special relationships between Greek men and teenagers. *Erastes* and *eromenos*— lover and loved.

Most women resented their husband's intimate companions. How could she compete? It was an inherently unfair playing ground. The wife remained sequestered in the home while the men trained for war, debated philosophy and attended symposia—all forbidden to her. She could never join one of their drinking clubs. Only entertainers, temple girls and *hetaerae* were allowed.

It was painfully obvious that Antinous was the youth's *erastes,* his teacher and mentor. If they were sexually intimate—and I was convinced they were—Antinous was the penetrator.

I felt an irrational, visceral reaction to the vision of Antinous screwing this beautiful boy. I had no right to be jealous, but I was. I suspected that the youth was the reason Antinous had declined my invitation; he preferred the teenager to me. By the look of his touch and his warm smile, his affection for the boy was profound. He loved him, and it wrenched me in a wholly irrational way to witness it.

We weren't married now. Our love had been centuries ago.

The teen left Antinous to stand before me and bow his head just enough to show respect.

"Peace be with you, Lady," he said politely.

His eyes were the most astonishing blue; I was quite startled just looking into them. Alexander the Great was said to have eyes like these, eyes that mesmerized everyone he met.

He passed by me, past Jason, and out the door. The slave Ajax stepped far aside and bowed his head deeply, chin on his chest. This teenager was someone important, or the son of someone important, which is the same thing.

Antinous smiled at me and put his hand on Jason's head. He displayed no signs of discomfort.

"You may leave Jason in my safekeeping," he assured me. "I shall return him to you knowing how to read."

His blue eyes said nothing about what he felt about the teenage beauty with Alexander's eyes—or about me.

Ajax followed me to the *agora*, the market south of the row of waterfront warehouses along the docks. A covered peristyle *stoa* surrounding the central plaza provided shelter for shopkeepers. In the open square, temporary booths with tarp coverings lined up in slipshod rows under the full wrath of the African sun.

Shouts and arguments of merchants and traders mixed with the wail of flutes and pounding of drums. I stopped for a few moments to applaud a troupe of minstrels and acrobats. Ajax tossed them three copper *obols*, and they turned a string of somersaults as thanks.

"Greek priestess! Come!" shouted an Egyptian astrologer from behind a pile of scrolls. "I see change in the future. Let me read your stars."

Next to the astrologer's tent, legs twisted into the lotus position, sat a lone Hindu in the coral robe of a *sadhu*. A brass begging bowl stood on the ground in front of him. His skin was the darkest of browns but not the ebony black of a Nubian. With an expression of utter calm, he appeared oblivious to the chaos around him. When I instructed Ajax to give him a copper obol, and the coin clinked in the empty bowl, he didn't open his eyes. Not a muscle twitched.

"Hey, Lady!" The old Nubian woman, surrounded by dried snakes, rodents and herbs, stretched out under a makeshift canopy of orange linen. Her arms and legs were so thin and her skin so dry, she might have been a mummy.

I smiled at her, and she smiled back. She had one upper tooth in her black gums.

"A beautiful lady like you has need of a real man." She ignored proper protocol and addressed me directly in informal speech. "Let me make you a potion. I promise your husband will be powerful as a bull and hard as stone the whole night."

After my sleepless night, I couldn't help beaming. "I assure you that is most certainly not necessary."

"Then take this potion to make him limp as a worm. Or this for yourself, if you desire to keep up with him—and your lovers."

She was a mischievous old lady with a spark in her black eyes, so I bought a small clay vial with an oil she claimed would make my skin as soft as a young boy's. *As soft as the young friend of Antinous?*

A few zealots ranted here and there around the square; one or two drew a small crowd. The *agora* is the heart and soul of any Greek city. Speeches are made here. Revolutions start here. Governments fall here.

Ajax held the parasol over my head to protect me from the fierce spring sun while I wandered among the stalls, stopping to sniff spices and handle vegetables and cloth.

I idly sorted through an old painted chest filled with poor quality rings and bracelets. Sunlight glinted off gold. I picked up a ring. Two gold horns framed a grape-sized, deep blue, gold-veined stone.

I stared, hardly daring to believe my eyes. The second Hathor ring—it must be the second. The first was delivered with the ransom note. Odd that Ptolemy hadn't returned it to me.

I slipped the ring on my right middle finger. It fit perfectly.

"How much?" I asked.

"Excellent choice, my Lady. Ramses the Great had this ring made for his daughter-wife, the White Queen."

"How much?" I repeated.

"Six *drachmas*. A special price only for the Lady."

"Two *drachmas*. And not an *obol* more. The stone is not real—it is faience. Anyone can see that. The metal is Lydian copper used to create counterfeit coins."

What I claimed was nonsense, of course. But certainly not more ridiculous than his claim of Ramses the Great. It was all part of the posture of bargaining, and we both knew it.

"Five. The Lady has a keen eye for beauty. The ring belongs on her hand."

"Three *drachmas*. I am feeling generous today."

The large brown and gray striped tent occupied a prime spot under a portico roof. Only a reputable businessman dealing in quality goods could afford the high rent of such a desirable location. At my nod, Ajax opened the flap, and I stepped inside.

Thick camel wool muffled the clamor of the agora. The interior was dark and quiet; I blinked and waited for my eyes to adapt.

An old Jew in a richly embroidered gown lounged on a tapestry-covered divan, smoking a brass pipe with a long, slender neck. He was surrounded by stacks of lush, colorful carpets.

"*Shalom!*" he greeted me in Hebrew. "Peace to the Lady."

"*Shalom,*" I answered politely.

He waved his horsehair whisk around the tent as if to say 'Look.' Then he settled back with his pipe, but his eyes never left me; I could feel them follow as I wandered.

A familiar red glow pulsed in the shadows at the far side of the tent. I tried to hide my excitement, knowing that the Old Jew would be carefully monitoring my enthusiasm to see where he might start the bidding. But I walked too quickly past gilt chests and tall black-and-red glazed urns painted with athletes and Gods.

The bronze mirror needed replacing, but the red lacquer frame was in perfect condition. The Hathor ring and now *this*—what were the odds to find them both in one morning, in one marketplace?

The Red Mirror. My ticket home whenever it suited me.

In spite of the trembling excitement inside, I kept my exterior as cool as a marble statue. But I'd already lost my advantage. The old man had seen me head directly here, passing every treasure along the way without so much as a glance.

"How much?" I asked with a tone of idle interest.

"How much does the Lady wish to pay?" he countered in an equally casual tone.

Rings of smoke swirled around his neatly coiled red turban.

"As little as possible," I answered.

"Do we not all?" he said, chuckling. He scratched his chin through the gray bush of his beard.

I could tell he was enjoying our repartee, but he didn't waver.

"What price would the Lady find reasonable?"

By forcing me to state my first offer, he ensured he wouldn't set the price too low.

"I would find it reasonable if you earned a 25 percent finder's fee plus 10 percent warehousing."

The Old Jew mulled that over for a moment. He flicked the horsehair whisk at a giant black fly.

"It is a fair profit," he agreed in a congenial tone. "Perhaps on the low side for warehousing. Let us say 40 percent in all, and we have a deal."

He took a long draw on his pipe and blew out a series of smoke rings. They drifted quite a distance in the still air before melting away.

I said nothing, sensing that he had more to add. Never talk too much during a negotiation.

"But rather than merely agreeing to the equation is not our dilemma to determine the base figure from which we start? How does the Lady know I am honest?"

"Your stall looks to be permanent. Repeat business depends upon honesty. Would you risk your good reputation when we may easily come to an equitable arrangement?"

He beamed and gestured to the divan at right angle to his.

"Do me the honor of taking refreshment with me, Lady, and we shall arrive at a fair price."

"Eben! Bring a tisane," he shouted.

He must have been here all along, but I hadn't seen him. Eben had the same long, slightly unkempt hair and the straggly beginnings of a beard as when we sailed the Nile three hundred years before.

I knew at once by his eyes that he recognized me. I smiled at him, and he smiled shyly back. Did he still sing psalms while he played his lyre? Did he still practice Kabbalah?

"My youngest son," explained the Old Jew.

The scent of the flowery tea served in small, clay, handleless cups held a hint of mint. Eben's father tore off a chunk of dark bread, passed the round, flat loaf to me, and then dipped his piece into olive oil. A silver bowl with five-pointed stars around the rim overflowed with fat, glossy dates. A dozen pigeon eggs, boiled and peeled, rested on a bed of coarse brown salt.

We nibbled on dates tasting like caramel; I dipped bread in the oil. We sipped the honey-sweetened brew. The old man was in no hurry to discuss an outcome we both knew to be inevitable. I wouldn't leave today without the Red Mirror, regardless of the price.

He offered me smoke from a pipe, but I declined politely and waited for him to speak first.

"The Lady has taken a long time to arrive."

"Pardon me?" I thought I must have misheard.

"The Lady was expected weeks ago."

How he knew I was the priestess from Korinth, I couldn't say. Perhaps by my accent. I assumed he'd heard gossip of my kidnapping. There were few secrets in a marketplace. I'd seen his eye go to the Hathor ring on my right hand more than once.

"I was delayed."

"We were concerned."

"Who are *we*?"

He drew more smoke and idly flicked his fly whisk, moving his wrist back and forth with lazy snaps. He glanced at my slave Ajax, standing next to the tent flap, pretending not to listen. But slaves hear everything.

"Ajax," I commanded. "I believe I have forgotten my shawl at the ring vendor's stall. Fetch it before he sells it."

Ajax didn't look at the shawl on the sofa beside me but left the tent without a change in his expression. Eben followed to make certain he didn't listen from outside the woolen flap.

"Who are *we*?" I repeated.

"We? We who wait for you." As soon as we were alone, he switched to informal speech and addressed me as "you"—as an equal. "Did you think the Oracle would give you a task without providing assistance?"

"Oracle?" I repeated the word as if I were too dense to get its simple meaning.

"You cannot find the answers to the Emerald Tablet on your own."

He studied me. His eyelids were fat and heavy, giving him a hooded look. But from under those fleshy lids, his keen eyes missed nothing.

"There is someone you must meet. Eben will come for you when the first stars come out."

Eben busied himself with the tray. Ajax returned empty-handed, of course. I rose to leave and gathered the shawl with me.

"How silly of me. Here it has been all the time."

"I shall have the mirror delivered to the Lady's quarters today." The Old Jew addressed me formally again. "We shall make arrangements for proper payment at another time."

I didn't bother to ask how he knew where I lived. If he knew about the Oracle, there could be little he didn't know about me.

CHAPTER 21 JEWISH QUARTER

"First have a definite, clear practical objective. Second, have the necessary means to achieve your ends—wisdom, money, materials and men." – Aristotle

Antinous worked at his marble slab desk when I returned to the Library for Jason. He left his papyri immediately and greeted me warmly and enthusiastically.

"Jason had a good day. He is very quick and made remarkable progress."

"Thank you, Antinous of Kos, for your interest in him."

I kept my reserve, still a little off balance from seeing him this morning with the golden youth. But Antinous was unperturbed.

"Your invitation to dine yesterday eve was most kind. I regret I had a previous engagement."

"Yes, you must sup with us again, Antinous of Kos. Your company enlightens and educates."

An awkward moment passed while he waited for the invitation that didn't come. It wouldn't be tonight. I expected Eben.

"This afternoon I am to interview my new secretary and begin forming a staff," I said, maneuvering our conversation to business. "Might I impose upon you to arrange appointments with the names on the list you provided?"

"Of course," he replied smoothly.

Even Antinous, with his head in the cosmos, couldn't fail to notice the formality that hadn't been there before I saw his hand on the youth's shoulder.

"Shall we meet in the morning, Athena of Korinth?" An ice-blue twinkle sparkled in his eye. "It seems you are occupied for the rest of this day."

Sunshine bathed his blond curls. His lower lip was slightly fuller than his upper in a sensitive mouth set above a cleft chin, the mark of Venus. Antinous was the most beautiful man I'd ever seen—except for the boy-god this morning.

The Red Mirror arrived mid-afternoon. I stood it against the white marble wall of my bedchamber, close by where I slept. I felt a wonderful sense of control; I didn't need Barb's help to get back. Well, at least as long as I was close to the Mirror.

Jason played with Kallisto and jabbered on about Epicureans, Skeptics and Stoics. I tried to concentrate on my papyri, but my mind kept wandering back to the Old Jew and wondering who of the 'we who wait for you' I would meet tonight.

Ptolemy's Chancellor Sosibius sent me an old fat Egyptian scribe with a correct and subservient demeanor. The letter of introduction identified him as Platon, a common Greek name. The letter went on to say that he held a degree from the Civil Service Academy. I'd seen the building on the Library campus. Egyptians were trained there to carry out the day-to-day functions of the vast Ptolemaic bureaucracy of tax collectors and scribes.

I didn't detect malice in his eyes, but as he came from the Lord Chancellor, I knew I had to keep everything from him except business details of the Temples—mine in Korinth and the new one in Alexandria.

I showed him to a cypress desk and gave him the task of compiling my notes for a return response to my assistant Irene on the Akrokorinth. He set to work at once, needing almost no instruction. At least, the Chancellor had sent a capable man.

The light of the Pharos blazed brighter as darkness fell. Antinous had explained that at sunset, slaves stoke a giant bonfire at the base of an internal shaft. The flames rise forty stories to the cupola top where a mammoth lens reflects the fire all through the night.

I watched the light until the stars came out, and at last, Eben arrived.

"Please come with me. Alone is best."

Over the objections of Ajax, I wrapped my hooded dark green cloak around me, told Jason I was going to the Library, not to linger for bed, and stepped out to go I knew not where.

We went a short distance on the Street of the Soma and entered the Jewish Quarter through an arched portal not far from the Gate of the Moon. The guards were closing the heavy wooden gates for the night.

The Greek Quarter's straight, well-lit avenues built for chariot traffic disappeared. The streets here were much narrower and lined with three-story white-washed, mud buildings topped with roof terraces.

More Jews lived in Alexandria than in Jerusalem or Babylon, but the Jewish Quarter was also home to Assyrians, Persians and almost anyone else who wasn't Greek or Egyptian. The richest merchants built Persian-style mansions with brightly painted walls and crenellated tops trimmed in jewel-colored geometric patterns.

Rows of naked awning poles stuck out from houses along the full length of the street. If I had come by day, I would have used corner shops as landmarks—turn left at the silk merchant, right at brass pots. Now every street looked the same. The exotic Eastern goods of a chaotic sidewalk day market were packed away for the night.

The moon had yet to rise. Unlike the Greek Quarters, the streets were dark; all houses were tightly shuttered. Cats by the dozens fled into alleyways when we passed. A dog howled. Shrouded in robes, faces hidden, dark figures scurried like rats from shadow to shadow. No one called out to their neighbor.

We turned down a tiny alley and stopped at a rough wooden door. Eben knocked three short raps, and the door opened. He kissed his fingers and touched the *Mezuzah* with Hebrew letters on the right door jamb before we went through, and the door closed behind us.

The whitewashed room was small with a terracotta tile floor and one shuttered window. Two brass oil lanterns shaped like Aladdin's lamp hung by chains from the beamed ceiling. In front of the hearth, a man in a hooded black and gray striped cloak sat at a rough wooden table.

"Welcome. It gives me great joy to see you again," he greeted me in Egyptian.

Without the telltale voice of a eunuch, it took me a moment to realize the man was my old companion, the priest Qeb-ha. I last saw him three centuries before when I escaped the fate I feared that he'd suffered.

A cane leaned against the table, and he didn't rise to greet me, so I embraced him where he sat. I settled next to him on a small stool with my back also to the fire. Taking his old hand in mine, I kissed it and switched to Greek; my Egyptian wasn't fluent enough for the answers I sought.

"I made it out of Egypt safely, Qeb-ha, although I am certain you know. What of you—and Maia and the others?"

"Do not ask," he said with the patience of centuries. "Some things are best not known. The Fate and the Fortune, they come from the Gods."

My mind flooded with terrible images of torture and death.

He touched my blond hair, saying wistfully, "Even you are Greek now. Everything is Greek. Egyptians are no better than slaves in our own land."

Black Falcon had said exactly the same, that nightmare day in his cabin when he sent me away. He, too, saw me as Greek—as the enemy.

Qeb-ha patted my hand and leaned back in his chair. "It has been that way since the Persians," he sighed. "I fear Egypt is but a shadow of what we knew."

I detected no bitterness in him; I had the sense that disappointment had worn down his anger. At any rate, I felt no anger toward me, but rather a resigned sadness, perhaps more like regret at the Fate the Gods had imposed on us.

Eben had taken a chair in the corner, near the door. Behind me, the flames of the fire crackled. Qeb-ha's and my silhouette danced on the opposite wall.

"They allow us to worship our Gods," he told me. "But how could we worship theirs? Greek gods are jealous, vain creatures who play out their petty rivalries through the lives of mortal men."

He continued in a tone that said he couldn't fathom how anyone might choose another path. "Our Gods command us only to follow the Mystery leading to eternal life."

"But surely, Qeb-ha, the gods are all the same, but with different names."

"You have not changed, Isis. Always the doubter."

He squeezed my hand and then spoke earnestly and a little hurriedly, as if we had run out of time.

"You have come about the Emerald Tablet."

"The Oracle of Delphi sent me here. Do you know where the Tablet is?"

He shook his head. "Alexander is the last I know to possess it. He received the Tablet from the Oracle of Amun in Siwa before he set out to conquer the world."

"But he did not succeed, Qeb-ha. His troops mutinied in India. He died in Babylon. What happened? The Tablet is supposed to give complete power."

Qeb-ha shrugged. "It is the Mystery."

Then he put his hand on my cheek in the tender way of a doting uncle.

"You shall find the Tablet because the Gods put you here. But you cannot manage alone. The Tablet needs protectors. Eben is young. I am old. You must recruit others—only those you trust unconditionally."

"And after I find the Tablet? What then?"

"All shall be revealed. Look for the signs; they are there."

"How shall I know them?"

"You are the Chosen One. The Light is revealed to you."

The way back seemed shorter, as it always does. The guards at the gate questioned Eben, glancing at me suspiciously. If I were a woman of the night, why did I visit the Jewish Quarter? They had their own women.

Just when I was about to intercede, the taller of the two accepted a small pouch from Eben and opened the wood door of the postern beside the tall gate.

We had crossed over the Street of the Soma when I stumbled in the shadows on an uneven stone and fell, hitting my head on a marble column. I heard Eben saying my name, but his voice grew fainter, as from further and further away—and then there was silence.

CHAPTER 22   METROPOLITAN

"Affairs are easier of entrance than of exit; and it is but common prudence to see our way out before we venture in." – Aesop

I woke to the white marble tiles of my condo, not the paving stones of the Alexandrian street.

"Welcome back," Barb greeted me with a teasing smile. "Did I take you from the arms of a lover?"

"No," I answered with a laugh. "This time you've saved me from a bad headache."

We stayed up late, sipping Merlot. Barb was spellbound by my description of Alexandria. I focused on the beauty and vibrancy of the city and its magical complexity. I didn't tell her about the evil Scribe Setne incarnated as Lord Chancellor Sosibius, or the Crown Prince Psamtik as Pharaoh Ptolemy.

I didn't tell her either about the second Red Mirror—well actually, the same mirror, but in the past. As much as she resisted helping me, I decided it would frighten her more to realize I could go back and forth without her help, without her knowing. In truth, I wanted her to know about my trips. Barb was my anchor to this life.

"Have you become a mother?" she asked as soon as I mentioned Jason. "It's not too late for us, you know. I'd like to have a child—if I could find the right father."

She raised both eyebrows when I told about the night with Hektor of Naukratis.

"Does this change your feelings about Hector?"

"Maybe. If he's anything like he is in Alexandria, I've been missing out."

I decided right then that I'd see him as soon as I got back from New York. If the business with his uncle's estate wasn't finished, I'd fly to BA, and we'd do more than tango.

It was like the old days with Barb. Probably convinced I had come to my senses, she teased me about silly stuff, and we left the hard subjects alone.

Packing my suitcase for New York, I went for a sophisticated look with a black Chanel suit and patent pumps, tossing in a couple of evening tops and a cocktail dress.

When I emptied my red clutch, a business card fluttered to the bed.

Anthony Callis, PhD
Director of Cosmology
Institute of Advanced Studies
Princeton NJ

It was the card Tony had given me the night I ran into him at Caesars Palace. He hadn't recognized me, but I knew him the moment I heard his voice. Antinous.

On a wild impulse, I sent a quick email asking if he remembered an Isis from Cleopatra's Barge in Las Vegas. You bought me a martini, I reminded him. A reply came from his Blackberry about one minute later.

To: Isis
From: Tony
How many beautiful women named Isis does a rocket scientist meet?
To: Tony
From: Isis
I'm going to be in New York. Is it too far from Princeton to meet me for a drink?
To: Isis
From: Tony
Martinis? When and where?

I checked into the hotel and got upgraded to a room overlooking Central Park; the horse carriage station was below.

That would be fun. But I decided against it as too romantic; Tony might get the wrong message.

After changing into jeans and boots comfortable enough for walking, I took the elevator to the lobby a few minutes late. Tony was at the bar with two red-brown cocktails in frosted stem glasses and garnished with plump maraschino cherries.

The blue oxford cloth shirt matched his eyes; his muscular thighs pulled at the khaki trousers. His blonde curls weren't sculpted with gel. He wore no aftershave. None of that metro male stuff for Tony.

"I promised you a martini," he said smiling, "but did you know that the Manhattan was invented right here in this bar? Back in the days it was the Ritz. 'Stirred, not shaken' is the right way to make them—or so the bartender tells me. I thought we had to try one."

He was relaxed, like we were the oldest of friends, although 'friends' might not be a totally accurate characterization. Tony tried to be discreet, but I caught his quick assessment of my fitted jeans and soft V-neck sweater. I started to wonder if meeting him had been a good idea.

He asked if I had plans for the rest of the afternoon; he had the day off and could catch one of several trains back to Princeton.

"Well, I had thought of going up to the Metropolitan Museum. It's about twenty blocks. Shall we grab a cab?"

I had this vague hope that the Greco-Roman sculptures might joggle his memory. Rasheed, Hector and the General all knew me from our past life. Why not Tony?

He was quiet when we walked through the Greek Sculpture Court. He'd stand in front of a marble torso, shaking his head in wonder.

"How did they do it with the tools they had?"

I answered, "How did they do it with *any* tools?"

When he admired the athlete *Diadoumenos*, I explained that it was a Roman period marble copy of an original bronze by the Greek genius Polykleitos.

"Polykleitos was the first to use *contrapposto*. That's Italian for the relaxed way the athlete is standing—with the shifted balance of weight on one leg. The pose had its revival with the great sculptors Michelangelo and Donatello."

The athlete, a dead ringer for Antinous, stood poised for eternity between rest and movement.

"None of Polykleitos' work has survived. Bronze was his media. We only have a few copies of statues that were probably melted down. Anyway, he developed a *Kanon* which combined mathematics, music and art. A kind of aesthetic ideal based on Pythagoras and the musical scale. I can't remember the ratios."

"1:2 – octave, 2:3 – harmonic fifth, and 3:4 – harmonic fourth," he said without a moment's hesitation.

"Of course, you would know that off the top of your head," I teased. "I forget you're a math geek."

"Who knows nothing about art."

"The *Kanon* was a kind of bible for all classical sculpture, until it was lost—or rather the concepts were—through the Dark Ages. Then, more and more Roman statues were uncovered; it became the rage to own them. So when the next wave of geniuses came along, they revived the ideal. And *voilà*! The Renaissance."

I hadn't meant to go on like that, but Tony seemed to soak it up.

"You really know your stuff," he said with a look of admiration.

"Not really. I'm an amateur." I played modest but admit it felt good to bask in his respect.

"This guy looks familiar." He stopped at a Greek marble head of a teenage boy. "I feel as if I've seen him before. But I can't imagine where. I never go to museums."

I clearly saw the beautiful golden youth in Antinous' office at the Library—an observation I didn't share with Tony, who would doubtless think me a total nutcase if I breathed a word about reincarnation.

At the marble statue of a nearly nude Aphrodite, he remarked, "I hope you don't think I'm being too forward, but you could have modeled for this."

Too forward. I laughed, thinking how sweet he was. And fun. He was so curious about everything, reading all the labels, commenting on similarities, contrasts and timelines.

The air was balmy for this time of year; we decided to walk back through Central Park. Everywhere was incredibly fresh and green compared to Las Vegas. The path moved from late afternoon sun to shade and back again.

"Thank you for that, Isis. I'm so busy looking into the universe that I don't pay much attention to what's around me, unless it's at the top of a mountain."

"The Greeks saw the cosmos reflected in the world around them."

"Macrocosm and microcosm," he interjected. "They were actually the first cosmologists. I've never fully appreciated their art, though. I had no idea you were so accomplished. But then, you haven't told me much about yourself."

He glanced over and added, "Unless you think I'm being too personal."

"Not at all, Tony. It *is* what people do." I was thinking, *Can anybody be this innocent?*

"Well, the elevator version is that I'm not married, live in Las Vegas and am here for an art auction."

When he didn't jump in with his own story, I prodded, "What about you? I know you're a scientist and that you live in Princeton, but nothing else. Do you have any children?"

It was a pretty obvious way of asking if he was married, but he didn't seem to pick up on it.

"I have a daughter, Jenny—Jen—who's twelve going on twenty."

I waited, but he didn't add more. He wasn't particularly skilled with subtlety.

"And her mother?"

He didn't answer right away and looked down as we walked. I expected him to reveal a nasty divorce.

"You see, it's only Jen and me. My wife died of ovarian cancer two years ago. I haven't quite gotten over it."

"I'm so sorry, Tony." I touched his forearm. "You may never get over her completely. I mean…if you truly loved her."

"I loved her," he said.

The sounds of the city were a constant hum in the background. Inside the park, walking under a thick green canopy with freshly mowed grass on both sides of the paved path, the squeals of children playing and the trills of birds singing were in our ears.

We had almost come out of the park, back to the hustle of traffic on Central Park South, before we spoke again.

"Do you have a business card?" he asked.

"I don't have any with me," I fibbed, then felt a stab of guilt. He had been so honest with me.

"This auction thing is brand new, Tony. In fact, this is my first one. I was trying to impress you. Silly of me, really. Why should you care one way or the other?"

Tony stopped and said, "I care, Isis."

He'd sobered since talking about his wife; there was a new earnestness about him. "Look, we barely know each other, but that's not how I feel. You're so easy to be with—as if we've known each other for years. I can't explain it. Does it sound stupid? Yes—it sounds stupid. Forget I said anything."

Refreshingly forthright, that was Tony. With none of the macho issues that afflict most men. Hector was like that, too. I felt a stab of guilt and pushed it away. *We have only this moment—only here and now.*

"Do you want to grab something to eat," I suggested. "Or do you have to get back to Princeton?"

"Jen's sleeping over at a friend's tonight. I can catch a late train."

I smiled at him and tucked my arm in his. He smiled back and looked first at me, then up at the Manhattan skyline and then back to me. He had the most electric blue eyes made even more intense by the twilight. I saw more than intelligence and enthusiasm in them now; I saw the distinct glow of affection.

"Isn't it great to be alive, Isis?"

"Yes, Tony, it is."

We had a few moments of awkwardness in the lobby. I wanted to do something with my hair and get a jacket, maybe change my boots, which were starting to pinch.

"Would you like to wash up before we go out?"

"Thanks," Tony smiled. "That would be great."

All the way up the elevator, we didn't look at each other or speak. I kept seeing him as muscular *Diadoumenos* cast forever in marble. I wondered if he saw me as Aphrodite, and then told myself to stop it. I was asking for trouble.

The door to my room opened with the keycard, and I stepped in. It all happened so fast, I didn't have time to turn on the light.

Tony pinned me to the door with his perfect body. He didn't put his hands on me but placed his forearms on either side of my head. The light from the city through the floor-to-ceiling windows was just enough to see his face. His features sharpened as my eyes adapted.

He asked me without words, looking intently into my eyes. His eyelashes were thick and curly. A halo of loose blond ringlets framed his face. He didn't make a move, waiting for me.

I bit my lower lip. *"Don't do it! You'll be sorry."*

But I ignored the shouting voice in my head and nodded ever so slightly, giving my consent. Tony kissed me so hard I thought my head would go through the reinforced door. I suspected he hadn't slept with a woman since his wife died. The pent-up passion exploded into a force of nature.

Tony ate me alive; his lips crushed mine with his tongue down my throat. His hands on my shoulders, then my waist, and then my hips were those of a wrestler crushing his opponent. I cried out once or twice when he was too rough, and he slowed down, but not for long.

He ripped my sweater over my head and unzipped my jeans. His hands were under my panties in front, then in back, and then in front again. He kissed my neck, my throat, my shoulders and my lips. I could feel him hard as iron pressing against my stomach. Pinned to the door, I could barely move.

Pulling his shirt over his head without unbuttoning, his lips were back on mine the moment the cloth cleared his face. His chest was as perfect as *Diadoumenos*. My fingertips caressed his taut skin, and if I thought he had been wild before, it was nothing compared to the beast my touch unleashed.

With his hands gripping my buttocks, his fingers digging into my flesh, he lifted me with no more effort than he heaved a climber's backpack. My legs locked around his waist. I held onto the back of his neck with one hand while stroking his gorgeous chest and bulging biceps with the other. He carried me to the desk, shoving the lamp aside. It tumbled and crashed. I heard the shatter of broken glass.

Nothing slowed him. Using his toes on the heel, he pried off one of his sneakers, then the other. He unzipped his khakis with one hand while the other gripped my hip as if I might run away. I would have helped him, but he moved so fast and with such intensity, I was afraid to get in the way.

He pulled his slacks down to his ankles and kicked them across the room. He tugged my left boot off and then the right. I clung to the desk, else he would have yanked me to the floor. Peeling my jeans from me in one movement, he tossed them aside without so much as a glance.

I reached behind and unfastened my bra; he buried his face in my breasts at the same time he yanked down my panties. I had been stripped naked in less than a minute. His boxers disappeared somewhere in the dark room.

Then he stopped. He put his forehead on the top of my head and breathed heavily for a few moments, his chest heaving. I caught a faint whiff of locker room sweat—unabashedly male.

"I'm sorry," he apologized. "It's been so long."

I kissed him to let him know everything was fine, and he squeezed me all over, his hands so strong I knew his fingers left red marks. It felt wonderful to be ravaged in such a delicious, unthreatening way.

I rode the frenzy with him. He never actually hurt me, and if he went too far, he listened to my whimpers and backed off.

He pounded me, my legs locked around his waist, our bodies rocking the desk, slamming it against the wallpapered wall. I expected the phone to ring with a warning from Security to quiet down.

With a great convulsing, he came. His body shook, then trembled, then shook again. Gooseflesh rose all over him; I caressed the millions of hair follicles electrifying his skin.

Taking time only to catch his breath, he lifted me and carried me to the bed. He was already hard again. Rolling me to my stomach, he shoved a pillow under my belly. I reached out for the headboard and grabbed hold of the edge. With his hands gripping my hips, he plunged into me, over and over.

The bed rocked, and the headboard banged the wall. I held on, pushed back—and again feared the phone might ring. But I didn't try to calm him.

He dragged me to the foot of the bed, with my breasts squashed into the bedspread and my knees on the floor. His hands were none too gentle, but still he never hurt me. My cries, loud before, changed to wild shouts. Clutching the bedspread in my fists, I buried my face in it, thrusting myself back into him.

With a kind of wrestler-lover hold, he clutched me with one powerful arm gripped around my waist and the other tight around my chest and shoulders while he plunged. I cried out in a sound more cat than human as release rolled through my pelvis in waves.

Tony dropped me on the bed and rolled me over. My arms lay limp, stretched out, palms up. He thrust inside me again, once, twice, three times, and then his back arched, and he actually howled.

I started laughing; I couldn't help myself. "That good, huh?"

He collapsed next to me, roaring as loud as a lion. We laughed until tears came, lying next to each other on the bedspread, stark naked, drenched in sweat.

"I'm starving," he declared. "Let's order room service."

When I came out of the bathroom, he sat with his back against the headboard, still naked. His perfect body glowed in the soft light of two shaded lamps; a giant smile spread across his face.

"Man, that was great!" he announced. "Can we do it again?"

I laughed and started to slip on the white terry cloth hotel robe.

"Wait!" he shouted, ripping the bedspread back and jerking a sheet off the bed. He draped the sheet around me, lifted my arms and adjusted my hips so I stood in the classic *contrapposto* position.

Raising the TV remote in the pose of an emperor with his scepter, he commanded in a theatrical voice, "I am the god Ares. You are my sex slave. I forbid you to wear blue jeans again."

I envisioned a laurel wreath around his head—the champion of the Games.

We managed another quick round and were under the sheets laughing and giggling when room service knocked on the door. We devoured the hamburgers and guzzled the cold beer; Tony threw most of the French fries at me. We slept on salty, stained sheets.

I woke to sunshine streaming in the windows, Tony's hands on my breasts and his hard-on against my butt.

"You're insatiable. Don't you ever get enough?" But I giggled like a college girl and only pretended to struggle.

He maneuvered me into one of his wrestling holds and ran his fingers over my body until he found where it tickled.

"Stop," I shouted. "You're a sadist!"

He beamed, relaxed his hold and then kissed me quite tenderly, asking, "Has sex ever been this much fun?"

"Order some breakfast while I hop in the shower."

But the hot water had just come when he slipped into the glass stall with me. His erection was huge, and so was his grin. He soaped me all over, and then I soaped him, massaging his balls and his penis until he exploded, his back leaning against the marble tiles of the shower. Hot water rained down on us.

"Go," I commanded. "I have to get dressed. Room service should be here by now."

Hair washed and hanging wet on my shoulders, I wrapped the second white hotel robe around me and called out, "Tony! Has breakfast arrived?"

Standing in the middle of the room was not room service with a linen tablecloth-covered trolley, but Hector.

They faced each other—Tony, all wet from the shower in a white terry cloth robe matching mine, and Hector in his bomber jacket and jeans, half a head taller, an overnight case in one hand and a bouquet of red roses in the other. They both turned to me when I opened the bathroom door.

I'm not sure how Tony's face looked; I only saw Hector. He stared as if he didn't recognize me. Then he glanced around the room, and I saw it through his eyes—broken lamp, bed linen stained, tossed and tumbled, dinner dishes piled on the nightstand, clothes all over the place. I felt sick when I saw my panties by his big foot in tasseled cordovan loafers.

I started to speak, but the look in Hector's eyes stopped me.

"You!" Hector said to Tony.

There was no doubt he recognized Antinous the Greek. He'd given me over to him back on the Nile. Not because he wanted to, but to save me.

"Hector," I started, but what words could follow?

"*No digas nada,*" he snapped. "Nothing you say can fix this. Anything you say will make it worse."

Tossing the roses on the battlefield bed, Hector turned, strode to the door, opened it and walked out. The heavy reinforced door shut firmly behind him. The click of the latch was loud and final.

Gradually I became aware of noise from the street drifting through the double glass windows. I heard a siren, far away, as if from the end of a very long tunnel.

"Guess you weren't expecting him, huh?"

I was vaguely aware of sounds coming from Tony. I forced myself to make them into words with meaning.

"What did he mean by *you*?" he asked in a puzzled tone. "Should I know him?"

I could hardly tell Tony, world-respected scientist, that Hector recognized him from a previous life.

"I'm sorry, Isis," Tony was saying from the end of the same tunnel as the siren. "I'm truly sorry."

I stared at the closed door. *Should I go after him?*

"Was that your date from Cleopatra's Barge? He seems taller."

I shook my head, slowly and numbly. Rasheed had been my date the night Tony and I met in Vegas.

"Well, you certainly lead a complicated life."

If only you knew...

Then I came back, really back. I told Tony I was sorry, too.

"You must think I'm a slut."

"I don't think that at all," he assured me. "We didn't plan for this to happen. Okay, maybe I hoped *something* would happen. But I didn't expect anything like last night."

I don't know what I'd expected. I email a guy I met in a bar. I go to a museum to look at nude statues and then invite him up to my hotel room. I knew what Barb would say.

Hello! What did you think would happen?

Tony moved next to me and lifted wet strands of hair from my face.

"You have my number, Isis. You know where I am."

I looked at him and blinked.

He continued in a matter-of-fact tone, as if he were explaining one of his mathematical axioms.

"I come with baggage—a lot of it—starting with instant motherhood. And Princeton is not Las Vegas. I'd love to give us a shot—if you can't fix it with this guy. But I hope you can fix it. I honestly do."

I didn't know what to say. I didn't expect anything he was saying.

"I like him, Isis. He took it a lot better than I would have. Some guys would've tried to kill us both. He was humiliated but kept his cool. You've got to respect that."

"Humiliated?" Is that how men think?

I called Hector's cell. It rang three times and then went to voicemail. I sent him a text that I wanted to talk. He ignored it. I think it would have been less painful if he had text back 'no.' At least the lines of communication wouldn't be dead.

I left a message with Isabel asking her to have Hector call me—that it was urgent—but I knew I wouldn't hear back. This was the ammunition she needed to eliminate me, and I had handed her the loaded gun.

CHAPTER 23   IBIS MAN

"Injuries may be forgiven, but not forgotten." – Aesop

When the cab dropped me off at Bonham's Auction House on Madison Avenue between 56th and 57th Streets, I had fifteen minutes to spare. After registering and picking up my numbered paddle, I found one empty seat in the row third from the back. I could see most of the other bidders, which gave me an edge. If there is a *feng shui* power position, it's at the back of the room.

Isabel had to have seen me arrive and find a seat; her chair commanded the room. But it wasn't until I had settled and politely greeted the two men on each side that she turned toward me with a look on her face that said, *I warned you.* For a tiny moment, I resented that Hector had run to his mother. *Good riddance to him*! Only I didn't believe it for more than a second.

Phone banks lined one wall. A clump of academic types probably representing university museums sat together. The auction today was a collection of antiquities. In all other ways, the setup and mood were the same as the art auction at the Venetian. The air crackled in anticipation.

The auctioneer, again British, took the podium and welcomed us. Curtains up! The show started.

I waited for the ibis to be announced, forcing myself to focus on the bidders and bidding, pushing Hector out of my mind, calming my nerves. I wasn't prepared for him to be there, but he showed up after about thirty minutes in an unwrinkled suit and open-necked starched shirt. Had he carried them in his little overnight satchel?

He took the empty seat next to Isabel, who spoke in his ear. He didn't turn in my direction but stared stonily ahead. I closed my eyes to stop the tears.

You made your bed. Now lie in it. Visions of the hotel bed with tangled and stained sheets played and replayed. I rationalized that Hector shouldn't have shown up without calling, but it was a pathetic excuse, even for me.

At last, the rose granite ibis was carried to the front and placed in the spotlight. Even after the catalogue photo convinced me that it could be the same statue from the Abydos dock, my heart skipped a beat when I saw it. There was no doubt. I'd traded a necklace for that bird twenty-five centuries before.

After a brief description, the auctioneer asked for the minimum bid. Before I could react, a man with black hair two rows in front of me raised his paddle.

Be present, I chastised. *This is the real thing.*

A counter bid came from the phones. I raised the ante, followed by the man. Wherever the auctioneer led us, we went. A fourth bidder, a redhead with a ponytail, stepped in; the audience stirred.

We had gone through several volleys, the bid bouncing between the phones, the man, the redhead and me, when Isabel raised her paddle. A murmur ran through the room, and heads turned.

I could hear the mob cheering, "Let the Games begin!" If Isabel wanted something, she played for blood.

The auctioneer pushed us higher and higher; the redhead dropped out. The bidder on the phone dropped out with a shake of the brunette's head above her laptop screen. That left the man two rows in front, Isabel and me.

I raised my paddle; the auctioneer upped the bid, and the man raised his paddle. Isabel didn't hesitate, but ever so slightly nodded her head. All eyes were back on me. I left the paddle on my knee and nodded, mimicking Isabel.

She turned toward me for the first time since the bidding had started, and I answered her look with an Athena one—cool and aloof. I would have been more effective if icy blonde like Athena, but I willed my eyes to glitter like glass.

I felt sweat in my armpits and thought crazily, *I've ruined this silk blouse.*

The auctioneer jumped the next bid a hundred thousand; the murmur in the room swelled. A bit heady, I nodded without hesitation. It was the General's money; I wasn't going to leave without the ibis.

Back and forth we went in a frenzy until we far exceeded the catalogue price range. The piece was not Old Kingdom or New Kingdom and burdened with a shaky *provenance.* Even three thousand years old, the rose granite and bronze ibis wasn't worth the bid.

Isabel, always the businesswoman, dropped out. The crowd sighed but understood. That left the man two rows in front and me. Ibis Man. He wouldn't give in.

I began to worry if the General had enough funds in the special account to cover my bids. It crossed my mind to call him and ask if he wanted to go on. How badly did he want the statue? But I knew the answer. He wanted it bad.

Finally, as in all auctions, there was a final bid.

"Going once, going twice," the auctioneer looked directly at the man with black hair. "This is your last chance, sir."

We all waited, a bit breathless. At last, he shook his head, and the hammer came down.

"Sold to the young lady at the back of the room! Congratulations."

The room burst into applause, and I felt like I'd won Wimbledon.

Isabel gave me a grudging half-smile of respect. Hector steadfastly stared at the podium. Suddenly, out of a nightmare, Ibis Man turned to face me and my heart stopped. Lord Chancellor Sosibius in a gray worsted suit. Those sinister hawk eyes couldn't belong to anyone else.

I called the General right away, but he already knew.

"Congratulations, Ishtar. I believe you have a new career. Why don't you celebrate tonight with one of your men?" he suggested. "My treat."

"Excuse me?"

He only chuckled and said, "Check one off your list."

Did he mean his wish list—or my men? I didn't have time for his games.

"There was a man bidding against me. Do you know him?"

"We both know him, Ishtar, don't we?"

I was silent.

"I don't think I need to tell you to be very careful."

"What has he to do with all this?" I insisted. "Why did he want the ibis?"

"It has nothing to do with the ibis, Ishtar. It is personal. He is after me. He undoubtedly knows you represent me."

I looked all around, expecting to see the General's thugs in the crowd at the back of the room. When I went to confirm my purchase and arrange for payment and delivery, I felt eyes on me. I looked over my shoulder to see two bruisers, massive chests bulging in their suits.

In a panic, I turned to Hector, but his seat was empty. I would have gone to him, even with what happened this morning. Who else could I trust? The irony wasn't lost on me: trust and Hector in the same thought. What would he think about trust and me?

Several taxis waited outside, motors running. I ducked into one, constantly watching the glass doors of Bonham's. The two men came out and got into the next cab. When my car pulled out into the traffic moving uptown, theirs did too.

Instead of turning on 57th Street and heading back to the hotel, I told the driver to keep going.

"I've changed my mind. Take me to the Metropolitan Museum, 82nd & Fifth."

The cab behind us also went straight. Madison Avenue is a major thoroughfare to the Upper East Side; it didn't mean they were actually following me. The traffic was heavy, and I soon lost sight of them in a sea of yellow cabs.

But when the driver dropped me off at the 82nd Street entrance of the museum and I turned to look from the steps, their taxi pulled in down the street, and the men got out. There was no doubt now.

I hurried into the Great Hall. The place was jammed with long lines of chattering visitors. *Doesn't anybody have a day job in New York?* But the Luck Gods were with me, and I managed to squeeze in front of a family of six.

Convinced that there had to be a way to disappear in the vast Metropolitan Museum of Art, I devised one strategy and then another, rejecting all. I even thought of making directly for the ladies room, but that would be like entering a box canyon; I'd be trapped. My instincts told me to lose these guys now.

Just as the cashier handed me my ticket, the two came through the tall doors and stopped, one looking to his left, the other to the right.

I pretended I didn't see them and headed up the steps, my high heels clicking on the polished stone, not going too fast but still moving past other visitors intent on their brochures.

As soon as I hit the second floor, I took a quick left, slipped off my heels and ran past Drawings and Photographs, turned left again, and made for the elevator by Ancient Near Eastern Art.

I kept glancing back to the end of the corridor, expecting the two men to come around the corner. The elevator took forever to arrive. I pushed the button twice more and kept my eye on the hallway.

Two white-haired ladies in sneakers waited with me, scowling at my stocking feet, frowning at my impatience. I slipped in as soon as the doors opened, rudely brushing against a man exiting.

The elevator stopped on the first floor, emptied and refilled. It took an eternity to descend to the ground floor. I ran out before the doors were fully open, bumping a baby stroller, almost knocking down a man on crutches, only daring to look back when I reached the exit to the parking garage.

Once inside the garage, I hid behind a pillar for a couple of minutes and when the men didn't show, I ran out to 80th Street, still in my stocking feet, and hailed a cab heading into Central Park.

The General answered on the first ring.

"Yes, Ishtar."

"Do you have men following me?"

"Could you describe them?"

"So you *do* have men following me. Why didn't you tell me? They scared me to death."

"Where are you now?"

"I'm in a cab. I'm not telling you where."

"Are they still following you?"

"No. I lost them in the museum. At least, I think I did."

"I'm impressed. If they are my men, they're usually quite good."

"What do you mean, *if* they are your men?"

"You didn't describe them."

This is crazy. I went to an auction and bought an old granite bird, and now I'm trying to figure out if the guys following me are the General's goons or someone else's.

"Ishtar, are you still there?"

"I'm still here, and I'm scared."

"You have nothing to fear from me."

"I don't know that. Why should I trust you?"

"Who else do you have?"

That stunned me into a moment of silence.

"Rein your guys in, General. If they're supposed to follow me, then at least introduce us."

I rang off before he could answer.

The bed was made. Housekeeping had folded my clothes neatly, and a new lamp stood on the desk. The hotel room was perfectly tidy with no trace of last night's wild sex. The ghost of Hector hovered in the center of the room.

I sat on the edge of the bed and breathed deep and slow. When I slipped my heels off, the bottoms of my pantyhose were in shreds and the soles of my feet black with grime from the parking garage.

Alone. I felt so alone. I had more allies in Alexandria than New York. I hadn't messed things up with Hektor of Naukratis—at least not yet.

My stockings went in the trash. I washed my feet in the *bidet*, stuffed my clothes into the suitcase and hurried down to the lobby.

"I'm checking out. Please email my bill."

"Is there a problem, ma'am, that we should know about?"

"Not at all. I've had a change of plans."

When the porter hailed my cab, I had no idea where I was going. I didn't know anyone in New York. For a brief moment, I thought of going to Penn Station and catching the next train to Princeton. In the end, the cab had driven only a few hundred feet past 6th Avenue when I told him to stop at the Plaza Hotel.

The lobby was stupendously elegant, but I scarcely noticed as I crossed to the front desk.

"Do you have a room for tonight?" I didn't care what it cost.

"Certainly, Madam, I can offer you a king or two queens."

"May I ask you an enormous favor?"

"Yes, Madam, certainly. How may we serve you?"

"I'd like to pay cash. Is there anyway you can hold my credit card and not charge it?"

"That can be arranged, but we are required to see identification."

A diplomatic way of telling me I couldn't avoid registering under my name. What do people do in the movies? Obviously they are more prepared.

My Plaza Room, understated yet luxurious, with muted colors and overstuffed furniture, faced the interior courtyard. It was eerily still. I tipped the bellboy $30 and hurried him out of the room, locking the door in all possible ways behind him.

The tip was designed to get his attention, to garner an ally of sorts. The word would get out among staff; I didn't feel quite so alone.

When I came out of the shower, a voicemail message waited.

"We need to talk," was all Hector said.

I nearly sobbed. I had a chance. A long shot, for sure. But at least he wanted to see me.

In the corner past the grand piano, Hector sat by a window. A beer in a frosted glass and a martini—probably Plymouth—stood on the table. A sophisticated crowd, smartly-dressed without any of the flamboyance of Vegas, quietly jammed the bar.

I wore a black silk Armani suit with a pencil skirt ending a couple of inches above the knee. The open top buttons of the French-blue silk blouse exposed some skin and a tiny bit of cleavage. A long strand of baroque pearls I'd inherited from my aunt doubled at my throat. Conservative black patent pumps, only two inches high, completed what I hoped was a sufficiently chastised look.

As if reflecting my angst, my hair refused to cooperate, and I had to put it back up in a French roll. Wispy bangs, curly from the shower, softened what was otherwise a look too severe for seduction.

Hector, ever the Argentine gentleman, stood and pulled out the second chair.

He didn't comment on how I looked, as he always did.

What if I never again hear him tell me how beautiful I am?

My stomach was so full of butterflies that I thought I might throw up right there in the world-famous Oak Bar.

"I needed to confront you in person, Isis. I do not want to keep ignoring your calls."

Confront? This was not starting out well. I dreaded what would follow. I couldn't think of anything appropriate to say, so kept silent, all the while wishing I could go back in time. Not to Egypt, but to yesterday afternoon.

"Was he the reason you didn't stay in the same hotel as my mother?"

"No, Hector! I didn't plan for it to happen." I started to say, *I don't lie to you,* but stopped myself. When hadn't I told him half-truths?

"So you just happened to run into him, here in the big city of New York?"

I found myself counting the red flecks in his eyes to keep from crying.

"I played all your silly games, Isis. All the waiting. All the 'I'm not ready' *mierda*. What kind of an idiot do you think I am?"

He didn't expect an answer; I sat there feeling sick and fighting tears.

"You know what bothers me most?" He made a little snorting sound, only a slight, sharp exhalation that said everything about his disgust.

"I could have made you happy—really happy. *We* could have been happy. But you never gave me a chance."

"I'm sorry, so sorry." I spoke to him so earnestly, my voice choked. "No! I'm not *sorry*. I'm *heartbroken*. I never meant for this to happen. It...it just did," I finished lamely.

"Did it have to be the Greek?" Hector had been through the mirror once to himself as Hetmus-hor; he remembered only too well what Tony was oblivious to—giving me over to Antinous on River God's ship.

"Can you ever forgive me?"

"No. I don't think so."

He could have said 'never.' His words, paltry as they were, gave me some hope.

"Remember, Hector, the conversations we had about commitment? How lousy I am with it? I want to, I truly do. But I'm driven by something I don't understand. It pushes me to...to do things."

"That is precisely the *problema*, Isis. It is all about you."

He told the waiter to put the drinks on his room and stood. He was so tall that, seated in my chair, I had to look up at the ceiling to see his face. His lush cedar-colored waves were combed back from his forehead. One stray, glossy strand fell to his eyebrow. I blinked back tears.

"Do not call me," he said. "Do not text me. Do not Skype. I will come to you, if and when I am ever ready."

"Hector," I asked as he went past me. "Did you tell your mother about Tony?"

"Could you give me some credit, *por favor?*"

And then he walked past the piano, winding his way through the chic New Yorkers and out the door of the Oak Bar.

CHAPTER 24   OAK ROOM

"There are only two people who can tell you the truth about yourself—an angry enemy and a loving friend." – Antisthenes

My cell rang, and seeing it was the General, I almost let it go to voicemail before considering that he might have something important to tell me about the men at the Met.

"I'm worried about you, Ishtar."

"Thanks," I said acidly.

He really did have the most annoying timing. Hector was barely out the door. I hadn't had a moment to collect myself.

"I'm in New York—small universe, isn't it?"

I wasn't particularly surprised.

"My offer to celebrate still stands. Your choice of restaurants. Any place in Manhattan. What do you say, Ishtar? I'd like to talk about the next acquisition."

"There aren't going to be any more 'acquisitions'—at least not by me. You crossed the line today, General."

"I thought you liked to walk on the wild side, Ishtar. At least that's always been my impression."

There was a long moment of silence, the kind on a cell phone when you're not sure if you're still connected.

"Why don't you join me for dinner next door in the Oak Room?"

I almost repeated 'next door' but stopped myself. I looked all around until I found him sitting at the bar, looking at me and smiling. He raised his glass.

"So you had your first taste of a win today. Exhilarating, isn't it?"

The General sat across from me at a two-person table, he in the brown leather booth and me in a curved back, upholstered chair. Oak paneling lined the walls. The white barrel-vaulted ceiling was Gothic-inspired with arched windows; murals of German feudal castles filled three niches. A tall crystal chandelier hung over a round table set with a floral arrangement at least five feet tall.

"Those were my men today, Ishtar. Let's call it a little test. You passed with flying colors—except for your move to the Plaza. It was too predictable, what with Señora de Segovia staying here and all."

I stared at him.

"Do you like your scotch?" he asked.

The General had ordered 30-year-old Macallan served in a crystal brandy snifter with a tiny splash of water to 'open it up.'

I refused to let him act like everything was normal.

"You had someone at my hotel all the time, didn't you?"

He chuckled again.

"Don't ask me to give away trade secrets, Ishtar. At least, not yet."

Our first course arrived with a flurry of waiters and ground pepper. When I reached for my wine glass, the General leaned forward and touched the edge of the blue silk ruffle at my wrist with his thick middle finger. The white of his starched cuff held a gold crocodile cufflink with an emerald eye.

"I like this look," he said. "I approve—classy yet sexy. It's that little bit of your skin at the open neck that teases."

"I didn't do it for you."

"*Touché.*"

He took a bite and then spoke with his mouth full.

"Not terribly successful, though, was it? Too bad. The man's not thinking straight. A part of you is worth more than the whole of most women."

He had watched Hector walk out on me. He probably knew about Tony, too. I might as well have been naked, I felt that exposed.

"The next acquisition will be at an auction in Paris." He suddenly turned all business. "I'll email you the information."

"I told you there won't be any more."

"My beautiful Ishtar, this is but the beginning. You're a natural. You're only going to get better. We're almost partners now."

"I don't want to work with you anymore. It's not as much fun as I thought it would be."

"We're not talking about fun. The man at the auction today, he knows you work for me. Who else would have fought him so hard for the ibis? He will try to get to me through you."

Barb's voice whispered in my ear. *What if you can't get out, once you're in?*

"What do you really want from me, General?"

"Why, I thought you had figured that out, Ishtar. I want what we all want—the Emerald Tablet."

I stood up from the chair, grateful I'd declined the booth seat which would have meant moving the table for me to escape. The General smiled and tipped his glass toward me.

"Have a pleasant flight back. The details about Paris will be in your email tomorrow morning."

My nerves were too shot to sleep. I took an Ambien, but before it kicked in, I relived the day a hundred times. Tony and Hector. Then Sosibius as Ibis Man at the auction, followed by the two thugs in the museum. And finally the General's comment about the Tablet.

Why these games? If the General wanted the Emerald Tablet, he could have one of his goons torture me until I gave it up—or offer to buy it. I'd protect the Tablet, but within limits. I wasn't interested in suffering. I certainly wouldn't die for it.

Just before I drifted off, I wondered if I should warn Hector. He was the one who found the Tablet in the antique mall; he knew I stored it in the bank vault. And Barb. She knew, too.

"How was the auction? Did you get the ibis?" Barb was full of questions, none of them relevant.

"I got it. That's the good part of the trip."

"The good part? What happened?"

It was like swallowing a bitter pill to tell her about Tony and Hector.

"How could you be so stupid?" she asked with disgust.

"How could I have known Hector would show up?"

"Oh, so now it's his fault."

But when I told her about the General and his goons, her breath caught in her throat.

"I told you not to get involved with him."

"That's not all, Barb. He mentioned the Emerald Tablet."

"What! I thought you hadn't told anyone."

"He knows. I don't know how."

Barb should have pooh-poohed me and said something about being ridiculous. But I got no reassurances.

"He's a very frightening man," she said simply.

When I got off the phone, I sat for a few long moments, stroking Aisha, gazing into the Red Mirror.

I might be the protector of the Tablet, but shouldn't the Tablet also protect me? How did I make that happen? I couldn't think of any other way to find out except to go back to the source.

Carla didn't pick up until after three rings; she took her time deciding to answer my call. We hadn't talked since her party when I first met Hector in this life, and he left her for me. I'd heard through the grapevine she was now seeing a blond hunk from Berlin.

"Carla, we've been friends for too long not to talk again."

She didn't comment. She used to be one of my best friends—that's the worst person to steal your boyfriend.

"Carla, *please*. Hector and I aren't together anymore."

That got her interest. I sensed a change in the silence.

"Well, that's all in the past," she said in a flat, unconvincing voice. "I have Günter now; he's much more my type."

She didn't offer to introduce us.

"Carla, do you have the number of the psychic who was at your party—the weird guy in the cheap suit?"

I ended the call with, "Let's meet for drinks." But I didn't think it would be for a while. Carla's voice was ice cold to the end.

The phone rang and rang until finally he answered.

"Hello?" His voice was cautious, as if he were fearful of who might be at the other end.

"Eben?"

He didn't answer.

"Eben, this is Isis."

Still no answer. He had to know who I was. He's a psychic, isn't he?

"Eben," I repeated with as much patience as I could muster.

I was about to speak again when he answered.

"Hello, Isis." He didn't say anything after that.

I heard his too rapid breathing into the phone; there was a raspy quality to it. He had struck me the night of Carla's party as heavily autistic. Was he capable of carrying on a conversation?

I was searching for the right words to draw him out when he went straight to the point.

"You know that your destiny is on the green stone."

"Will you help me, Eben?"

"I have always helped you."

"Can you tell me anything about who is after the Tablet and why?"

"They want power, like they always have."

"Who are they?"

"Too many to name."

I struggled again to keep the irritation from my voice.

"What can you tell me about the General?"

"You already know."

I made one more attempt.

"Eben, if the Tablet is so powerful, why hasn't it given more power to me?"

"The Oracle told you where to find the answers, Isis. There are no shortcuts. You must make the journey. Choose your path carefully."

CHAPTER 25   SLAVE MARKET

"There is no harm in repeating a good thing." – Plato

If I had injured myself with the fall on the Street of the Soma, there was no cut; my forehead felt smooth without the trace of a scar. I felt nauseous; could I have suffered a concussion? The sun was well up; bright light poured in from the balcony.

Kallisto had grown as kittens quickly do. She chased a fly round the room. Jason was nowhere in sight, but his sleeping pallet still lay on the floor at the foot of my bed.

A slave held a silver bowl under my face while I vomited. Was I ill? There must be hundreds of diseases to catch—the water from the Canopic canal was often foul, barely fit for bathing.

Once my stomach emptied, I felt better. Another slave brought chamomile tea and warm bread.

Platon, the fat old scribe sent to me by the Chancellor, begged permission to enter. Although his arms overflowed with scrolls, he appeared calm and not harried.

"Peace be with the Lady. I have documents for perusal and signature."

Long lines of figures swam across the papyri. Some of the accounts dealt with the Temple of Korinth, some with Ptolemy's project. A new site had been selected on a stretch of sandy coastline between Alexandria and the resort city of Canopus which lay to the east at the mouth of the Nile. The construction budget had been increased to cover additional transport costs, but every expense required my approval.

Jason, curls freshly barbered, appeared in his white tunic with blue trim. He jabbered about a new wrestling hold he had mastered, and that today he would exercise with Nikandros who was older by two years.

I called for the dressing slaves to bring a *peplos* and left the choice of color to them. They quickly twisted locks of hair around my face to join a mass of braids at the back of my neck, finishing the arrangement with a wide headband of teal linen interwoven with silver threads. I didn't have the patience for curls. The queasiness in my stomach persisted.

The owl necklace from Hektor went round my neck. Delicate gold pendants in the form of a single floret, lapis lazuli bead and tiny owl dangled from my earlobes. More jewelry from Hektor, who never tired of showering me with gifts. The Hathor ring from the *agora* was on the middle finger of my right hand.

Jason ran happily off to his class as soon as we reached the gates of the Library grounds. I went directly to my offices and settled at my desk.

"Peace be with our Lady," greeted each of my staff.

I was reminded by an Egyptian scribe that I was to visit the new site with Antinous in the late afternoon. I thought only of the Emerald Tablet and the impossible task of locating it.

Qeb-ha had told me that the clues would be all around me, but there was nothing in the tedious accounting papyri that hinted at the Mystery. At mid-morning, I gave up trying to concentrate and sent for Ajax to accompany me to the *agora*.

The sun was unmistakably hotter than on my last visit to the market, the day I found the second Hathor ring and the Red Mirror. When we arrived at the *agora*, a noisy crowd had gathered close to the docks.

"Go and find out what is happening, Ajax."

He left me for a few moments while I held the parasol and craned to see.

"It is the slave market, Mistress. A fresh cargo has arrived from Syracuse."

"Let us see, Ajax, what draws the crowd's interest."

A score of men, full-bodied and strong like warriors, stood naked near the platform. Shackles around their ankles bound them together; their hands were chained behind their backs. The hot sun blazed down without mercy. Greek Alexandrians kept to the shade of the half-circle portico; I was reminded of a theatre with standing room only.

I saw him right away. Massive chest, thighs like tree trunks, his limp manhood longer and thicker than most men's when erect. His matted hair hung in heavy locks; his dark beard was long and filthy.

"Who is the beast?" I asked Ajax.

He went into the crowd and returned.

"He is a Carthaginian general, Mistress. Captured in Syracuse."

The crowd booed when two giant Nubians pulled him to the block. Bits of garbage flew through the air; some splattered on his massive chest, while a few pieces hit him in the face. He didn't flinch but sneered at the crowd, holding himself proud as Hercules.

The bidding started. I tipped the parasol to signal I was in. The crowd stirred.

"Please, Mistress. May I be allowed to speak?" Ajax's eyes were wide with alarm. "Carthaginians are not suitable as house slaves. They cannot be trusted; they murder their masters in the night. Even in the mines, they cause trouble and refuse to obey. They are only useful as galley slaves."

I saw the doomed rowers on our ship, chained to their oars, facing their death by angry waves or fire. Those were the lucky ones. Most galley slaves died slowly of malnutrition and exhaustion, thrown overboard, still breathing, when they could no longer row.

I tipped my parasol again to counterbid a tall man in miner's garb. The crowd watched as the bidding went back and forth, neither of us relenting. The price went beyond what a galley slave was worth. A slave in the mines met death even faster. But still the man insisted, and I bested every increase.

And then, as in every auction, there was a final bid, and it was mine.

"Arrange to have the Carthaginian delivered to the villa," I ordered. "See that he is fed and bathed. Keep him chained at all times."

By the time Ajax and I got to the black and brown striped tent, the Old Jew was at prayers with Eben. His Egyptian servant couldn't say when they would return. I despaired of finding my way in the Jewish Quarter and left the message that I wished to speak with Eben as soon as possible.

Antinous had arranged for a chariot and took the reins himself to drive us to the Mediterranean site proposed for Ptolemy's grand Temple of Aphrodite. I wore a cotton cape and a pointed straw hat with a scarf draped around my face to protect my skin from the unforgiving sun.

We left the Library to rattle down the Street of the Soma into the heart of the Greek Quarter where the magnificent mausoleum, the *Soma,* housed the honey-mummified body of Alexander the Great.

As every day, a throng of tourists crowded the square, waiting to file past Alexander's gold coffin kidnapped by General Ptolemy a hundred years earlier on its journey from Babylon home to Greece.

We went east along the boulevard of the Canopic Way, passing through the hectic Jewish Quarter. The deserted streets of my night visit to Qeb-ha were now jammed with wagons and carts plowing their way through hundreds of pedestrians. Everyone shouted obscenities. Some threw garbage. Not at us, though. Perhaps awed, maybe intimidated, by Antinous' god-like Greek beauty, the crowd parted, albeit slowly, for our chariot.

Once through the Canopic Gate and out of the city, we made good time. We skirted the *Hippodrome* to avoid the crush of spectators gathering for the afternoon horseraces.

The new site turned out to be a graceful rise above a long sandy beach. Somewhere along this stretch of empty shore, an ancient Hathor Temple had long disappeared under the shifting coastline sands.

Fresh northerly breezes dulled the sharp rays of the sun. Sand dunes stretched inland as far as I could see. The seaside resort town of Canopus, offering pleasures of every kind, was not far to the east.

It was the most perfect of sites for a temple to the Goddess of Beauty. Even demanding Ptolemy couldn't help but be pleased.

Papyrus drawings in hand, Antinous paced the plot, marking a circle with sticks and ropes, pointing out where columns would stand. Mounds of sand showed where workers dug to reach the bedrock needed to support tons of gleaming marble.

I had not been prepared for his genius. The old concept was gone. Without sacrificing harmony, Antinous incorporated the mystic elements of Egyptian iconography into the mathematical aesthetics of Greek architecture. His drawings showed a true fusion of two extraordinary worlds.

He planned a circular layout with a wide *stoa* arcade of columns painted in vivid colors and decorated with Egyptian hieroglyphs. A massive open portico facing the Mediterranean would catch the sea breezes. The unique mosaic dome of lapis blue and turquoise faience tiles was sure to satiate even Ptolemy's voracious appetite for extravagance and drama.

Antinous was not the first to think of a closed dome, but until now, all other attempts had collapsed.

"Look at my calculations, Athena. I am certain they are correct."

I couldn't follow his rapid explanation or the maze of numbers and equations that covered his papyri.

The sky in the west changed from azure to gold. Pink smeary clouds streaked where the sun kissed the desert. Above the sea, a pastel rainbow mist lined the horizon.

We drank watered Cretan wine and ate goat cheese, chewy dates, green almonds and full-grain bread with salty butter. Antinous stretched out beside me, his glorious profile silhouetted against the rosy sunset. The final golden rays of the sun glinted off his windswept curls.

He leaned on his elbows, head back, tan legs with strong graceful ankles and perfect feet thrust in front of him. When he turned toward me, his eyes were so blue, they rivaled a spring sky on Delos.

"You were wise, Athena, to insist on a new site. And on a new design. I admire your judgment greatly."

Admire. It wasn't exactly what I had in mind, but I'd take it as a starting point. I rather enjoyed his purity; I felt lighter just being around him. When I laughed for no reason, the sound to my ears was carefree and lilting.

"You are quite remarkable, Athena of Korinth. It is rare to find such beauty and intelligence in one person, and even rarer in a woman. If I closed my eyes and heard only your words, I might think I spoke with a man."

I was so intelligent, I could be mistaken for a man.

I thought he might kiss me, but he made no move. I had a vision of Antinous pounding the beautiful youth I'd seen in his office in the way Tony had ravaged me in New York.

Just when we thought to pack up and travel back to the city, we heard a stifled cry followed by loud whispers. We should have been alone. The digging stopped at sunset for the workers' evening meal.

The young workers immediately prostrated themselves and kissed our feet, crying out in rapid Egyptian. I asked them to speak slowly.

"We took but small things, Lady. We can return them all."

Everything on the site belonged to the Pharaoh; they trembled in terror of punishment.

"Tell no one else," I said in halting Egyptian. "I cannot protect you if you do."

Antinous watched our back and forth with a puzzled look, no doubt surprised by what he must have perceived as my fluency. Like all Hellenes, no matter how long they lived in Alexandria, he didn't speak a word of Egyptian.

They ran immediately away, leaving behind a handful of amulets—and most important—the sealed chest they argued over.

Carved seven-pointed stars covered the soapstone lid. It was in remarkably good condition, probably buried for a long time, but not hundreds or thousands of years.

Antinous found a bronze chisel and pried the lid open. My heart pounded at the sight of an antelope skin packet the size of a thick atlas. When Antinous moved to unwrap it, I grabbed his hand.

"Wait! Please wait."

Our torch burned alone on the rise. The moon, two nights past full, had risen to sparkle on the white sand. Campfires burned inland at a small oasis where the laborers ate and slept.

"I must tell you something first, Antinous. What you are about to see is something significant and secret. I need to trust you. Can I trust you?"

If he wondered how I knew what was wrapped inside, he didn't ask. I couldn't very well tell him that, in a previous life, he'd help create a magical tablet with the power to rule the world. Instead, I settled for "very old, mystical, all-powerful Cosmic Code that, if in the wrong hands, could be used to harm others." And then there it was. The first stanza.

the following to be the truth…
And as all things came from the one,
through the meditation of the one,
so all things were born from one thing by adaptation.

As it turned out, after reading the entire chiseled text, Antinous was at once captured by the concept of *as above, so below*. Macrocosm and microcosm are core to Greek cosmic harmony and order.

"I do not understand, Athena, but I see how important it is to you that I keep this in confidence. You may rely fully on my discretion."

Qeb-ha would be most pleased. I had recruited a third Protector.

CHAPTER 26   THE CARTHAGINIAN

"All human actions have one or more of these seven causes: chance, nature, compulsion, habit, reason, passion, desire." – Aristotle

Moonlight lit the sandy fields and swampland. Our heavy chariot bumped and shook instead of flying over the ruts and stone as would its lightweight Egyptian cousin. Greece being too hilly and rocky for a wheeled vehicle to be effective in war, there is little tradition for chariots, other than racing on a track. My jaws clenched to keep my teeth from rattling.

The two-horse wooden *biga* could be adapted to four horses with the driver usually standing. Antinous and I sat on a bench resting over the axle, with the soapstone chest containing the Emerald Tablet between us. A brass railing curved around the front and sides. A footboard separated us from the hind legs of the horses, and short sideboards from the spoke wheels.

I was reluctant to take the Tablet home where my secretary Platon might find it. I made certain he never saw anything I didn't want immediately reported to Lord Chancellor Sosibius.

"Antinous, I need you to keep the Tablet in your office, hidden away from all eyes. Can you assure me that no one shall see it?"

"Of course."

"And you will not speak of the Tablet? Not even to the young man—"

"Athena, I gave you my word," he interrupted, turning toward me. "I am quite capable of separating one part of my life from another."

From the direct and knowing look in his eye, he spoke of more than the Tablet.

An unhappy-looking Ajax waited at the Library to walk me home.

"What is it now?"

"The household is most unsettled with the presence of the Carthaginian, Mistress. They call him the Crocodile."

"Is he restrained?"

"Yes, Mistress, he is chained in the slave quarters."

"Does he speak any Greek?"

"I cannot say, Mistress. He has not spoken."

My whole body ached from the jarring bumps and jolts of the chariot trip; I ordered Dead Sea salts added to a hot bath. A slave massaged my stiff muscles with lavender-scented oil from *millefiori* bottles fused from tiny colored-glass rods. Exhausted, I slipped into the steaming water. When I closed my eyes, I saw the Emerald Tablet in its soft suede wrapping.

I must have dozed. Jason touched my shoulder.

"Mistress, the cook and Ajax are arguing. Ajax has told the others they must sleep in their quarters, but they won't enter, because the new slave is there."

"Send Ajax to me."

When he arrived, I had him test one of the columns that held the roof of the portico around my bath.

"Push as hard as you can. Ask another to help you."

When I was assured that the pillar was solid, I ordered Ajax to bring the Carthaginian. Dousing the small brass lanterns around me, I watched from the shadows while they shackled his massive legs to the marble column.

"Leave us," I commanded.

Ajax and the other slave hesitated, glancing at each other.

"Wait outside. I shall call when I need you."

Once we were alone, I asked him, "Do you speak Greek?"

He grunted. I took it as a yes.

His face above the bushy beard was bruised; battle scars covered his arms and legs. His massive bull chest strained the cloth of the chiton. My slaves had managed to braid his long hair; they must have been terrified being that close to him.

"Do you know who I am?" I asked.

If he said his new mistress, I would know that he didn't recognize me.

"It would seem that the tables are turned, Ishtar."

Scabs from a whipping streaked across his cantaloupe-sized biceps. I flashed on the red welts my whip raised on his flesh when Isis—Ishtar as he called me—was his sex slave three centuries earlier in his Persian tent.

"Yes, General, indeed they are. You owned me once—and now I own you."

I rose slowly and deliberately from the bath; the water licked at my thighs. Pulling the pins from my hair, the mass of blonde waves fell around my shoulders.

The General didn't look away or lower his eyes as a slave should, but stared straight at me, lust on his face. He even smirked. I could have ordered him killed for less.

But I didn't want him dead. I wanted him to suffer. My revenge was for him to look at me and crave what he could never have.

I draped a thin shawl around myself, not to cover myself—the sheer cloth clung to my wet body—but to be more seductive, as *hetaerae* prefer the tease of a transparent gown over nudity.

The General's erection bulged under his tunic. I let my eyes linger on the swollen mound before I stepped slowly out of the pool and stretched on a divan covered in soft fur. The silk of my shawl tugged at my flesh like a second skin. My golden hair streamed around my shoulders.

"I would command you to bathe me as I once bathed you, General, but that would pleasure you, not punish. What am I to do? You were the predator and I the prey. You would like nothing better than that, I suppose—for me now to 'prey' upon you?"

The General chuckled; his dark eyes glittered from under thick lids.

"Are you so sure about which of us was the predator? Who lost his life?"

I should whip him for such insolence, but a whip in my hand only thrilled him.

I sipped unwatered wine, regarding him over my cup; the Pharos flamed behind him. He never turned his eyes away but challenged me, thrusting his swollen monster of manhood toward me in defiance.

A fresh breeze came up, and I felt a chill; his eyes went to my nipples pointing through the sheer cloth. Even chained to the pillar, he unsettled me. I covered myself with a heavy turquoise wool shawl and took a more businesslike pose on the sofa.

The General watched every move with hooded eye; he didn't try to hide his hunger. He held himself straight as the column behind him, his massive chest heaving with each breath, his giant feet spread as far as the shackles would allow. A slave necklace glinted in the tangle of black hair at his throat. He hadn't yet been branded on the forehead.

"I did not want to kill you, General, but you gave me no choice. In time, I would have run out of ways to please you. Was that not the attraction? To see what new tricks I could invent? But a sweet thing tasted too often is no longer sweet."

He smiled, but only one side of his mouth turned up. He found me amusing. I found him maddening. I should have left him for the mines.

"Admit it, General. You would have done the same in my place."

"That is where you and I are different, Ishtar. A man seldom eliminates a woman who pleases him—and you pleased me very much. Who knows how long we might have had together? Maybe one more night—maybe all our lives."

I took another sip of wine, studying him. He stared back.

"You are not going to force me to kill you again, are you?" I demanded.

He only chuckled and shifted his weight slightly so that his chains rattled. His erection was still huge.

"A man like you should never be in chains!"

In spite of my efforts to be in control, my voice was too full of accusation. It was his fault to end up like this.

He eyes travelled the length of my body.

"Your breasts are full. Your belly is rounding. Are you with child?"

I blinked. I had thrown up this morning and was tired before the day began. Why hadn't I thought of it?

He maneuvered to put me on the defense. I ignored his question and returned the subject to him.

"How *did* you end up a slave, General? Are Carthaginians not like Spartans? Rather die in battle than surrender?"

"I believed she was you. I let down my guard," he said with a shrug.

I stared at him, stunned by his admission. I'd never realized the full extent of his hunger for me.

"She had emerald eyes like yours, green as a cat. It was the eyes that fooled me. But she was a spy and drugged my wine. When I woke, I was in chains on a ship."

"So you were undone by your penis!" I laughed. "The Gods, too, are fond of a joke."

I drank more unwatered wine. Warmth spread through my cells. The wool shawl slipped from my shoulders, and the General's eyes followed. I pulled the shawl back up to cover me.

"What am I going to do with you?"

"Unchain me," he answered without hesitation.

"They say you cannot be tamed, that Carthage is a land of savages. My slaves call you the Crocodile and won't sleep in their beds for fear of being in the same room."

He smirked again. Fear of him was yet another of his pleasures. I'm certain he thought us fools.

"If I undo your chains, what is my guarantee you won't slit my throat—and those of my household?"

"You might trust my word. There are those who think it means something." He grinned. "But then, there are others who might wish they had been more wary."

"I saved you today from the mines or a warship galley, General. Do you not owe me something? Even in your brutal, vengeful world?"

"I owe you nothing. You did what you did for your own reasons, whatever they may be. Only you know them."

"I bought you to save you! Can you not understand how much it saddens me to see a man like you die on an oar?"

"And what kind of man is that, Ishtar? I am not one to fetch your curling irons and bend to your every whim. There are only two ways I can serve you. I would gladly do both with no disappointment on your part."

He shifted his weight. The chains rattled. For a terrified second, I thought I saw the pillar move.

"I can protect you. A woman with your beauty and position always needs protection."

His eyes wandered down my body, pausing on my breasts and then my loins.

"We both know how else I can serve you."

I suppressed an insane impulse to free him so he could ravage me into submission. Suddenly exhausted, I wanted nothing more than to sleep. I rang on the brass bowl.

"Have they given you food?"

"I could have more," he answered.

Ajax must have been waiting right outside the door, because he entered immediately. Jason was on his heels. When Jason saw the General chained to the column, his hazel eyes grew enormous.

"Come, Jason," I said gently. "Do not be afraid."

The General's hooded eyes followed Jason as he came to me and settled on the floor beside my hand. The two of them stared at each other, Jason with round eyes and the General from beneath heavy lids. He looked first surprised, then suspicious when I stroked Jason's curls.

"Tonight the Carthaginian will sleep in the grain storeroom," I told Ajax. "Chain him and lock the door. Let him eat his fill and give him beer, but only with his food. We shall see what tomorrow brings."

"Mistress has a visitor," Ajax announced. "I explained the hour was too late, but he insists. He claims he is expected."

Eben took a small stool next to me while I reclined on my divan on the balcony. Jason slept on his pallet at the foot of my bed.

The city around the harbor was dark. Here and there, I saw torches; some of the buildings in the Royal Palace were lit. There was no light that I could see at the Library. The older students probably reveled at symposia in the Beta District, home to wealthy Greeks. The Pharos blazed as it did every night.

"I have the Tablet, Eben—or rather, Antinous has it. Only the three of us know. I want you to ask Qeb-ha what my next course of action must be."

"I shall do that, but I believe he shall say that only you can choose the path."

"Can he not give me guidance? What assistance is he, if I cannot make use of his wisdom?"

Eben shrugged. He wore his usual heavy dark robe. His long natural waves hadn't been combed since he slept.

"You are the one chosen by Hermes *Trismegistus*. Everything comes back to you."

CHAPTER 27   BIRTHDAY

"You don't develop courage by being happy every day. You develop it by surviving difficult times and challenging adversity." – Epicurus

My slaves had orders that I be allowed to sleep in the morning, but I woke with the sun and vomited soon after. The signs were obvious now; I couldn't ignore them. Was this how I spent my past lives—at the mercy of my uterus? This was no time to carry a child; I needed my focus to be on the Tablet. I was scared, too. Women died in childbirth on a regular basis. I reassured myself that I would go back through the Mirror long before the birth.

There was nothing to feel when I put my hand on my stomach. It was much too soon for the movement of life. I tried to imagine the baby as a miniature Black Falcon, but with caring eyes.

I don't know why it took me so long to think of Hektor.

The child could be his. And as if merely thinking of him were a kind of magical mantra that manifested his presence, Ajax hurried in with a letter.

After a long introduction of formal titles and flowery salutations, Hektor wrote that he would join me at Ptolemy's birthday celebration that afternoon. He finished with, *"I look forward to toasting your beauty. Kallistei!*—To the most beautiful!" Just as he had declared at the symposion in Korinth.

His signature was followed by the date and name of his Naukratis estate.

The slaves took hours at my toilet. I felt nauseous the entire time. And so bloated. The Hathor ring dug into my swollen finger; a slave had to use oil to pry it from my hand.

They dusted my face with white lead powder, rouged my lips and shadowed my eyes, expertly camouflaging the dark circles. My hair was such an elaborate maze of braids and curls, it took two pairs of hands to accomplish. I prayed to the Luck Gods for a windless afternoon.

I had trouble deciding which gown to wear and called for Jason who had returned from the Library early.

"There are no classes this afternoon," he reported with regret. "It is the Pharaoh's birthday."

A turquoise silk with bands of gold embroidery twice as wide as my hand was his immediate choice. The color reminded me of Black Falcon—the color of my gown the first night in his cabin and the color of the sea the day he sent me away.

"May I go, Mistress?" Jason begged.

I remembered Ptolemy's eyes on him that first audience in the Presence Chamber.

"Not today. Today is not for children."

When the litter came to carry me to the festivities, I saw the General chained to a *persea* tree in the yard. No one knew what to do with him, least of all me.

He sneered at me from the deep shade.

Trumpeters and elephants lined Soma Street from the Gate of the Moon south to the Gate of the Sun. Swags of greenery and chains of lotus connected the hundreds of carved columns lining the avenue. More trumpeters, elephants, and decorated columns stretched on the Canopic Way east from the Canopic Gate west to the Necropic Gate at the City of the Dead.

Four slaves carried my litter through streets jammed with foot traffic, other litters and chariots. The clamor of voices and blaring trumpets was a roar in my ears. Rose petals showered down from the rooftops, carpeting the paving stones in a thick layer of pink and red snow.

Already drunk on the Pharaoh's free wine, a mob surrounded the *Hippodrome*. Soldiers broke up the frenzied crowd with shields and spears to allow dignitaries to pass. At last we were through the roped cordon marked by giant yellow flags emblazoned with Ptolemy's cartouche.

A ring of yellow canopies circled the racetrack. Greeks, foreign diplomats and Egyptian priests feasted in pavilions furnished with divans and carved chairs set on lush carpets. Hundreds of long wooden tables nearly buckled from the weight of roast hippopotamus, aardvark and oryx.

The Pharaoh's private party gathered on a dais populated with men in dazzling gold parade armor and winged, plumed helmets. I was greeted by a Nubian slave in a blue and yellow striped headdress who led me to a fuchsia upholstered divan next to Antinous.

"I have studied the Tablet," he spoke into my ear. "I have much to share."

Antinous could have shouted, and no one would have heard. Trumpets blared, flutes bleated and drums pounded. I felt exhausted and had only just arrived but fought back nausea to pay my respects to Ptolemy.

He was seated in the middle of the dais on a silver throne with a whole roasted giraffe on the ground in front of him. At his right hand, reclined the Lord Chancellor Sosibius on a divan.

"Our Supreme Priestess honors Us with her presence." Ptolemy beamed the silly grin of a man quite drunk.

"Accept my birthday wishes, Your Majesty, for a long life filled with happiness and prosperity. Each day I entreat the Goddess to continue Her generous blessing of Your Royal Personage, the glorious Alexandria and all Egypt."

"We thank you for your prayers, Athena of Korinth," Ptolemy offered cheerfully as he reached out for the hand of the handsome woman beside him. "We believe you have not had the privilege of meeting Our sister, Our Queen."

When the Royal sister-wife pulled her hand away to pick up a small fan, his silly grin melted, and his face went sour.

The Queen of Egypt stared at me for a very long moment before nodding her head to signal that I was permitted to speak. She didn't deign to smile, but there was the slightest glint of amusement in her inky black eyes. I was certain she recognized me. I knew so well the subtle changes in Sit-hathor's—Isabel's—expression.

"I am most grateful for this opportunity, Queen Arsinoë. Your Majesty is held in the highest regard throughout the Greek world as a patroness of learning and the arts. Nothing would honor me more than your esteemed opinion of our design for Ptolemy's Temple to Aphrodite."

"We must become friends, Athena of Korinth," she commanded. "Women of intelligence should form alliances, do you not agree?"

"Already the Queen plots with Our friend!" Ptolemy exclaimed to the group. "These impossible women! How they do get around Us. Can't live with them or without them."

Everyone laughed loudly as if the wit were Ptolemy's own and not a direct steal from the poet Aristophanes.

A man wearing the chain of Royal Steward leaned to the olive-skinned woman lying next to him and whispered something that made her smile in a most unpleasant way. Dressed in the Egyptian fashion with ripe breasts barely covered by pleated bands of gauzy fabric attached to a clinging crimson gown, she exposed her sumptuous body as much as decorum allowed.

There was something cruel in the set of her mouth, lush as it was. And unmistakable cruelty in her eyes. Carla's eyes. They bore right through me.

Although I saw nothing in her expression that said she recognized me from the future, this incarnation of Carla hated me instantly. I suspected this woman would despise anyone she viewed as competition.

I thought I might escape to my place next to Antinous when Ptolemy stopped me, waving his drinking cup, sloshing wine over his gold-encrusted gown.

"Where is that delightful little slave boy of yours? We had hoped you might offer him as a birthday gift."

All conversation around us stopped. The circle of silence grew larger and larger, and with it the tension. I felt everyone looking at me, waiting for my response.

"Your Majesty knows that anything I own is his." I smiled graciously. "But I cannot offer that which belongs to the Goddess. I shall consult Her, and She shall instruct me in Her wishes."

Ptolemy's eyes took on the soulless stare of a cobra. Oh, how cold his tone when he said, "We trust the Goddess would grant Our birthday wish, Athena of Korinth. Are We not building the most magnificent edifice in all the world to honor Her?"

"I am certain all shall be as Your Majesty desires," I assured him in a voice far calmer that I felt. "The Goddess is ever grateful for the generosity of the House of Ptolemy."

I bowed my head again to Ptolemy and then to the Queen. I don't know how I walked on my shaking legs. My whole body quaked. I was afraid to pick up the wine goblet, my hand trembled so.

Antinous leaned over and urged in my ear, "You must send Jason away at once."

My head throbbed. My heart pounded. Nausea overwhelmed me. I wanted nothing more but to leave, but I couldn't. I was trapped. Jason was trapped.

It was then Hektor joined us, bullying the man on the sofa next to me to move. But he bullied with charm, and the man acquiesced. I was beginning to comprehend Hektor's power in Alexandria; it was said that his family was so rich that even Ptolemy left them alone.

"You dare take on the Pharaoh, Athena of Korinth? Take heed or you will have need of my protection."

His tone was teasing, but both of us knew the danger of refusing Ptolemy.

If only I could get to my apartments and the Red Mirror. Could I take Jason back with me? Could a soul pass if there were no physical body on the other side to enter?

It was not long before a royal slave presented me with a message from the Queen. I should join her for a cup of wine in her pavilion behind the platform.

Queen Arsinoë welcomed me warmly enough, but without any further sign that she knew me from another life.

"Sit here, my dear. You are quite pale."

She motioned toward the sofa across from her, placed quite close considering her station as queen. Her black eyes, heavy with *kohl* in the Egyptian way, almost smiled.

Accepting her offer of wine, I asked for it to be diluted more. Nausea wracked my body; my esophagus was on fire. Blood pounded in my temples. I longed to lie down in my cool marble room by the sea, away from the heat, away from the chaos and clamor.

"Did you notice the whore with the Royal Steward Agathon?" she asked.

"I saw a woman with the Steward, Your Majesty," I answered cautiously. "We were not introduced."

"She is Agatha, the Steward Agathon's twin sister and my husband's mistress. The twins Agathon and Agatha battle constantly with the Lord Chancellor Sosibius to control Ptolemy. All three encourage my brother's excesses. Who can judge who is the more evil?"

She stopped to sip more wine and looked at me over the rim of the cup. I didn't take her pause to mean that she expected me to comment. How could I know who was the evilest? They all frightened me. Especially Agatha with the hatred in her eyes. As wild as it seemed, I couldn't help but fear that Carla might seek revenge for Hector dumping her for me. If she had recognized me, that is. I couldn't tell for certain.

"They are fearsome in their cruelty," Arsinoë was saying. "I am certain they provoked my husband to kill our mother and brother."

Inside her tent, the air was still and hot in spite of the towering palmiform fans waved by young copper-skinned boys in white loincloths and black wigs.

I took a small sip of wine to calm my nerves. Her intimacy made me most ill at ease; her words smacked of treason.

"Our mother died in agony, poisoned by my husband—her own son. But our poor brother Magas suffered most. He was first tortured and then boiled alive."

I could only stare. The horror must have been etched into my face.

"They would also see me dead," she went on. "But Ptolemy needs a Queen, and it pleases the Egyptians that the Pharaoh's wife is his sister. The Goddess Isis was wed to her brother Osiris, as I'm sure you know."

She took another sip of wine before musing, "So perhaps I am safe—who knows?"

She closed her eyes. Green mica covered her lids to the eyebrows. Her black wig sparkled with a thousand emeralds entwined in tiny braids. She had remarkable flawless skin and a long, gracious neck.

"Our mother Berenike truly loved our father," she continued, speaking softly with eyes still closed. "She cut her hair when he went to war and gave it as an offering to Aphrodite that her husband, Ptolemy III—Ptolemy *Euergetes*—would return."

She paused for a moment and looked directly at me. "She always feared her son. She knew she was not safe without the protection of my father. None of us were—are."

The tent did little to muffle the noise of the celebration. The blare of the trumpets pierced my aching head. Arsinoë resumed in a more idle, conversational tone.

"Some claim that Aphrodite created a constellation with my mother's hair. Callimachus even wrote a poem about it. He was a great admirer of my mother. They both were from Cyrene. Perhaps you have read the 'Lock of Berenike'?"

But before I could answer, she said, "But, of course, you have read it. You are an educated woman. That is your problem."

She smiled at me, showing only a hint of her straight teeth, slightly yellowed from chewing herbs.

"Why do you think my husband wishes to build this extravagant monument to the Goddess? The ghost of the mother he poisoned haunts his sleep. He hopes Aphrodite will quiet his dreams."

She leaned toward me, across the narrow space, almost close enough to touch my arm.

"They all have sex together," she hissed. "The vile Steward Agathon, his whore sister Agatha and my little brother Ptolemy."

I glanced anxiously at the row of boys waving fans, wondering that she dared be so critical of her perverse and vindictive brother in front of the slaves.

"Do not mind them," she said. "They can neither hear nor speak."

I took another sip of wine. It burned all the way down. Did protocol allow me to ask for ginger tea?

"My husband desires me to join in their perversions," she murmured, "but I will have none of it. I do not care for them to touch my body."

She waved for a servant to bring more wine. When her chalice was refilled, she drank again, her eyes over the rim holding mine, commanding my full presence.

"Do you think I enjoy sex with my vain and lascivious brother? He disgusts me."

She no longer looked at me. The tent did little to stifle the wild noise of the crowd outside, but Arsinoë seemed too far away to notice. Her honey voice took on a dreamlike cadence.

"The great tragedy of my life was the murder of my brother Magas. I loved him over all others. Perhaps that is why he had to die."

She stopped. I imagined she saw images of a screaming Magas being boiled. Then she brought herself back; her voice lost the dreamy quality. It turned out she didn't want to speak only of herself.

"Ptolemy and his vile Steward also share a taste for young boys. This is an evil the whore sister must tolerate; Agatha's heart is not in it. If a child steals too much attention, he soon disappears."

Jason. Bile came up in my throat again. It was suddenly too hot in the tent for me to breathe. The servants waving fans moved no air at all.

"I see you are shocked, Athena of Korinth. Perhaps you have led a sheltered life in your temple on a hill."

"Sex with children, Your Majesty, and between brothers and sisters is not acceptable in Korinth. And certainly not all at the same time."

The trumpets blared again. The first chariot race started. Having waited all day, the frenzied crowd erupted into a deafening roar. The poles of the pavilion trembled, and I felt the vibration of thundering hooves travel up the legs of my divan.

"Leave us," she commanded, clapping her hands.

The tent emptied, and we were alone. I couldn't imagine what she would tell me that was more dangerous than her accounts of incest and murder.

"You have angered the Pharaoh, Isis," she whispered. At last, she acknowledged that she recognized me. "He fears the Goddess, and so She offers you some protection. But beware. The Lord Chancellor and Royal Steward plot against you."

Her words sent a chill across my shoulders; I dreaded those two more than Ptolemy. In that moment, I wanted nothing more than to return at once to my villa and go back through the Mirror. But what would happen to Jason? And the Emerald Tablet? I knew no more about its secret than before.

"I would leave Egypt, Your Majesty, but I am not yet free to do so."

"I shall help you in any way I can. But we must be cautious. Everything is at stake. It might not be pretty for those you leave behind."

My head pounded. I wanted out of her tent, away from the stifling heat. Surely she had nothing else to say.

She leaned back against the raised arm of the divan and gave me a sly, secretive half-smile. "Do you not find it odd that Hektor's wife is not in attendance for my husband's birthday? The Pharaoh surely takes offense."

Hektor's wife. I tried but couldn't keep my face a mask, and she laughed in notes as high as a bell.

"You did not know? Oh, our dearest Hektor, Hunter of Women, is at it again! He has quite the reputation in Alexandria. But you, of course, have not been here long enough to understand the full extent."

With that, the Queen of Egypt dismissed me to return to Hektor and Antinous, one with a wife, the other with a teenage boy lover. But I could add one more Protector to my list: Qeb-ha, Eben, Antinous and now the Queen.

As quickly as the racing chariots passed, slaves ran onto the track to throw basins of water to settle the dust. But thick clouds still rose, making it difficult to breathe. My intent had been to retire to my divan and close my eyes, hoping to quell the hammering in my head. But the world went black, and when I opened my eyes again, I was not on the platform, but on a litter not far from the Queen's tent and away from the dust.

Both Hektor and Antinous knelt beside me. A slave wiped my forehead with a damp cloth. When I leaned over the side and retched on the ground, the concern on their faces changed to alarm. Antinous insisted on sending to the Library for a physician. I pleaded to be taken home.

Every street was filled with drunks, and night had not yet fallen when the mad reveling would begin in earnest. The Alexandrian mob was notorious for arsons and revolts, both minor and major; it didn't require much to set them off.

After a great deal of shoving accompanied by Hektor's aggressive threats, we made it home without incident. The slaves settled me in bed.

A colleague of Antinous from the Medical *Akademy* politely asked Hektor and Antinous to leave the room while he examined me. It took him no time to make the obvious diagnosis.

"You must avoid extreme conditions, eat sensibly and rest much."

"This is a most indelicate situation for a woman in my position, as I'm certain you can appreciate. May I count on your discretion?"

"A priestess is first a woman," he answered matter-of-factly. "You must treat your body without concern for gods—or those who believe in them. I have no interest other than your health and that of the child."

He rewrapped his utensils in a long linen cloth and called for Antinous.

"The Lady is exhausted. I recommend bed rest and an infusion. The herbs are here. I bid you a good night."

"Thank you, Antinous, for everything." I said as soon as the physician left. "May I have a moment alone with Hektor?"

If he was surprised by my request, Antinous was gracious enough not to show it. Hektor was so ungracious as to give him a triumphant look before perching himself on the edge of the bed.

He didn't wait for Antinous to be out of the room to take my hand and raise it to his lips. His brown eyes with red flecks smiled warmly down on me.

When he leaned over to kiss me, I put my fingers to his mouth to stop him. "Why did you not tell me that you are married?"

He blinked in surprise and sat straight up.

"Of course I am married—how could I not be? Every man of my station is married. But that has nothing to do with us."

"You might have told me and let me make that decision."

He appeared genuinely confused. "You are wed to the Goddess. Does that change what we have together?"

We might have a child together; that would certainly change things.

"You did not bring your wife today. Was that because of me? You risked insulting the Pharaoh, endangering both you and your family."

"Let me worry about Ptolemy, Athena. As for my wife, she and I were betrothed at birth to unite our families. Eugenia is an intelligent woman with interests of her own. Her life is the quiet of the country and mine is—well, you know the life that I love. We understand each other; she accepts my needs and is content to live apart."

"What of your children? Do you not wish to spend more time with them?"

"We have no children. It is one of the sorrows we bear."

If Hektor's wife Eugenia was barren, he could still be the father of my child. But if Hektor were sterile, then the father had to be Black Falcon. I wanted to ask him if he had sired children with other women, but that might trigger questions—questions I wasn't ready to answer.

I asked Hektor to send in Antinous, but the herb tea took effect, and I couldn't keep my eyes open. The last thing I saw was the Red Mirror hanging beside my bed.

CHAPTER 28   ESCAPE

"Love is all we have, the only way that each can help the other." – Euripides

The sky was still dark when I woke. The beacon of the Pharos shone far out over a mercury sea shrouded in pre-dawn mist. The sun wouldn't rise for another hour.

Jason snored lightly on his pallet at the foot of my bed. Kallisto chased a fly on the balcony.

I slipped on a yellow linen robe and made my way silently in murky shadow down the backstairs to the kitchen. Faint red embers glowed in the cooking fire; not even the first slave was awake.

My bare feet were silent in the stone corridor leading to the storerooms. I inched the bolt back and slipped inside, the heavy door closing behind me with a faint sucking sound.

The storeroom was a long narrow space, not more than six feet wide, lit by air vents on the end wall up near the vaulted brick ceiling. The General, awake and alerted by my fumbling at the door, sat straight up on a narrow pallet barely squeezed in among the coarse sacks filled with grain. His hands were chained together in front and ankles shackled.

I sank to my knees onto dirty straw covering a rough stone floor; pieces of gravel, loose grain and straw ground into my flesh. I eased onto a sack, curled my legs up close and leaned back against the hard wall. My hair in a thick braid was a rope on my spine.

"I am aware of the risk of being here with you," I said softly.

He said nothing. Not a muscle moved in his powerful frame. He could strangle me in a heartbeat, with his bare hands shackled in front, or with the chains that held them.

"I need your help."

There was just enough light to see his pupils dilate when I said I needed him.

My eyes filled with tears, and I rested the back of my head on the wall, closing my lids, almost wishing that he would strangle me, that I wouldn't have to deal with what was coming.

I could have gone back through the Mirror this morning, and no one would have known. But I stayed for Jason. Maybe more than I stayed for the Tablet.

"I have nowhere else to turn."

He shifted his weight ever so slightly. I could see each scar on his battered face. His legs stretched out in front of him with monster feet stuck up at right angles from the floor, as far apart as the chains allowed. The skin around the shackles was covered with open sores and crusty scabs. I wondered how long the rough metal had rubbed his wrists and ankles. Since Syracuse?

"Tell me what I need to unlock your chains."

"Do you trust me that much?" he growled.

"I have no choice. If you kill me, I shall know nothing of the events that follow. If you do not kill me, then you may help me."

"Have you not left out a third possibility?"

I knew his hunger for me; I had foolishly taunted him in my bathchamber, never dreaming that this moment would come.

"I am at your mercy, General. You have long desired to have me once again in your power. Whatever you do is on your conscience—if you have one. I am staking my life that you do."

He snorted, nodding his head slightly. A tiny flash sparked in those black, black eyes. "You have even more guts than I gave you credit for."

"I shall free you from your chains, General, but you must agree to do one thing for me. You must give me your word."

"Who do you want me to kill?"

Oh-h-h, how tempting. I thought immediately of Ptolemy and Sosibius whose deaths would make my life easier and save Jason's.

Instead, I said, "I do not want you to kill anyone. On the contrary, I want you to save someone's life."

He didn't try to hide his surprise. He never hid his feelings from me; he was that confident.

"You must take the boy, Jason, and leave at once. Do not tell me where. No one must know where. Ptolemy's torturers can extract any secret; in the end, everyone talks."

I found a chisel and hammer in the tool room, wrapped sacking around the metal to dampen the sound and handed them to the General. He was lightning fast; the chains fell away.

He rubbed his wrists and his ankles and then, so quickly that I had no time to react, grabbed me by the throat with one giant paw and pulled me to him.

I choked and put my hands on both sides of his head, not sinking in my nails or trying to scratch. I didn't struggle but went limp as a cat surrendering to a dominant.

My look told him I couldn't breathe, and he relaxed his grip. His face was only inches away; I saw each tiny red capillary in the whites of his eyes. His beard had a few strands of gray. His breath was sour with a hint of stale beer.

With a jerk of his forearm, he pulled me full into him and kissed me with such force that my lip split, and I tasted blood. His hunger sucked the air from my lungs. Opening my lips, I let him devour me but didn't give back. I might have been unconscious, I was that passive.

The more pliant I was, the more he crushed me against him. His arm locked around my waist with such force, I feared he might snap my spine. Knife pains pierced my tender breasts. At my rounded belly, his monster manhood menaced.

Oddly, I was calm. He could choke the life from me with one hand, but his desperate need oozing from every pore gave me power.

Then, much like Black Falcon on the ship, he buried his face in my hair and inhaled my scent. Vulnerable. He was so vulnerable.

"We have no time," I urged. "Listen to me. Listen to why I came."

His hand around my throat relaxed more, but not enough for me to move.

"We had a child, General. Ishtar and Sher. Conceived in the desert. In your tent."

He stared at me. I wondered if he understood.

"A son. *We had a son.* And I believe our son's soul is Jason. Think! How else could I love him so deeply—and have done so from the first moment?"

He sank back, releasing his grip on my neck and his arm from around my waist.

"A son?" he asked dumbly.

"Yes, *your* son. And he needs you. Ptolemy wants him. He *will* have him. Do you wish him to be defiled by these perverted Greeks and then cast away, broken with no hope ever to be a man?"

By his face, I thought he still didn't comprehend. He stared at me with empty eyes. Minutes passed. He seemed incapable of decision; I had never imagined him so weak.

"You must act *now*," I insisted. "Do you hear me? Now!"

I tugged at his arms to pull him to his feet, but he was like the carcass of a dead bull.

"A son, General. A son! You can save him!"

I was thinking of slapping his face, when a light came into his eyes—a look of wonder. He suddenly stood, dragging me to my feet with him.

Quietly opening the door, he took the chisel and pried off the iron bands of the bolt, catching them in his hand and scattering them silently on the floor of the corridor. He wrapped his shackles, chains and the iron tools in grain sacks to muffle any sound.

In the kitchen, a lone slave built the morning fire. We waited until he stepped out to draw water before we hurried up the backstairs, stepping into my bedchamber when the light on the sea told me the sun was near the horizon.

I kissed Jason's sleepy face in a dozen places.

"I love you, Jason," I told him. I would not let him see my tears.

Holding him to my breast, I unfastened the slave necklace that said he belonged to me. Then I went to my knees and held him by the shoulders.

"Go with the General. Obey him in all things. Never tell anyone your name. Never mention mine. Do not speak Greek."

I kissed him again on the forehead.

"Be brave. We shall see each other again one day, I promise."

I replaced the General's slave collar with a leather thong attached to a pouch of silver *drachmas,* all the while giving him quick directions while he stuffed Jason into a grain sack.

"To the east is the Jewish Quarter with thousands of foreigners. To the west is the Egyptian Quarter, Rhakotis, with its own port. The docks and slave market lie between here and there."

The General threw the sack with his shackles and the sack with Jason onto his back and dropped easily and silently over the balcony to the ground. He didn't look back and was gone among the trees and bushes of the garden before I shed my first tear.

I called for Ajax, and he came with the silver bowl, but instead of being sick, I told him, "I am hungry."

When he moved to fetch my breakfast, I idly asked, "Where is Jason? Is he in the kitchen?"

"No, Mistress. I have not seen him this morning."

"Send him to me."

I settled back on my pillows and waited. It didn't take long.

"The Carthaginian is gone!" Ajax shouted. His eyes were wide with alarm. The pox scars on his red face popped like white polka dots.

"What can you mean—gone?" I asked in an incredulous tone. "Was he not locked in as I instructed?"

"Yes, Mistress. Certainly, Mistress. I bolted the door myself last night, but he forced it from the inside. He has escaped, chains and all. I never imagined him so strong."

It took the household only a few minutes longer to realize that Jason was also missing. By the time the scribe Platon arrived for his daily instructions, I lay on my bed, surrounded by cowering slaves seeking to console me.

"You understand, Platon," I said with my hand over my eyes, "I am too distraught over this loss to the Goddess to concentrate."

He bowed, expressed his condolences and scurried away. I knew he would head straight to Sosibius to report Jason's disappearance. And the Lord Chancellor would go to Ptolemy. My great gamble lay in whether they would believe this charade.

Slaves rarely escape. If caught, they face whipping and mutilation, if not a most unpleasant death. Yet a newly acquired slave in my household had kidnapped a boy slave in which the Pharaoh had shown interest. Of course, it would look suspicious, especially to a devious mind like that of Sosibius.

I sent for Antinous, a perfectly natural thing for me to do. We worked together daily; Antinous schooled Jason. But that was for outside eyes to see. With Jason out of danger from the Pharaoh, I was free to focus on the Tablet.

When Antinous arrived, visibly off-balance, I was alone in my apartments. I had locked the slaves in their quarters with the excuse they awaited punishment. I wanted no witnesses or eavesdropping.

"I can understand the Carthaginian's escape," Antinous reasoned. "They are a race who cannot be tamed. They welcome death over servitude. But why would he take Jason?"

He paced the room. His blond curls stood out as if shot through with electricity; his eyes were electric blue. I wanted to tell him the truth, to ease his worry, but couldn't take the risk of him knowing.

"What have you learned, Antinous, about the Tablet? Perhaps it can help us with Jason."

He stopped pacing and leaned back against a rich wall tapestry of Dionysos carrying off a bare-breasted Ariadne.

"We have the original or a copy of every book, play, treatise and *kanon* in the world—and a catalogue system to itemize everything—but there is no trace of an Emerald Tablet in the Library. I could not find one credible reference."

"But what about the Code? Have you deciphered that?'

"The text says nothing that is not in other sources. The tenets are the basis of many teachings."

"Could it be, perhaps, because the Tablet speaks the Truth?"

He came over to sit next to me on the bed, close but not intimate.

"Let us say, Athena, for the sake of argument, that you are right about the Tablet having mystical power. So why am I not suddenly powerful? Why can I not manifest Jason—or understand the movement of the planets?"

Thinking of the Tablet in the Las Vegas safe deposit box, I answered, "I have asked myself the same question."

He lay back on the bed and put his arms behind his head. His feet still rested on the floor. He stared at the ceiling. I imagined the turmoil of conflicting theories battling in his head. The acceptance of the Tablet's power was a quantum leap for his pragmatic mind.

"What if?" he mused. His brain turned some more before he began to speak quickly. "Consider this. What if I cannot access the power of the Tablet because to possess the stone is not enough."

He paused again, but only for a breath or two. When he spoke, it was with confidence. He had developed a theory, as incomplete as it was.

"We are missing something. An unknown. Some X factor that is needed to activate the Tablet's potential."

He stared up. Did he see Eros flying among lyres? Lying on my bed, did he think of me at all?

"Should you not be married, Antinous?"

"What?" He jerked his head toward me with a start. Of course, my question, out of the blue, startled him.

"A man of your age and your station is always married. Should you not be siring sons?"

He sat up and faced me, his brow furrowing in the way it does when he is puzzled and thinking hard.

We sat so close, I had only to put out my hand to touch him. I wanted to—not from desire, but from my need for intimacy. I felt so alone. But the vision of Antinous and his touch on the boy-god's shoulder paralyzed me.

I saw he struggled with how he should answer, as if he loathed to offend me, but felt compelled to tell the truth.

"Menander says, 'Marriage, if one faces the truth, is an evil, but a necessary one.' I have not yet conceded, Athena, that it is necessary."

He had the most earnest expression, speaking carefully, searching for the right words.

"My work is my world," he explained. "A wife would be a…distraction. My household is small and uncomplicated—I have my scrolls and my tools. My slaves take care of my physical needs."

"What of your emotional needs? Who takes care of those?"

I saw in his eyes he knew that I referred to the beautiful youth in his office. I thought I had put him on the spot, but instead, he smiled. His eyes were warm and full of affection.

"Is the Lady offering herself for that duty?"

At that moment, Hektor burst into my bedchambers, red cape flying, sturdy sandals pounding the pink granite floor.

"No one answers at the door," he shouted. "Where are your slaves?"

When he saw Antinous beside me on the bed, his expression changed from alarm to shock. Antinous stood to his feet and bowed his head.

"Good day, Hektor of Naukratis."

Hektor barely nodded his head in return, glancing only briefly at Antinous before saying drily, "I see you are recovered well enough from last evening, Athena of Korinth."

"I am. Thank you, Hektor of Naukratis. But a new drama has struck.

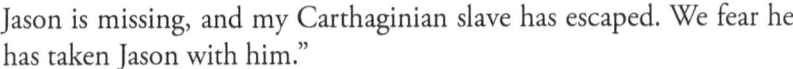

Jason is missing, and my Carthaginian slave has escaped. We fear he has taken Jason with him."

"What Carthaginian slave?" he demanded. "What were you thinking, Athena? No one keeps a Carthaginian in the house."

Hektor insisted on interviewing each slave. He inspected the storeroom. He moved sacks of grain and lifted the sleeping pallet, his big feet disturbing the straw-covered floor and raising small clouds of dust.

After carefully examining the door and then the broken bolt on the corridor floor, he picked up the pieces and put them into my hand, closing my fingers around the chunks of rough metal.

We stood for a long moment facing each other, Hektor probing my eyes, not saying a word. I tried to keep my face innocent; I didn't have to feign sadness.

He raised his hand and plucked a piece of straw from my hair, holding it in his fingers in front of our eyes for a moment before letting it float to the floor.

We both glanced at Antinous to see if he noticed, but Antinous leaned against the corridor wall, lost in his thoughts, probably sorting through theories, examining the logic and supporting evidence of each.

Hektor leaned to my ear and whispered, "Cover your neck, Athena. I see the bruises."

The rest of the afternoon passed uneventfully. My slaves went quietly about the house, whispering, hardly believing their good fortune that they'd been spared the whip. I rested as well as I could, but even the physician's herbs didn't bring sleep. Kallisto meowed and meowed, missing Jason.

I wondered where the General and Jason would sleep tonight. Jason must be frightened, although he had been through more in his short years than most experience their whole lives. I told myself that he was safer now than with me. At least, I prayed so. And, I was free to focus fully on the Tablet.

Sunshine reflected off the stone floor onto the polished bronze mirror; the red lacquer frame glowed. I decided to stay yet another day.

CHAPTER 29   RHAKOTIS

"Try to take for your mate, a person of your own neighborhood." – Hesiod

A jax first dared enter my chamber as the sun was near setting. Having avoided me since his news of the General's escape, he kept his eyes fixed on the floor.

"A man is here, Mistress," he said, placing a small pink seashell in my palm. "Egyptian."

"Tell him to enter."

"He refuses, Mistress, and waits outside."

I scarcely let myself hope what the seashell could mean. I changed quickly from my lounging gown into a simple white chiton woven in a blend of fine wool and linen. It tied at my shoulders with silver twine.

A slave hurriedly twisted my hair into a thick braid at the back of my head. I didn't take the time to curl the loose tendrils around my face or put on a fancy headband. I slipped on sturdy sandals and called for my green, hooded priestess cloak.

My dressing went silently. I don't know what the slaves thought of my hurried exit; they were afraid to look me in the eye. I might yet change my mind and bring out the whip.

Waiting outside the door in the early shadow of evening was Black Falcon's second-most-trusted man. His face turned toward the harbor; the scar on his cheek flamed in the light of the lamp in my hand.

I told Ajax I was going to the Library, stepped outside and closed the door.

"Follow me," Scarface said in Egyptian.

We went quickly through the gardens and down to the water. A small boat waited at a short pier used for delivering supplies to the Library. We rowed through purple waters to the main docks with massive seagoing ships moored at the stone quays. When we came ashore, it was a few yards from the *Heptastadion* leading out to Pharos Island.

From the docks, we went on foot across the empty agora and into the winding alleyways of Rhakotis, the Egyptian Quarter. We might have stepped off the end of the earth. The meandering streets of Rhakotis, barely wide enough for foot traffic, were more like Korinth than Alexandria. There was nothing Greek about the wild splash of color and exotic smells.

The quarter was crowded with noisy men, mysterious women and running children. Garish murals of Egyptian Gods jumped out from flat-roofed, mud brick houses crammed against each other. Even the poorest hovel had crude ankhs painted on the walls. Eyes-of-Horus were above every door.

The narrow alley widened into a square with a teeming market of spices and food stuffs. Skewers of meat roasted on open charcoal fires; black smoke billowed to mix with the heavy scent of frankincense and myrrh. As we hurried past, vendors called out to me in Egyptian. Everywhere were the sounds of Egyptian; I heard no Greek at all.

I plastered myself to a cobra-painted wall to avoid a cart loaded with fish. I stepped on a dazed snake in a small tattered basket. Chickens squawked and water birds wailed. A screeching monkey, tethered by a rope to a blind beggar, grabbed at the hem of my cloak.

The light was failing fast; trade carried on without pause by lantern and torch. So many people jammed the streets, it might have been midday.

Then I saw Goliath standing guard like a giant statue, his arms crossed on his massive chest. When he saw me, his eyes glowed, but he shook his head slightly, warning me not to react—to show nothing.

He had to bend to open the short door into a mud house with no windows on the street. The Eye-of-Horus stared back at me from above the lintel as I passed through into a pitch-black room. Thick walls muffled almost all sound.

It took a few seconds for my eyes to adjust to the dark. Closed double doors and shuttered long windows faced me on the opposite wall. I guessed an inner courtyard lay beyond. I heard the cackling of hens and the cooing of pigeons.

I felt his heat before his touch. He unwrapped my cape slowly, as if opening a delicate and much anticipated package. Leaning back into him, I relaxed against his chest and rubbed my temple against his jaw. His breathing was fast and shallow in my ear.

He loosened my braid; my hair tumbled onto my shoulders and covered his bare arm holding me. Then he wrapped a handful of my hair around our faces, breathing on my neck, blowing in my ear.

His hands moved over my breasts, down my midriff, along my waist, across my belly and over my hips. He caressed my thighs, on the outside, up the inside, everywhere he could reach. He relived every curve of my body with his fingertips.

He moved my hair aside, exposing the back of my neck. Every inch he kissed, along my shoulders, down my spine. When he settled at the magic door that opens all doors—that spot just where my neck joins the shoulder—he sucked gently and then licked. His breath, hot and moist, sent chills everywhere. My canal throbbed.

I pressed into him, rocking back and forth against his iron manhood pressing at the curve of my spine. He gently massaged my full, tender breasts. The slightest touch on my nipples, hypersensitive with early pregnancy, jolted me. His thumbs circled the tips slowly through the soft cloth while I sang *O-o-o-o-o-o* into the dark.

Only then did he untie the silver twine at my shoulders; the light linen fell like silk in one long slide to my ankles. His hands stroked my belly and caressed my loins. Finally, he slipped over my mound into the wet.

He explored my valley and caressed my lotus; his fingers dipped into my canal. I loosened his loincloth and stood on his feet to be higher and closer. He put his hardness between my thighs.

One arm encircling my waist, he lifted me up and into him—his fingers still exploring—and entered me from behind. I gripped his forearm, hooked my other arm around his neck and moved with him. There was nothing between us; we shared the same skin.

The door rattled as our bodies rubbed against it. The thought of Goliath listening and guarding on the other side entered my mind for a millisecond and then was gone.

There was nothing in the world for me at the moment except the euphoria of being one with Black Falcon.

We never lighted a lamp. The narrow bed had fresh straw and a blanket smelling of sun. Black Falcon lay on his side, supported by his elbow, his head resting on his palm. He traced every line of my body with his fingers, along my face, my jaw, down my neck, and over my breasts. He counted my ribs and caressed my mound, memorizing me again.

My fingertips trailed across his chest and down his biceps. I explored each feature of his face—his black eyes deep as a desert well, his sharp cheekbones, his proud nose with narrow nostrils. Even the hard lines etched around his perfectly carved mouth were beautiful to me.

He lifted strands of my hair and pulled them through his lips. Once he held a curl under his nose and inhaled deeply.

"I have never seen hair such as yours—like spun gold, but alive."

He bent and kissed me tenderly and then tickled the end of my nose with the lock of my hair.

"I had to see you," he said simply, switching to Egyptian.

I was afraid to ask why he was in Alexandria, afraid he would tell me that it was for his 'cause' and that I was a convenience he worked into his schedule.

"How is the slave boy?" he asked idly.

I considered telling him, but I'd vowed to tell no one. I had to think of Jason. The abbreviated truth served me well.

"He is no longer with me."

"That surprises me. I thought you would never part from him."

"I do not wish to speak of it."

He looked hard at me for a moment, and I thought he might ask more. But instead, he went back to memorizing with his eyes and his fingers. I felt him grow hard again.

"Your body is fuller now," he teased. "Did we not feed you enough on the ship?"

His harsh face was so tender in that moment, I wanted more than anything to believe he was the father.

"I am with child," I said, bracing myself for his questions.

"You are carrying my son?"

His reaction astonished me; he immediately assumed the child was his—and a boy.

"She might be a girl," I dared to suggest. But relief washed over me that he had no questions for which I had no answers.

A rapping on the door signaled it was time for me to leave. He said nothing about when I might see him again. Goliath had to peel me from his arms.

"Tell no one about tonight. No one," Black Falcon warned. "For me, for you—and for the life of my son."

The door closed between us, and I followed Scarface down the narrow, winding streets still jammed with Egyptians.

Ajax must have stood alert waiting for me, as the door opened only a moment after I knocked and called out to him.

"Welcome home, Mistress," he said a little too urgently.

"Has something more happened?" I asked.

"Hektor of Naukratis called this evening. I informed him that you were at the Library."

"Did he leave a message?"

"No, Mistress, he did not."

He avoided my eyes, but it didn't require great skill to see he had something to say.

"So what is it, Ajax? Speak freely."

"My impression is that he was not pleased."

Hektor. Not easily fooled.

"Thank you. I have no further need of you tonight," I said without comment on Hektor. "You may retire to your quarters."

He bowed his head lower than usual and made to leave the entry hall. "Ajax."

He stopped and turned, daring finally to look directly at me.

"What happened today was a terrible thing. My heart is broken that Jason is gone. But it is not your fault. Carthaginians do not make worthy house slaves."

It was really quite painful to see his relief.

CHAPTER 30 SUMMONS

"You will never do anything in this world without courage." – Aristotle

R ising early, I attended to paperwork and prepared a list of chores for Platon. Nausea came, and I vomited once.

The dressing slaves took special pains to apply powder to the bruises, arranging an emerald green silk scarf around my neck and shoulders—without comment, of course. The marks could be from Hektor or Antinous. I was often alone with either one of them.

The swelling in my hands was less, and for the first time in days, I slipped the Hathor ring from the *agora* onto my middle finger.

"Health and good wishes," greeted Platon. "I am pleased to see the Lady is herself today."

"Thank you. The loss of a slave boy cannot delay our work. It is the will of the Goddess that he be gone. How else could it have happened? The wishes of men are different from what the Gods dispose. Who are we to understand Their plan?"

Antinous was buried in scrolls. They covered his desk in multiple layers and tumbled to the marble tiles. Above the shelves behind him, inscribed in stone, were the words of Sophocles. WHO SEEKS SHALL FIND.

I wondered that he could find anything in the disorder, but when an assistant appeared with a request, he put his hand immediately on the relevant papyrus and handed it over without a glance.

"A waste of time and money," he grumbled.

He pored over a large drawing of an enormous warship with five banks of oars on each side.

"Four hundred and twenty feet long! Impossible! The engineering is all wrong. A ridiculous folly. It will never leave the harbor but will sink immediately. Ptolemy should stick to writing bad plays and leave the navy alone."

Two assistants in short chitons hurried back and forth, bringing new scrolls and taking away others.

At last we were alone.

"Antinous, I have remembered something Qeb-ha told me."

He looked up, mildly astonished I was still there.

"Qeb-ha?" he asked with a blank look in his eyes.

"I told you about him. The old Egyptian priest who knows more than anyone about the Emerald Tablet?"

Antinous put down his stylus; I finally had his attention.

"Qeb-ha insists that Alexander received the Tablet from the Oracle of Siwa before going on to conquer Persia and the Indus Valley."

"Siwa? Here in Egypt?"

"Yes. Perhaps there we can discover the missing component."

"It is a hard journey, Athena—several days across the desert, to the west and then south. You must consult the physician before you travel."

"I am not fragile, Antinous; I shall not break. Can you arrange everything for me?"

I took his writing hand in both of mine. He almost pulled it away in surprise, but in the end, he only blinked and then focused on me. I had the impression that for once, he was one hundred percent present.

"I believe it best, Antinous, if you do not travel with me. You are next in line for Director of the Library. You must not jeopardize your life work."

"Every end does not appear with its beginning, Athena. As Heraclitus teaches, big results require big risks. I go with you. There is no purpose in further discussion."

"And of all possessions a friend is the most precious." I squeezed his hand in gratitude and let it go. "Thank you."

With that, he smiled absentmindedly and went back to his work.

We lunched together in his office fountain courtyard under a broad trellis overgrown with grape wines. His personal slave served much-diluted Delta wine with grilled eel, fresh goat cheese and ripe olives. We dipped bread, hot from the oven, in olive oil and sea salt.

We both missed Jason. Antinous was pensive; a cloud of sadness hung over him that I hadn't seen in his office. I believe he threw himself into his work to keep his emotions in check.

The beautiful youth, who Antinous introduced as Leandros, *lion-man*, joined us for mint tea.

Antinous and he talked as easily as two brothers. They often touched each other, not in an overly affectionate way, but communicating a deep intimacy.

Leandros was clever and witty with a ready laugh, wise in spite of his age, which I guessed to be about sixteen. When he turned his clear blue eyes on me, my heart actually skipped a beat. I thought again of Alexander and the legendary power of his eyes described as blue fire.

I had thought perfection defined by Antinous, but Leandros was without flaw. I surrendered all thought of competing with him. I couldn't offer what he offered—their Y chromosomes spoke to each other in a way I never could.

I felt quite left out until Antinous took my hand and told Leandros that I was the most intelligent woman he had ever met. Always that qualifier—*woman*.

"Mistress!" Ajax appeared suddenly. "A message from the Pharaoh. He requires your presence at the Palace at once."

Leandros jumped to his feet.

"I shall find Hektor of Naukratis to accompany you, Lady. Please remain in this courtyard until we return."

I didn't think twice about obeying a sixteen year-old boy. I hadn't thought of Hektor—I hadn't thought of anything except escaping through the Red Mirror.

We didn't wait long for Leandros to return with Hektor drenched in sweat. When in Alexandria, he exercised daily at the *Musaeum,* and Leandros had known exactly where to find him.

A slave quickly wiped the sweat from Hektor's muscles; a clean chiton appeared. The sponge bath and change of dress took place in the courtyard without awkwardness. There was much discussion with various theories about why I was being summoned, none of them reassuring.

I couldn't stop thinking of Arsinoë's warning of plots against me.

"Life must be lived as a play," Hektor said without his usual levity. "This is only the next act."

His uncharacteristic solemn tone made me more anxious.

He took hold of my chin and looked me in the eyes. "Courage is knowing what not to fear, Athena of Korinth. You are the Supreme Priestess of Aphrodite and beyond the Pharaoh's reach."

We arrived at the palace and were admitted at once into the Presence Chamber. The Lord Chancellor Sosibius stood on the right side of Ptolemy's throne and the Royal Steward Agathon on the left.

The porter announced, "Athena of Korinth."

The room stilled, and every head turned toward in my direction.

Ptolemy beckoned me forward with a hand covered in rings. He wore a traditional Pharaoh's headdress crowned with the heads of a cobra and a vulture; his eyes were outlined in *kohl* in the Egyptian fashion.

I hoped I didn't visibly tremble. Surely the Pharaoh wouldn't make this fuss over a missing slave boy. I steeled myself but was still unprepared for what came next.

"Welcome, Athena of Korinth. We have great news."

I waited. Great news?

"We have captured the rebel Black Falcon."

I prayed my face didn't show my shock or give away my terror.

When I didn't answer, he demanded, "Well, Athena of Korinth, have you nothing to say? Are you not overjoyed that your tormentor is to be punished?"

"I but wonder what role Your Majesty envisions for me. I care nothing for politics. My life is the Goddess."

I could see he was irritated at my dispassionate reaction to his momentous news.

"We have summoned you to identify him as the man who held you hostage."

If they needed me to confirm his identity, they might not have captured Black Falcon after all! I held my hands together to control their shaking.

"As always, I am at Your Majesty's disposal."

Two Royal Guards dragged forward a tall, slim, muscular man in chains and dropped him to his knees ten feet away. They pulled his head back. He had been beaten so brutally, there was little left of his face. I turned away quickly and struggled to mask my horror.

"I do not recognize this man." It was easy to lie when my words were so close to the truth.

A loud murmur rippled through the Presence Chamber.

"Look again," Ptolemy commanded.

"I must ask for Your Majesty's forbearance. I wish not to look upon this man's dreadful face. The Goddess deplores violence."

The murmur grew louder. Ptolemy shifted on his throne; I kept my eyes fixed on him, blocking out everyone else.

The evil Sosibius handed something to a slave, who in turn brought it to me. I glanced at it briefly. It was the Hathor ring Black Falcon had taken from me on the ship. The slave held the ring out to me for an awkward moment, but I refused to take it.

"Is this not the ring the Pharaoh gifted you in Korinth?" Agathon demanded. "How do you explain that it was found on this Egyptian when captured?"

"I know nothing of this ring. The ring I was given in Korinth is on my finger as it is every day."

I raised my hand for all to see. The room buzzed louder than a hive. The sergeant-at-arms pounded the staff of his spear on the marble floor and bellowed, "Order!"

Sosibius and Agathon first looked stunned and then confused. Sweat beaded on their brows.

"How can there be two rings?" hissed Ptolemy. "What does this mean?"

The chamber buzzed again as Ptolemy's question of two rings repeated from person to person.

"Silence!" roared the sergeant-at-arms. The hall resounded again with the crack of his staff on stone.

Herodotus wrote that the best men reflect on everything that can happen but are bold in the moment of action. I dared to speak without being addressed.

"I do not understand why there are two rings, Your Majesty. But I have absolute faith in the authenticity of the ring that I wear. The Goddess sees all. She would have revealed to me—and most certainly to Your Grace—if my ring were a forgery."

The three of them, Ptolemy, Sosibius and Agathon, stared at me as if I spoke a language they had never heard.

"Would Your Majesty care to examine my ring to assure himself?"

Ptolemy no longer sat up straight on the throne but slumped back. He stared at me with cold, serpent eyes. I'd bested him, and we both knew it.

There wasn't a sound in the Presence Chamber until Sosibius snapped his fingers and waved impatiently to the slave, commanding, "Give me the pirate's ring."

When the slave crossed over the marble with the Hathor ring, Sosibius made a grand show of examining it carefully.

"Clearly this ring is a forgery," he declared. "The gold is not pure, and the quality of the workmanship is inferior. I assure Your Majesty that the man who appraised this copy shall be punished."

Ptolemy leaned forward; in a trick of the light, his eyes yellowed, taking on the color of the eyes of the leopards chained at his feet. If I had not been a Supreme Priestess, he would have ordered me killed in that moment for the sheer pleasure of it.

"We hear that your precious slave boy—*Our Omen of Good Fortune*—has been kidnapped. We wonder what portent the Goddess gives to *that?*"

"As Your Majesty, of course, is aware," I said in a matter-of-fact tone, "kidnapping is common among the Gods. We mortals cannot guess what jealousies motivate the Immortals. The weak accept what they must endure."

Managing a small shrug of false resignation, I continued, "I have accepted what the Goddess has ordained. I have relinquished my anger. The Gods first make angry those They wish to destroy."

I hardly recognized my calm and logical voice. I spoke as if everything I said was such common sense that no thinking man could dispute it.

"Athena of Korinth is well-schooled that the wise words of philosophers are so ready on her lips," snarled Ptolemy. "What think you of the words of Sophocles that the oaths of a woman are inscribed on water?"

"I think that even a woman recognizes much wisdom goes with fewest words."

Ptolemy snorted and sank back into his throne. He challenged me no more, and I was dismissed at last. I didn't look again at battered Black Falcon.

Hektor stepped out from the audience and took my arm.

"Allow me, Supreme Priestess, to escort you to your apartments."

I felt every eye in the room follow us until the tall gilt doors closed. If all of Alexandria hadn't known of Hektor's attachment to me before, it did now.

My hands shook. My knees shook. My whole body trembled. I smelled the acrid stench of my nervous sweat. Without Hektor, I'm not sure I could have stood upright.

He didn't speak until we were clear of the long corridor and well into the reception gardens.

"You may not take an interest in politics, Athena of Korinth, but that does not keep politics from taking an interest in you."

"What will happen to the captive? Will he be killed?"

"Death is not the worst that can happen to a man."

My nausea came back full force.

We didn't speak again until at my villa. My mind reeled at the capture of Black Falcon and the horrible beating he'd endured. As hard as I tried, I couldn't erase the image of him on his knees, chained, face battered beyond recognition.

Hektor's face was as serious as I'd ever seen it; there was not a trace of his confident smile. First he touched the gleaming garnet in the snake bracelet, and then the lapis lazuli stone of my Hathor ring. He toyed briefly with the green silk covering the bruises on my neck.

"I cannot begin to guess what games you play, Athena, but they are dangerous. I advise you to restrict your movements to your quarters until I return."

He kissed me lightly on the lips, holding my chin with his fingers. I looked him straight in the eye, not blinking, trying to muster innocence, trying not to show him anything.

"You hide many secrets behind those emerald eyes. I ask you no questions, as you tell me only what you want me to know. I shall do everything I can to protect you, but do not make my task too difficult."

As soon as he left, I called for Ajax.

"We go to the agora."

CHAPTER 31   OKTODRACHMA

"Make me useful to my friends, rather than agreeable." – Crates

The Old Jew, called Isaac I'd discovered, was in his usual place, reclining among his carpets and smoking his pipe. He waved for tea as soon as I entered.

After instructing Ajax to wait outside, I came straight to the point and skipped all the niceties of wishing each other peace and inquiring of health and family.

"I need to speak with Eben."

"He is at his work in the Library," Isaac replied in the calmest of voices. If I were anxious and hurried, he would not let it affect him.

"The Library?" My surprise at this news pulled me off purpose for an instant. This was the first I'd heard of Eben in connection with the *Musaeum*. I had never seen him there, but then it was a large campus with dozens of buildings.

"He works on the translation of the Torah of Moses from Hebrew to Greek."

The old man must have seen my puzzlement because he went on to say, "The five sacred books of the Torah tell the story of our people from the first day of creation."

"I must go," I said rudely.

I had only to find Eben at the Library, and he could take me to Qeb-ha. There was a time when Qeb-ha could see the future. And the future was exactly what I needed to see. Now.

Isaac continued to spew meaningless words in spite of my standing to leave.

"It was the Pharaoh's grandfather, Ptolemy II, who commissioned the translation. He desired the Library to have a copy of every book ever written, no matter the origin."

"I apologize, but I cannot stay. I must speak with Eben."

"Eben can wait," he said, motioning with his whisk for me to sit again. "Please take some tea, Athena of Korinth. Humor an old man bored with his day among dusty relics and old carpets."

I reluctantly retook my seat. My mind raced. I could appeal to Qeb-ha; he would help me save a fellow Egyptian. O Aphrodite, please! Someone, somewhere had to help me.

I wasn't listening to old Isaac's chatter until I heard 'Black Falcon.'

"What! What did you say?"

"The market is full of news about the capture of the Black Falcon," he repeated.

I held my breath and watched his fleshy lips, surrounded by thick gray hair, open and close to form words. I forced myself to concentrate to make sense of them.

"He was captured before dawn in Rhakotis, the Egyptian Quarter. No one understands why he dared enter the city. There has been a price on his head for years. You can trust no one in the Rhakotis; there are spies everywhere."

I had to see you.

I leaned forward and put my head on my knees. Had I been followed last night? Were his brutalized face and broken body my fault? He hadn't sent my Hathor ring with the ransom letter but carried it on him. He'd risked everything for *me*.

My eyes must have been filled with terror when I raised them.

"What will they do to him?" I whispered.

"He shall die, of course. But in what manner? He is surely be tortured to death. The Pharaoh employs Persians for that task. If torture is his sentence, it shall take place in public, perhaps in the *Hippodrome* before a crowd. The Pharaoh is fond of that."

I sobbed out loud. Isaac whisked at a fly and drew more smoke from his pipe.

"There can be another possibility for convicted criminals."

I stared at him, daring to hope that he meant to tell me of a more merciful end.

"It is the custom to give criminals to the Medical Akademy for use in vivisection."

"Vivisection?" I mouthed.

"Yes, they dissect living beings to advance the science of anatomy. The practice is forbidden by most religions—and abhorred by other Greeks. But no one objects to the knowledge gained from the research."

I vomited my tea on the plush wool carpet at my feet. Had the physician who treated me after Ptolemy's feast performed such abominations in the name of his science?

The outcome promised to be more horrible than my worst imaginings. I couldn't string two coherent thoughts together. Monstrous images of ripped-open ribs and beating hearts played over and over in my mind.

"I-I really have to go now," I stammered as I stumbled to my feet. My head was down, and hair fell around my face. I forced myself to breathe slowly and deeply.

Isaac placed a leather thong bracelet with a tiny pouch in my sweating palm.

"A few drops and it is quickly over."

My head came up.

"Go in peace, my child."

He went back to his pipe and even closed his eyes as if to nap.

I went straight to the Library with Ajax hurrying to keep up. After several inquiries, I found an annex filled with cubicles where seventy Jewish scholars each independently translated the Torah. Eben hunched over a small cypress table with a stylus in his hand. So different than Antinous, his desk held only two scrolls—one that he read from and one on which he wrote.

He sent his assistant away, and we were alone.

"I need Qeb-ha to tell me the future."

"You already know it."

"Do not say that. There must be something I can do."

"You cannot alter the outcome, Lady, but you can affect the means."

"Is there no hope, no hope at all?"

When he didn't answer, I leaned back on my stool and squeezed my eyelids to stop the tears. A crushed Black Falcon swirled among uncoiling intestines and exposed lungs. I didn't know if I would ever be able to close my eyes again.

"The Tablet. Do not forget the Tablet!" Eben warned. "Remember Qeb-ha's words. You *must* fulfill your destiny."

"Qeb-ha is no use to me! He gives me no guidance."

"You are the Chosen One. The Light is revealed only to you."

As usual, Antinous worked at a desk piled high with papyri. I quite startled him by rushing into his office without knocking.

"Where is the prison for a condemned man?" I didn't bother greeting him.

He looked up, a little open-mouthed. I'm sure my eyes were wild with panic.

"There are several. The specific one might depend upon the crime. Why do you ask?"

I couldn't tell him why I wanted to know, but not because I didn't trust him. I already trusted him with the Tablet. Antinous could not be privy to anything I was about to do; he already risked too much.

"Do not ask me," I answered.

Antinous put down his scroll and leaned back into his hard-backed ebony chair. He studied me for a moment with eyes that seemed never to have known deceit before knowing me.

"I cannot help you unless you tell me whom you seek. I can only give you possibilities which would be of no practical assistance. If I know the name, I can make inquiries."

I was tempted to confide in him but decided that for the sake of the Tablet, Antinous had to be protected from all else.

"No, Antinous," I said firmly. "I cannot tell you."

The sun was setting; the harbor and the sea beyond began their daily transformation through a pastel palette. I saw no beauty in the calm sea and cloudless sky; I saw only Black Falcon and the nightmare that awaited him.

As ever, the Pharos burned bright at the mouth of the Great Harbor. If only I could sail back to those golden days when I bathed each morning in the sea and tasted Black Falcon each night.

Out of desperation, I sent a message with Ajax to the Queen and lay on my divan on the balcony to wait. The first stars came out. Kallisto played with the silvery ties of my chiton and tried to gnaw on the leather thong bracelet with the deadly vial.

Ajax was quick to return. The Queen had been in her apartments preparing for a feast at the Palace; she agreed to see me if I came at once. Ajax already had my dark green cape in his hand.

The opulence of marble, flower and fountain of the Queen's terrace overlooking the sea would have awed me if I had not been in such a frantic state of mind.

Arsinoë appeared in a cloud of shimmering golden cloth that looked as if spun on Mt. Olympus. I don't know how she stood upright under the weight of her gold and jewels. She wore a shoulder-length black wig twisted with gold; each braid ended in a tiny ball encrusted with jewels. Her eyes were outlined in *kohl* and her lips darkened with carmine. In the shadows, she was ageless.

With one look at my distressed face, she said, "This does not concern the Emerald Tablet, does it?"

"No, it does not. But still, will you help me?"

She guided me by the elbow to a far balcony, away from eyes and ears. The waves of the sea crashed against the rocks below. I detected impatience below the surface; she was dressed in her best finery and expected elsewhere.

"Do you know where they keep the prisoner who was in the Presence Chamber today?" I asked.

"You mean the rebel Black Falcon?"

I opened my mouth to refute the man was Black Falcon, but she interrupted, "Do not pretend with me. We have no time for that."

She gripped my arm so tightly, her long hennaed nails dug into my skin.

"There is no hope for his escape. Do not even think of it."

"I must see him one last time. Can you understand that? Did you not wish to comfort Magas? Did you not long to ease his agony?"

When I said her brother's name, she dropped my arm and leaned against the carved railing. Her eyes closed. The night was balmy, without any chill. The shimmering folds of her caftan were liquid gold in the sea breeze.

High in the sky, Jupiter glowed. Would the planet of good fortune smile on me tonight? In the distance, a night dove cooed. Hunting dogs bayed somewhere on the Palace grounds.

I thought of dropping to my knees and grabbing hers, begging her to help. But she spoke before I could make my next desperate move.

"Wait here. Send your slave away."

Ajax was reluctant to leave, but I told him the Queen had invited me to stay.

"Go back, Ajax, and tell the others I am safe and well. The Queen will send me home with an escort."

An eternity passed before Arsinoë returned with a short, stocky man in a black tunic and cape. A black turban coiled around his head; the black beard on his chin ended in a point. His hard, obsidian eyes glittered in the starlight.

"Follow him," she told me. "Obey him without question."

I nodded, holding back tears. *O Aphrodite! Thank You for Your Grace.*

"You shall need this."

She handed me a soft suede pouch with drawstrings. I heard the clink of heavy coin when I tucked the bag into a hidden pocket sewn in the folds of my chiton.

"*Oktodrachmas*," she explained. "It will be expensive."

The black-robed man was leading me away when the Arsinoë grabbed my upper arm and hissed into my ear.

"I shall deny everything. You were never here."

CHAPTER 32   EMERALD SCARF

"Extreme remedies are very appropriate for extreme diseases." – Hippocrates

We left the Queen's gardens by a small postern in the wall, far from the main gates and well-hidden by overgrown jasmine. Within minutes, we were at the Gate of the Moon with the Royal Harbor on one side and the Street of the Soma on the other.

We didn't enter the city but waited in the shadows by the gate. Soldiers stood guard, but not seriously. They joked with each other about a Thracian woman at the docks they had both enjoyed the night before.

The black-turbaned man never spoke, but used hand signals to guide me. I took his cue and was as quiet as possible, fearful of breathing too loud. The eerie cry of an alley cat echoed from down a narrow shadowy lane between two bulky marble buildings. He motioned for me to follow, and we moved toward the sound.

Another man, tall and thin, waited. He also wore a black turban and cape, but his beard was dyed indigo blue. They spoke in low tones; I understood nothing. I had never heard their language before. It was guttural, maybe a dialect of Arabic, certainly nothing like Greek. The first man held out his palm and wiggled his fingers.

I took out an *oktodrachma* and put it in his hand. He waved his fingers again. Metal clinked in the dead silence of the alley when I placed two more coins in his palm. If not for the Arsinoë's protection, I'm certain they would have slit my throat and taken the whole purse.

He disappeared, and I was left with Blue Beard. I had no choice but to follow him into the night.

A small boat moored to a short jetty bobbed in the gentle waves. We climbed aboard. Blue Beard began to row. The blades slid in and out of the water noiselessly, although the squeak of the oarlocks deafened me. No one else was on the water.

The island prison lay just offshore. I had seen it every day from my balcony as I reclined on my sofa, eating my breakfast, enjoying the change of colors on the water. Never had I dreamed of the horrors that went on there.

There was nothing unsavory to see from the outside. A low building of marble with the usual columns and statues rose a few feet from the beach. We didn't tie onto the dock but came ashore in a tiny cove on the far side of the island. The rocks were steep; Blue Beard took my arm to drag me up. I tripped once on my long cape, but he kept me on my feet. When his cape opened, I saw the flash of steel in his belt.

He wiggled his fingers and wasn't satisfied until I placed six coins in his square palm. Would he now leave me, too, for yet another man to appear in black turban and cape?

I waited in the dark of the portico. Somewhere I heard laughter broken by the excited shout of a gambler. I couldn't make out how many voices. My heart hammered in my chest. Dry as the desert, my mouth had no saliva when I tried to moisten my lips. I couldn't swallow; an invisible giant hand gripped my throat, allowing nothing to pass.

When Blue Beard came back, he put his finger to his lips and signaled for me to follow. Glued to the walls of the villa, we moved silently toward a lighted open doorway. Laughter erupted from inside. From the sound of their voices, the men were deep in their cups. I heard the clink of dice, followed by more shouts.

A few yards before the light, we entered a small doorway that opened onto a narrow stone corridor. At the top of steps leading into blackness, a bulky guard with massive thighs and biceps stepped into our path. I pulled the folds of my hood over my face; the dark green cloak hid everything except the tips of my sandals.

Blue Beard signaled I should go with the guard and ducked into an alcove to wait. I could only hope he would be there on my return.

The guard stopped at the bottom of steps slippery from sea damp and moss. My nausea came back in force at the mixed stench of urine, feces, blood and rot.

He motioned for me to hold out my hands. When he started to untie the bracelet with the vial of poison that would end Black Falcon's suffering, I grabbed his wrist and pleaded, "No!"

But he peeled my fingers loose, and I was forced to let him fumble at the knot until the thong fell from my wrist and the tiny pouch into his hand.

O Aphrodite! Please do not forsake me—not after coming this far.

Then he opened my cloak and ran his hands quickly over my body, not out of lust, but to see if I carried a weapon. He grunted when he felt the weight of my purse. My hands shook so hard, I don't know how I opened the pouch to give him three heavy coins. Apparently satisfied, he grunted again and motioned for me to follow.

The gate to the damp cell was not locked. I thought the creak of the iron hinges more deafening that the oarlocks on the boat. High up near the ceiling, a tiny window with iron bars let in the sounds of the sea. I caught a whiff of salt over the foul odor of blood and urine. Shadows flickered on the wet walls from a single torch burning outside the cell.

"Alone," I insisted.

The guard grunted again and shrugged his shoulders. I heard his heavy footfall on the stairs.

Black Falcon was chained to the wall at a height that didn't allow him to sit. I thought he was unconscious until I was next to him, and he turned his battered face toward me. I think he was blind. It was impossible to see if he had eyes. But he had a tongue.

"You?" he mumbled in a wondering tone.

I don't know how he knew.

"Me." I said simply, kissing his chest and tasting dried blood.

Hundreds of slits covered his skin. I stifled a sob.

"Let me smell you," he pleaded. "Let me smell your hair."

I lowered my hood and raised a lock of hair to his once proud nose, now smashed into his face. I couldn't imagine he could smell anything but blood. The lips I worshipped, now mangled and bleeding, parted to show shattered gums where teeth used to be.

"Don't raise my son a Greek," he slurred. "Promise me."

"I promise," I whispered into his ear. I felt his agony right through to my bones.

We had little time. Every moment I was here was too long. I looked frantically around the cell to see anything I could use, but there was nothing. The chains at his wrists and the shackles at his ankles were too short to reach his neck.

I slid off the emerald silk scarf that covered the bruises from the General's fingers and quickly formed a loop. The tears streamed down my face as I slipped it over his head.

"Forgive me, my love," I begged him.

I yanked with all my strength. I pulled with every muscle in my body. He thrashed back and forth, but he didn't cry out. I think I pulled too tightly for him to scream.

He fought me. He struggled for his life with what little strength he had, kicking his legs in wild spasms and jerks. His bloodied feet rose and fell on the floor, first one then the other. Bits of foul dusty straw flew in the air when his legs crashed down and bounced up again.

Then finally, his heels digging and sliding in the filthy straw, he slowed. Terrible gagging sounds came from his open mouth, and I thought the guard would surely come.

Desperate to end it, I braced one foot against the wet wall next to him and leaned backward, using the wall as leverage, pulling with everything I had. My foot slipped in the slime; I stumbled once, and then regained my footing.

"Please let go," I pleaded. "Give in. *Please* give in!"

His arms twisted in the shackles above his head, and his legs still jerked in the chains. He wouldn't stop trying to draw breath. I willed him to surrender as I heaved harder. My whole body trembled; the muscles in my arms and thighs quivered uncontrollably. Choking back tears, I myself struggled to breathe.

"We shall be together again, I promise you. Please go now."

He shuddered. Both legs jerked at the same time. Then his right leg twitched once and went limp. His whole body went limp. Black Falcon, at last, was still.

I could scarcely see through my tears as I fumbled with the green scarf, sliding it from his neck and twisting it back around mine. The silk burned hot against my skin.

I doubled over from the pain in my chest. A vivisection surgeon's knife at the Medical Akademy might have opened my ribs and ripped out my living heart. Clenching my fists to stop my shaking hands, I swallowed the vomit in my mouth.

But Black Falcon felt pain no more. I touched his fractured face and bloodied lips one last time with my fingertips. He was at peace; his soul had passed into another dimension. How many lifetimes would go by before I would meet him as Rasheed?

The guard was coming down when I started up the steps. He looked past me into the cell. From where we stood, Black Falcon looked as he had when I entered—unconscious.

My hands shook so hard when I handed him the pouch with the remaining coins, that I was sure he would suspect something. But he only grunted and led me up to the corridor where Blue Beard waited.

The moment we pulled into the small jetty on the mainland, Blue Beard stepped up onto the wood planking to secure the line. Like Eben in a Kabbalah trance, I rocked back and forth on the hard bench, misery racking my body. The sea, the city and the sky disappeared. I saw only nightmare images of Black Falcon fighting for his last breath.

The scuffle brought me back. A thick figure of a man pinned Blue Beard to his chest. The curved steel of a sword flashed as it rose and then, quick as lightning, slashed Blue Beard's throat.

The spray of blood flew over my head; hot drops fell on my upturned face. When his body splashed into the water, cool droplets from the sea rained down on me. A scream ripped through my throat but was instantly muffled by a giant hand across my mouth. How could the man move so quickly from the jetty to the boat?

"Do not scream, Ishtar. The guards will be upon us at once."

The General!

"Why?" I whispered into his hand. "Why did you kill him?"

I looked around the dock.

"Where is Jason?"

"Jason is safe," he growled. "I am taking you to him."

"No! You do not understand. There is something I must do."

But the General was already lifting me from the boat. I pounded him with my fists and threw my body from side to side. When the little boat tipped and the sea poured in, he almost lost his footing.

"Do not make me hurt you," he warned.

He dragged me onto the jetty where I sank to my knees, refusing to walk.

"You are going with us," he hissed. His eyes were wild, like a crazed animal. "I am taking Jason and you to Carthage."

"No! You cannot have me. I am not yours."

He dragged me a few feet and then tossed me over his shoulder with no more effort than a sack of grain. I dug at his back with my nails, but I was only a fly on the hide of an elephant.

Hanging upside down, I lost my bearing, but I think we headed toward the main moorage. Once I was on a ship bound for Carthage, there would be no escape. I reached up and back to rip at his ear.

He dropped me on the ground and seized me by the throat. My hood slipped off; my hair was silver in the starlight against his dark skin.

"If you do not come with me, I shall kill Jason," he threatened.

I glared at him, and after a moment of hesitation, he loosened his grip.

"You would not kill your son. Do not threaten me with that."

Whack!

The General tumbled to his side, dark blood gushing from his temple. I caught a movement as someone swung to hit him again.

"Stop!" I shouted. "Do not kill him!"

Only the General knew where Jason was.

The club halted in mid-air.

I jumped to my feet to confront the attacker. Goliath! I threw my arms around his waist and buried my face in his chest.

The General moaned; he was not dead. Goliath and I dragged him behind a stack of *amphorae*. I took off the green scarf I had used to end Black Falcon's agony and dabbed at the wound on the General's head. The bleeding was already subsiding. I bound it tight, and the General opened his eyes. My face was inches from his, as close as in the storeroom of my villa, so close I again could see the tiny capillaries in the whites.

"Not now, General," I whispered. "Our time has not come."

Goliath pulled me to my feet and hurried me along the docks.

"He will have but a bad headache," the Nubian assured me. "He will walk away long before dawn."

I felt the General's eyes on me until we turned into the shadows of the warehouses.

Goliath knew his way around Alexandria; we sped through dark side streets and alleys. When he stopped, we were far from the docks and near the Gate of the Moon.

"I have followed you all evening," he said in his heavy Greek, "but could not tell who was friend or foe. I waited not far from the jetty, until a patrol of soldiers showed up, and I had to hide in an alley."

I put one hand on his massive forearm and the other on his cheek.

"He suffers no more." I said in Egyptian.

He didn't realize right away what I meant. Only when I nodded slowly to encourage him, caressing his cheek as one would a child, his eyes opened so wide that I could see white all around the black. He took my hand from his face and put it to his heart.

"The Gods bless you, Lady," he sobbed, slumping into my arms.

I thought he might wither before my eyes; he seemed already to have shrunk to half his size.

"Take me home, Goliath," I said softly. Then I took his hand in mine to lead the way.

Hektor and Antinous waited for me upstairs in my private rooms. Both looked dumbfounded when I entered my bedchamber with blood-soaked Goliath.

My cloak was soiled with human filth and wet from the sea. My hair flew in all directions; dried blood splattered my face and neck. I had held myself together through the dark gardens and pathways, but when I saw the two of them, I began to shake uncontrollably.

Hektor stripped my cape away and wrapped a wool shawl around my shoulders. He removed my filthy sandals and washed all traces of blood and grime from my face. He even tidied my hair before shouting for slaves to come draw a bath.

Antinous sent for boiling water to make one of the physician's infusions.

I perched on the edge of my bed and stared at the Red Mirror. *Now. Now would be good.*

The dressing slaves removed my gown and helped me into the warm, scented water. Goliath stood in profile at the entry to my bedchamber, careful not to look at me in the bath. Antinous paced the balcony.

Hektor watched me from a tripod stool, sitting bent forward, elbows on his thighs, boat feet spread apart, hands clasped between his open legs. He stared at the fresh bruises on my body and neck while the slave girl combed out my hair and piled it on top of my head with ivory pins.

"Leave us," he ordered.

The slaves looked at me. I nodded yes, and they slipped away.

"Well," Hektor demanded. "Are you going to tell us where you have been?"

I shook my head.

"Damn you, woman!" he snapped, jumping to his feet.

The tripod stool tipped over, hitting the arabesque tiles with a resounding crash. Before the stool had hit the ground, Goliath pivoted toward Hektor, drawing the curved dagger from the belt of his bloodied tunic.

"No, Goliath!" I commanded in Egyptian. "He intends me no harm."

Antinous rushed in from the balcony and gripped Hektor's shoulder.

"Can you not see her distress? Give her time, man. Give her time."

When I nodded to Goliath, he stepped back to the doorway and turned his face away again.

"There are things you cannot know, Hektor." My voice sounded flat and dead to my ear, but there was no mistaking my conviction. "Nothing you say or do can convince me otherwise."

"I insist that you come back to Naukratis with me tonight."

"I shall not."

"You *must.* I cannot protect you here."

"And how shall you introduce me to your wife?"

He didn't have a quick answer or, if he did, he didn't voice it. It turned out, though, that he had a surprise ally in Antinous.

"Hektor is right, Athena. It would be most prudent for you to leave Alexandria. You can be safe under Hektor's protection."

"But I thought *we* were leaving, Antinous."

I'd counted on going to Siwa as soon as possible, even as early as the next day. Once I had met with the Oracle of Amun, I could say goodbye forever to Alexandria and the Ptolemies.

"Not yet, Athena. I cannot leave my duties on such short notice," Antinous reasoned. "Go with Hektor. For now. For a few days. Give me time to arrange what I must."

It was then I made my decision.

"May I have some privacy?" I asked politely. "Please take the Nubian and wait in my reception room. Ask for food and drink for him. I need only a few moments to pack."

CHAPTER 33   NYHAVN

"I like not this great success of yours, for I know how jealous are the Gods."
– Herodotus

Icame back in an instant and with relief. I may not have learned how to activate the power of the Tablet, but it was time to get out of Alexandria. *The Light is revealed to you.* The Light told me to come back, and I listened.

Besides, I didn't want to meet Hektor's wife. I didn't want to be an unwelcome guest in her home.

My cell phone had the usual missed calls from unknown numbers, one from Tony, two from the General and many from Barb. But the ones from Barb stopped yesterday. There were no calls from Hector.

"I figured you went back to Alexandria when you didn't pick up or return my messages." Her voice was flat. She sounded as if she'd given up on me. Maybe she even sounded tired.

"How did you come back without me?" She hadn't entirely given up; she was still curious.

I told her about finding the Red Mirror in the agora, and then about meeting Eben, Qeb-ha, the General, and Isabel.

"I got pregnant again, Barb. No one seems to think of birth control. At least, I didn't."

"Who's the father this time?"

"I'm not sure if it was Black Falcon or Hektor."

"No DNA testing, I guess," she answered.

I saved the part about Black Falcon's death until the end. I knew she wouldn't hear anything else after that.

I called Tony next. He talked about New York. He said he hadn't laughed so hard in years—not since his wife first got sick. *He's lonely.* When he asked if I had heard from Hector and I said no, he sounded disappointed and glad at the same time.

"The man's a fool if he lets you go. Do you want me to call him?"

"I don't think that's such a good idea."

I kept the conversation light. The less Tony knew, the better for him. We ended with a promise to keep in touch but no fixed commitment. I didn't offer, and Tony didn't press.

The General answered right away. He sounded relieved to hear from me.

"A piece has come up on the market unexpectedly. I want you to acquire it."

I started to protest, but he stopped me.

"Listen first, then decide."

I breathed out.

"It's a Hathor ring, Ishtar. I've been after it for years, but it's been in a private collection."

"Hathor ring?" I repeated, not quite able to believe one still existed.

"It's going on auction in Copenhagen. I have already arranged your flight and a hotel. Can you leave tonight?"

"Tonight? No. I just got back."

I waited for the General to ask from where, but he didn't.

"Would you feel differently if I told you that Rasheed is rumored to be going? Apparently he also wants the ring."

He chuckled when he heard me take a sharp intake of air.

"Your ticket is in your email. I'll be adding a nice bonus for the short notice."

I hardly heard what he said. I was stuck back on the news about Rasheed.

"Have a good trip, Ishtar."

I didn't know I'd decided to go until I found myself googling Copenhagen weather. It was still cold there, freezing at night. When I called Sonny, he laughed and asked if I wanted him to adopt Aisha.

The bonus the General promised was as much as I earned all last year. The tickets were on SAS, non-stop from Chicago, first class. I easily got a seat on a connecting flight from Vegas. My passport was in the drawer where it was supposed to be.

The forecast was rain, rain and more rain. I packed wool suits, several sweaters and my boots. I grabbed a black Saga mink jacket I'd scored for $35 at the swap meet from an irate husband in the throes of divorce. At the last minute, I threw in the black and red garters from the night at the Wynn, the night I met Rasheed.

Barb was sarcastic when I called from the taxi on the way to airport.

"The General and Rasheed. Now there's two charming guys to hang out with. *Roads to honor* both."

"I have to do this, Barb."

"Yeah," she snorted. "You keep saying that."

"I'll call you as soon as I get back."

"Be careful what you wish for," she warned instead of saying goodbye.

My hotel turned out to be a converted warehouse in *Nyhavn,* New Harbor, although there was nothing new about it. A long row of seventeenth century Dutch-style buildings, painted in bright colors with pitched slate roofs, housed chic restaurants and trendy bars. Barges and sailboats of all sizes moored in the canal.

The stark white walls of my room were trimmed with thick wood beams on the ceiling and around the doors and windows. Every tall, narrow window framed wonderful views of the boat-filled canal and Copenhagen's medieval skyline.

The white-tiled bathroom was outfitted with ultra-modern chrome fixtures and soap dispensers mounted in the wall instead of little wrapped bars or plastic bottles. No bathtub.

I dressed carefully for the auction in a black wool suit with the buttoned jacket showing a hint of cleavage, three-inch black patent heels, my doubled strand of pearls, and hair up in the French roll softened by bangs.

I splashed Carolina Herrera 212 Sexy at my throat and slipped on the black and red garters. All for Rasheed. Would we ever have another night like the Wynn?

Bruun Rasmussen's Art Auction was on *Bredgade*, Broad Street, running between the Marble Church and the Queen's Palace. Rosewood tables stood on dark red Persian carpets scattered on gleaming parquet floors. Conversation hummed in a low murmur; it was rare for an Egyptian piece to be offered in Copenhagen.

The room filled quickly, and I took my seat. I didn't see Rasheed and felt the crush of disappointment. But just as the auctioneer introduced the item before the ring, he walked in the door and took a reserved seat.

I was relieved to see him upright, body in pristine condition, face handsome with his proud nose perfectly intact. He didn't look around the room before sitting. His bodyguards, Marcos and Gamel, stood at the side of the room. Marcos spotted me right away and spoke in Gamel's ear. They glanced over at Rasheed, who was engrossed in his catalogue.

The bidding on the ring began. There was a flurry of action with several bidders, and then only the two of us were left. Rasheed hadn't seen that his opponent was me; he sat a couple of rows in front of me to the right.

His cell must have vibrated, because he lifted it to his ear. He turned and looked right at me, shock on his face. I nodded my head to acknowledge him, and the auctioneer took it as a bid.

When we reached the top range listed in the catalogue, I made my decision. The bid came back to me. I shook my head.

Rasheed's eyes narrowed when he turned toward me. I kept my face blank with a Mona Lisa smile on my lips.

That's when my cell buzzed.

"I see the torch still burns brightly," the General said.

I looked around the room for his men.

"I never realized the full extent of your vulnerability, Ishtar."

My eyes followed Rasheed as he signed the paperwork and headed toward the exit. Marcos and Gamel fell in behind him.

"General, I've got to go."

I didn't exactly run after Rasheed, but a couple of Vikings had to move quickly out of my way.

Gamel was hailing a taxi when I yelled—yes, yelled—"Rasheed! Wait!"

He hesitated, and I thought he might climb in anyway. But he stepped to the side, away from the curb, and stood facing me. Gamel and Marcos stayed next to the taxi.

Exhaust from the running motor poured white smoke into the dense, cold air. Drizzling rain fell on the wet pavement. I could almost feel my bangs frizz.

He made me walk up to him; I wanted to slap his face.

"Are you going to leave without saying anything?" I asked.

"What is there to say?"

"What did I do, Rasheed, that was so wrong?"

"You hid things from me." His voice was cold. "I don't trust you."

If he felt any desire for me, it didn't show in his cold, glassy green eyes, or in his face, which was as hard as the evening I wrote the ransom letter on Black Falcon's ship.

Rasheed looked like he'd lost weight. The skin stretched tighter over his cheekbones.

"*I* hide things from *you*? Is that a joke? You won't give me your cell number. I don't know where you live or what you do. I don't know your last name. I don't even know for sure your name is Rasheed. I know nothing about you."

"And that's how it has to be."

He motioned to Gamel, who opened the taxi door. Rasheed got in the back, followed by Marcos. Gamel took the passenger seat, and the Mercedes taxi moved into the thin traffic of *Bredgade*. I stood in the cold rain and watched the red tail lights grow smaller and smaller. What was it Tony told me about red shift, speed and distance? Rasheed moved away from me at the speed of light.

I was numb on the ride back to Nyhavn. The cobbled streets shone. Green and red coronas glowed in the mist around traffic lights. I listened to the sound of the taxi tires splashing in puddles and the singing of rubber on wet pavement. The windshield wipers beat back and forth, back and forth.

I couldn't wait to get out of my suit. My humiliation hung in the fibers. I took another hot shower. Jet lag was hitting me hard, but the steaming water sharpened my brain cells, and I decided on dinner out. I refused to sit in my room and sulk over Rasheed.

When I asked the concierge to recommend a restaurant, he sent me to a place for locals.

"Excellent food and not so expensive," he confided.

A 30s-and-up crowd, dressed in leather jackets and boots, blazers with turtlenecks, and sweaters of quality wool, jammed Café Viktor.

I'd expected something Danish with intimate lighting and lots of wood, maybe a fireplace crackling in the corner. Viktor was more French bistro style, wide open and a bit on the noisy side with the clatter of heavy cutlery on solid porcelain.

The *maitre d'* asked me to wait at the bar. It would only be few moments. His English was perfect, like everyone else I met.

I ordered a *Kir Royale* and stood among natives speaking a language that sounded like English played backwards on a tape recorder.

"Isis! What are you doing in Copenhagen?"

"Lars! Is it really you?"

He kissed me on both cheeks and stood back, his hands still on my shoulders, his eyes assessing me from head to toe.

"You look great," he decided.

I didn't detect anything sexual; his look was more of an assessment, factual but with appreciation.

"How long has it been since Las Vegas?" he asked.

He towered over me. His straight platinum hair and long, angular arms and legs made him Barb's twin. We'd paired off that night. Barb and Lars. Rasheed and me. The first night I met Rasheed. The night of the Stirling Club, the night of the Wynn. The night of the black and red garters.

Lars looked around—I supposed to see if I was with anyone—Rasheed?—and then back at me and smiled.

"Join us for dinner."

'Us' turned out to be a Danish couple and Norwegian Lars. They spoke English for me. After the usual 'People actually live in Las Vegas?' reaction, we got round to the auction, and I gave my spiel about representing an anonymous collector. I could tell Lars was impressed.

They switched to skiing and which slopes in Italy were best at different times of the season. The woman Grethe talked about her trip last summer to the Argentine Alps. Argentina. Hector. I took a swig of wine.

The French-Danish cuisine was light, made with all fresh ingredients. Portions were tiny and served like flower arrangements on oversized white china plates. I ordered a half portion of the saffron-flavored *bouillabaisse* followed by a strong Roquefort cheese with a French Bordeaux.

"Have you ever been rowing?" Grethe asked.

Did being rowed around the Mediterranean and the Great Harbor count?

"We're going out tomorrow, if you're interested. The Hellerup Ladies

Rowing Club. Here's my number. Call me in the morning."

"What have you heard from Rasheed?" Lars asked as soon as he settled next to me in the back seat of the gray Mercedes taxi.

"I saw him today at the auction."

"Rasheed is here in Copenhagen?"

"Yes, but he wants nothing to do with me."

He exhaled through his nose, making the slightest of snorts, not unlike Barb.

"The man is a fool," he declared, patting my hand. His touch was like that of a brother—but not a Ptolemy.

"Come in for a nightcap?" I suggested.

We sat in the lobby and drank port wine.

"Don't you see Rasheed anymore, Lars?"

"Not lately," he answered. "We're moving in different circles."

That was a polite way of putting it. Lars didn't seem like the type to do—what had Isabel called it?—shady business.

Finally, Lars asked about Barb.

"She's great, working hard, selling lots of real estate." I wanted to make her sound successful—and available.

"I'm glad we ran into each other, Isis. Will you be around a few days?"

I put his business card in my pocket and kissed him good night on the cheek.

The sky was gray when I woke early, but at least it wasn't raining.

Grethe answered in a cheery voice, "*Det er Grethe.*"

"Now that you're going to row," she declared, "we'll be four plus. I'm cox today."

I had no idea what she was talking about.

The *Roklub* nestled among beautiful coastal homes at the northern edge of the city in the upscale suburb of Hellerup. Neat racks of long, skinny, highly varnished wooden boats filled a well-maintained, red brick nineteenth century boathouse with stone floor.

"Shells," Grethe corrected me when I called them rowboats.

Three supremely healthy and fit-looking Norse goddesses in tight latex pants joined us. They assured me that my jogging suit was appropriate but likely to get wet.

"Where are we going to row?" I asked, imagining we would hug the coast.

"Sweden," they said in unison.

"Do you think I'll be warm enough?" I toyed with begging off.

"You'll be sweating within minutes," they assured me.

I was relieved when we all put on life vests—and when they pointed to a flat piece of land across the water. I had no idea Sweden was so close.

We hauled the shell down to the ramp and launched it. The oh-so-shallow boat dipped and bobbed in the slate waters. I was terrified I'd humiliate myself and capsize us all before we even left shore.

I took the second seat from coxswain Grethe, who faced our crew of four. As cox, she faced forward, steered the shell and set the stroke of the oars.

"It's called 'catch' when the oar blade goes in the water," Grethe explained. "You extend your legs at the same time and push the seat toward the bow of the boat."

I tried once. As promised, when I stretched my legs, my seat, gliding on rails, slid back.

"Good! Now 'drive' is the pressure you put on the blade when it moves through the water."

I tried that.

"Last is 'recovery.' That's when you take the oar out of the water and bend your knees so the seat slides forward—and you're ready to 'catch' again."

I had already begun to sweat, and we were five feet from shore.

"This might have been a little ambitious for me."

They laughed.

"It's all about rhythm. You'll get the hang of it."

I watched the fluid, coordinated movements of Anne-Lise in front of me and tried to mimic her, but my oar kept bouncing along the surface of the water, and my seat slid backward at the wrong time. I wasn't the least bit cold in spite of the wind moving across the icy Øresund where the frigid North Sea meets the freezing Baltic. My thigh muscles were soon on fire.

"Not much room," I joked, my knees to my chest only inches above the water.

"You'd be surprised," said Grethe. "During the German occupation, the girls in the Hellerup *Roklub* smuggled Jews to Sweden in this boat and others like it."

I looked at the tiny spaces on the sides of the rails. Anne-Lise turned in her seat to face me.

"The Nazis didn't consider Hellerup a threat. The German guards stationed in our little harbor were, for the most part, homesick teenagers."

"The girls, just teenagers themselves, rowed every day," added Helene from behind me. "The soldiers got used to them. They were, in fact, very glad to see young blonde girls in shorts and tight sweaters."

"They rowed right past the Germans," said Grethe with a laugh. "Waving and smiling—with the guards waving back—and the Jews lying on their backs under blankets."

"Entire Jewish families escaped, one person in a shell per trip. Maybe two children."

I tried to imagine the terror of a small child not daring to make a sound, listening to soldiers calling out friendly greetings in German. It seemed impossible that anyone could fit in the boat besides rowers. The hull wasn't more than a foot deep, and the seats slid constantly back and forth.

The rain was coming down steadily before we got the shell back on its rack. The sea and sky were slate gray. Hundreds of seagulls flew in wide circles, gliding, diving and soaring again.

A black sedan was still parked under the bare branches of a tall tree on the tiny side street. Two men sat in the front seat. I wouldn't have given it a second thought, except I remembered seeing it from the boathouse when I arrived. It seemed a long time to be parked there, next to the Rowing Club among private homes.

"Coffee?" Grethe asked, pointing to the Clubhouse.

"Sure, just a sec. I'll be right in."

With my drenched jogging suit clinging to my body and my wet hair hanging in my face, I walked straight over to the car and rapped on the driver's side.

The electric window slid down halfway.

I leaned in just a bit to look directly at the driver and said, "Tell the General to stop."

He had a swarthy face, pitted with acne scars. His menacing eyes peered out from puffy pouches. The second man's face was half-hidden by a charcoal fedora with the brim snapped down in front.

Neither one spoke. The driver curled his lips in a silent sneer, and the window slid up again with a quiet *whir*.

I stood for a moment longer, seeing only my own reflection in the glass, and then crossed back to the Clubhouse. The black sedan with the two men was still there when I closed the half-glass door with lace curtains.

"Who was that?" Grethe asked.

"I don't know. They've been here since I arrived. I saw the car from the boathouse before we went out."

Anne-Lise and Grethe exchanged looks. They had to think it odd I approached strangers in a car parked on a public street.

Helene and Sofia came out of the locker room in athletic sweatsuits, and I went back to change. When I reached into the pocket of my trench coat to find a tissue, I pulled out Lars' card.

"Can you meet me right away?"

"Half an hour?" He answered immediately without questioning why. I'm sure I sounded panicked.

My next call was to the General.

"Do you have more goons following me?"

"Describe them."

This time I wasn't playing any games. I described the driver exactly as I had seen him—very scary-looking.

"Perhaps you should think about coming home, Ishtar."

Grethe appeared to ask, "Are you okay? Your coffee's getting cold."

I smiled bravely and followed her out, butterflies swarming in my stomach.

CHAPTER 34   THE ROUND TOWER

"I know one thing, that I know nothing." – Socrates

The black sedan pulled away minutes before Lars arrived at the Clubhouse in his navy blue BMW. I watched the traffic as we drove into the center of the city but didn't see the black car with two men.

I told Lars as much as possible without telling him anything about the Red Mirror, the Emerald Tablet or past lives. I needed him to believe in my sanity. Not mentioning any specifics, I let him know what kind of man the General was and that he did business with Rasheed.

"Rasheed and you have gotten mixed up with a tough crowd."

"*Rasheed and I* don't exist, Lars. I would best describe myself as a nonperson in his eyes."

"I don't buy that. I guarantee you exist for him. That's why he pushes you away. Rasheed doesn't let himself get close to anyone."

Lars took me for coffee at the *Konditori Antoinette* on the car-free shopping street *Strøget*. He called it *gågade*, or walking street.

My fears seemed foolish among the ladies sampling elegant pastries off *Flora Danica* plates. The two men probably had nothing to do with me and thought me crazy when I tapped on their car window. I didn't believe it, though; the driver's eyes were too menacing.

Our thick black coffee came in a graceful white porcelain pot with delicate matching cups and saucers, a creamer with real cream and a sugar bowl with miniature cubes and tiny silver tongs.

"I'd call him," Lars offered, "but Rasheed changes cell phones a lot."

He looked at his watch. The cuffs of his white shirt were starched stiff. He wore *intaglio* cufflinks, each with a seven-pointed star carved into the dark green stone.

"I'm sorry," I said quickly. "You must have a meeting or something."

"Do you want to go to the police?"

"What could they do? I'm not even sure myself."

"Can I get you a taxi to your hotel? I'd drop you off, but I'm running late."

"No, I'm okay, really. The street is jammed with people. Go do what you have to do."

"What about dinner tonight? You can't get a decent flight out of here until tomorrow."

When he paid the check, I again noticed the seven-pointed stars on his cuffs.

"I like your cufflinks, Lars. Unusual. Were they a gift?"

"I inherited them from my grandfather. Family legend is that they've been passed down for generations. But we have lots of stories in my family—mostly untrue."

My city map showed I was quite close to the hotel. But when I stepped out onto *Strøget*, it stopped raining. The throng of foot traffic gave me new confidence. How many times would I be in Copenhagen? I didn't want to spend my afternoon hiding out in my hotel.

Instead of turning toward *Kongens Nytorv* in the direction of Nyhavn, I went the opposite way to a small *torv* where *Strøget* joined another walking street leading to the Round Tower.

"Don't miss the view from the top," the concierge had suggested. "The Tower was built in 1637 as an observatory by Christian IV, the builder king. You'll have a splendid 360-degree vista of the city—if it doesn't rain."

A wide interior brick ramp wound upwards in a continuous spiral through an ice grotto-like interior with no hard edges. Curved white ceilings flowed into white walls. The only light came from recessed Gothic-arched windows.

The brochure said that while on a visit to the King of Denmark, Czar Peter the Great and Empress Catherine had driven to the rooftop viewing deck in their royal carriage.

Schoolchildren filled a gallery about halfway up the ramp. Once past that point, I had the place to myself. But the way the ramp turned, anyone could be a few yards ahead or behind. I wouldn't know they were there unless they spoke.

A few drops of rain began to fall as I stepped onto the empty roof terrace. A biting wet wind blew right through my trench coat and wool sweater.

I played around with the functions on my new smartphone until the screen suddenly popped into video mode. Walking slowly around the wrought-iron fencing, I recorded the panorama of a medieval cityscape of copper spires unblemished by skyscrapers.

Two men in trench coats filled the screen; one wore a charcoal fedora. I almost dropped my phone. They were the men from the black sedan this morning. I looked around—still alone except for the men. They must have waited outside the *Konditori*; I hadn't looked when I came out. If they had followed us from the Rowing Club, I hadn't seen their car.

For one paranoid moment, I suspected Lars. Did he call them and give our location?

"What do you want from me?" I tried to keep the fear from my voice, but don't think I was convincing.

"My employer would like a few words with you," said the man in the hat. His accent was Eastern European—maybe Russian.

"I'm not going anywhere with you."

"I think you will," he answered, showing me a small, black pistol.

"You won't shoot me here. There is no way for you to get out."

"Do you want to test me? I hear gunshot wounds are painful and can cause lifelong damage. You seem young to face that."

The likelihood of him shooting me seemed small, but his eyes were so cold, I thought him capable of anything.

I remembered the phone in my palm and put my hands in the pockets of my trench coat.

He took my arm and steered me toward the doorway onto the ramp. We walked three abreast, with the gun in my ribs. I kept saying to myself that this could not be happening to me. But hadn't Antinous once told me that Pythagoras believed anything that can happen, can happen to you?

All the way down, I schemed of making a break for it when we came out on the walking street.

"Do not try anything stupid," he whispered in my ear. "I can get away easier here than at the top."

We walked down a narrow alley to a tiny street behind the Round Tower. Only one car could pass by the waiting black Mercedes with tinted windows—and it would have to be small.

The rear door opened, and the man with the gun pushed me in.

Ptolemy's Royal Steward Agathon wrapped in a cashmere overcoat waited; his lips curled up in a sick kind of smile.

I couldn't stop shaking. I thought I might even wet my pants; the pressure on my bladder was intense.

"You are cold, my dear," he remarked. "Sasha, turn up the heat a little."

I took that as a good sign. If he was about to kill me, would he think of my comfort?

"What do you want from me?"

Whatever it was, he could have it. If he wanted the Emerald Tablet, it was his. None of this was worth it. The Tablet was useless anyway. It wasn't doing me much good.

"I want to know where Bayoumi is."

"Bayoumi? Is that a place? Or a person?" For a wild moment, I thought that all this was a big misunderstanding, a case of mistaken identity.

"Please do not play dumb. It is not convincing. You were seen with him yesterday at the auction."

Rasheed! He was talking about Rasheed.

"I don't know where he is. I didn't even know Bayoumi was his last name. If you ask your spies, they'll tell you that he drove off and left me standing in the rain."

He studied me. I met his eyes without blinking. I hid nothing because I knew nothing. *Thank you, Rasheed, for never telling me anything about yourself.*

He sighed and looked ahead at the rain beating down on the windshield. The idling motor purred. The two men from the black sedan stood against a brick building, under a small overhang.

Sasha the driver watched me in the rearview mirror. My eyes met his reflection, and he looked away.

"I can't tell you what I don't know," I said in a voice so level it surprised me. "I met him in Las Vegas and saw him a couple of times. He never told me anything about himself. Now he won't even talk to me."

I didn't plead for him to believe me. I spoke the truth in a matter-of-fact tone and played Athena accustomed to everyone following my logic.

The new Agathon listened without comment. I saw him analyze me, deciding if I were telling the truth, maybe even deciding if I were to live or die. Sasha met my eyes in the rearview mirror.

The only sound was the hum of the motor and the clatter of rain on the moon roof and windshield.

"May I give you a ride back to your hotel?" Agathon asked politely.

"No thanks. I'll find my own way."

"*Do svidaniya.*"

No one tried to stop me from opening the car door, and I was out in the rain and running down the narrow street before he had a chance to change his mind. A taxi crossed through the intersection; I waved it down, hopped in and started shaking all over again.

The General promised he'd identify the men in the video I sent him.

"He said something like *Do svidaniya* when I got out of the car. Do you know what that means?"

"It's Russian, Ishtar. *Until the next meeting.*"

"What next meeting? I don't ever want to see him again."

"Rasheed seems more trouble than he's worth," he chuckled.

"I don't find this funny. I've never been threatened with a gun before."

"You handled yourself well, Ishtar. I congratulate you. The Russian considered eliminating you but decided you are more valuable alive. I would have done the same."

He let those words sink in. I waited, my heart pounding and my throat dry. Once, not so long ago, all my dangers had been on the other side of the Red Mirror.

"I wouldn't advise any further contact with Rasheed, *ma bella*. They know there is something between you. They'll be waiting when he comes back."

CHAPTER 35   ALADDIN'S LAMP

"It is not once nor twice, but times without number that the same ideas make their appearance in the world." – Aristotle

I lay on my back and stared up at the leaden sky. Cold water washed over me; I shivered under a sodden wool blanket. Grethe shouted in Danish to Anne-Lise.

The oars moved faster in the choppy water: catch, drive, then recovery followed by catch, drive and recovery. Only inches away, Anne-Lise's seat slid back and forth past my head. I hoped my hair wouldn't catch in the rails.

My back hurt; my legs cramped; I could no longer feel my toes.

"Out," Lars whispered in my ear. "Out before it's too late."

He took my arm to help me stand, but when I looked, it was the General. The Russian Agathon grabbed my other arm, and the two men pulled at me in a tug of war. My arms stretched and stretched until they were twice as long, and still they didn't let go.

I woke in a sweat in my hotel room in *Nyhavn*. My cell was ringing.

"It's Lars. Is 5:30 okay with you?"

Lars was exactly on time. When I got off the elevator, he whistled and smiled.

I wore one of those black knit dresses that follows curves without clinging. My aunt's long strand of baroque pearls hung down the front. My hair was tucked up with loose tendrils at the neck; Tiffany diamond studs sparkled in my earlobes.

"You are very charming tonight. Rasheed is a fool."

The drive was short. I let Lars talk about the fun he had in Las Vegas. I didn't mention my afternoon until we were settled at a table in *Sankt Gertruds Kloster,* a cavernous restaurant buried in the bowels of a 14th century convent. Arched brick ceilings with thick wood beams curved into brick walls lighted with candle torches. The only lighting came from candles—hundreds of them.

Rows of knives marched outward on one side of our plates with lines of forks on the other. We looked at each other over a sea of sparkling glass goblets.

I waited until the server brought our champagne cocktails before I told Lars about the Round Tower, the two men, the gun and the Russian in the black Mercedes.

Lars barely blinked. His eyes were sky blue, but a paler shade than Tony's. He took my hand and squeezed it.

"Please, forgive me for not taking you more seriously. I feel terrible I left you alone."

"I'm worried about Rasheed, Lars. What will they do if they find him?"

"There's a reason Rasheed never told you about himself, Isis. Now you understand."

"I know nothing about him, Lars. Not even where he's from."

"He told me once that he was born in Cairo but went to boarding school in Vermont or New Hampshire. I can't remember which. We met skiing. He's not married—if that's what you want to know. His family had money, but they lost it. Something to do with politics. Rasheed's Coptic. Apparently there's a large Christian population in Egypt—since Roman times."

"So, you don't see him much any more?"

"No, not lately. We did some business together for a while. That's why we were in Las Vegas."

The first courses arrived with mustard and parsley in cream for the fish, then raspberries with hazelnut oil for the ham. The rosy pink lamb was served with a rosemary glaze.

We left off talking about Rasheed. Lars told me about himself, his company based out of Oslo, his sister who lives in Paris and his brother who lives in Soho in Manhattan.

"I'll give you their numbers, in case you want to look them up if you're there."

He wasn't married. *Barb will like that.* But he had a steady girlfriend who flew with SAS. They shared an apartment in Copenhagen and both travelled a lot.

"Two ships passing in the night," he said with a smile. "But the nights are good."

I was stuffed when the chocolate pyramid arrived and begged off. The waiter brought me two tiny scoops of freshly made sorbet, one champagne, the other red currant. They tasted like a *Kir Royale.*

It was only nine o'clock when we left the restaurant.

"Want to have a nightcap at my place?" he asked casually. "It's close by, in *Søerne,* The Lakes."

Thinking of Tony in New York, I answered, "I'm not sure that's such a good idea."

He grinned at me as he turned the ignition. "Playing it safe? I don't blame you. You're a beautiful woman, Isis. But you were always Rasheed's, right from the moment he saw you."

He pulled out onto the narrow, cobblestone street.

"You don't want to be alone after what you've been through today. I promise to behave."

Lars lived in a grand old, French-style mid-rise apartment house with attic dormers and slate roof. Tall, curtainless windows of paned glass looked onto a vast rectangle of still water lined by walkways. Broad-limbed, leafless trees waited for spring.

"The Lakes were dug to help fortify the old city walls. Back in medieval times. If you were here in the daytime, you'd see hundreds of swans."

His apartment had rooms arranged in what he called *en suite*—large, parquet-floored salons connected by glass French doors. Elaborate floral stucco work and crown molding at least two feet wide finished the high ceilings.

I settled on one of those ultra-modern, beige leather sofas you see in magazines. A low beechwood coffee table created an intimate conversation area in a room so sparsely furnished it echoed.

Huge abstract, bright-colored canvases, each with its own gallery light, plastered the white walls. They reminded me of the painting hanging behind Hector's head when we Skyped.

"My brother's work," Lars offered. "The one who lives in Soho."

He lowered the lighting with dimmer switches, turned on some

Brubeck with his Bang and Olufsen remote, and poured *Armagnac* into two oversized brandy snifters.

"All we're missing is the cigar," I joked.

"Do you want a Davidoff?" he asked as his cell buzzed.

He answered and looked over at me, mouthing, "Rasheed."

My heart stopped.

"Rasheed, there's someone here you should talk to."

He handed the cell to me.

"Rasheed, it's me."

Silence.

"Rasheed, listen to me. I met some ugly people today who want to find you. Russians maybe? I don't think you want to be found."

"Did they hurt you?" His voice was quiet and very deep.

"No, but they scared me to death."

"Get out of Copenhagen, Isis. Go back to the States."

"Rasheed, who are they?"

"Rasheed?"

But he had hung up.

Barb curled up on my red sofa with a black-and-white polka dot throw pillow clutched to her chest. Her blue eyes, usually small and half-hidden by her bangs, were round as a china doll's. She brushed off the news about Lars and his stewardess girlfriend with a wave of her hand.

"We had a terrific time that night. But Lars lives in Europe. I'm here. Did you go to the police?"

No," I admitted. "There would have been too many...questions."

Barb studied me for a moment before stretching out her long, never-ending legs and reaching for the glass of chardonnay.

"How many bad guys are after you? Have we lost count?"

Her sharp look told me she didn't expect an answer. I heard an ice cube drop in the fridge ice maker. Off in the distance, a siren blared.

She drained the glass, set it a bit hard on the coffee table and stood to go. "I'm not sure I feel safe visiting you anymore."

After Barb left, I sat a long time in my gray leather armchair, Aisha purring in my lap. The Red Mirror reflected a strange me with hair a little too wild, like my eyes.

My condo has double security—uniformed guards at the main gates and iron grates with code access for the parking garage. But I didn't think for a minute that would stop the men I'd met lately.

Only the Emerald Table could do that.

I rubbed and rubbed with the same cloth I'd used on the Red Mirror. Rubbing worked on Aladdin's lamp, didn't it? But nothing happened. No spirits appeared. No surge of power. I rewrapped the package and put the Tablet back in the safety deposit box.

I checked the other cars in the Bank of America parking lot when I got behind the wheel. I watched in my rearview mirror the whole way home to see if I was being followed, just like I had watched during the drive there.

I couldn't live like this. I didn't need to live like this. The Tablet should make all my problems go away. There must be a way to activate it.

"Go to Siwa," the Light told me. *"Go to the Oracle of Amun."*

"I'm not going to waste my breath trying to talk you out of it," Barb said in a disgusted tone. "Call me when—and IF—you get back."

"Boy, your life has changed," Sonny remarked with a smile as he took Aisha from my arms.

The General didn't ask why I'd be out of touch or where I was going, but instead said, "Good luck, Ishtar."

Why did he wish me luck?

CHAPTER 36   EUGENIA

"What house ever became prosperous without a woman's excellence?" –
Sophocles

A warm breeze rustled palm fronds. All around me was the song
of a hundred birds. The music of a fountain and small children's
laughter tickled my ears. It was hotter than Alexandria and
markedly more humid; the heavy, moist air pressed on my skin.

When I opened my eyes, I saw Barb. Thinking that she might have
travelled through the Red Mirror with me, I almost said her name
out loud.

She reclined a few feet from me in a slim, sleeveless gown of blue
linen tied at each shoulder and under the breasts with yellow silk cord.
Her hair was the same gleaming flaxen blond but twisted into precisely
plaited cornrows secured with blue ribbon. She looked not at me, but
at a handful of fair, sunny children playing on green grass.

Fountains sparkled in a long marble pool stretching the length of
a rectangular peristyle garden enclosed on three sides by a columned
porch with pillars carved into flowering vines. Colorful murals of
flowers and birds covered the walls between paneled doors and grilled
windows. The far end of the gardens opened onto a graveled corridor
passing through date palms to the Nile.

The woman smiled as she watched the children; her blue eyes were
warm and adoring, not at all sharp and quick like Barb's.

"Aunt Eugenia!" a towheaded boy called. "Come see the frog with red stripes."

Eugenia. Hektor's wife. Barb.

"Bring him to me, Georgios," she answered in lilting Greek.

Her light, happy laugh was the tinkle of small bells. When she moved her head, sunbeams sparkled in her hair.

"Are they not perfection?" she asked me.

They were beautiful children, with glowing skin and shiny hair, radiating that particular confidence of those deeply loved.

"My sister's children—all of them. She is blessed by Hathor."

I must have shown my surprise at her mention of the Egyptian Goddess, because she smiled at me in a slightly amused way.

"Yes, I worship Hathor," she said in a quiet, assured voice. "Do you find that uncommon? My family has been a thousand years in Egypt. We long ago learned that the Egyptian Gods are stronger in this land than our Greek ones."

An exotic slave girl with slanted eyes served us pomegranate juice in two-handled golden cups embossed with rosettes. A silver tray with fresh black figs and amber dates balanced on a low tripod between us. The fragrance of a citron tree perfumed the air.

Eugenia sipped at her juice and watched the children for a few moments before turning her attention to me. She seemed not at all uncomfortable that I was here, in her home.

"Hathor, Isis and Aphrodite are all champions of women, are they not, Athena of Korinth? Do not all women wish for the same thing? Love and motherhood."

She looked longingly toward the children, squealing and giggling among rose bushes and ivy topiaries shaped into gazelles.

"I went on pilgrimage once," she confided, "to make sacrifice to the Persian Goddess Ishtar that she might allow just one child to live in my womb." She sighed and turned her face toward me. Her eyes were so incredibly sad. "But, alas, the Goddesses have all forsaken me."

My heart broke for this beautiful and tragic woman. She had everything, yet she had nothing, because she couldn't have a child. I couldn't seem to avoid it.

"Hektor is a kind man and a good man, no matter his reputation," she continued in a wistful voice, watching the children again. "He could have taken a new wife—one who would bear him sons. But he lives honorably by the Greek code. Our union was desired by our families and planned before our births. Hektor and I come from the same ancient line."

Enthralled, I watched her in profile, her lips moving as she talked about Hektor. How had he explained me, my coming here?

"Shall you return to Korinth, Athena, when your temple here is completed?"

"Yes, of course. I am the Supreme Priestess. Since the day my father gave me to the Goddess, I have dedicated my life to her. The Akrokorinth is the only home I have ever known."

Eugenia took a long, deep breath and then exhaled slowly. The garnet eyes of the gold cobra coiled around her upper arm winked at me. Did Hektor have a chest full of snake bracelets to give to his conquests?

"Shall you take the child with you?" she asked, at long last looking directly at me. "Is there a place in your world for him?"

"Child?" I repeated dumbly.

"My slaves told me of your morning sickness."

Slaves. Of course. They know everything.

"Is that why my husband brought you here—because of the child? He has never brought another of his women to our home."

His women. She didn't say it in a particularly insulting tone, but I felt her words as a slap in the face.

"Hektor does not know about the child," I warned.

"Then we must tell him."

"No, I do not think we should. I am not certain the child is his."

"But can you be certain that he is *not* the father?"

I hesitated before answering, "I cannot."

She waved away the slave girl who came to refill our goblets.

"Athena of Korinth, may I speak from the heart, as do sisters?" She waited for my nod before continuing.

I thought her a Goddess, perhaps Hera herself. Such poise and dignity in the face of a husband's betrayal.

"If there is any possibility that the child you carry is my husband's— *any* possibility—would you consider allowing us to raise him as our own?"

Eugenia took me quite off guard. A surrogate mother. I'd never remotely considered it.

"Hektor would be overjoyed to have a son whom he believed to be his," she persisted in her gentle way. "He does not have to know anything else. This can be our secret, Athena of Korinth."

Sons. Always sons. I wanted to ask, what if the child is a girl? But instead I gave my standard answer when avoiding a commitment.

"It is most flattering that you would raise a child of mine as yours, Lady Eugenia; I can imagine no finer mother. But as in all matters of importance, I must consult the Goddess and follow Her wisdom."

"Of course," she agreed graciously. "I understand."

But her yearning was impossible to disguise.

A delicate girl of about five climbed onto Eugenia's lap. She had the same silver hair as Eugenia and wore it in long coils that fell about her face. Fragile gold owls dangled from her tiny earlobes. Her tunic was the purest of whites with bright blue and sunny yellow bands woven around the neck and hem. Henna darkened each toenail of her perfect little feet.

"Hektor will return today from Alexandria," Eugenia said brightly. "He stays there not so long when you are here."

"What is this about Hektor?" Hektor's voice boomed in the walled garden. "What are my two favorite ladies saying about me?"

He beamed down on both of us, kissed Eugenia on the brow, above the nose, and then crossed to me and kissed me at the same spot, only his fingers lingered longer on my face.

I caught the envy in Eugenia's eyes before she looked away.

"And how is the city, my husband?"

"The riots have calmed." He looked sideways at me.

"Riots?" I asked.

"The Greeks took to the streets when Ptolemy announced there would be no public execution of the rebel Black Falcon. The Egyptians attacked the Greek Quarter after hearing rumors of the Falcon's assassination in prison. As usual, the Libyans and Syrians joined in the looting."

"What of my household? Are they safe?"

"Ptolemy's men have placed them in protective custody."

Hektor's expression warned me there was more but not to speak of it in front of Eugenia and the children.

"I thank you both for your hospitality and shelter during these turbulent times, but I must return to Alexandria. Hektor, would you be so kind as to make the arrangements?"

Hektor and Eugenia both started to object. I couldn't imagine that Eugenia wanted me here, unless she believed I would stay sequestered in her home until I gave birth.

"My decision is made. I have not only the Temple here to complete, but also one to manage in Korinth. I have rested. I am strong. I must return to my duties."

I didn't sleep but waited for Hektor, knowing he would come. I worried about my slaves. I worried about Jason. I schemed how to get to Siwa. I would send word first thing in the morning to Eben and Antinous of my homecoming.

The night was absolutely still; gauzy pink linen curtains hung limp in the open doorway. The same sheer fabric canopied my bed and kept swarms of buzzing mosquitoes at bay. The breezeless air was heavy with the perfume of gardenia, rose and jasmine.

My rooms were at ground level on the smallest of the villa's three peristyle gardens. Double doors opened onto a mosaic-tiled patio with a golden fountain statue of the cupid-god Eros; water tinkled from his tiny penis all through the day and night. A life-sized marble Aphrodite poised gracefully in an alcove on the other side of the courtyard.

Hektor was first a shadow, then a solid form in a long white linen robe. Opening a gap in the bed curtains, he started to lower himself.

"No!" I said emphatically. "Not in your wife's home."

He first stood up straight, then plumped down on the edge of the low bed, his knees sticking up at an angle into the air.

"Why not? What has changed? You know that Eugenia and I have an understanding."

"No woman wants to share her husband, Hektor, and certainly not under the same roof. You delude yourself. Eugenia accepts the terms of your marriage because she has no choice."

He looked more confused than disappointed, but to his credit, didn't try to press himself on me.

"Tell me about my slaves," I demanded. "What protective custody?"

"The ones you left behind were questioned about your whereabouts the night of the Falcon's death."

"Questioned?"

When I closed my eyes, I saw Black Falcon's mangled body and then the mangled faces of my innocent kitchen slaves and gardeners. I reached for the bowl and gagged into it, but nothing came up.

"All that is known is that a woman came to the prison, and the Falcon was dead the next morning. The Lord Chancellor tried to plant the

seed of your involvement, but Ptolemy found the idea too audacious—
even for you. You are safe, for now. The torturing of your slaves was an
accommodation, more to prove the theory wrong than right."

Hektor didn't come right out and say he knew the woman was me,
but he didn't need to. He had cleaned the filth and blood from my
body that night. I had refused him explanation.

"As far as the Royal Court is concerned, you were here on my estates
the whole evening. I have spoken personally with Ptolemy."

"I must return tomorrow, Hektor."

"Why?"

"Do not ask me."

"More secrets, Athena? You tread a treacherous path."

Eugenia was up in the pre-dawn to kiss me goodbye. Her long platinum
hair hung loose on her shoulders and shimmered on the celadon green
of her silk robe.

"We must think of ourselves as sisters," she whispered in my ear.
"Your child would have every advantage of wealth and education. My
heart is already filled with love for him."

I pressed Kallisto into her arms and asked her to give some of that
love to the kitten.

Apparently Eugenia hadn't told Hektor about the child; I saw nothing
in his face or eyes other than irritation and concern that I insisted upon
returning to Alexandria.

Rich, verdant fields flowed past. Oxen circled round water wheels
to the music of pan pipes. The river was ours, save for a few lone
fishermen balancing on their shallow canoes, casting their nets on still,
golden waters.

The sun rose, and it was immediately hot. The air hummed with
insects. My slaves waved broad palmiform fans while I reclined on a
cushioned divan under a green and yellow striped canopy with golden
fringe.

Hektor tried to make conversation, but I was lost in my plans for
Siwa. He gave up and played *senet* with Ajax. Goliath in the stern never
took his eyes off me.

No one answered our knock at my villa; the house echoed when we
entered. Ptolemy had not returned my tortured slaves. When I asked

Hektor if he thought them dead, he merely shrugged. I hadn't learned all of their names, and they had suffered, perhaps to death, for me.

I gathered those who had travelled to Naukratis with me into the reception chambers, and with Hektor as witness, gave them their freedom. Instead of being grateful, the women burst into tears, falling to their knees, sobbing hysterically.

"Where can we go?" they wailed. "We shall have to become prostitutes!"

"We are members of your household, Mistress," urged Ajax. "Please do not send us away."

I sent three messages: one to Antinous, one to Eben and a cryptic note to Queen Arsinoë inquiring after her health and asking her opinion of the healing powers of desert springs.

Antinous had made the preparations for our journey. First we would sail from Alexandria west to the small port city of Amunia, and from there travel by horseback southwest across the desert to the Oasis of Siwa, known to locals as the Land of Palms.

Hektor was furious that I travelled with Antinous and not him.

"The Goddess has spoken to me, Hektor. This is Temple business."

"You do not believe in that nonsense anymore than I do. And Antinous believes only in his numbers," he fumed. "What is the real purpose of this journey?"

"You must accept my decision, Hektor. But there are ways you can help me, if you truly care for my well-being."

His tall frame, leaning against the balcony of my bedchamber, was silhouetted against Pharos, the cerulean sky and cobalt sea.

"Are you set on self-destruction?" he demanded. "What will you have of me now?"

"You must say that I have returned to Naukratis with you."

He glared out at the harbor.

"And please take my servants—not slaves any longer, Hektor—home with you. Care for them."

I'd never seen him angry. He was always cheerful and positive, so confident he could have what he wanted.

"Can you do that for me, Hektor?"

He finally turned toward me. The anger flashed in his eyes, then softened, and when he answered, his voice was resigned.

"We have come a long way since those first days when you so distrusted me, have we not, Athena of Korinth?"

I took it as a yes.

A return message came from the Queen. She strongly recommended taking the desert waters, the cure being quite remarkable.

Arsinoë sent two men in black turbans and black robes, both with curved swords at their waists. They wore the same pointed beards as Blue Beard, but one dyed his jet black, and the other hennaed his red. They must have known of their comrade's death the night of our visit to Black Falcon's prison island, but if they resented Blue Beard's slaughter, I couldn't read it in their expressions.

They didn't introduce themselves, and I didn't ask their names. Goliath assessed them quickly and gave me the nod of approval.

Eben arrived to travel with us. He retreated to a quiet corner to consult his scrolls, calculate number combinations and occasionally break into hypnotic trances, swaying back and forth, muttering incomprehensible incantations.

Qeb-ha had consulted the Egyptian omens. His message said the signs were favorable, if we choose the right path.

Isn't it always so?

I toyed with taking the Red Mirror with me, but Antinous insisted we travel light.

"It is much too cumbersome. Why would you need such a large mirror in the desert?"

I could come up with no logical explanation that would satisfy any thinking person, much less analytical Antinous, so I resigned to travel without it.

Antinous undoubtedly took my concern with the Red Mirror as a woman's vanity, and we didn't speak of it again. He was preoccupied with a million details—assigning his classes at the *Musaeum,* handing off administrative duties to his assistants, writing last minute instructions for the foreman who oversaw foundation work at the Temple site.

I understood well his preoccupation with responsibilities. I finished the last of my correspondence to Korinth and approved expenditures from another contingency fund.

Ajax returned from errands, and we left for the docks.

PART THREE

THE PROTECTORS

CHAPTER 37   SIWA

"Shrines! Shrines! Surely you don't believe in the gods. What's your argument? Where's your proof?" – Aristophanes

T he port of Amunia proved to be little more than a village on a white sand harbor protected by a natural breakwater. A handful of cargo ships anchored in clear, azure waters. Naval installations for the Egyptian Fleet lay to the west of the port, but only one *trireme* moored there. The crew was not in the town.

In the little marketplace next to the harbor, desert Berbers traded exotic skins, spices, slaves and Nubian gold for iron weapons, grain and beer—the 'Libyan wine' they drank at each meal.

Our arrival caused something of a stir. As much as we tried to avoid notice, the vision of a blonde Goddess traveling with an entourage composed of an untidy Jew, a giant Nubian, two black-robed assassins and a magnificent, muscled Greek sent rumors flying from the port all through the town.

Ajax also travelled with us; he refused to stay behind. The remainder of my household had packed up and returned to Naukratis with Hektor.

Antinous' bright blue eyes brought cries of "Alexander! Alexander!" as we passed through the narrow, twisting alleys.

No sooner than out of sight of the Mediterranean, the moist sea air changed to bone dry. Ahead stretched unrelenting rock and sand into the heart of the Sahara. Not a cloud marred an endless blue sky. Although the sun blazed and heat rose off the sand in waves, we didn't stop to rest at midday but continued through the furnace.

We rode proud Bedouin horses with burnished coats and braided manes. They danced among the stones polished by wind and never lost their footing when their hooves sank in the soft sand of the dunes.

Our saddles were blankets on top of animal hide. No stirrups supported my feet, and my thigh muscles began to burn after only a few miles. But I couldn't complain about my discomfort. Everyone was here because of me.

The sky flamed orange, faded to copper, and then to pale coral before losing its color altogether, and the stars came out.

We stopped for a meal, rested the horses and remounted. When at last our guide called a halt for the night, Jupiter shone precisely overhead. Orion the Hunter hovered above the southern horizon.

"You must have heard the fable, Athena," Antinous said as he pointed out the constellation *Coma Berenices* not far from Ursa Major, the Big Bear. "They say Aphrodite raised Queen Berenike's hair to the heavens in honor of the Queen's love for her husband. Pure nonsense, of course. The stars have been in that arrangement for as long as astronomers have studied the sky."

He named each star in Orion, and then Ursa Major. His voice droned on and on in the cadence of a soothing lullaby until, huddled under a coarse wool blanket, I fell into an exhausted sleep on cold sand.

We were back on the horses with first light. Long, monotonous hours passed without any change in the flat desert. Then without warning, we came over a rise to look out over the vast oasis of Siwa, known to the locals as the Land of Palms.

Miles of green-topped date palms ended abruptly at a craggy escarpment flanked by sand dunes. In the near distance rose two low peaks.

"The Mountain of the Dead." Our guide pointed with his riding crop. "The one peppered with tombs. Over there, on the other hill, you shall find the Temple of Amun. And the Oracle you seek."

We rode down the rise, into the oasis and soon arrived at a village of sorts.

"Trust no one here," he warned. "These Berber savages traffic in slaves for Carthage and would slit your throat for a *drachma*."

Carthage. The General. Jason.

Men in flowing tunics made from supple goatskin roamed the sandy streets or clustered in small groups in the meager shade. Their heads were shaved except for long, thick braids hanging from the crowns, like a Chinese queue. The only women I saw carried water jars balanced on their covered heads.

Conversation and all activity stopped when we passed. In spite of my hooded cloak, every eye seemed to follow. I had the feeling they'd never seen a Greek woman up close. Maybe they hadn't seen one at all.

Shouting boys in knee-length, loose tunics pursued us from the edge of the oasis, leaping alongside and running ahead of the horses. Their heads had been shaved to create a circle of soft brown curls in the shape of a skullcap.

A boy about Jason's age with his same startling hazel eyes and happy smile handed me a branch of sticky golden dates.

"*Ansuf!*" he shouted up to me. "Welcome, Goddess!"

The guide led us directly to an inn where clay pitchers of beer and flat loaves of warm bread tempted from a rough wooden table. I was hungry and exhausted, but refused to rest for long.

"The Lady must go to the Temple in the morning with sunrise," insisted the Innkeeper. "That is the preferred time."

"The Oracle shall see me tonight."

We were cautioned that the ascent to the Temple of Amun would be steep and rocky. Not long after passing the healing hot springs, we abandoned the horses to a village boy to guard for an *obol*.

Antinous carried the Emerald Tablet, wrapped with the antelope skin, in an ordinary tool bag such as any architect would use.

The sun had set; we made our way on the path in rosy twilight. When we neared the summit, a stooped Egyptian priest appeared from the shadows. I'm certain he had been waiting for us.

Without saying a word, he signaled us to follow him along a narrow trail that ended at a high-walled enclosure perched on the edge of a sheer cliff. Massive sandstone blocks clung to a craggy outcrop of wind-battered yellow rock. The wind whistled with the song of a thousand flutes.

A few lights flickered in the village below. In the center of the sweeping oasis of spiky palms, a large mirror lake reflected the orange sky. Beyond the oasis, golden dunes continued to the horizon.

Our guide stayed behind when Antinous and I followed the priest through double cedar doors set in thick stone walls. After a second set of double doors, we stopped in an open courtyard with vivid-painted fluted columns topped by palmiform capitals.

The priest put fire to a series of tall brass braziers. Neon colors popped out of the dark; row upon row of hieroglyphs glowed. He motioned for us to sit on a stone bench near the gilt doors of an inner sanctum, and then, silent as a shade, he disappeared.

All was still except for the flute song of the wind. From far away came the high-pitched howl of a jackal. A heartbeat later I heard another, and then a third. Antinous took my hand.

One by one the stars appeared. Antinous was still as a statue, breathing quietly. I was certain he took in every detail of the winged lintels and rich murals, working out the mathematics of the engineering and the geometry of the design.

Then quite unexpectedly, he turned and kissed me lightly. His eyes sparkled; torchlight glinted off his golden curls.

"Magical, is it not, Athena of Korinth?"

The stars formed a blazing canopy across the inky sky by the time the Oracle appeared on the bench opposite us.

"Hermes!" I blurted out.

My long journey from Delphi had brought me to Hermes *Trismegistus*, the creator himself of the Emerald Tablet. His white mane was gone; he had a shaved head, oiled and glowing in the lamplight. He didn't wear a flowing blue robe with silver stars; his bare bony shoulders poked at the leopard skin. But those familiar, kind, paler than pale eyes, now lined with *kohl* in the Egyptian fashion, smiled at me with deep affection.

"It gladdens my heart that we three are together again," he greeted us warmly.

"Together again?" an astonished Antinous asked. "Have we met, Sir?"

"Does he not *know*?" Hermes asked me. "How can that be?"

"Not everyone has the Sight, my father."

"Father?" Antinous asked. "Sight?"

Poor Antinous. I'd never seen him so completely bewildered.

"Later," I said gently, squeezing his hand.

The line was there between his eyes, the one that deepens when his computer brain struggles to make sense of divergent data. His pupils were huge and black. He'd never focused so intently on me before. At least, not in this lifetime.

"Trust me," I whispered.

I could see a million questions racing through his mind. But instead of insisting on answers, he hesitated for a moment or two and then said, "I have followed you this far, Athena of Korinth. You have my trust."

Was there ever another man who so believed in me? Well, perhaps Hermes *Trismegistus*. He had named me the Chosen One.

"I take it that you two have found the Emerald Tablet."

Antinous opened his mouth to speak—I'm certain to ask how Hermes knew—but ended by pursing his lips, the furrow between his eyes impossibly deeper.

I only allowed myself a heartbeat of surprise. I should have realized that I had no secrets from Hermes.

"We found it buried in the sand," I said as if telling him something no more improbable than how we'd found the path to his Temple. "Just as the Oracle of Delphi prophesied."

"And so," he answered, "you fulfill your destiny. Did Pythia not also foretell that?"

"She may have foreseen my destiny as written on the Tablet, but I cannot read it. Possessing the Tablet is not enough."

"Not enough?" His eyes twinkled, perhaps in amusement. "Indeed. Is that why you have come? You desire the Tablet's power?"

"Do you not trust me with it?"

"You are asking for much trust this night," he teased, patting my hand. He sat back, studying me. His eyes had gone serious.

I waited, meeting his look directly, letting him read my thoughts and my heart.

"I trust your intentions, Athena, but you are not as strong as you believe. The Tablet is a force for great Good—or great Evil. The stakes are high. If you lose control, you lose everything. There is no halfway."

Hermes paused and gazed up at the night sky filled with jewel-colored stars.

"Is the cosmos not glorious?" he pondered with true wonder in his tone.

For the first time, I considered that he might not tell me. That Hermes might judge me unworthy of the secret to so glorious a universe.

"Have you read the text, Antinous?" he asked, his head still back, his gaze drinking in the cosmos. "Do you understand its meaning?"

"I believe I do, Sir. The mind has the power to manifest the physical from the non-physical—to create form from energy. But as for the Tablet, I have concluded that there is a missing element—an X factor—required to activate its potential."

"A fair enough assessment," Hermes admitted, looking from the stars to us. "But do not envision that you can manifest an army from nothing, but rather understand that the cosmos will put an army at your disposal."

He must have seen our confusion, because he said emphatically, "*Influence.* I am talking about powerful, inexorable *influence.*"

Then he looked back up at the sky, and my eyes followed his to see Jupiter suddenly crest the wall. Hermes smiled and breathed out a long sigh. Did he take the sudden appearance of the planet of benevolence as an omen of my good intent? But I don't believe that Hermes had much use for omens. He has the Sight.

"I must caution you," he went on briskly, looking at Antinous and me in turn. He was all business. "I have placed limits on its power."

"Limits?" I asked. "As in how large an army?"

"No. Limits to the *quantity* of power. When the power is spent, the Tablet must recharge."

"How much power does it have?"

"However much is left."

Riddles. Oracles do love their riddles.

"But surely, Sir," Antinous insisted, "there must be a formula to calculate how much force has been expended and how much is in reserve."

"Precisely the dilemma, my boy! Some outcomes require more energy than others. You cannot know the limit until the moment the power is exhausted." Hermes chuckled, obviously pleased with his own ingenuity. "Call it my way of braking ambition and keeping events from moving too quickly—of giving the cosmos an opportunity to balance itself."

I thought only of balancing my little world; I didn't have the pretensions of Alexander the Great. My desire was for the Tablet to protect myself and those I loved—nothing more.

Hermes took both our hands into his warm, comforting palms; his calm, steady life force flowed into us. A noble corona of pure white light glowed around Antinous. My whole body pulsed. I felt every cell vibrate at higher and higher frequencies.

Without a word, Hermes let go of our hands, rose and disappeared through gilt doors into the *naos*.

We waited. Surely he meant to return. Antinous reached for my hand; his eyes smiled into mine. I squeezed his fingers, and he raised mine to his lips.

"You have led me on quite a journey, Athena of Korinth."

Flames sputtered in the braziers, and sparks flew with a rising wind. The music of the rocks grew louder. The jackal, closer this time, howled his high, lonely cry and was answered once more.

Finally, Hermes returned with a silver sword as long as my arm. I recognized it as the sword in my Abydos dream three centuries earlier. The double-edged silver blade burned fiery orange in the red glow of the embers.

"Kneel, Antinous," Hermes commanded.

Greeks do not kneel before any man, not even a king, but when I nodded, Antinous went to his knees.

Holding the golden guard in one hand and the emerald pommel in the other, Hermes offered me the sword. A cobra, etched into the deep groove at the center of the blade, snaked its way down the fuller to the tip.

I fully expected the heavy-looking sword to be weighty as iron and reached out with both hands to grasp the grip. The metal must have been a special alloy—luminous like silver yet strong as steel—because the blade was light in my hand and perfectly balanced to my strength.

First hot to the touch, the grip quickly cooled to my own heat. The rough-cut gemstones in the hilt colored my palms and fingers with rainbow light.

I tapped Antinous with the tip of the sword first on his right shoulder and then on his left.

"Antinous of Kos, I name you *Hippeus Smeraldos*, the Emerald Knight."

I admit to feeling a little ridiculous, as if we were Guinevere and Lancelot with Merlin in a Camelot play.

"The Order of the Tablet," Hermes instructed, "may have seven members. Choose wisely, Athena. Seven Protectors. Everything depends upon their loyalty."

"And now, if Antinous will excuse us, I shall explain the rules."

A priest opened the outside gate for me, and Antinous and the guide leapt to their feet. The guide was in a hurry to return to the inn; we slowed our pace and let him go on ahead. I handed Antinous the tool bag with the Emerald Tablet wrapped in antelope skin.

"What happened?"

"Please do not ask me what I cannot say."

When I'd placed my right palm on the Tablet and repeated the mantra, *Alpha to Omega, We are all One*, I might have asked for world peace. But my two desires were quite simple—first to see Jason settled and safe, and then to go home. Home to Las Vegas.

Antinous was silent for much of the descent. I imagined that he thought of what he would have asked of the Emerald Tablet in my place—how to build a dome that stands, how to explain the passage of seasons.

Dry earth and small stones crunched under our leather soles. The stars blazed over our heads.

We were about halfway down the path when he stopped and took me by the shoulders. His grip was firm, that of a wrestler. Instead of his usual detachment, he was intense and wholly present.

"How do you know the Oracle, Athena, and how does he know me? You must tell me at least this."

I searched for a way to explain our souls meeting in different lifetimes that wouldn't sound crazy to a nonbeliever like Antinous, but there was no explanation other than the truth.

"We knew each other in another lifetime three hundred years ago. Here in Egypt. In Saïs. Hermes was my father, and you were his assistant. You helped him create the Emerald Tablet."

I didn't consider telling him that we also knew each other in the future. Already the past would be more than he could accept. I expected him to be dismissive. Maybe I thought he might laugh. He didn't share Plato's belief in the transmigration of souls.

But it seemed that even pragmatic Antinous had succumbed to the magic of the Temple of Amun.

Instead of arguing the implausibility of consciousness surviving death, he asked, "And what was I to you?"

"You were my husband."

Of everything I'd told him, that seemed to stun him most. I had the sense our marriage in the past came as a revelation explaining the connection between us he must feel. A few seconds passed while he studied my face.

"Did I make you happy?" he asked most seriously.

"How could I be anything but happy with you?"

The oasis was silent save for the song of the wind rustling through palm fronds. In the starlight, Antinous might have been carved from marble, his beauty was so pure.

"Now I understand your questions about my marital status," he said matter-of-factly. Then he added, "And your unease with Leandros."

Brutally honest, that's Antinous. But without harmful intent. To him, the world was a collection of facts and observable behavior. Emotions and feelings were but one part of the equation.

I didn't intend for him to see me react to his mention of Leandros, but there isn't much the brilliant Antinous doesn't see when he chooses to.

He touched my cheek and said gently, "There are many kinds of love, Athena."

"Yes," I answered, "I know."

There in the still of the night, perhaps a little high on the magic of the Oracle, Antinous kissed me as a lover for the first time in this life.

But instead of the wild exuberance typical of him, his lips pressed on mine in a kiss as sweet as poetry. His hands moved tenderly across my shoulders and up the sides of my neck; his fingers gently combed through my hair.

I leaned into him, my tongue in his mouth, and he pulled away.

"Not like this," he said. His tone was husky but firm; his mind was in control.

I imagined his pulse rate only slightly above normal.

He kissed me again softly; his lips were a cool breeze on mine. Surrounded by curling lashes, his eyes were all pupils. In the starlight, his curls were more silver than gold.

"I would have you, Athena, knowing that you could never give me all. Would you have me, knowing the same?"

The specter of the beautiful boy-god Leandros slithered between us.

When I didn't answer, he smiled knowingly and took my hand, leading me through the swaying palms under a glorious field of stars.

CHAPTER 38   TOMB OF THE CROCODILE

"Fear is pain arising from the anticipation of evil." – Aristotle

Filthy from travel, muscles aching, I longed to bathe in the healing waters of Siwa. I was both euphoric from my encounter with Hermes and melancholic over Black Falcon, Jason and now Antinous.

I wanted to free myself of the inhibitions that allowed Leandros to come between Antinous and me, I truly did. Would my feelings of inadequacy be different if I competed with another woman and not a boy?

As much as I desired it otherwise, my heart couldn't ignore that the youth satisfied a special need in Antinous—occupied a special place in his male affection—that a woman could never fill. And never to reach that level of intimacy was more than I was ready to accept.

"Do you still sing your psalms, Eben?" I asked wistfully. "It has been so long since your sweet voice soothed my soul. Will you not come with me to the springs?"

I insisted that Goliath and the two black-turbaned men were ample protection. Antinous stayed behind with the Tablet. Over the protests of the innkeeper and our guide, we rode through the sleeping oasis back along the trail to the hot pool nestled in a grove of palm trees.

We passed a pack of mangy dogs scavenging for food but saw no villagers out on this moonless night.

Seven words. I repeated them in my mind. *Alpha to Omega, We are all One.* That short phrase encapsulated the essence of the cosmos.

I had only to place my palm on the Emerald Tablet and say the mantra. Utter simplicity, really. How could it be otherwise?

Eben brought his lyre and sang the ancient psalms of his people. I soaked in the steaming sweet waters. Layers of dust and sweat floated away. When I dipped my head back, my long, luxuriant hair swirled around me in the snaky tendrils of a mermaid.

Goliath stood guard, his back toward me. The Queen's black-robed men disappeared into the trees. It was so peaceful. White almond blossoms scented the air. Only the slightest of warm breezes kissed my skin. A night bird sang out, and then another. I didn't recognize their song.

It happened so fast, I didn't have time to scream. A cloth went over my mouth and nose. I breathed something acrid into my lungs, and then the world went black.

When I came to, I was bound, gagged and still naked. Where was I? Where was Goliath—and Eben?

It was pitch dark and dead quiet. My hair was damp; I hadn't been unconscious long. Rough sand with small stones ground into my naked flesh. As hard as I tried to subdue the panic, it overwhelmed me.

Men's voices warned me of their approach, and then light from their lanterns brightened the chamber. I was in a cave. A mural of Osiris, God of the Underworld, leapt into vivid relief. The cave was a tomb. I was surrounded by death.

A half-finished wall of inscriptions in hieroglyphs was not far away. Mallets, chisels and paintbrushes lay scattered at the base. I made out a sketch of a fox, and then an elegantly executed crocodile with a face full of cunning. The Tomb of the Crocodile.

The end and the beginning. That's what the Oracle of Delphi's prophecy had said about the crocodile. Was this the end of Athena and the beginning of my soul's journey to the next life?

What would happen to the Las Vegas me, if I experienced death here and now in this cave? I didn't want to make that journey, not knowing where death leads on this side of the Mirror.

My mind processed a thousand thoughts at once. Even the words of Thales rushed through. *What is the fastest? The mind. It travels through everything.*

I couldn't tell how many men were in the cave with me or make out their faces. They spoke in low tones to each other in Greek; they were not the desert Berbers who sold slaves to Carthage. I think I would have welcomed that evil over the sinister aura of these men.

"Barb, wake me up! Wake me up!"

Of course, Barb couldn't hear me. I hadn't wanted her help.

The nightmare became impossibly more terrifying when a voice whispered in my ear, "We meet again."

The voice of Zavan the merciless.

"I have waited long for this moment," he breathed into my face. He flicked his wrist, and a tiny steel blade flashed.

No matter how many centuries passed since he called for my death in the General's tent, I'd never forget his ogre bulging eyes and twisted, thick lips spewing acid droplets of hatred.

"I have not forgotten what you did to the General, whore. I have dreamed through time of my revenge."

Why does the pure soul of Antinous have no memories of our past life, while such evil as Zavan is gifted with the Sight?

"Alpha to Omega, We are all One. Alpha to Omega, We are all One." I chanted the mantra over and over in my mind, desperate for it to save me. At least, my thousand terrified thoughts coalesced into one.

"Do you see this?" Zavan asked, waving the sharp, shiny point back and forth at the tip of my nose.

I stared into his eyes, willing myself not to scream into my gag or turn my face away. I wanted more than anything to find the courage to defy him, but he saw my fear. How could he not?

"This blade is my own creation. I have found it most efficient."

He traced the knife from the base of my throat, down between my bare breasts, across my slightly swollen belly, over my white mound and stopped at the entrance to my dark valley.

"From here I peel the layers back, like skinning a rabbit."

But when he cut, he pressed the razor-sharp edge down the length of my left arm. He barely broke the skin; drops of blood swelled. I again tasted the dried blood from Black Falcon's chest covered in hundreds of slits and gagged into the cloth in my mouth.

"I can go deep or shallow," he continued in a conversational tone. His bulging, ogre eyes sparkled with delight.

He dangled the leather amulet in front of my face, the one the Old

Jew had given me to poison Black Falcon, the one the prison guard took from me.

"Do you recognize this, whore?"

My wrists were bound so tight blood no longer flowed to my hands, yet I felt the Hathor ring throbbing on my finger. I summoned the Power.

It rose. I felt the heat spread. The Power vibrated in my every cell. Then it flowed from me to fill the dark space of the tomb. My heart rhythm calmed. I no longer felt the burning where the blade had slit my arm.

If I could have seen my eyes, I believe they turned hard and glittery as emeralds, emitting splintering rays of piercing green light.

As if slapped in the face, Zavan fell back and then stumbled to his feet.

"You did not say she is a witch," he snarled.

I stared in disbelief when Zavan dragged Ajax forward, his eyes wide with terror in a horrified face dotted with those luminescent white pox scars of his. His whole body trembled; he wouldn't look at me.

With shock, I realized that Ajax had probably spied on me all along. He'd been with me in the market; he carried my messages to the Queen. He journeyed to Siwa. The connections he witnessed were damning.

"The Royal Steward wants only the Tablet!" Ajax shrieked. "Let her tell us what she knows and then kill her quickly."

I felt more kindly toward him with his plea for a quick kill. *Death is not the worst that can happen to men.*

I once said on the other side that I wouldn't die for the Tablet. Now I welcomed death, if it ended the coming pain. Socrates believed death might be the greatest of all human blessings.

They say that time can stand still. It happened to me in the Tomb of the Crocodile dug into the hillside of the Mountain of the Dead. But rather than standing still, I believe one minute stretched to fill an eternity.

The men argued. Zavan was the most forceful; their voices came from afar. I was no longer in my body but floated above, looking down on a nude woman menaced by men and surrounded by symbols of death.

A sharp pain brought me back. Zavan had sliced off the tip of my right earlobe. Hot blood flowed down my neck. He leaned right into my face. To my horror, he placed the tiny piece of my own flesh in his mouth, chewed and then swallowed.

"How long do you think you can live if I take you apart in pieces as small as this?" He grinned an evil smile; his words sprayed filth in my face. "Tell me about the Tablet. Tell me everything you know."

"How can she speak while gagged?" Ajax screamed in panic.

Zavan pulled away the cloth binding my mouth, and I spat out bloodied saliva. I had bitten my tongue in my terror, but it didn't keep me from speaking.

"I know that the Tablet is useless without me."

Those were not the words they expected. The murmuring stopped. In the silence, the oil lamps spluttered like the hissing of snakes.

Dozens of carved cobras reared their heads above the sandstone lintel, swaying in the flickering light as if to the strains of a snake charmer's flute.

"I am the Chosen One," I insisted in a voice so strong, it could only have come from the Goddess. "Without me, the Emerald Tablet is merely a green stone. Nothing you do to me can change that."

"What she says was foretold by the Oracle of Delphi," whispered a man with a torch.

I recognized him from Ptolemy's delegation to Korinth.

"I heard the Oracle myself," he continued in a hushed, awed tone. *"She is the One. Her destiny is the green stone."*

Whatever deceives men produces a magical enchantment that clouds the exact memory of words and events. "My destiny written *on* the stone" had become in his mind "My destiny *is* the stone."

After a brief discussion, they agreed they wouldn't risk Steward Agathon's wrath by returning with a possibly useless stone. Zavan wasn't convinced. He grumbled and argued, but the others were firm. They insisted that they needed the Tablet *and* me.

They left me again in the pitch-dark, but not before I spotted the leather amulet with poison on the ground a few yards away. I wiggled my way toward it, slithering like a snake. Gravel scraped my skin. I reached the amulet with the tips of my fingers and clutched it in my fist tied behind my back.

I slept, but my dreams gave me no rest. I was back in the yellow silk bed beside the sea, but the four shadowy men now brandished small, sharp-edged knives. A blade flashed silver in the moonlight and pierced my right eye. I awoke from the blinding pain in my dream to the vivid pain of Zavan's special knife.

He hovered over me, holding the nasty small blade between our eyes, turning it from side to side to reflect the light from the torch burning beside us. Warm liquid oozed from my eyebrow; I didn't need to see it or taste it to know it was blood.

"Sorceress," he hissed. "You think I do not know your tricks? You may hypnotize the others, as you bewitched the General, but you do not fool me. Your power is in your green eyes. When they are gone, it is gone."

I squeezed my lids in hopeless defense; I saw Black Falcon's bloody slits where his eyes had once been.

How could the Tablet have failed me? I had asked for so little.

Zavan grabbed hold of my face; his coarse fingers dug into my flesh. I twisted back and forth and tried to bite his wrist. He stabbed me once in the left cheek—deep.

I felt the cold tip of the blade on my tongue. More blood flowed. I couldn't think of the Tablet's mantra. Only a white glow of terror filled my mind.

"Let her go, Zavan."

Zavan released his grip immediately at the sound of the voice and jumped to his feet.

"General!" he exclaimed.

"Move away from her, or I kill you where you stand."

Zavan had to be as stunned to see the General in the cave as I was, but he spoke as if centuries hadn't passed since we were last together.

"But, General, this is the Hathor whore who butchered you. Do you not wish revenge?"

"I want her—and in one piece. I said move away."

In the dim light of the torch, the General could have been a gorilla from deep in Nubia. He crouched. His arms swung low. On his toes with knees bent, a heavy broad sword in his hand, he poised to pounce.

Zavan hesitated and then stepped away from me. The tiny steel blade in his hand was no match for an iron sword. Zavan's weapon was death by a thousand cuts; the General could take off a head in one stroke.

In a movement so quick it was a blur, the General wrested the knife from Zavan's hand and shoved him against the wall, his massive forearm pressing on Zavan's throat.

Zavan gagged and put up his hands, palms out in the sign of surrender.

"If you have harmed her more than I can see, Zavan, I will take you apart limb by limb. Stand here. Do not move. Do not test me."

The General knelt, untied my bindings, put one arm around my back and the other under my knees and lifted me from the ground. Zavan didn't move from the wall.

"I kill you not today, Zavan, as I wish to do. You saved my life once in battle. The next time we meet, you die."

With that final warning, the General carried me out of the tomb. Three bodies lay outside. Black blood pooled on the pale sand. Ajax's throat had been slashed so deep, his head was attached only at the spine. I hung onto the General's neck and clutched in my hand the amulet with the poison vial.

"Get a physician," the General barked at the terrified family.

They understood enough Greek for a young boy to disappear into the night.

The women of the house appeared with a heavy wool cloak, and the General wrapped me gently and lay me on a mat. He wiped away the blood and examined my cuts. Only one oil lamp and a smoky cooking fire gave light.

"Not serious," he growled.

I felt his relief.

When he opened my hand and saw the amulet, I begged him, "Please, put it on my wrist. It makes me strong and keeps me from harm."

A bald priest arrived with a rolled leather kit. He quickly prepared a draught of poppy, sweetened it with honey and held it to my lips. Within minutes, my lids drooped and my nose tingled. After washing the wounds with water from a clay jug, he took out a needle and silk thread.

The deepest cut was on my left cheek. He took several small stitches on the outside and tied off the thread; the General held my lip while he stitched the inside. Next he closed the gap at the tip of my ear.

He applied a poultice of herbs on the stitches and the incision above my eye, and then turned to the long slit down my arm. The wound was very shallow, barely breaking the skin. He dabbed a line of honey along the length of the cut.

I was half awake, half dreaming during the procedure. Blurry faces peered at me; the General's face was close by, behind the physician's. The priest-doctor ran his fingers over my limbs and then my belly. The General watched every move; I watched the General.

Finally, the priest burned frankincense, waving the fumes over me and muttering magic spells. I caught only *Neferie'ri,* 'beautiful eye.'

I couldn't make out what the priest and the General said to each other; the broken Greek in strange accents jumbled in my drugged ear. When the priest made a small mound over his stomach with his hand, the General nodded his head.

Before he left, the priest removed the poultices and coated my facial wounds with honey.

"No bath," he said to me in pidgin Greek.

"Thank you," I answered him in Egyptian and fell instantly to sleep.

When I woke I was tied to a litter on the back of a horse in the empty desert. The sky was light, but the sun had not yet risen. The eastern horizon glowed rosy gold. My horse was tethered to the General's horse; he rode beside and slightly in front.

My cheek burned. My arm burned. My earlobe throbbed. I touched the silk stitches on the inside of my cheek with my tongue. I tried to sit up, but ropes held me.

"General," I called out. "I need to move. I need to relieve myself."

He stopped the horses and dismounted. Before he untied the ropes, he cautioned me.

"Do not try to run."

"Where?" I asked.

He helped me down and handed me a goatskin of water. He busied himself with bread and dates while I relieved my full bladder. I was still naked under the cloak. The rough fabric rubbed on my cut arm, and tiny hairs from the wool stuck in the honey.

"I need something else to wear."

He grunted and handed me a piece of dried goat.

"Where are you taking me?"

"To the sea."

"And after that?"

"To Carthage, of course."

I needed time to think of a strategy, so kept silent for a while. The sun came up as we ate, and the day was immediately hot.

"What happened to the Nubian and the Hebrew?"

He shrugged.

"General, I must get word to my companions."

"They know," he answered. "Everyone in the village knows of the physician's night visit. There are no secrets in Siwa."

It was some comfort that Antinous knew I was alive.

"How did you find me?"

"When I arrived by sea to Amunia, I heard nothing but talk of a Greek Goddess traveling with Alexander the Great. Who else could it be?"

"And how did you know I was in the tomb?"

"The artisans stopped working. They had silver to spend. Someone had to have paid them to stay away. I told you that there are no secrets in Siwa."

He looked at me expectantly—I supposed to hear thanks.

"I am grateful, General, that you saved me from Zavan, but you did it not for me. You have your own reasons." I gave him back his own words from my bathchamber the night I bought him in the slave market.

He laughed. "Clever, Ishtar. Always so clever."

"Let me go, General. There is more at stake than our game."

"This is not a game."

I chewed more of the dried goat and swallowed more sweet Siwa water. To keep calm, I told myself the Tablet would still save me.

"What have you done with Jason?"

Our agreement was never to tell me where Jason was, but I had to know. I had counted on the General to get Jason away; I'd had no other choice. But with the General, I could never be sure. He might have killed Jason the morning they left my villa in the Royal Gardens.

"He is safe."

"Is he still in Egypt?"

"No."

"Tell me what you have done with him. Assure me that he is safe. Make me believe it."

"I sent him to Carthage."

"Carthage?" I repeated dumbly.

"You said I should treat him as my own son. My son will be a warrior. What else would you expect?"

Only news of Jason's death could have twisted my heart more. I had considered the risk when I used the ploy of fatherhood to win the General's protection but never considered this outcome.

Be careful what you wish for was what Barb had said.

I envisioned so much for Jason—that he would grow up learned and noble—that he would be Greek. First Jason, now the child I carried, looked fated to be raised in savage Carthage.

"I cannot go with you to Carthage. I have never lived the life of a normal Greek woman," I argued, "much less a Carthaginian. You lock your women away, prisoners for life in your fortress houses."

One path leads to honor, the other to slavery.

"I would be like a slave," I pleaded.

Silence. He stared at the northern horizon, our route to the sea.

"Tell me that you do not prefer death over life as a slave," I demanded.

He refused to answer.

"General, if you do not let me go, one of us must die. If not today, then tomorrow or the day after."

When he still didn't speak, I made one last pitch.

"Generals are crucified in Carthage for losing one battle. What will they do to *you*—disgraced and enslaved? You cannot return there."

"Enough!" he snarled. "We have a long ride."

With that, we remounted. He tossed the litter aside and kept my horse tethered to his. He didn't bind my hands; there was no risk of my fleeing. Where would I run in my bare feet?

My tears over Jason evaporated into the dry air. I despaired of ever seeing him again in this lifetime. I glanced often at the leather amulet on my wrist with the deadly vial and its promise of the final escape.

With every mile we drew nearer to the sea, a bright future seemed to slip further away. But even a man with nothing has hope.

CHAPTER 39   REUNION

"Force has no place when there is need of skill." – Herodotus

From the top of a rocky ridge, we had a view of the harbor. A great broad-bowed vessel moored there now. A ship built to sail through the Pillars of Hercules and north on the stormy seas to the land of the Gauls and Celts. Before heading west into the Atlantic, such a ship stops in Carthage.

Warning me that if I signaled for help or tried to escape, he would kill the whole family, the General pounded on the wooden gate of a mud hovel on the outskirts of town. After a brief exchange, the old man turned over a Berber woman's tattered robe, sandals and sparkly head scarf for a coin.

I let the hood of my cloak slip to my shoulders, exposing my blonde hair, knowing that word would spread like wildfire that the Golden Goddess was back, but without Alexander.

We stopped for me to change on an isolated low rise overlooking the ship with green sails that might soon carry me to Carthage. Wispy clouds turned bright pink when the sun sank below the flat line of the desert. The air instantly cooled but was still balmy and mild with no wind.

The General had a problem, and we both knew it. How could he get me on the ship without my cooperation? He had no leverage with which to threaten me. He could gag me and bind me and put me in a sack, but not without a struggle. He would have to knock me out.

"Are you going to hurt me?" I asked.

He had tethered the horses to stones; they nibbled at scruffy shrubs growing between rocks. The coarse-woven linen of the Berber gown was soft against my skin after the scratch of the wool cape. I couldn't see the wounds on my face, but the slit on my arm showed no sign of infection or swelling.

"What shall you do if my child is a girl? Kill her, as is your custom?"

He glared at me. I wondered how far I could push him. I even wondered if I could overpower him and pour the poison from the vial down his throat.

"Would you really rather die than go with me?" he asked suddenly.

He must have been thinking about my words all day. I put my hand on his massive forearm scarred from a life of battle. His skin was dark next to mine; tiny black hairs rose in gooseflesh at my touch.

He closed his eyes. Dust coated his thick, wavy beard. His bull's chest rose and fell.

"I have a life in Greece," I whispered, "given only to a handful. I am burdened with responsibility, but I am respected. In many ways, I am free—more free than any woman anywhere in this world."

He didn't open his eyes.

"You once said you could never bend to my every whim. Could you expect me to bend to yours?"

"Would it be different if I offered you other than Carthage?" he growled.

His question took me off guard. I hesitated, trying to imagine where a Carthaginian renegade and a Greek priestess could go.

"No."

His sigh was heavy when he stood to his feet. His massive tree trunk thighs, fuzzy with curled black hairs, were within reach, but what could I do? I could hardly overpower him. I found myself focused on his hands clenched into powerful fists and his thick fingers that could crush my throat with one squeeze.

"Would you live with the father of your child?" He didn't look at me.

"No," I answered immediately.

Black Falcon was gone, Hektor married. I would return to my life as priestess. Then I held my breath when the words sunk in. Had he truly said *would*? Did he offer hope of the possibility of a future without him?

"That, at least, is some consolation," he grunted. His lips formed a bittersweet smile around words tinged with irony. "I told myself that if I could not have you, no one could. It seems no one shall."

It took me a moment longer to dare let myself believe that he spoke of letting me go. He turned abruptly and sat on his haunches, facing me. I thought he might yet kill me right there on the sandy rise overlooking the sea.

"I lied to you, Ishtar."

His face was inches from mine. I could smell his breath, not sweet, a little sour, but not unpleasant.

I waited, staring at him, not daring to breathe or blink for fear of him changing his mind.

"Jason is not in Carthage. He is in the port."

"Jason is *here*? He is *here*!"

I can't explain my reaction. I couldn't control the shaking. I leaned into the General, put my arms around his neck and sobbed into his chest.

At first he stiffened. Then he put his powerful arms around my waist and crushed me to him, lifting me off the ground even while he crouched.

"Thank you! Thank you!" I cried into his mouth.

And then I kissed him. We breathed together, filling our lungs with each other's air. I don't know if I ever loved any man more than I did in that moment.

He spread the cloak on the hard, rocky ground and lowered me gently, careful of my arm, careful not to brush against my stitched cheek. As he lay me down, I saw on the horizon the sliver of the crescent moon with the brilliant evening star Ishtar at the tip of its horn.

With great care, he pulled the Berber gown over my head and kissed my breasts and my swollen belly. He leaned into my ear, his coarse beard brushing my stitched cheek, and rumbled so deep from his throat that his words were more growl than speech.

"My regret of that life is not that you killed me, but that you did not let me see my son grow in your womb. That I did not suckle your milk."

I untied his sash, letting it fall across my loins. With my cut arm throbbing, I pulled his tunic over his head and buried my face in the mass of black hair on his chest. I breathed deep of his animal scent.

My fingers barely reached around his engorged manhood. I didn't feel the sharp edges of rocks poking through the wool, except to register pleasure. With the General, it is always that delicious sliding back and forth between pain and rapture.

When he lifted my hips, I locked my legs around his waist and hung onto his neck, suspended above the desert floor. My mouth hung on his. I forgot the stitches and begged him to devour me. Our feral cries frightened the horses; I was vaguely aware that they whinnied wildly and tugged at their tethers.

He was at my gate, pushing like a log into my canal.

I called out to the Goddess when he split me to ram up against the bottom of my womb. My legs around him tightened; I lifted myself into his thrust. The skin popped on my arm as the wound spread, but pain was so utterly confused with pleasure that I purred in delight.

He tore his mouth away from mine and, like a raged bull, snorted in my ear. Tiny droplets of his saliva sprayed my face. I bit his earlobe until I tasted blood and then licked and swallowed and sucked more. The harder I sucked, the harder he pounded me. I grabbed handfuls of his hair in my fists and pulled myself still closer into him.

His arm across my back arched my spine. My breasts crushed into the hot tangled hair of his chest. My head went back with my thick mass of waves swinging in the dust.

Suddenly his hand was around my throat, squeezing so tight I couldn't breathe. I gasped and choked, and still he didn't let go. I thought he was going to kill me, but when I looked into his eyes, I didn't see a killer.

I let go of his hair, and he loosened his grip. Our eyes locked. Then he squeezed again, and this time I felt the thrill.

I knew it was wrong; I knew it was sick. But still I felt it. He saw the pleasure in my eyes and squeezed harder.

I frightened myself more than he frightened me.

Frenzied, I pulled at his hair. I couldn't breathe; his hand crushed my larynx. The world went fuzzy and then sharpened in the purest and clearest of colors before exploding into radiant white light.

At the edge of losing consciousness, I dropped my hands, and he released my throat so I could breathe again. Even though he had let go, I still throbbed where each of his steel fingers had pressed.

He drove into me again and again, pushing me to my limit while every cell screamed for more. He gnawed at my neck like an animal, sucking the skin with his thick lips as if he could draw blood through my pores. I scored his grizzly bear shoulders with my nails. Each time I dug in, he snarled and crushed me in his arms.

We developed a rhythm. When the pain was too great, I loosened my grip on his hair. I became passive to his dominant. When I wanted more, I pulled hard again. He unleashed a fire I thought could never be quenched.

The pressure started low in my buttocks, like a warm flame spreading down my loins and over my belly, burning hotter and hotter until my lotus erupted in a *Kundalini* wave that travelled up through my womb, stopped my breath and exploded in my ears.

When he climaxed, his great gorilla body shook with such force, I thought his heart might stop. He heaved and trembled, his animal growls savage in my ear.

I let go of his hair when he relaxed his arm holding my back, and my shoulders fell to the ground. But my legs, with ankles locked, still gripped around his waist. He supported his massive weight on his forearms and knees; his head hung down with his long, coarse hair in my face.

We panted together as wild animals after a chase. We should have been drenched in sweat, but the droplets dissolved into the sere desert air before beading on our skin.

When our breathing calmed, he lifted his head and looked into my eyes.

"What a pity we have to wait until another lifetime to soar to the stars each night."

He kissed me tenderly with his fat thick lips, and then even more gently, kissed my wounded eye and my stitched cheek.

"You will always be flawless to me," he whispered next to my mutilated earlobe.

But when he looked at my arm, he frowned and found the waterskin to wash away the fresh blood. He reapplied a stream of honey slowly and carefully, precisely as the priest had done.

"Why did you deceive me about Jason?"

"I hoped for your gratitude when you saw him safe."

I should have been angry he lied, but instead I *was* grateful—for Jason, for my freedom, for the lessons I learned from every game he played. Today he taught me the dark secret that I could feel shame and thrill at the same time.

The stars shone in the wine dark sky. A fiery red crescent with the cool evening star sank below the horizon before he handed me my robe.

"It is time now," he said, "to go to Jason."

The General had left Jason at an Egyptian inn near the port. I found him in the kitchen, playing with a puppy near the cooking fire. He ran to me at once, throwing his arms around my waist, burying his face in my breasts while I clutched him to me and rocked back and forth, kissing the top of his head.

When he pulled away to look in my face and saw my wounds, his hazel eyes widened in shock and then filled with tears.

"How could anyone harm someone as beautiful as you?"

"I am not harmed, Jason. The wounds will heal; *I* have not been touched."

"How can there be such evil in the world?"

"To live without evil belongs only to the Gods."

"I know that!" he exclaimed proudly. "That is Sophocles."

He had so much promise. I kissed Jason again, and thanked the General with a smile. He grunted and turned away, but not before I saw satisfaction mixed with sorrow.

We supped on fish stew and warm bread with beer at a long, rough-hewn table in the inn dining hall when Antinous rushed in the door. At first he saw only me. When his eye fell on the General sitting across the table, his huge frame silhouetted by the fire, he stopped, and his hand went to Hermes' silver sword in his belt.

"Antinous! I am safe and well."

I went straight to him and put my hand on his around the jeweled grip. The General was on his feet with a steel dagger flashing in the firelight.

"He saved me, Antinous. I am here of my own free will."

I didn't have to ask how Antinous came to the inn, knowing that the streets must be full of nothing but the news of the return of the Golden Goddess. As in Siwa, there are no secrets in Amunia. Audience to our drama, the townspeople watched our every move. Someone probably stopped 'Alexander' every few feet to tell him that I was in the inn.

"Your escaped slave, Athena? I do not understand."

Then he saw Jason. I'd never seen Antinous smile so bright. He grabbed Jason by his thin shoulders and swung him in the air, holding him out, examining him from head to toe.

"Are you well?"

"My life is perfect now," Jason replied.

The General watched us. His thick eyelids drooped, but I saw the envy in his eyes. My heart wrenched for him. Had he ever known love and devotion in his whole brutal life?

Seated under a grape arbor in the inn courtyard, Antinous and I talked quietly among cackling black-and-white chickens. I told him my terrible saga of the Tomb of the Crocodile, about Ajax's betrayal and the General rescuing me.

"The Egyptian did an excellent job on your wounds. There is no sign of infection. You will have scars, of course; that cannot be avoided."

The matter-of-fact tone of his voice communicated more clearly than anything that scars were irrelevant to pragmatic Antinous.

He blessed me with the news that Goliath and Eben should soon arrive. They had survived the attack but sustained injuries—Goliath less, Eben more. The Queen's assassins returned in time to save their lives, but only after I'd been carried off.

"I went straight to Hermes. He assured me that I would find you here at the sea. I don't know how he knew."

"That is why he is called an Oracle," I teased.

He smiled and raised my fingers to kiss the Hathor ring. He moved to kiss my lips, but I stopped him with my fingertips on his mouth.

"May Jason sleep in your chamber tonight?"

At first, he stared at me with that blank look he often has when processing new information. When I saw the shock come into his eyes, I knew he'd realized that the General was the reason why.

"There are many kinds of love, Antinous. Do not try to understand."

I kissed him briefly on the lips, and then tenderly on each eye.

"Did we have a family together?" he asked quite unexpectedly.

"The Sight is a peculiar phenomenon. I have visions of people, like characters, in vivid scenes—but cannot remember the whole play. I cannot tell you how our story ended. Except that my last memory of you is one of love and trust."

"How many lives have we known each other?"

He truly astonished me with his acceptance of a premise quite impossible in his mathematical world.

"Three—that I know of."

"Three? Was there another before the Library of Neith, or between then and now?"

"The third is in the future."

"Thales says only the past is certain and that the future is obscure."

"Thales was wrong. He did not understand time."

The General sat with Jason, who played with the puppy. They talked low, but I heard snippets of an unfamiliar language and realized they must be speaking Punic. They both looked up as we came back inside; Jason smiled, and the General frowned.

"Do not raise him to be soft," he growled at Antinous.

"We Greeks hold beauty and learning highest—but we do not lose our manliness."

"You Greeks are arrogant fools," the General snapped. "Your 'manliness' is an ideal, like one of your statues. Do you think wars are won by wrestling?"

"Greeks have won more wars than Carthage has waged battles," Antinous countered.

"You call the petty squabbles among yourselves *war*?" the General snorted. "While you bicker among your many kings and grow weak, looking always to the East for enemies, Rome devours the West. Only Carthage stops them."

"Then it is up to you, Carthaginian, who so loves war. While you and Rome battle each other in your senseless slaughter, we cultivate our minds. It is knowledge that will prevail in the end."

"With Rome, there is only victory or annihilation. Your turn at slavery is near, Greek. Of what use will your cultivated mind be as a slave?"

I took Jason's worried face in my fingers and kissed him gently on the forehead.

"Do not concern yourself with Rome, Jason. They are yet far from our world. You must give Antinous the joy of your company tonight. He wants to hear all of your adventures."

When the General closed the bedchamber door in the tiny inn with thin walls, I put my hands on his bull chest and made him promise only one thing—quiet. He bound my mouth with a cloth and then his.

CHAPTER 40 ALPHA TO OMEGA

"The bravest have the clearest vision of what is before them, glory and danger alike, and go out to meet it." – Thucydides

I was up with the sun to go in search of a stone carver. Jason would not let me out of his sight; he had been asleep outside my room when I opened the door.

The craftsman was drinking his morning beer and dipping his warm bread in olive oil when we found his small stall at the end of a narrow alley. Jason greeted the man in Berber. We used a mix of hand signals, rudimentary Greek and Jason's meager Berber to negotiate.

He would start at once and deliver by the end of day. Awed by the visit of the Golden Goddess, even dressed in a tattered Berber robe, he promised to work without stop until finished.

Goliath and Eben had arrived when I returned to the inn. Eben, gravely wounded with several knife stabs to his chest and back, assured me that the priest-physician in Amunia had administered the appropriate treatment.

"I have been meditating while we journeyed," he explained. "I have been in communion with the Light. It is my destiny to survive."

I wished him success with his translation of the words of Moses to Greek.

"Your work is the foundation for three great religions."

"There is only one God," he replied. "We are all one."

Goliath had one arm bound and a bloodied cloth around his head.

The light in his face said he was as relieved to see me alive as I was him. It left his face just as quickly when he saw the flaming wound on my cheek and my swollen, bruised eye.

"It was not your fault," I hurried to assure him. "It was I who insisted on bathing that night."

In the courtyard, again among the cackling chickens, I asked him to be a Protector, using Egyptian where I could, simple Greek for the rest. When I began to explain the Emerald Tablet's mystic power and cosmic principles, he stopped me.

"I vow to protect you and all that is yours. I need not know more."

"Please watch over Jason for me, Goliath. Guard him with your life."

"I failed you once," he said. "Never again."

The artisan finished as promised and came at the end of the day with a leather pouch. Antinous gave him a small purse with silver *drachmas*, but he refused them, kissing my hand and asking as payment that the Goddess bless his wife with a child. I put the coins back in his hand and told him to save them for his son.

I felt guilty when he wept from joy, knowing his wife's barren womb wouldn't be so easily filled. But his elation was so great when he left, that I rationalized any moment of happiness in his hard life to be a blessing.

A septagram etched each small circlet of green faience—an exact match to the cufflinks Lars wore in Copenhagen.

I pressed two in Eben's palm, one for him and one for Qeb-ha.

"We are all One," I told him, squeezing his hand three times.

I gave one to Goliath with the same three squeezes, then two medallions to Antinous.

"One is for the Queen. Discretion is paramount."

"We are The Six Protectors. The Order of the Tablet. I have not yet named the Seventh."

When Antinous tried to give me the silver sword, I put my hand on his arm.

"You are the Emerald Knight. It belongs with you."

"Remember," I said to them. "We are all One."

As the sun set in a blaze of red glory, Hektor's gilded yacht sailed through burgundy waters into port. I judged the restrained and elegant opulence of his custom *bireme* to be Eugenia's taste.

Ever the gentleman, he raised his silver *kylix* in a toast when he saw my face.

"*Kallistei!*" To the most beautiful. Just as our first evening together at the symposion in Korinth.

"All shall heal," he assured me. "Small scars cannot detract from your beauty, but you should bathe and change at once. It pains me to see you in rags."

He led me to a luxurious suite, complete with marble bath and yellow canaries in gold cages. The sweet perfume of gardenia filled my nose.

Two of my freed slaves from Alexandria were filling the bath with warm, scented water. They beamed their joy at seeing me until they saw the stitches on my face and the angry cut on my arm. They immediately averted their eyes and wouldn't look directly at me again.

"I come bearing gifts," Hektor joked.

"When do you not?"

My two chests carved with my name—Αθηνα Κορινθος, Athena of Korinth—stood by a bed covered in rose-colored silk and piled high with down pillows. I resisted the urge to lie down.

"Leave us," I told the girls.

Hektor smiled, glancing at the bath and then the bed.

"Eugenia told me about my child," he said as he poured dark wine into a second *kylix*. "I woke from deep sleep with one thought—to come to you as quickly as possible."

"How did you know to come to Amunia?"

"I cannot say for sure. I heard many rumors but sailed here."

He handed me the silver drinking cup embossed with Dionysus embracing Ariadne. We both took a sip, looking at each other over the rims of our cups.

"Did a dream speak to you?" I dared ask.

"A dream? You know I have no faith in the meaning of dreams, Athena."

"But did Pindar not say that there comes to men a gleam of splendor given of heaven? Perhaps heaven spoke to you, Hektor."

He took the *kylix* from my hand, set it back on the ebony and gold table and moved right next to me, taking my chin in his fingers and lifting my face so that I looked directly into his eyes.

"The heavens do not speak, Athena. The Gods do not listen. If they did, all men would have perished by now, for we are forever praying for evil against each other."

I wouldn't ask Hektor to be a Protector. He wasn't ready to believe in the Emerald Tablet.

"I have thought of nothing but you," he whispered in my ear. In his smooth, expert way, he started to lift my robe to ease over my head.

I took his hands firmly in mine and held them.

"No, Hektor."

"Why not? You please me more than any woman. I know I please you. What else is there?"

Life was so simple for Hektor born to ease and fulfillment.

"It is not so simple for me. I love you, Hektor, I do—but I also love Eugenia."

"Eugenia? But you barely know her."

How could I explain Barb in a distant future to Hektor? I took refuge in a cushioned chair with low straight back and massive, unforgiving arms mounted with fierce, gold lion heads.

"Hektor, there is something you must do for me."

"Always that," he said glumly, picking up his cup of wine again. "You have no trouble asking for my help when you need it."

"I want you to adopt Jason. Ptolemy would not dare covet your son. Would you do that for me, Hektor?"

He straightened and turned away, taking a large swig of wine.

"Jason. Always Jason," he said resentfully.

"I love him with all my heart, Hektor, but he cannot be with me in the Temple. Men are not allowed in the sacred area. You, of all people, should know that."

It was not hard for my soft voice to conjure up those intimate, forbidden moments we had shared in my office high above the Gulf of Korinth.

I rose and went to him, putting my hand up to his smooth, newly-pumiced cheek. He softened ever so slightly. I made my next demand.

"I want him to be educated by Antinous."

"Why does *he* not adopt him?" he asked in a tone close to that of a spoiled child.

"Because Antinous is unlikely to marry, and I want Jason to know a mother's love. Eugenia can provide that affection. I know her heart."

He didn't answer. His jaw set in that stubborn way of a man not wanting to admit defeat, but knowing it's inevitable.

"Hektor, please. Jason is part of me. If you truly love me, then you must love him, too."

"What of *my* child? What happens to *him*?"

I followed Eugenia's lead and didn't tell him that paternity was in question. I wanted to say nothing that might sabotage my unborn child's happiness.

"If the child is a boy, you and Eugenia may adopt him as your own. You may choose his name; he need never know about me. But you must vow he speak Egyptian as well as Greek—and worship their Gods if he so desires."

But in my heart, it was Black Falcon I begged for understanding. His last request was for his son not to be Greek. *Forgive me!* I had to live with a compromise position, but it was the best I could do for a child who might not even be his.

"If my child is a girl, I shall raise her in the Temple. She can grow to be her own person without the permission of a father or husband."

I waited for Hektor's decision. The air in the plush cabin was thick with his disappointment. He sat down on a low tripod stool, long legs bent at the knees, leaning forward with his forearms on his thighs, hands clasped together. He had sat in that exact position in my bathchamber the night of Black Falcon's death. But today, he had the air of defeat about him.

He said nothing; he glowered and refused to look at me. I'd even say he pouted. There was a chance he might not agree to my terms; he was a man used to having his way. But when he finally sighed, and I saw resignation in the slump of his shoulders, I knew I'd won.

"I brought along something else of yours," he said flatly. "I thought you might want it."

He turned his face toward the bed. "There. Under the green silk."

A wrapped rectangle leaned against the tapestry-covered wall. I didn't need to fold back the cloth. I knew. The Red Mirror. My ticket home.

The Emerald Tablet does not manifest armies from thin air, but puts an army at your disposal.

"O Hektor! I owe you everything. I shall always love you. You must know that. You *must* believe that."

My heart nearly broke as I let myself dream, for a breath, of the life we might have if we were free. I resisted running my fingers through his rich chestnut waves and barbered curls. I resisted kissing his lips, letting my love and gratitude flow into him, easing his tension.

But we weren't free. There was Eugenia. There was the Temple of Aphrodite on the Akrokorinth.

I stood close to him, but not so close as to invite him to take me in his arms.

"You showed me, Hektor, that life must be enjoyed. You gave me the greatest pleasure when I needed it most."

He looked at me then, and seeing the glimmer of hope in his eyes, I quickly added, "But tomorrow I sail to Cyrene with the morning tide, and from there to take the first ship north to Greece. Tonight I return to the inn."

I didn't tell him that I would sail to Cyrene with the Carthaginian slave.

He didn't try to talk me out of it. He didn't move to kiss me or convince me with embraces. His long, beautiful body was so tense, he would shatter into a thousand pieces if I were to touch him.

He bit his bottom lip and turned his face away, avoiding my eyes. I think he didn't trust himself to look at me.

"You refuse to be with me because of a decision my family made before I was born," he said bitterly. "I had no choice in my marriage. Where is the justice in that?"

I felt his pain and frustration like my own. I, too, lived with heartbreak. Even in this moment, if I let myself, I could see Black Falcon gasping in those last terrible moments. Life is ruled by Fortune, not wisdom.

"We never went to the theatre," he said into the melancholy air.

As always with Hektor, my resolve softened.

"Greece is yet another world," I said very softly, leaving the door open a crack.

I think he was too lost in his misery to hear me, because he didn't seize that tiny hopeful opening as I found myself wishing he would. Why else would I have offered it?

He, who believed most in seizing the moment, did not make his move. It seemed our fate was sealed. I sighed. This was goodbye.

"Hektor, I must ask you something. Will you respond honestly with no charm or clever quotes?"

He turned to me then and looked straight into my eyes; a knife stabbed my heart when I saw the hurt in his. Glistening tears made the red specks iridescent against the warm brown.

"Ask me anything, Athena. You see my soul. You know I can refuse you nothing."

I was a bit startled to hear Hektor speak of his soul. Was he beginning, after all, to believe?

"Why did you pour wine on my breasts that first night? It was so crude. And you angered me so. You made me feel used and manipulated. Now that I know you so well, it was not at all like you."

That brought an ironic smile to his lips.

"I felt the heat under your frigid façade; I recognized the need in your eyes. But you were wound so tight, Athena of Korinth, that only shock would break through your cold wall."

There was the touch of Apollo in his smile now. "And in the end, it is you who used me. But I have enjoyed every minute."

I raised his long, graceful fingers, the ones that went straight to the Spot no other man knew, and kissed the tips.

"I pray, Hektor, that the Goddess gives you a son."

I sat at the rose marble desk in the sumptuous suite on Hektor's yacht and composed a careful letter to Ptolemy advising him that the Goddess commanded my presence in Korinth. He would no doubt be furious, but what mortal, even a Pharaoh, can dispute the will of the Gods?

> Your Majesty's Temple to Aphrodite is under construction. Your Royal Architect is well-disposed to the task and in possession of exemplary skills to oversee its fruitful completion. Be confident that I shall continue to collaborate and the Goddess to offer Her Gracious Guidance and Blessings.

I signed the scroll *Your Majesty's humble and most grateful servant, Athena of Korinth, Supreme Priestess of Aphrodite* and set my seal in red wax. I would not see Alexandria again in this lifetime.

Jason sobbed when I told him that Hektor would take him home without me.

"You must study with Antinous and become a great mathematician. You might even write plays or beautiful poems. Eben shall teach you Aramaic and Hebrew; you shall be a master of languages. I shall be so very proud of you."

When he argued that he could study in Greece, I reminded him that males are forbidden to live on the Akrokorinth. I would be forced to send him away.

"Is it not better to study with Antinous at the finest university in the world than be sent to Athens where you know no one?"

He fought back tears and only brightened a little when I told him that Kallisto missed him and waited in Naukratis.

To see him so shattered tore at my heart, but I resigned myself to a decision that was the best for him, if not for me. I was leaving all whom I loved behind. Until I might meet them on the other side of the Mirror—or in yet another life.

"We shall see each other again, Jason. Did we not meet here, as I promised?"

I kissed him and sent him again to sleep with Antinous the last night in the inn, my last night in Egypt.

"Where shall you go?" I whispered to the General as he licked my spine.

"It is not only Carthage that fights Rome. There are many who are willing to pay handsomely for my skills."

He took a fistful of my hair and pulled my head back to look into his eyes.

"But wherever it is," he growled, "it is after Cyrene."

The Red Mirror reflected back his long, thick black hair mingled with my blonde.

I gave myself over to the moment. Pleasure—and pain. That was the General.

But I didn't fear him. In fact, I wasn't afraid of anything anymore. My worries surely were over. I had the Emerald Tablet; I knew the mantra that unlocked its power. I was convinced no one could touch me, not here or in Vegas. I knew it was time to go back, but I wasn't in a hurry.

I had one remaining task—name the seventh Protector, but not tonight. No, not tonight.

The General mounted me from behind and held his hand over my mouth. I cried out when he rammed his thick log in me and bit down on his palm to taste blood.

O comet ride! O delicious stars!

How easily I might have passed from this life in that moment. With a single thought I could be back home in Las Vegas. But not before Cyrene. Oh no, not before Cyrene.

I prayed to the Goddess for headwinds to slow our sail.

CHAPTER 41 - NIGHT VISITORS

"This is the root from which a tyrant springs; when he first appears he is a protector." – Plato

A ruby glow from the red-shaded lamp set on a timer was the only light when I came back to my condo. I checked my cell phone and saw it was Saturday. I couldn't get to the Emerald Tablet until the bank opened on Monday morning.

A message from the General said to call him as soon as I got back.

My knock on Sonny's door brought no response. Saturday night in Las Vegas. He could be anywhere, could come home any time. I scribbled a note and stuck it under the door. Aisha would have to wait.

My call to Barb went to voicemail. I left her a quick message and hopped in the shower. By the time I dried my hair, shaved my legs and smeared myself in lotion, the clock had gone ten. I slipped into white silk pajamas, put on Norah Jones and waited for Barb to call back.

When the knock came, I thought, *Oh good, at least I'll have Aisha for company.* But it wasn't Sonny. It was Rasheed.

He leaned against the stucco wall, dressed for a business meeting in a dark blue suit with starched white shirt and muted olive green paisley tie, the color of his eyes when he's moody. Always impeccable, he looked like he'd just stepped out of GQ magazine. I tried to remember if I'd ever seen him in this life without a suit—well, except naked, of course.

He stood upright the instant the door opened. His black hair glistened in the overhead lights. The shadows sharpened his cheekbones.

For a heartbeat, my mind filled with the terrible image of his mangled face in the prison dungeon. How much memory did Rasheed have of Black Falcon?

Gamel stood not far away. I automatically looked around for Marcos, spotting him where the walkway turns for the elevator. How did they get past the security guards?

Rasheed stared at me, and I stared back. I'm sure I looked stunned; I felt shell-shocked. I didn't move to open the door wider.

"Are you going to let me in?"

The light that brightened his face when I opened the door had dimmed. He looked very serious. I don't think it had occurred to him that I might not welcome seeing him.

I actually considered shutting the door like he shut the taxi door in Copenhagen. Too bad he wasn't standing in the rain.

"I need to talk to you, Isis."

To be honest, I was torn. One part of me wanted to rip his clothes off and pull him on top of me. The other wanted to slip a scarf around his neck and choke the life from him—and not from mercy.

"You told me in Copenhagen there was nothing to say."

"I was wrong. Have you ever been wrong, Isis? Have you never regretted a mistake?"

The scene in New York with Tony and Hector flashed for a moment. I still hoped Hector would forgive me—give me another chance. But I was not in a forgiving mood with Rasheed.

"Why are you here?"

"Don't make me do this standing outside, Isis."

"Why not? You left me standing in the street."

How many times did he think he could humiliate and reject me before I got a backbone? *Thank you, Barb!*

Out of the corner of my eye, I saw Gamel shift his weight from one foot to the other. Marcos watched us without expression. Those two guys had certainly seen their share of our drama. I wondered what they thought of me. Had Rasheed been happy in the beginning, only to turn sullen? Was I bad news for their boss?

I relented, opened the door and stepped back. Of course, I wanted to hear what he had to say. Most of all, I wanted to see him grovel.

We stood in the narrow, mirrored entry with our reflection repeated into infinity. Rasheed put his hands on the mirror wall on each side of my head. His face was inches away. Neither one of us blinked. His piercing eyes were almost brittle, like green glass.

They shouted at me, *Stop it!*

As hard as I tried, I couldn't ignore his heat; his special Hathor Power for men oozed from every pore. It would have been so easy to slip my arms under his suit jacket and slide them along his narrow waist. If he had touched me, I don't think I could have resisted dissolving into him.

He leaned forward to kiss me, and I ducked my head under his arm and moved toward the living room. I was not going to give in that easily. He'd hurt me. No! He'd broken my heart. And now he thinks he can show up at my doorstep, breathe heavy on me, and I'll melt.

If I asked him to have a drink, it was an invitation to stay. My hands shook, and I hated them. He followed me into the room and looked around. Rasheed had never been to my home, never sat, like Hector, in the gray leather chair.

Without invitation, he lowered himself to Barb's spot on my red sofa. He stretched his legs out on the zebra carpet; his Italian handmade shoes didn't have a scratch. His thigh muscles pulled at the cashmere of his slacks. When he lifted his arms and clasped his fingers at the back of his head, I saw the bulge in his crotch.

I dropped into the gray chair to keep myself from unzipping his pants and straddling him.

Rasheed looked at me. Silence sat like a fat elephant between us. I could see he was assessing the situation, but I couldn't read anything in his face or eyes—not even desire, although I knew he wanted me. He was here. I saw the bulge.

My cell buzzed. It was Barb.

"Can I call you back?" I asked, never taking my eyes off Rasheed.

"You sound strange," Barb commented. "Are you okay?"

"I'm okay. There's someone here."

"Who?"

I didn't want to say Rasheed's name; I didn't want him to know that Barb understood his importance.

"I'll call you later," I told her and rang off.

I heard the fridge motor kick in and a couple of ice cubes fall in the ice maker.

"Every time I see you, Isis, I realize I'd forgotten how beautiful you are."

That was the first time Rasheed ever told me what Hector used to tell me all the time—not about the forgetting, but about being beautiful.

"Thank you Rasheed, although it's not a big compliment to be forgotten."

"Don't play games, Isis. It doesn't become you. I've never forgotten you for one moment, and you know it."

That edge of impatience was in his voice; Rasheed didn't like to waste time with words.

"And how would I know that, Rasheed? You disappear and reappear without explanation. I don't know what you feel. Or think."

"I think you and I belong together, Isis. I think that after everything we've been through in the past, we deserve to enjoy each other."

I was afraid I'd burst into tears. There was no guile in his face or voice; he spoke the truth, pure and simple, in words that until now, I had only dared dream.

"What you and I have, Isis, we don't have with anybody else. It might be different with another; it might even be good—very good—but someone else wouldn't work for me. It has to be you."

Not long ago, I'd have given everything I had—or ever hoped to have—to hear Rasheed say I was the one, that he couldn't live without me. But things had changed. I'd changed. Not totally, of course. I still craved his touch. I still craved his lips—but at what cost?

He reached into his pocket and slid a royal blue velvet sachet across the glass surface of the coffee table.

"It belongs to you. It should be yours."

Inside was the Hathor ring, the one from the auction in Copenhagen. My hands shook when I tried put it on my right middle finger. Too tight.

Rasheed reached over and slipped it on my left ring finger. It fit.

"I had it sized," he said simply.

Engagement ring? I stared at him.

"Come to Dubai with me," he said as casually as if he invited me to New York.

"Dubai?"

"Yes. I want you to be with me. I want to be with you."

"Isn't that in the Persian Gulf? Don't women wear veils there?"

I was so focused on the idea that he invited me to what I saw as a modern day Carthage, I forgot he was asking me to live with him.

"Some do, yes," he answered with a laugh. "But you won't."

It was the first time I saw him laugh. The harsh angles of his face softened. He was so handsome and warm when he smiled. Trouble is, he doesn't smile often, except for his special half-smile when I'm in his favor. Would that change if I went to Dubai?

"I live in a high-rise, Isis. We have TV and air conditioning, even restaurants. It's not that different from Las Vegas."

He had to be kidding. Did he expect me to wait in his glass and steel skyscraper in the Middle East while he disappeared to who knows where, doing who knows what?

Before I could stop him, he slid down the sofa and took the hand with the Hathor ring, raising my fingers to his lips. I felt his wet tongue and remembered each time he tasted my body. I felt him in every secret place. Goose bumps rose on my arms; my face flushed. My breasts throbbed for his electric touch, and I couldn't stop my nipples from rising in the white silk of the Chinese pajamas.

"I won't try to deny that I feel you in every cell of my body, Rasheed. I can hardly breathe when you're in the room."

He moved toward me. I pulled my hand away, and he sat back into the sofa again. I could see he was a little unnerved, and I found the strength to press on.

"But that's not enough to build a life in Dubai. I have a new career. I won't ask your permission."

He studied me. The tic at his eye was very slight, but I saw it. It always popped up when he felt himself losing control of events. His pupils were huge in the low light, making his eyes black as coal with no trace of green. He looked so much like Black Falcon in that moment, so much like River God.

"And I couldn't live with your jealousy," I added in a rush of bravery.

Rasheed put his hands behind his head again. He didn't say anything, but stared at me, clearly weighing the implication of my words. Then he looked over at the Red Mirror before taking in the rest of the room.

I prayed he wasn't thinking that it shouldn't be hard for me to give up my little condo for his Pasha Palace in Dubai. I couldn't have forgiven him that.

He looked back at me, his hands still behind his head, his elbows sticking out, his legs stretched under the glass coffee table. The bulge was gone.

"Are you naming your terms?" he asked.

"Yes, maybe I am."

Rasheed didn't say anything else. He dropped his arms, putting his palms on the sofa on each side of his legs. He smiled ever so slightly, all the time appraising me, or perhaps the scene. A light in his eyes flashed; he might have been both surprised and amused. I don't know what he expected when he showed up, but I don't think it was this.

"You couldn't ask about my business dealings, Rasheed. And I would be free to travel when and where I need."

He cocked his eyebrow at that.

I hurried to say, "And I won't ask you about your business or where you go."

Instead of raising immediate objections to my living a life secret to him, he surprised me by not answering right away. His slow nodding of the head was almost imperceptible as he considered my proposal.

"Okay, Isis. But I have one condition myself. In business you are free, but no other men. I couldn't live with that."

"That means you'd have to trust me. Trust is not your strong suit," I reminded him.

"I know," he admitted. "I don't have a good track record, do I? It's not easy for me, but I'm willing to try."

I'd gotten everything I wanted. At least it seemed so at the moment. But the problem with 'trying' is that it doesn't mean you succeed.

"I need time to think, Rasheed. If I decide to give us a chance, you must agree to a trial period—say three to six months—with no talk of long-range commitments. With no pressure."

He laughed out loud. If he knew how he melted me with that smile, he'd smile all the time.

"I'd agree to almost anything right now, Isis, and you know it."

But there was one last nagging, frightening detail I couldn't ignore.

"What about those men in Copenhagen? I don't want a life looking over my shoulder."

His jaw set, and his eyes turned smoky. A black cloud moved quickly across his face but was as quickly gone.

"They've been taken care of."

I stopped myself from asking how he'd taken care of them. No questions from him and no questions from me. I already could see how this wasn't going to work and wished I had the excuse of needing permission from the Goddess.

"Are you finished?" He had a wry twist to his mouth as if he found it ironic to find himself where he was. At my mercy. "Any more demands? I'm giving you everything you want—even time to make up your mind."

"I'll let you know if there's anything else," I said with a grin.

He returned my smile before sliding to his knees on the carpet in front of me. I started to reach for him, but his hands slid under my silk top to my bare waist and stopped everything—my breath and all thought. I closed my eyes and luxuriated in the feel of his heat on my flesh. No one had a touch like Rasheed.

His hot palms moved up my ribs, and I felt sparks like static electricity. His lips were only inches from mine, but still he didn't kiss me. He didn't say a word. He let his hands talk as he stroked the length of my smooth, strapless back.

I ran my fingers through his thick black hair and then traced his sculptured lips, rediscovering each curve, remembering with vivid sensation each of his kisses in every crevice of my body. As always, he mesmerized me; I couldn't define where Rasheed ended and I began.

He pulled me closer, sliding his knees between mine, pushing them apart. He put his face in my valley and licked me through my silk pajamas and panties, sucking on my bud—teasing me.

A current shot from his lips straight through me. All my muscles and nerves seized at once.

He licked my nipple through the silk, then pulled gently with his teeth until a rock hard point stood out in the wet, dark circle. He licked again, but only once, and then slowly traced his tongue around the edge of my ear. His hot breath on my neck sent chills down my spine.

"Now can we have what we both want?" he whispered.

I wanted to be nowhere else.

It was after three before he left, not because he wanted to go, and not because I wanted him to, but out of pity for Marcos and Gamel, who waited in the corridor. My condo was too small to have them inside. Rasheed asked me to go with him, but I said no, fearful that I would keep on going and never have the strength to come back.

Making love with Rasheed is always a slow, sensuous dance that starts with pleasure and ends in bliss. Tasting each inch of my body as I taste his, he leads me through rose liquid lands.

He's never in a hurry, never rough, never forceful; his lips and fingers find places on my body I didn't know were erotic. With Rasheed, everywhere is erotic.

The Touch. Could I dare believe I could have it in Dubai, that I could have it all my life? So far destiny had not been kind to us.

I had just dozed off when I heard the knock. Certain that Rasheed had returned, I opened the door a second time without looking first through the peephole. But it wasn't Rasheed; it was the General. His bodyguards, whom I knew were with him, made themselves invisible.

"Do you always answer your door without checking to see who it is?"

"Do you realize it's almost four in the morning?"

"You came back and didn't call."

He stepped by me into the mirrored entry before I could invite him in, before I could close the door on him.

I didn't bother to ask him how he knew where I lived. I did wonder if security was on duty tonight.

His animal power filled the room. When he looked me over in my silk kimono, his eyes lingering on my breasts, I pointed to the bar, went into my bedroom, closed and locked the door to change into jeans and sweater—with a bra.

He was on the red sofa when I came out, sitting exactly where Rasheed had sat only hours ago. *Was the seat still warm?* He sipped whiskey—probably Macallan—and looked at the Red Mirror. Another crystal tumbler with amber liquid sat on the glass table.

"How was your trip?" he asked.

I sat in my gray chair and faced him.

"What do you want, General? What couldn't wait until morning?"

"It's morning somewhere," he chuckled.

"You're here. Talk."

He was much too large for the sofa. His massive chest and gorilla arms dwarfed the low back. He sat with his feet flat on the floor, knees bent, leaning forward a bit too much, like he was ready to pounce. Strangely, I wasn't afraid; I guess I deluded myself that Athena had tamed him.

"Did you find out what you needed?"

"I don't know what you're talking about."

"Don't play games," he snapped sharply.

My fear of him came back. I didn't like the look in his eyes.

"You're not strong enough to keep the Tablet, Ishtar. It will fall into the wrong hands. That's not what the Order would want."

I caught myself before I repeated 'Order.' How could he know? I wished I could remember if I'd made him a Protector. Surely Athena had been smart enough to see the General's greatest lust was for power, greater even than for her.

His eyes widened in surprise when he saw the Hathor ring. My eyes were a little too defiant. I wanted to be cool and unreadable, like Athena.

"Did Rasheed give you the ring tonight?"

It both unnerved and annoyed me that he was having me watched.

"I thought I warned you about seeing him, *ma bella*. About how dangerous that would be."

He glanced around the room and then focused a moment on the Red Mirror before studying me.

"You're too smart to have the Tablet here. Where is it? In a safety deposit box?"

I let him talk and took another sip of scotch.

"You're not safe here, you know that. Who do you think will knock on your door next? The Russian? It won't be pretty if they want the Tablet. It won't be pretty if they want Rasheed."

I didn't want to say that Rasheed had taken care of the problem—or that I'd been foolish enough to believe him. Maybe Rasheed believed it himself.

The Emerald Tablet was supposed to straighten out this mess; I planned to use its power to make these ugly people in my life disappear. Not a very noble cause, but important enough to me. I had more than 24 hours before the bank opened. *This wasn't a three-day weekend, was it?*

"I don't think you realize how dangerous these men are, Ishtar. Pack a bag."

When I protested, the General reached into his pocket and dropped a green faience circlet with a seven-pointed star on the table. The clink of ceramic on glass exploded, and then the disk clattered like a tossed coin before settling.

"Now will you get your things?"

CHAPTER 42 - TAHOE

"A common danger unites even the bitterest enemies." – Aristotle

One of the two men who had followed me into the Metropolitan Museum in New York opened the back door of a waiting black Mercedes sedan. He acknowledged me with a nod but didn't speak. I climbed onto the back seat, and the General joined me. Behind the wheel sat the second man. We exchanged glances in the rearview mirror.

As we drove out the security gates onto Flamingo, another black Mercedes pulled in behind us. We moved together through the early morning traffic heading north.

"I have an important meeting today," the General said in a casual tone as we turned into Northtown Airport.

A sea plane waited on the tarmac, twin engines revving up.

"I can't go out of town, General. I have to be here tomorrow morning." *Tomorrow. Monday. The bank. The Emerald Tablet that would stop this craziness.* My voice sounded a little tight to my ear but not too panicked.

"We're not going far." He smiled and actually patted my hand.

I pulled away and put both hands in the pockets of my fleece jacket.

"Trust me, Ishtar." There wasn't much in his tone to engender confidence.

What was I doing here? Was I as insane as Barb believed?

"You are safe with me," he oozed in an oily voice I didn't like at all. "Rasheed believes he can protect you. But only I can do that."

Then my cell buzzed, and I jumped. It was a text from Tony.

Call me. Strange dream. Silver sword/green stone. Fighting 4 our life.

At the moment I started to press dial, the General put his gorilla paw on my phone and said, "Maybe it's better you turn it off."

I almost told him not to be ridiculous, but even the remote possibility that I could be tracked made me power off. He took the phone from me, opened the back and removed the battery.

With a flurry of opening car doors and purposeful exiting, we went up the steps to the plane. No sooner had we boarded and buckled up, than the seaplane taxied down the runway. Five bulky men, all in dark business suits, clumped together in the seats behind us.

A golden sun rose just above the horizon when we splashed down on sapphire Lake Tahoe sparkling among deep green mountains capped with snow. The bodyguards changed into black leather jackets, and I caught a glimpse of handguns in the holsters at their armpits.

The sun hadn't yet come over the mountains; the sky was Persian blue with white wispy clouds. A wooden motorboat left a wooden pier and headed toward us, leaving a V-wake of small waves on the glassy water. A yellow flag with a black crocodile waved from the stern.

When we arrived at the dock, I firmly resisted the man from the Met reaching to take my bag with my laptop, toothbrush and change of underwear. He dropped his hand at a signal from the General.

Heads of moose and bear hung on the stone walls. To the right, a solid cedar staircase led to a second floor balcony open to the hall below. Massive open beams supported the roof. Bright sunlight streamed through leaded glass skylights, casting rainbows on gleaming oak floors.

"Breakfast?" the General asked casually, opening a door into a cedar-paneled dining room.

A long polished oak table had been laid with hot breads and steaming coffee, plates of cheese and bowls of fruit salad. Floor-to-ceiling windows looked over the sapphire lake; giant Ponderosa pines blocked views to both sides. Scattered patches of snow covered bits of rocky ground carpeted with pine needles.

I downed a glass of water and stared at my coffee. Tendrils of steam rose from a white porcelain cup. Not far from the table, a fire roared in a castle-sized stone hearth.

"Seems like a long way to go to a meeting, General. What's this about?"

"We are forming a new Order, Ishtar. I'm afraid you no longer will be its head."

Doors opened from another room, and two men, one in a cream cable knit sweater and the other in a brown corduroy sports jacket, took seats at the table directly across from me. The General sat at the head. Russian Agathon from Copenhagen wore the sweater; the jacket was Ibis Man Sosibius from the New York auction. I stared at them, quite frankly dumbfounded. They smiled smugly back.

"We know, " the General said in a matter-of-fact tone, "you will resist giving the Tablet to us, Ishtar, and so we have a proposal."

The three men looked at me benignly. It was obvious they expected to dictate terms. Not feeling in a position to negotiate, I didn't bother to ask what kind of proposal.

The General reached into my bag and placed my laptop in front of me on the oak table.

"Let's see what your friend in Princeton has to say."

A baseball bat into my stomach couldn't have had more impact. Innocent Tony, lost in his stars. He had nothing to do with this. But that wasn't entirely true: he was the Emerald Knight, a Protector. Even his dreams had changed; his text to me said he was waking up.

I logged onto the Wi-fi, and a request from Tony popped up on Skype.

My heart stopped when the video call filled my laptop screen. A girl of about twelve stared at me from a terrified face, a gag over her mouth. The girl had to be Tony's daughter Jenny, but I knew immediately by her startling hazel eyes that she was Jason.

Until now, no soul I recognized had changed gender, but there didn't seem to be any hard and fast rules about knowing and not knowing, or seeing and not seeing. Why would there be rules about gender?

"You wouldn't harm your son, General." I tried the same ploy that had worked so well for Athena.

"In peace, sons bury their fathers. In war, fathers bury their sons," he answered. "The Greeks understood everything, didn't they? Most of all, they understood human tragedy."

"I hate you." I knew it sounded childish, but I couldn't help saying it.

Someone ended the call; the screen went blank for an instant before my screensaver, a photo of the Great Pyramid, came back.

"What will you do when I give you the Tablet?" I never doubted the outcome. I didn't want to find out how much pain I could endure. I certainly didn't want Jenny to suffer until I gave the General what he was sure to get in the end. Who might suffer next—Barb?

"You will tell us where the Tablet is. You will tell us what you found out when you went back." The General didn't leave any room for argument; it would be as it had to be. "After that, you'll live your life as you did before. Your death has no value to us."

I didn't believe any of it, except about my telling them what they wanted to know. What had the General said about the Russian? *He considered eliminating you, but decided you were more valuable alive.* What value would my life have after they got the Tablet?

I glared at the General, my eyes burning with fury. But that wouldn't get me anywhere with him. I closed my lids. I forced myself to cool into Athena, taking my time, counting slowly to ten, before opening my eyes again. If I gave in too easily, they wouldn't believe me.

"I have visions. Crystal clear visions—like scenes from a movie, but unconnected. Almost like…trailers. Yes. Like a movie trailer. I get the gist of the story, but it jumps around. I recognize all of you. I can't tell you how I see what I see—I don't know where the visions come from. They just…*are.*"

There was nothing in their expressions that said they didn't believe me. The General had never once mentioned the Red Mirror.

"What did you learn at Siwa?" asked the Russian Agathon.

I was beyond wondering how he knew about Siwa. "The Oracle instructed me to create the Order, and I was due to go back the next morning to hear more. But as you surely know, I was kidnapped by your men."

I worked hard to keep the loathing from my tone. These two men would have let Zavan carve me alive.

The Russian stared back. I saw him considering my words; he had the same expression in his eyes as in the back seat of his Mercedes in Copenhagen.

"And you, General, took me away from Siwa. I never had a chance to return to the Oracle."

The three glanced at each other. I dared to let myself believe I had passed the test.

"I don't remember anything else, General, except I trusted you. Apparently that is my weakness."

The fire crackled, and cups clinked on saucers; they drank their coffee as if today was any ordinary morning. The Russian smeared butter and dark red jam on a crusty roll.

"If it's the Tablet you want, why did you pretend you were interested in Bayoumi?" I asked him.

"That is another business," he said as he chewed.

"Why did you want the ibis?" I demanded of Sosibius.

He shrugged and nibbled on a slice of fresh pineapple.

"That was another time."

The General did business with Rasheed, and the General was involved with these men. He might have promised Rasheed to get rid of the problem with the Russian. He might have promised the Russian to get rid of Rasheed.

There was no loyalty in this band of thieves. Like a pack of wild dogs, I knew they would tear themselves apart to get the Power. I didn't want myself or anyone I loved to be in the middle.

"This was a pretty elaborate scheme, General—the phone calls, the meetings, the auctions—to gain my trust."

The General's smile was non-committal. Did he become more evil with each incarnation?

"Why didn't you just steal me away, like now? Why the charade?"

"You weren't ready. You hadn't made the trip back. You hadn't visited the Oracle of Amun."

A heavyset man with fat jowls escorted me to an upstairs bedroom overlooking the lake. He handed me my bag, minus laptop and cellphone.

"Sleep," he growled and locked the door from the outside.

I wondered why they didn't torture me to learn what they hoped I knew. But they could never be certain I told them the truth unless they held the Emerald Tablet in their hands. I had until tomorrow when the bank opened to live. Jenny had until tomorrow to live in terror.

The windows were locked; it was at least three stories to the hard ground. Even if I found a way, I don't think I would have tried to escape. Jenny was their guarantee of my cooperation.

I couldn't think of sleeping and settled onto the cedar window seat upholstered in brown wool. From my upstairs vantage point, I could see a broad wooden deck below with a glimpse of a driveway between tall, straight Ponderosa pines. Here and there grew a regal Sequoia.

Two black sedans arrived, followed by a small fleet of Land Rovers with a single white Range Rover. A tall man in a leather bomber jacket got out of the Range Rover; a wide-brimmed bush hat, like Australians wear, hid his face. Hector had a jacket like that. Hector drove a white Range Rover.

He had come through the Red Mirror once to save me when I was Isis in Egypt. For a wild, hopeful moment, I imagined him rushing now to the rescue.

But there was no crossing the Mirror to get here. I couldn't escape this reality. Barb couldn't wake me up. This was the lifetime I always came back to and never really left.

A dozen men dressed in sweaters or leather jackets came out on the deck, their breaths white vapor in the chilled air.

Among the trees roamed bodyguards with rifles or automatic weapons like in the movies—the little Uzi-like guns that fire off hundreds of bullets at once.

When the tall man from the Range Rover joined the men on the deck, they went inside.

I must have dozed off because a knock on the door startled me.

"May I come in?" asked the General politely.

"Do I have a choice?"

He chuckled.

The sun was setting; the lake was the deepest of blues with a magenta sheen. Smooth as a mirror, the water reflected the mountains and sky; not even the slightest breeze raised a whitecap.

"You're a monster!" I spat at him. "A child!" I hissed. "An innocent child. *Your* child. You are even less human than I thought."

I stayed put on the window seat while the General sank into a cream-colored armchair facing me. His gorilla hands with thick fingers hung down from the wide armrests. I remembered with horror those hands around my throat and then on my body; I shuddered at the memory of Amunia. How could I have lusted for him?

"There are many things you don't understand, Ishtar."

"Who are these men? What is this meeting?"

"You might call them a 'New World Order.' Yes, you might call them that."

Then he asked, "Are you hungry?"

I saw him chained to a column in my bathchamber in the Alexandria villa. I had offered him food; he had been my slave then.

He didn't wait for my answer. The snap of his fingers cracked in the room, and the door opened immediately.

"Bring a tray," he ordered.

He stared at me in much the same way he'd watched me in his Persian tent. I saw his mind work through scenarios of my life or death.

"What am I going to do with you?" he asked idly, using the same words I'd said to him that night in my marble Alexandrian bath.

"Let me go," I said without a moment's hesitation.

"Clever," he responded. "Always so clever. But you must learn not to trust so easily."

"Will I have time to learn?"

"That is up to you," he answered.

The tray arrived with sliced duck, wild rice, arugula salad and two glasses of red wine. The smell of the food made me nauseous.

"People will be looking for me, you know."

"But not here, Ishtar."

I flashed on him removing the battery from my cellphone under the pretense of protecting me.

He took a long sip and held the glass by its stem, turning it in the light as if to judge the wine's color and clarity.

Set on timers, two brass lamps with large, ivory-colored shades switched on.

"You should eat. Never let yourself weaken."

I chewed mechanically on the duck, but the lump in my throat and my cotton mouth made it hard to swallow.

"I have told them, Ishtar, that I want you for me. They have agreed. It is part of our arrangement."

He held up his hand to stop me from speaking.

"I know what you're thinking. *Now I will be his slave.* But contrary to your opinion of me, I don't want you like that."

I held my breath in anticipation of learning how he wanted me. I'll admit that I never expected his proposal.

"I told you that I've never met a woman like you. I don't want to break your spirit. I can have a thousand slaves. I want us to be partners."

"Partners? Partners in what?"

"In everything, Ishtar. In life."

"Is that my choice? Be your partner or die? Shouldn't a partnership involve negotiation?"

The lines around his eyes crinkled, and his smile was so big, I could see his strong, square teeth.

"You see, Ishtar? That's exactly my point. Who else would say that to me?"

Then he suddenly switched gears.

"Where is the Tablet? You wouldn't keep it in your home, but I have men there now. They can tear everything apart, or you can save us the inconvenience. My guess is you have it in a bank vault. Where's the key?"

This was the second time he mentioned the bank box. I stared at him stubbornly, all the time knowing I had no real position of strength from which to maneuver. All I had was the General's hunger for me. It had been enough in the past, but there were others involved now.

"If the key is in your apartment, we'll find it. If you have it with you, we will find it. If it's somewhere else, we'll be forced to use persuasion. I will not be able to stop my colleagues, Ishtar, if you do not cooperate."

He took another sip of wine, his eyes never leaving mine.

"Please, Ishtar, don't make me do what I do not wish to do. You can resist and suffer, make the girl suffer—or you can join me. You can be part of the new Order. Is that really such a difficult decision to make?"

One road leads to honor, the other to slavery. My paths at that moment led to death or to life. I rose from the window seat and dug the safety deposit box key from the bottom of my bag.

The General spoke quietly into his cell and then gave me a small, satisfied smile.

"Wise move, Ishtar. It is always best to fold your cards and wait for a better hand."

He rose easily from the chair. His bulky grace always amazed me.

"My laptop?"

He chuckled. "Always negotiating? You'll get it back, but not tonight. Get some sleep. We'll be at the bank when it opens in the morning. You're safe. You are under my protection."

He closed the door behind him, and I heard the lock click.

CHAPTER 43 - WE ARE ALL ONE

"I'm not afraid of storms, for I'm learning to sail my ship." – Aeschylus

Early morning traffic snarled along at a snail pace on the Las Vegas Expressway. After sitting in gridlock for twenty minutes, our driver got off at the next exit and travelled side streets to the little Bank of America on Sahara. Instead of arriving early as planned, we pulled into the parking lot at 9:23.

The General assessed the quiet surroundings. He noted the security cameras and the two security guards and decided his men should stay in the car. He took my arm, not roughly, but firmly, and guided me toward the entrance. In my other hand, I carried my bag with laptop.

Early as it was, people were already coming out of the bank to a bright, sunny Monday morning.

I was startled when Omphale, Xenon's *hetaera* from the symposion in Korinth, came through the glass doors and waved at me, beaming. Only now she was platinum blonde with a rich tan and huge white Dior sunglasses. Instead of a skin-clinging sheer gown, she wore tight white leather pants with matching jacket and white leather, high-heeled boots.

"Hey, girl! I haven't seen you at the Stirling Club in ages. Whatcha been up to?"

I blinked. The voice. Where had I met her? Then I remembered. Esperanza. We'd run into each other at a vintage shop; she'd called me The Dancer and invited me to be on her TV show. That was the afternoon I bought that sizzling red satin dress—the dress I wore to

Caesars Palace and met Tony at the bar. The night I met the General in this lifetime. The night he severed Rasheed from me.

I glanced at the General; his face was blank, but his eyes were wary. *Oh please, Esperanza, just go! Don't mess everything up.*

She flashed her huge smile on both of us; her teeth were too perfect and almost as white as her sunglass frames. I don't know why I decided in that moment that they were veneers. I don't know why I thought about her teeth at all.

"I've been traveling a lot," I answered vaguely, managing a tight smile.

The General's grip on my arm tightened to propel me forward.

"Esperanza Montelongo, *con mucho gusto.*" She held out her hand to the General.

The General paused, then dropped my arm and swallowed up Esperanza's slender hand in his bear paw. He didn't tell her his name, though.

"*Que hombre!*" She beamed in appreciation first at him and then at me.

I thought for a second of running when he released me, before thinking of Jenny and accepting I had no choice but to follow wherever he led.

"Hey amiga, call me this time. Promise?" She pressed her glossy business card into the General's hand and then mine. "We'll go shopping. You're gonna love that little vintage shop in North Vegas."

She beamed at the General and went off to a navy blue Porsche. The General had my arm again and steered me past the security guard and into the bank.

When I told the receptionist that I wanted to access my deposit box, she was very polite and asked us to have a seat. A line had formed for the tellers. I imagined everyone in the lobby looking at us. The General dropped my arm when we settled in rigid, chrome-armed, burgundy plastic upholstered chairs.

"Good morning. May I assist you?"

His name tag read 'Miguel Lopez, Branch Manager.' He looked to be about thirty and had neatly combed, straight black hair. He blinked constantly, and beads of sweat swelled on his upper lip. There was the slightest of tremors in his hands at his sides.

I could feel the General's tension; the savage beast in him whiffed the scent of danger.

"Would you care to wait here, Sir? Our bank policy only allows the owner of the box in the vault." Miguel was exceedingly courteous and his voice a touch too high.

I clutched the key in my hand, half expecting the General to grab it and make a run for the door.

Beads of sweat popped up on Miguel the manager's forehead. A security guard stepped conspicuously near the door. The General, Miguel and I formed a little circle in a room charged with energy.

Transfixed, I stared at the General, waiting for his next move. My eyes shouted at him, *It's not my fault!*

I thought he would argue with Miguel and say he'd never heard of such a policy, maybe even pull out a gun. I thought he would take my arm and hurry me back to his goons.

But instead, he turned and said, "I will wait in the car."

There was a momentary glint in his eyes of something I couldn't quite define—almost amusement. He turned and walked past the security guard, through the glass doors and out of sight. I nearly sobbed from relief, but it wasn't over. As long as the General had Jenny, he had me.

Miguel took my arm so gently, that after the General's clutch, I scarcely felt it.

"Are you okay, ma'am? Should I call the police?"

Beyond wondering how he knew anything was amiss, I shook my head and said I needed to get into the vault.

Once inside and alone, I unwrapped the Tablet. The Greek letters were a jumble of symbols in my blurred vision.

When I put my hand on the glassy surface and repeated the mantra, *Alpha to Omega, We are all One*, the stone warmed slightly. I couldn't tell if the heat radiated from the stone or from my fingers. I repeated the mantra. *Alpha to Omega, We are all One.* The Tablet glowed brighter.

The third time I said the mantra, an intense green aura dampened the blue florescent lighting and infused the room in turquoise light. The Tablet burned hot as a dish from the oven. I almost dropped it on the vault floor.

My requests were as simple as they had been in Siwa. I asked for Jenny and me to come safely home. I knew in order for that to happen, I was most likely asking for the death of someone, maybe many. I didn't name names but counted on the cosmos to put an army at my disposal and remove the obstacles from my path.

When I came out of the vault, Hector was there.

He had to be a vision. But he looked as real as the morning he stood next to Tony in my hotel room in New York—only he held no overnight bag and no red roses. I touched the sleeve of his bomber jacket.

"Hector?" I said in wonder. "What are *you* doing here?"

He smiled to reassure me and took my hand, leading me into the manager's office.

"He is gone, Isis. Security says he drove off, but the bank has everything on tape."

Miguel bobbed his head up and down; his face was flushed, and his eyelids fluttered faster than ever. I don't think I've ever seen a man so relieved. Brave Miguel Lopez. I'd recommend him for Employee of the Year.

But they didn't understand. It wasn't over. The General still had Jenny.

When I opened my bag to get my laptop for Tony's number, my cell phone was on top. When had the General returned it? And why?

I powered on, the battery was charged and in place. Impatiently waiting for service, I stared at the little screen, biting my lower lip to keep from crying. Hector and the bank manager watched without saying a word. I ignored the voicemail alerts and went straight to contacts.

Tony answered on the first ring.

"Tony! Tony! I'm sorry, I'm so sorry," I sobbed into the phone. "I never wanted to involve you. I'm so sorry about Jenny, Tony. I'm so sorry."

"Isis, listen! Jen is with me. She's okay."

"What?…She's okay?…She's with you?"

"She came home yesterday. I tried to call you a dozen times, but it went straight to voicemail."

"She came back…yesterday?" Yesterday before the General's proposal, before I told him where to find the Emerald Tablet?

Jenny, unharmed except for the shock, had been dropped off an hour after the Skype call. He'd been bluffing. *There are many things you do not understand, Ishtar.*

Hector's white Range Rover was parked in the lot next door; I slid onto the passenger seat. The Emerald Tablet was back in the deposit box—for now. Until I could think more clearly, until I had a plan.

I thanked the cosmos for putting the traffic jam and Esperanza in the General's path and giving Hector time to alert the bank manager. Hector. How had the Tablet arranged for Hector to be at the bank?

"Barb called me. She said you needed help."

Don't call me, Isis. Don't Skype me.

"You came for me?"

Hector squeezed my hand.

"You were in trouble, Isis. *Te amo.* Nothing you do could stop me from loving you."

"But how did you know I'd be here—this morning?"

"Barb told me everything. *Todo.* About the people who threatened you in Copenhagen. How the General wanted the Emerald Tablet. What else would you do, but go to the bank vault?"

I nodded my head as he talked. I wanted to trust him—truly I did. He simply used the same logic I would have used. I'd told him about the bank box. He knew. But I kept seeing the tall man arriving at the lodge in the bomber jacket.

"It was the only thing I knew to do, Isis, so that is what I did."

"I didn't know you were in Vegas, Hector."

"I wasn't. I was in Tahoe. I flew in last night."

"You were in Tahoe?" A pressure in my gut pushed on my diaphragm. Did I dare believe in coincidence?

"We have a family retreat there, Isis. On the North Shore—Incline Village. I tried to reach you. Didn't you get my message?" He stopped, alarm on his face. "*Que pasa?* You are so pale."

I stared down at my hands clasped so tightly in my lap that my knuckles had gone white. The lapis lazuli in the Hathor Ring on my middle finger looked the size of a quail egg. If I called on its power, could I read Hector's mind?

You must learn not to trust so easily.

"Isis, do you need to see a doctor?" He seemed genuine enough in his concern.

But I kept hearing Isabel. *Hector is not the man you think he is.*

"No, Hector," I said sadly. "I want to go home."

Sonny, Barb and Hector sat with me while I petted Aisha. Sonny insisted on making Bloody Marys, and no one refused. They wanted to hear everything, but I was evasive with Hector there. Barb, normally so restrained was nervous and effusive. I felt a sharp pang of guilt to see the deep furrows developing between Barb's eyebrows. Worry. Worry about me.

"You sounded so weird Saturday night. And then you didn't answer my calls. So when Sonny called me and asked if I knew where you were, I decided you were in trouble and—"

"Your note said you were home," Sonny interrupted.

"And then when Sonny called back and said he saw two men fiddling with the lock to your condo—"

"Very scary-looking guys," Sonny cut Barb off again. "I called the police, but you know how long it takes Metro to respond."

"That's when I called Hector," Barb finished.

My cell rang. It was the General.

"I'm impressed, Ishtar. I don't know how you managed it."

"You lied to me about Jenny, like you did about Jason."

"Isn't that a happy lie?" He chuckled. "You like the Greeks so much, Ishtar. Didn't they say that in war, truth is the first casualty?"

"When did you become such a Greek scholar?"

He laughed as I knew he would and then took me off guard; he never lost the ability to surprise me.

"My offer about being partners still stands, you know. Nothing between us has changed. Strictly business, if you prefer."

I was silent. I couldn't believe I even considered it for one instant.

"By the way," he asked before hanging up, "have you seen the news?"

A private jet had exploded in flight from Lake Tahoe; there were no survivors.

"A team of federal investigators is on the scene," reported the KTNV website. "Authorities say it is too early to rule out terrorism."

Names of the victims hadn't been released, but I suspected the Russian or Ibis Man, if not both, were on the flight manifest.

Sonny and Barb left for work, but Hector stayed glued to the gray leather chair.

"It is not safe for you to be here," he insisted. "*Por favor*, let me check you into a hotel."

I didn't need a hotel. My faith in the Emerald Tablet was restored—Jenny and I were home safe, exactly as I'd asked, although I had never imagined the cosmos would arrange a plane crash. That I had the power to cause people to die was heady and scary at the same time. I tried not to think about the pilot. Was the plane chartered?

"I don't feel afraid," I told him in a flat voice. "Except maybe of you."

"Afraid of me? *Por qué?*"

His face was guileless. The red specks made his brown eyes glow. His chestnut hair was brushed back rather than falling in curls around his face like Alexandrian Hektor. Long, muscular, equestrian thighs stretched his blue jeans. Hektor's aristocratic fingers that went straight to the Spot rested completely relaxed on the arms of my favorite chair.

My cell rang again. It was Rasheed.

"Why haven't you answered my calls?" he demanded. "Are you home? I'm coming right over."

"I don't think that's a good idea, Rasheed. I'll call you back."

Then I realized how cold I sounded and added 'I promise' in the husky intimate croon of a lover.

"Rasheed?" Hector asked.

I imagined him ticking off a list on his fingers—Tony, the General and now Rasheed.

"Is there anyone else I should know about?"

"I need some answers, Hector."

"Answers about what? I think I've proven myself once or twice."

When my cell rang and it was Tony, Hector stood out of the chair, came over to me and took the phone from my hand.

"Give us a moment, Tony," he said and ended the call.

He put his hands on each side of my face and lifted my head so that I looked straight into his eyes. My cell in his palm was cold on my cheek.

"I do not understand what is in your head, Isis. You have nothing to fear from me—*nada*. *Te amo*. Why would I want to harm you?"

He appeared utterly sincere. I tried to probe deep, but couldn't see evil. It would be easy enough to check if Hector had a place in Tahoe. There *are* such things as coincidences. Not everything has meaning.

"I said I would wait until you were ready, Isis. I must admit I never imagined so much competition. But *por qué no?* If I want you, why would the others not want you, too?"

He kissed me so gently and with such love, I wanted nothing more than to let him wrap me in his cocoon and protect me from everything. As always with Hector, my resolve wavered. If I couldn't trust Hector, who was there?

His tongue went in my mouth, and he pulled me into him, his long arms strong and confident. Hektor's stunning Apollo virility. It had probably been there all along, if I'd let myself feel it. My Spot throbbed; I ached for the touch of his fingers.

But he stopped. He took hold of my upper arms and held me out from him. He stared down at me, searching my face, looking for answers in my eyes. I knew he was waiting for me to say what I wasn't going to say. What I couldn't bring myself to say.

When he saw that the words weren't coming, his lips pursed slightly. The red specks in his eyes floated on a glistening sheen.

"Call me when you make up your mind, Isis."

He handed me my cell phone.

"I think Tony is waiting."

He leaned down and stroked Aisha swirling at his ankles, before he closed the front door quietly behind him with a final-sounding click.

My old college roommate Elaine answered right away. I pictured her in the two-story colonial Pennsylvania house with comfortable furnishings and gleaming wood paneling and floors. Was she in her big country kitchen fixing a snack for the kids? Had they just come home from school?

"Have you got a minute?" I asked.

"All the time you need."

That was Elaine. Always there to listen in her soothing, nurturing manner, so like the Goddess Hathor's benevolent aspects. Elaine had first introduced me to the idea of life as lessons learned and lessons failed. And that the lessons don't stop with one lifetime but continue until we learn what we need to learn from each other. Reincarnating circles of souls.

When I went through the pluses and minuses of Rasheed and Dubai, of Tony and Jen, and of Hector with his mother Isabel and my paranoid doubts, she listened carefully and asked simple questions that went right to the heart of everything.

I even talked about the General and how, in spite of all I had been through with him, I was seduced by what he proposed—the power of earning my own money and lots of it. I didn't tell Elaine what else he offered. In truth, I was ashamed of—and feared—the part of me that hungered for his dark side and craved his thrill.

"It's not simple like I used to think, Elaine. I'm not sure anymore that there is a Mr. Right. I don't know who—or what—to choose."

I knew Barb would say Hector. He was, in all rational ways, the perfect match. But her judgment wasn't unbiased. She had, after all, been married to Hektor in Alexandria; it's pretty obvious that she was still in love with him. One day soon, at the right moment, I'd tell her about Eugenia. I think the news best delivered over a glass of wine.

Tony would be Elaine's choice. Like Euripides, she believes that the good and the wise lead quiet lives. But Elaine knows a quiet life is not for me. At least, not now. Not yet.

Neither would choose Rasheed, but then they'd never felt his touch; they'd never felt the sear of his heat on their skin. Rasheed had never turned his Hathor Power on them.

No one in their right mind would take the General—except me.

"Do you have to choose?" Elaine asked.

"What? Of course, I have to." I'd never considered any other possibility. "You always have to choose, don't you?"

"You have the Emerald Tablet. You have the Power."

Gentle Elaine, always steady and confident. I suppose her calm strength derives from seeing our entangled lives as an evolving experience transcending time.

"Can't you have them all, Isis, if that's what you want?"

EPILOGUE

"Happiness depends upon ourselves." – Aristotle

Do you wonder what happens to Athena after sailing to Cyrene with the General? Does the Pharaoh stop my ship at sea? Did Antinous build his dome? Is it buried beneath the sands of time? And the child. Do I have a son for Hektor? Or a daughter to dedicate to the Temple? I've been tempted many times to return to Korinth to see how the play ends. Comedy or tragedy? Pleasure or pain?

Once knowing the love of her four men, it's quite impossible to imagine Athena satisfied with the role of untouchable Goddess. I entertain fantasies of a sunny villa on the seaside at the base of the Akrokorinth where a smiling Hektor plays with his young son.

How do I know the boy is his? My first child, named for Eugenia, has golden hair like mine and green eyes. No clue as to the father. But the second child is most definitely Hektor's son.

Hektor came to me after Eugenia's death from the single bite of the smallest of insects. As heartbroken as I was at the news in his letter, I was elated to see him free. We were both free to choose pleasure over pain.

"Mommy!" calls out little Eugenia. "Come see the green-striped frog Goliath has found. Do you think Aunt Eugenia would like it in her pond?"

Eugenia's shrine stands at the foot of the garden, closest to the beach. I like to relax there among the roses in the cool shade and imagine she sips pomegranate juice as we watch the children play.

"Come now," I call out. "It is time for your lessons. You must learn all you can before Jason returns to Alexandria."

"But he promised we would act out a play before supper! I want to be Antigone."

"And so we shall," Jason croons as he swings her onto his broad shoulders. "But first I want to teach you some letters from a new alphabet. 'Latin,' the Romans call it."

His voice is much deeper this summer than last. He's taller, too. It's always a surprise to see how much he's grown over the winter. My life is complete when he arrives each summer with faithful Goliath.

Can you imagine as I do the General sailing into port on a grand galley ship with an army of mercenary soldiers? We soar to the stars for a few wild nights before he goes off to another battle. But that, of course, would never work with Hektor by my side. And Hektor is my vision with the most Light. I have made my choice, and I am content.

The Athena incarnation is finished for now. I will go back—but not to her. I'm a different person because of Athena, and she was a different woman because of me. My future changed the past, as my past changed the present.

Three hundred years will pass in Egypt before I cross through the Red Mirror into the life of Elektra. My next incarnation is a tale of Roman North Africa and the clash of cultures—Greek, Egyptian, Roman, Jewish and Christian. Raw power in all its forms determines the survivors.

I won't tell you who I meet in Hadrian's Egypt, but you can probably guess. Hermes *Trismegistus* isn't finished; my role as Protector of the Emerald Tablet isn't finished. The circle of souls continues.

The Black Scroll
Book Three of the Isis Trilogy
One life is not enough…

AUTHOR'S COMMENTS AND GLOSSARY

My novel *The Emerald Tablet* is a fictional work with historical plausibility that takes place during the Ptolemaic Greek Period of Egyptian history. Ptolemy IV, Ptolemy *Philopater*, or Ptolemy Father-lover, ruled as Pharaoh from 222 to 204 BCE. This story takes place mid in his reign, about 300 years later than the story of Isis and the Red Mirror.

The characters that are both in this book and *The Red Mirror* are listed at the end of this appendix. A pronunciation guide to foreign names is included.

The Temple of Aphrodite with one thousand sacred prostitutes on the *Akrokorinth* was famous throughout the ancient world. The city of Korinth was renowned for its wealth and the pleasures *drachmas* could buy.

Ptolemy I, II and III established Alexandria as a world center of culture. The Pharos Lighthouse is one of the seven wonders of the ancient world. The Library of Alexandria was one of the greatest centers of learning and research in human history.

The reign of Ptolemy IV (*Ptolemy Philopater*) is considered the beginning of the decline of the House of Ptolemy. He poisoned his mother, boiled his brother and married his sister Arsinoë, siring one son with her, Ptolemy V.

A Sosibius served Ptolemy IV as his Chancellor and competed for power with Agathocles and his sister Agathoclea, who was Ptolemy's mistress.

The Emerald Tablet itself is a mythical artifact said to be created by Hermes *Trismegistus,* Thrice-Greatest, a legendary personality similar to Merlin of King Arthur. If you are interested in more information about the Emerald Tablet and Hermes, you can read my research at:

www.SandraOfftheStrip.com/The Emerald Tablet

Throughout the book I have included both paraphrased and direct quotations from Greek poems, plays, writings, and proverbs. The complete list is found in the last pages of this appendix.

The Red Mirror, red sofa, bust of Antinous, and other images mentioned in the book are posted on my author website at www.SLGore.com.

note: The classical carved column superimposed on the papyrus icon is of the Corinthian order.

GLOSSARY

CITIES

Abydos. This ancient holy site on the Nile goes back to the earliest days of Egypt and was believed to be the burial place of the head of Osiris, king of Egyptian gods and god of the underworld.

Akrokorinth. Similar in structure to the Acropolis in Athens, the Akrokorinth rose above the city of Korinth and was the site of the Temple of Aphrodite with one thousand sacred prostitutes. Destroyed by the Romans, a temple likely as beautiful as the Parthenon had existed there for centuries.

Akropolis. Site of the Parthenon in Athens, the temple complex atop the mesa rising above the city is one of the best examples of Classical Greek architecture in the world.

Alexandria. Perhaps the greatest city in the ancient world before Rome, the site on the Mediterranean coast of Egypt was chosen by Alexander the Great because he could create a great harbor that would not be flooded annually as so many Egyptian cities risked. He ordered the construction of a Greek *polis* (city) before he left for the east to conquer Persia. His general Ptolemy returned after Alexander's death and claimed Egypt as his own. Ptolemy I, II and III (grandfather, father and son) built the Lighthouse, the Library and a magnificent city that amazed Julius Caesar and enthralled Hadrian who considered himself an Egyptophile. Alexandria continued as a great city of learning until the Christian era about 400 AD.

Amunia/Paraitonion. The town was a small Egyptian port serving as the Mediterranean gateway to the Oasis of Siwa with the Oracle of Amun. The Ptolemaic Greeks called it *Paraitonion*, but I used Amunia for simplicity. Today it is known as Mersa Matruh.

Athens. One of the great cities of the ancient world, Athens was home to Socrates, Plato and Aristotle among dozens of other famous Greeks we study today. It was the birthplace of all we think of as Greek: philosophy, theatre and democracy.

Babylon. One of the great cities of the ancient world, Babylon was the home to a population of Jewish scholars exiled there from Jerusalem by Nebuchadnezzar II in 588 BCE. He allowed them to continue to worship their one god and transcribe the oral tradition of the Torah to Hebrew. Babylon was the site of Alexander the Great's death at age 33 in 323 BCE. The site of the ancient city is in modern day Iraq.

Canopus. One of the pleasure resorts of the ancient world, the coastal town was outside of Alexandria where the now silted-in Canopic Branch of the Nile used to meet the Mediterranean.

Carthage. One of the great cities of the ancient world, Carthage was home to the Punics who had a reputation as savage and brutal war-mongers. Hannibal is the most famous of Punic generals and led elephants across the Alps in an attempt to defeat Rome. There is almost nothing left of the city laid to waste by the Romans who salted the land to prevent agriculture. A few ruins still exist in modern day Tunisia.

Cyrene. This ancient Greek colony in present day Libya was settled by Greeks in 600 BCE and continued to be a thriving region under the Romans. The terrain was lush for North Africa and not dissimilar to the rocky hills of Greece.

Delphi. This is the location of one of the most well-known of all ancient religious sites, the Oracle of Delphi. Pythia, always an elderly woman, pronounced prophesies in Apollo's voice and was considered one of the most powerful women of her time. Delphi is located on the Greek mainland at Mt. Parnassus close to the Gulf of Corinth.

Ephesus. Another of the great cities of antiquity, the Greeks built magnificent temples and theatres on the Turkish coast in the region known to them as Ionia.

Korinth/Corinth. Known to the Greeks as a city of pleasure and luxury, it was famous for its Temple of Aphrodite with a thousand sacred prostitutes. Korinth settled the colony of Syracuse on today's island of Sicily and amassed great wealth in trade. It gave its name to the most elaborate of Greek décor styles, Corinthian. The name itself became synonymous with opulence. The city was destroyed by the Romans in 146 BCE and its vast wealth sent to Rome.

Naukratis/Naucratis. Invited by Pharaohs to establish their own trading city, Greeks settled in Naukratis on the Canopic branch of the Nile centuries before Alexandria was built by the Ptolemies. Archeological evidence goes back to 1500 BCE during the Mycenaean Age.

Sais. Greek name for Egyptian *Sa* or *Zau*; Arabic *Sa el-Hagar*. The capital city of the Saite Dynasty in the Late Period (26th Dynasty), Sais was located in the Nile Delta, 50 miles from the Mediterranean on the Rosetta (*Bolbitine*) Branch of the Nile. Virtually nothing of the ancient city exists today.

CITY OF ALEXANDRIA

Agora. Market place.

Amphitheater. Open-air theatre associated with the Library.

Beta Quarter. Area of city designed for aristocratic and wealthy Greeks.

Canopic Branch of Nile. Now silted over, it was one of the seven branches of the Nile that existed in antiquity. The closest navigable branch to Alexandria.

Canopic Canal. Canal that led from Alexandria to the Canopic Nile. Source of city drinking water.

Canopic Gate. Gate in eastern city walls at the end of the Canopic Way. The Hippodrome was located outside the gate.

Canopic Way. One of the main broad avenues (200 ft wide) going east-west, connecting the Necropic Gate and the Canopic Gate and intersecting with the Street of the Soma.

City of the Dead. Burial grounds with tombs located outside western edge of city.

Delta Quarter (Jewish Quarter). Area of the city designated for non-Egyptians and non-Greeks.

Egyptian Quarter (Rhakotis or Gamma Quarter). Area of the city designated for Egyptians at the site of the ancient fishing village of Rhakotis. The Serapeum stands on a hill at the southern edge.

Gate of the Moon. Gate in northern city walls at the end of the Street of the Soma and the entrance to the Royal Harbor.

Gate of the Sun. Gate in southern city walls at the end of the Street of the Soma and the entrance to the Lake Mareotis Harbor.

Great Harbor. One of two harbors created by the Heptastadion, the causeway built by Alexander the Great. The Great Harbor is entered by passing between the Lighthouse and the Royal Promontory.

Harbor of Good Return (Eunostus). One of two harbors created by the Heptastadion, the causeway built by Alexander the Great. Shallow with dangerous shoals, it contains the Cibotus Harbor dug by hand at the mouth of Nile.

Heptastadion. A giant causeway built by Alexander the Great to connect Pharos Island to the mainland and create two harbors, it gets its name from Hepta (7) and stadia (approx 600 ft).

Hippodrome. A stadium for horse racing and chariot racing. *Hippos* (horse) and *dromos* (race or course.)

Jewish Quarter. Area of the city designated for non-Egyptians and non-Greeks, also called Delta Quarter.

Lake Mareotis. An great lake south of Alexandria stretching 100 miles from east to west.

Library. Considered to be the greatest library of the ancient world, it was charged with collecting the world's knowledge and copies of all books ever written. It was home to international scholars and scientists including astronomers, mathematicians, geographers, physicians, architects, engineers, poets and dramatists. Built like a university campus with many buildings in a park setting, the Musaeum (House of Muses) was the world's greatest institution of learning in its day.

Necrotic Gate. Gate in the western walls of the city that led to the City of the Dead.

Pharos Island. Offshore island location of the Lighthouse of Alexandria, one of the seven wonders of the ancient world, that the *Heptastadion* connected to the mainland. The name of the island evolved into the word for lighthouse in many languages, especially Latin-based. The island was home to pirates, the Posidium (Temple of Poseidon) and the Temple of Isis.

Rhakotis or Egyptian Quarter of Gamma Quarter. Area of the city designated for Egyptians built on the site of an ancient fishing village. The Serapeum stands on a hill at the southern edge of the quarter.

Royal Harbor. Harbor inside the Great Harbor for use of the Royal Complex.

Royal Promontory. Finger of land jutting out from mainland on which Royal Palace Complex was constructed. A narrow neck between the Promontory and the Lighthouse on Pharos Island is the entry into the Great Harbor.

Royal Quarter. Royal Palace complex and site of the Library of Alexandria. Also known as the Alpha Quarter or the *Brucheion*.

Serapeum. The Temple to Serapis at the southern end of the Egyptian Quarter built on the only hill in Alexandria.

Soma. The mausoleum of Alexander the Great was visited by many Roman emperors, including the last recorded visit by Caracalla in 215 AD. The tomb had disappeared by the 4th century.

Street of the Soma. The main north south avenue, reputed to be 200 feet wide, that connected the Gate of the Moon with the Gate of the Sun and supposedly passed by the Soma, the mausoleum of Alexander the Great.

COUNTRIES/REGIONS

Achaean League. The League was a confederation of Greek City States on the northern and central Peloponnese from 280-146 BC ruled by an elected top general known as a *strategos*.

Carthage. This North African powerhouse was founded by Phoenicians and feared by its neighbors for savagery and brutality. Carthage fought the Greeks for the island of Sicily known as Syracuse as well as other lands and then battled Rome for dominance in the western Mediterranean. It was defeated in the final Punic War. The ancient capital city was located in modern day Tunisia.

Cyrene. The Greeks founded a colony on the Mediterranean coast of North Africa in 630 BCE. The ruins are located in modern day Libya near the Egyptian border.

Iberia. Latin name for present day Spain and Portugal known as the Iberian Peninsula.

Indus Valley. The furthest eastern region conquered by Alexander the Great and the location of the mutiny that forced him to give up his dream of an empire from sea to sea.

Libya. Greek *Libyes* for region of Northwestern Africa. The name derives from *Libu*, Egyptian for a specific Berber tribe. The Greeks considered all Berbers *Libyans*, while the Egyptians differentiated between the many tribes.

Nubia. An independent kingdom in ancient times, Nubia refers to the region of southern Egypt along the Nile (25% of ancient Nubia) with the remainder (75%) extending into modern day northern Sudan. This area was also part of the Kingdom of Kush.

Persia. The ancient empire threatened both Egypt and Greece for centuries. The heart of the empire is in the modern country of Iran.

Syracuse. The ancient Greek city-state founded by Korinth and the site of numerous battles between Greeks, with Carthage and then Rome. Syracuse is located on the island of Sicily.

LANGUAGES

Arabic. Proto-Arabic can be traced to the 8th century BCE. The dialect referred to in this book would be pre-Classical Arabic of which a few inscriptions can be dated to the 2nd century BCE.

Aramaic. Originally the native language of the Arameans, Aramaic became the *lingua franca* of the Assyrian and Persian Empires. It was adopted and spoken by many conquered peoples, including the Hebrews and belongs to the Semitic group of languages.

Berber. This group of ancient Semitic dialects of North Africa is still spoken today by native tribes in the mountains of Morocco and Algeria. It is considered a close relative to ancient Egyptian.

Egyptian. The ancient Egyptians spoke a branch of the Afro-Asiatic language family which also includes Arabic, Hebrew and Berber. The Coptic language is considered to be an extant form of ancient Egyptian.

Greek. The ancient Greeks spoke several dialects until the conquests of Macedonian Alexander the Great established the Koine dialect as common Greek. Athena of Korinth in Alexandria would have spoken Koine. The Greek Translation of the Old Testament was written in Koine. Pre-Koine dialects included Aeolic, Doric, and Ionic. The *Iliad* was composed in Ionic. Plato and Aristotle wrote in Attic Greek, the subset of the Ionic dialect spoken in ancient Athens.

Hebrew. A Semitic language of the Afro-asiatic group, ancient Hebrew is referred to as the Holy Language by the Jewish people. Modern Hebrew is spoken in Israel. Biblical Hebrew was the written language used by Jewish scholars to write the Torah during the Babylonian exile in 6th century BCE. The term "Hebrew" is one of several names for the Jewish people.

Lingua franca. Italian for "Frankish language." This term refers to any language used to communicate between diverse peoples over a large geographical area. The *lingua franca* of the Persian Empire was Aramaic. The *lingua franca* of the Hellenistic world was Koine Greek. Latin was the *lingua franca* of the Roman Empire and the Catholic Church. The *lingua franca* during the time of the Crusades was French, thus the term *franca* (Frankish). English is considered today's *lingua franca*.

Punic. Also known as Carthaginian, Punic is an extinct Semitic language formerly spoken in ancient Carthage on the north coast of Africa. The city of Carthage was located in modern day Tunis. Punic was a dialect of Phoenician.

GODS

Note: The gods and goddesses listed below are not a complete list of the Egyptian or Greek pantheon, but only the deities mentioned in The Emerald Tablet.

Apis. The Egyptian bull deity was originally worshipped in Memphis, the traditional capital of ancient Egyptian Pharaohs. He was the most important of all sacred animals to the Egyptians. Ptolemy I combined him with Osiris and Jupiter or Pluto into the Alexandrian god Sarapis.

Aphrodite. The Greek goddess of love, beauty and sexuality was based on the Phoenician goddess Astarte. She had many lovers among the Greek gods, including Poseidon and Ares as well as among mortal men. She was reputed to have been born of the foam of the sea. The Greeks associated her with both Isis and Hathor. The Romans called her Venus.

Apollo. The Greek god of the sun and light was best known as the patron of Delphi who issued prophesies through his intermediary Pythia, the Oracle of Delphi. He had no direct Roman equivalent.

Dionysus. Officially the Greek god of the grape and wine, he became associated with revelry and ecstatic rituals and was the patron of the Greek theater. He was also called Bacchus which is the name the Romans adopted.

Eros. His name means "intimate love" in Greek and he was the god of sexual love and beauty as well as a fertility deity. Most mythology places him as the son of Aphrodite, Greek goddess of love and Ares, Greek god of war. The Romans called him Cupid or Amor.

Hades. The Greek god of the underworld was also called Plouton by the Greeks and Pluto by the Romans.

Hathor. The Egyptian goddess of love, motherhood, music, and dance was blended with Isis during the Greco-roman period. The Cow Goddess was associated with Ishtar by the Persians, Aphrodite by the Greeks, and Venus by the Romans.

Hera. The wife of Zeus, king of the gods is called Juno by the Romans. She was the goddess of women and marriage. Mythology has her suffering multiple betrayals by her philandering husband and brother Zeus.

Isis. The Egyptian goddess of the moon, the earth and women eventually supplanted Hathor as the Queen of the gods. She was worshipped widely by both Greeks and Romans and became identified with Aphrodite the Greek goddess of love and later Venus, the Roman version.

Jupiter. The Supreme Roman god of good fortune and benevolence was borrowed from the Greek Zeus.

Mars. The Roman god of war was borrowed from Ares the Greek god of war and courage and lover of Aphrodite.

Poseidon. The Greek god of the sea was known to the Romans as Neptune. He was yet another lover of Aphrodite.

Osiris. The Egyptian god of the underworld was blended with Apis the Bull and the anthropomorphic Pluto/Hades to create Serapis in Alexandria, giving Greeks and Egyptians a common deity.

Plouton/Pluto/Hades. The god of the underworld, known as Pluto by the Romans and Plouton or Hades by the Greeks, was the anthropomorphic form of Serapis, the Ptolemaic blend of Osiris and Apis.

Sarapis or Serapis. Ptolemy I created a god for Alexandria that appealed to both Egyptians and Greeks. Sarapis (Greek) or Serapis (Roman) was a blend of the Egyptian deities Apis the Bull and Osiris, the god of the underworld, with the anthropomorphic form of the Greek gods Zeus or Hades. His temple in Alexandria was called the Serapeum. He was also a popular god with the Romans.

GREEK NAMES

Ancient Greeks typically used one name plus an identifier (most often the person's origin.) Athena of Korinth (the city), Hektor of Naukratis (the city), Antinous of Kos (the island), and Callimachus of Cyrene (the city) are examples. Alexander the Great was known as Alexander III of Macedon (the city-state.) The use of the identifier was akin to a formal way of addressing or referring to the person as with a last name.

The first son and heir of the House of Ptolemy was always named after Alexander the Great's general, Ptolemy, who founded the dynasty. They chose a qualifier name when they took the throne: Ptolemy I was Ptolemy *Soter*, or the Savior; Ptolemy II was *Philadelphu*s, Brother-loving; Ptolemy III *Euergetes*, the Benefactor; Ptolemy IV was *Philopater*, Father-lover. Daughters (subsequent Queens) were usually named Berenike, Arsinoë or Kleopatra. Fourteen Ptolemy Pharaohs and one Queen, Kleopatra VII, *Philopater*, the Father-lover, ruled Egypt.

ARCHITECTURE

capitals. The top of a classical column. The pillar is called a shaft.

Corinthian/Korinthian columns. The third order of classical Greek columns. The capital, or top, is heavily carved, usually with the leaves of the acanthus plant below a small scroll. The name derives from the city-state of Korinth. This order of columns was more popular with Romans than with Greeks.

Doric columns. The oldest of three orders of classical Greek columns. The capital, or top, of the column is a plain circle topped by a square. The best extant example is the Parthenon in Athens. The name derives from a dialect of Greek spoken in the Peloponnese and mainland.

Ionic columns. The second of three orders of classical Greek columns. The shafts are taller than Doric which gives them a more slender appearance. The capital, or top, of the column is carved into a scroll-like pattern and is more decorative than the Doric order but plainer than Corinthian. The name derives from the area of ancient Greece known as Ionia in modern day Asia Minor.

lintel. The horizontal block that spans the space between two supports. Its use in classical time could be strictly ornamental.

mosaic. A design or picture made by setting small colored pieces, usually squares, of stone or glass into a surface.

naos. Greek for "temple." It referred to the sanctuary or innermost chamber of a temple. Also known as Holy-of-Holies or inner sanctum.

palmiform. Egyptian style of abstract design representing palm fronds. Palmiform fans and sunscreens were in the shape of single palm fronds. Columns were carved in a motif of eight palm fronds lashed to a pole.

peristyle. A columned porch or open colonnade surrounding a courtyard, often with a garden.

portico. A porch or walkway with a roof supported by columns, often leading to the entrance of a building.

postern. A small single door in a protective wall.

stoa. A covered porch constructed with two rows of columns supporting a roof with a wall on one side.

Syracuse style. A form of classical Hellenist design considered over exuberant by Greek contemporaries. Syracuse was a Greek city-state on the island of Sicily founded by the city-state of Korinth.

OBJECTS and MISC TERMINOLOGY

acanthus. A plant with spiky leaves commonly found in the Mediterranean region. Acanthus leaves inspired Greek and Roman decorative elements, including the capitals of Corinthian columns.

amulet. Symbols or objects believed to have magical powers used as talismans against evil or injury.

amphora/amphorae. A type of ceramic vase with two handles and a long neck rising from a thicker body used for the storage of various liquids, but especially oils and wine.

bireme. The Greek wooden galley ship propelled with sails and two banks of oars.

brazier. A container for fire, the brazier can stand upright or be suspended. It was a common source of lighting and heat in antiquity.

chiton. The traditional Greek dress was worn by men and women, with or without sleeves, girdled or loose at the waist. A woman's chiton was always long, but a man's could be long or end mid-thigh.

contrapposto. The Italian term refers to the stance of a human figure standing with most of its weight on one foot as if poised between repose and action. Polykleitos, the Classical Greek sculptor is credited with "inventing" the stance which was revitalized during the Renaissance.

drachm/drachma. The silver coin in the form of the *tetradrachm* became universal currency with the conquests of Alexander the Great. There were several weights of silver drachma which were identified by numerical prefixes: *didrachm* (2), *tetradrachm* (4), *pentadrachm* (5), *oktodrachm* (8) and *dekdrachm* (10). A *drachm* might be thought of as a silver dollar with each upgrade being 2 dollar coins, 5 dollar coins, 8 dollar coins etc.

erastes-eromenos. Lover and loved. The terms describe the relationship between mature man and youth in ancient Greece. The *erastes* is the mentor and penetrator. The *eromenos* is the pupil and youth who must forego being penetrated when a beard appears.

Herakles knot. Ubiquitous in Greek and Roman symbolism, the knot may have originated in ancient Egypt as a healing charm. In jewelry, two intertwined gold or silver ropes are looped to form a strong knot which symbolized marriage for the Greeks and Romans. It could be the source of the expression "tying the knot."

hetaera/hetaerae. These courtesans of ancient Greece were independent and wealthy women. Usually freed slaves or foreigners, they were supported by benefactors and the only women allowed at *symposia* other than entertainers. Trained in music and dance, they were well-read and their opinion in politics and philosophy respected.

kithara. An ancient stringed instrument in the lyre family with strings of equal length was played by professionals in public performances.

krater. The massive wine jars with broad bodies and wide mouths were used for mixing wine and water at parties. Designed to be carried by two men, wine would be ladled into the guests own cups, often a *kylix*. They also were the target for the drinking games called *kottabos* where players swirled the dregs of their wine and flung them at a *krater*.

kylix. A favorite of drinking parties or *symposia*, this drinking cup had a broad shallow body on a short stem with a foot and two handles. Artists delighted in painting erotic scenes at the bottom of the cup which were revealed when the wine was drained.

lapis lazuli. This semi-precious stone has been prized since antiquity for its intense blue color. The finest quality was imported from Afghanistan and often combined in patterns with turquoise.

lute. The ancient stringed instrument had a long neck and deep round back was usually plucked. It is more properly called a chordophone.

lyre. The ancient stringed instrument somewhat resembles a small harp which was strummed rather than plucked. It accompanied recitations of poetry or songs.

Milesian wool. This particular type of wool from the city-state of Miletus on the coast of modern day Turkey was treasured above all others in the Greek and Roman worlds. Its texture and weave were so fine that we might compare it to cashmere.

naos. This was the inner sanctum of a temple also known as the holy of holies.

obol. This small copper coin was commonly used through Greece. We might compare an *obol* to the *drachm* as a penny to a dollar.

Orcheisthai. This section of the Greek theatre set was the stage where the chorus danced and sang.

Orion. The constellation of Orion or the Hunter is visible from anywhere on the planet depending on the season, with a different orientation depending on whether in the Northern or Southern Hemisphere. Orion's belt is a row of three very bright stars.

peplos. This woman's gown was the most traditional and was replaced by the chiton. The tubular cloth was folded and gathered at the waist and pinned at the shoulders.

proskenion. This section of the Greek theatre was the stage where the actors performed. It was directly in front of the *skene*.

Punic. This term refers both to the culture of Carthage as well as the language. Punics were probably a mix of native North African Berbers and the conquering Phoenicians from the Middle East. The series of long and bloody wars between Rome and Carthage are called the Punic Wars. The Romans adopted "Punic" to describe having a treacherous or betraying nature.

Pythia. All Oracles of Delphi were called Pythia, the name originally given by the god Apollo to the first of the purest older native women.

Satyr. These half-men, half-beast creatures were companions of Dionysus and generally considered to be roguish lovers of wine and women and all other forms of wild physical pleasure. Satyr plays were short, light-hearted pieces performed after tragedies at drama festivals.

skene. This section of the Greek theatre was the background building which not only provided the scenery for the actors playing on the *proskenion* in front, but also served as storage for props and audio/visual machinery as well as a place for costume changes and off-stage action.

strategos/strategoi. Meaning literally "army leader," the *strategos* was a general elected to rule the military as well as civil matters in the Achaean League to which Korinth belonged.

symposion/symposia. The Greeks loved their wine and the men drinking parties called *symposia*. Entertained by professional musicians, they competed in oratory, poetry, and drinking games called *kottabos*. Held in private homes in the *andron*, the men's part of the house, guests reclined on divans, drinking from double-handled cups. The only women allowed to attend were flute girls or *hetaerae*. The Romans borrowed from the Greeks, but allowed women and introduced orgies.

trireme. The Greek wooden galley ship propelled with sails and three banks of oars.

Links to the three statues referenced in the scene with Isis and Tony at the Metropolitan Museum of Art in New York:

Image of Roman marble copy of Greek Aphrodite: http://www.metmuseum.org/toah/works-of-art/52.11.5

Image of Roman marble copy of Polykleitos bronze statue of Diadoumenos: http://www.metmuseum.org/toah/works-of-art/25.78.56

Image of Roman marble copy of Polykleitos bronze head of youth: http://www.metmuseum.org/collections/search-the-collections/130008468

GREEK THINKERS AND QUOTES

I have attempted to give the reader a feel for Greek thought by starting each chapter with a quote from a Greek philosopher. Greek quotations are woven all through the story, sometimes in dialogue when the philosopher is quoted directly, and sometimes when he is paraphrased by various characters.

The indirect quotes might pass without notice when you're reading. Can you find them in the text? I have listed them in this section in order of use in the book.

It was quite common in ancient Greece to quote the great thinkers. Playwrights and thinkers were greatly respected. A ready knowledge of their thoughts and the ability to quote their works were considered essential parts of a Greek's education.

I find it fascinating that the ancient Greeks said almost everything there was to say about human nature and even more remarkable to realize how little we have changed in 2,500 years.

The following Greeks have been quoted either directly or indirectly.
All dates are approximate and BCE – before the Common Era.

Aeschylus – *playwright, father of tragedy* - 500
Aesop – *fabulist* - 600
Antisthenes – *philosopher, Cynicism* - 400
Aristophanes – *playwright, father of comedy* - 400
Aristotle – *philosopher, Formal Logic* - 350
Crates – *philosopher, Cynicism* - 350
Diogenes – *philosopher, Cynicism* - 350
Epicurus – *philosopher, Epicurean* - 300
Euripides – *playwright, tragedy* - 450
Heraclitus – *philosopher* - 500
Herodotus – *historian* - 450
Hesiod – *oral poet* - 700
Hippocrates – *physician* - 400
Homer – *oral poet, Iliad and Odyssey* - before 700
Menander – *playwright, comic* - 350
Pericles – *statesman/general* - 450
Plato – *philosopher, Dialogues* - 400
Pindar – *poet* - 500
Protagoras – *philosopher/mathematician, Sophism* - 450
Sappho – *woman poet* - 600
Socrates – *philosopher, Socratic Method* - 450
Sophocles – *playwright, tragedy* - 450
Thales – *mathematician* - 600
Theophrastus – *natural scientist* - 300
Thucydides – *historian* - 400

CHAPTER QUOTES

1 - "I know men in exile feed on dreams." – Aeschylus

2 - "I'd like nothing better than to achieve some bold adventure, worthy of our trip." – Aristophanes

3 - "The vine bears three kinds of grapes; the first of pleasure, the second of intoxication, the third of disgust." – Diogenes

4 - "Great deeds are usually wrought at great risks." – Herodotus

5 - "Happiness is a choice that requires effort at times." – Aeschylus

6 - "Once made equal to a man, woman becomes his superior." – Socrates

7 - "The secret of happiness is freedom. The secret of freedom is courage." – Thucydides

8 - "First secure an independent income, then practice virtue." – Greek Proverb

9 - "Faithful earth, unfaithful sea." – Greek Proverb

10 - "Remember that with her clothes, a woman puts off her modesty." – Socrates

11 - "The greatest pleasure of life is love." – Euripides

12 - "No one steps twice into the same river, for it is not the same river and not the same man." – Heraclitus

13 - "Happiness is brief. It will not stay. Gods batter at its sails." – Euripides

14 - "Nothing has more strength than dire necessity." – Euripides

15 - "A great city is not to be confounded with a populous one." – Aristotle

16 - "Often an entire city has suffered because of an evil man." – Hesiod

17 - "The gods are not averse to deceit in a holy cause." – Aeschylus

18 - "A library is a repository of medicine for the mind and a hospital for the soul." – Greek Proverb

19 - "In nine cases of out of ten, a woman had better show more affection than she feels." – Aristotle

20 - "What is there more kindly than the feeling between host and guest?" – Aeschylus

21 - "Affairs are easier of entrance than of exit; and it is but common prudence to see our way out before we venture in." – Aesop

22 - "First have a definite, clear practical objective. Second, have the necessary means to achieve your ends—wisdom, money, materials and men." – Aristotle

23 - "Injuries may be forgiven, but not forgotten." – Aesop

24 - "There are only two people who can tell you the truth about yourself—

an angry enemy and a loving friend." – Antisthenes

25 - "There is no harm in repeating a good thing." – Plato

26 - "All human actions have one or more of these seven causes: chance, nature, compulsion, habit, reason, passion, desire." – Aristotle

27 - "You don't develop courage by being happy every day. You develop it by surviving difficult times and challenging adversity." – Epicurus

28 - "Love is all we have, the only way that each can help the other." – Euripides

29 - "Try to take for your mate, a person of your own neighborhood." – Hesiod

30 - "You will never do anything in this world without courage." – Aristotle

31 - "Make me useful to my friends, rather than agreeable." – Crates

32 - "Extreme remedies are very appropriate for extreme diseases." – Hippocrates

33 - "I like not this great success of yours, for I know how jealous are the gods." – Herodotus

34 - "I know one thing, that I know nothing." – Socrates

35 - "It is not once nor twice but times without number that the same ideas make their appearance in the world." – Aristotle

36 - "What house ever became prosperous without a woman's excellence?" – Sophocles

37 - "Shrines! Shrines! Surely you don't believe in the gods. What's your argument? Where's your proof?" – Aristophanes

38 - "Fear is pain arising from the anticipation of evil." – Aristotle

39 - "Force has no place when there is need of skill." – Herodotus

40 - "The bravest have the clearest vision of what is before them, glory and danger alike, and go out to meet it." – Thucydides

41 - "This is the root from which a tyrant springs; when he first appears he is a protector." – Plato

42 - "A common danger unites even the bitterest enemies." – Aristotle

43 - "I'm not afraid of storms, for I'm learning to sail my ship."– Aeschylus

SOURCES OF DIRECT OR INDIRECT QUOTES

"Quick decisions are unsafe ones." – Sophocles

"In youth and beauty, wisdom is but rare." – Homer

"When the gods appoint, we must obey." – Greek Proverb

"Gods do not reward or punish humans; the universe is infinite and eternal; events are based on the motions and interactions of atoms moving in empty space." – Epicurus

"Fear the Danaans (Lacedaemeon or Spartan Greeks) even when bearing gifts." – Greek Proverb

"We live, not as we wish to be, but as we can." – Menander

"Is it not harder to conquer a woman than to subdue any wild beast?" – Aristophanes

"Life is too important to be taken seriously." – Aristophanes

"The uphill is followed by the downhill." – Greek Proverb

"Man—the measure of all things!" – Protagoras

"A sweet thing tasted too often is no longer sweet." – Greek Proverb

"Either with your shield or on it." – Spartan code of honor

"The gods too are fond of a joke." – Aristotle

"These impossible women! How they do get around us! The poet was right: Can't live with them, or without them." – Aristophanes

"The gods have entrusted me with myself." – Greek Proverb

"Marriage, if one faces the truth, is an evil, but a necessary one." - Menander

"Who seeks shall find." – Sophocles

"As the old saw says well: Every end does not appear together with its beginning." – Herodotus

"Big results require big ambitions." – Heraclitus

"Of all possessions a friend is the most precious." – Herodotus

"Life must be lived as a play." – Plato

"Courage is knowing what not to fear." – Plato

"He is the best man who, when making his plans, fears and reflects on everything that can happen to him, but in the moment of action is bold." – Herodotus

"Those whom the gods wish to destroy, they first make angry." – Euripides

"The strong do what they have to do and the weak accept what they have to accept." – Thucydides

"The oaths of a woman I inscribe on water." – Sophocles

"Much wisdom often goes with fewest words." – Sophocles

"Just because you do not take an interest in politics, does not mean politics won't take an interest in you." – Pericles

"Death is not the worst that can happen to a man." – Plato

"To a father growing old, nothing is dearer than a daughter." – Euripides

"What is the fastest? The mind. It travels through everything." – Thales

"Death may be the greatest of all human blessings." – Socrates

"Whatever deceives men seems to produce a magical enchantment." – Plato

"What is quite common? Hope. Because even those who have nothing, they do have that." – Thales

"Human things are a wheel." – Greek Proverb

"To live without evil belongs only to the gods." – Sophocles

"The past is certain, the future obscure." – Thales

"We (Greeks) are lovers of the beautiful; yet simple in our tastes, and we cultivate the mind without loss of manliness." – Thucydides

"But when there comes to men a gleam of splendor given of heaven, then rests on them a light of glory and blessed are their days." – Pindar

"If the gods listened to the prayers of men, all men would quickly have perished, for they are forever praying for evil against one another." – Epicurus

"Life is ruled by fortune not by wisdom." – Theophrastus

"In peace, sons bury their fathers. In war, fathers bury their sons." – Herodotus

"In war, truth is the first casualty." – Aeschylus

"The good and the wise lead quiet lives." – Euripides

"The gods help them that help themselves." – Aesop

🦉

Hymn to Aphrodite *by Sappho 700 BC*

Throned in splendor, immortal Aphrodite!
Child of Zeus, Enchantress, I implore thee
Slay me not in this distress and anguish,
Lady of beauty.

Hither come as once before thou camest,
When from afar thou heard'st my voice lamenting,
Heard'st and camest, leaving thy glorious father's Palace golden,
Yoking thy chariot. Fair the doves that bore thee;
Swift to the darksome earth their course directing,
Waving their thick wings from the highest heaven

Down through the ether. Quickly they came. Then thou, O blessed goddess,
All in smiling wreathed thy face immortal,
Bade me tell thee the cause of all my suffering,
Why now I called thee;
What for my maddened heart I most was longing.

"Whom," thou criest, "dost wish that sweet Persuasion
Now win over and lead to thy love, my Sappho?
Who is it wrongs thee?
"For, though now he flies, he soon shall follow,
Soon shall be giving gifts who now rejects them.

Even though now he love not, soon shall he love thee
Even though thou wouldst not."
Come then now, dear goddess, and release me
From my anguish. All my heart's desiring
Grant thou now. Now too again as aforetime
Be thou my ally.

Translated by Wm Hyde Appleton
Greek Poets in English Verse

CAST OF CHARACTERS

Modern	Greek Egypt	Pharaonic Egypt
Isis and her lovers		
Isis _Eye_ sis	**Athena** of Korinth	**Isenkhebe Nefrusobek**
		Ee sen ke bay Ne fru so bek
	Ishtar _Ish_ tar	**Isis, Ishtar, Isidora**
Hector	**Hektor** of Naukratis	**Hetmus-hor**
The General	**The General**	**General Sher**
Tony	**Antinous** _An tee no os_ of Kos	**Antinous**
Rasheed _Ra sheed_	**Black Falcon**	**River God**
Main characters		
Aisha _Eye sha_	**Kallisto**	**Pehtes**
Barb	**Eugenia** _Eu gee nee a_	
Carla	**Agatha**	
Eben _Ee ben_	**Eben**	**Eben**
Esperanza	**Omphale**	
Isabel	**Queen Arsinoë** _Are see no ee_	**Sit-hathor**
Jenny	**Jason**	
	Goliath	**Goliath**
	Qeb-ha _Keb_ ha	**Qeb-ha**
	Oracle of Amun	**Hermes Trismegistus**
		Err mes Tris me gist us
	Oracle of Delphi	**Kiya**
The Bad Guys		
	Ptolemy _Tall e may_ **IV**	**Psamtik IV**
Ibis Man	**Chancellor Sosibius**	**Setne the Scribe**
The Russian	**Royal Steward Agathon**	
	Zavan _Za van_	**Zavan**

About the Author

Born with wanderlust, forever living in a fantasy world, S. L. Gore escaped the prairies of Kansas to follow the yellow brick road on an odyssey that took her to Europe, Africa, Latin America and the Middle East.

Starting with a one way ticket to Iceland, she returned with a Viking husband, an art degree and speaking five languages.

Years in North Africa, with months on the Sahara and hundreds of hours haggling in *souks*, set the stage for the *Isis Trilogy*. A love of adventure and romance combined with a fascination for exotic lands, classical history, ancient and modern languages, mysticism, and fine dining led Gore to create **The Red Mirror**, **The Emerald Tablet** and **The Black Scroll**.

Her non-fiction publications include the self-help manual **Sex and the Zen of Shopping: *How to Live Rich by Shopping Smart*** and memoir contributions to three **Life Choices** anthologies. She is a regular columnist for Life Choices Magazine with the food and table art feature **Beauty and the Feast.**

Gore is always actively engaged in her community and has served as a School Board Trustee, a Planning Commissioner and a Parks, Recreation and Beautification Commissioner. A frequent guest on the Dave Congalton Radio Show, she discusses international news and foreign policy.

The joyously married Nielsens have a grown daughter and son and divide their time between a California beach house and a Las Vegas condo.

S. L. Gore's Books

Isis Trilogy ~ *One life is not enough*
Published by Tajine Publishing in print and eVersion
The Red Mirror ꭓ (Book One)
- Pharaonic Egypt, 525 BC
The Emerald Tablet 🐍 (Book Two)
- Greek Egypt, 215 BC
The Black Scroll 📜 (Book Three)
- Roman North Africa, 130 AD

Lovers of Isis *Vignettes* 🐦 S. L. Gore
Published by Tajine Publishing in print and eVersion

Isis *Erotica* 🐊 Sandra Gore
Published by Tajine Publishing in print and eVersion

Isis Beach Read 🐦 Sandra Gore
Published by Tajine Publishing in print and eVersion

Sex and the Zen of Shopping: Live Rich by Shopping Smart
Sandra Gore Nielsen
Published by Tajine Publishing

Life Choices Anthologies
Published by Turning Point International
Navigating Difficult Paths: "A True Love Story"
Pursuing Your Passion: "The Muses Whisper"
It's Never Too Late: "Road to Vegas"

Tajine Publishing
Las Vegas, NV 89121
tajinepublishing@gmail.com
702-279-6556

Author website: **www.SLGore.com**

www.ingramcontent.com/pod-product-compliance
Lightning Source LLC
Chambersburg PA
CBHW030415180626
46812CB00005B/2016